The Secret of Saint Olaf's Church

INDREK HARGLA is one of Estonia's best-known and most prolific crime writers. Hargla's *Apothecary Melchior Mysteries*, set in fifteenth-century Tallinn and starring a detective pharmacist named Melchior Wakenstede, have been translated into five languages, adapted for stage and were the basis for a popular Estonian film trilogy. *The Ghost of Rataskaevu Street* is also available from Pushkin Vertigo.

ADAM CULLEN is a freelance translator of Estonian prose, poetry, and drama. His translations include *The Cavemen Chronicle* by Mikhel Mutt, *The Brother and the Reconstruction* by Rein Raud and Indrek Hargla's *The Ghost of Rataskaevu Street*.

The Secret of Saint Olaf's Church

Indrek Hargla

Translated from the Estonian
by Adam Cullen

Pushkin Press
Somerset House, Strand
London WC2R 1LA

The Secret of Saint Olaf's Church was first published as *Apteeker Melchior ja Oleviste Mõistatus* by Varrak in Estonia, 2010

First published in English by Peter Owen Publishers in 2015
First published by Pushkin Press in 2026

ISBN 13: 978-1-80533-574-0

A CIP catalogue record for this title is available from the British Library

The authorised representative in the EEA is eucomply OÜ, Pärnu mnt. 139b-14, 11317, Tallinn, Estonia, hello@eucompliancepartner.com, +33757690241

Designed and typeset by Tetragon, London
Printed and bound in the United Kingdom by Clays Ltd, Elcograf S.p.A.

Pushkin Press is committed to a sustainable future for our business, our readers and our planet. This book is made from paper from forests that support responsible forestry.

www.pushkinpress.com

1 3 5 7 9 8 6 4 2

The Secret
of Saint Olaf's
Church

TOOMPEA IN
THE FIFTEENTH CENTURY

1. St Mary's Cathedral (Dome Church)
2. The Small Castle of the Teutonic Order; Commander's residence
3. Clingenstain's lodgings
4. Passage from Toompea to Tallinn
5. Bell Tower Gate (Dome Gate)
6. Short Hill guard tower

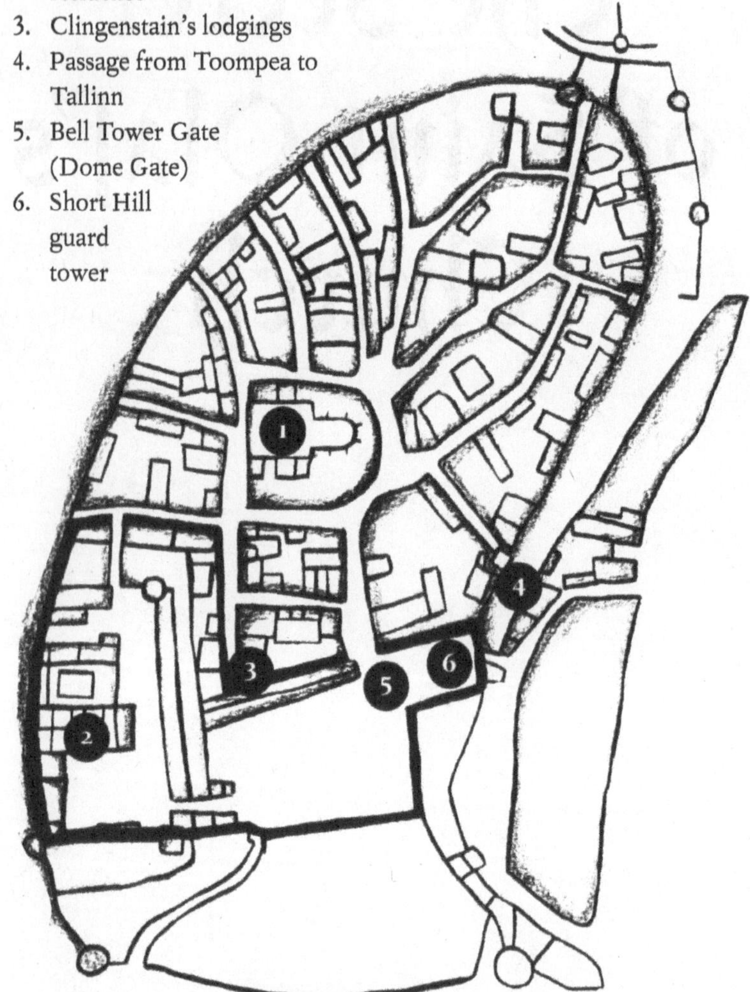

THE LOWER TOWN OF TALLINN IN THE FIFTEENTH CENTURY

1. St Olaf's Church
2. Melchior's Pharmacy
3. Town Hall Square
4. Dominican Monastery
5. St Nicholas's Church
6. Seppade Gate

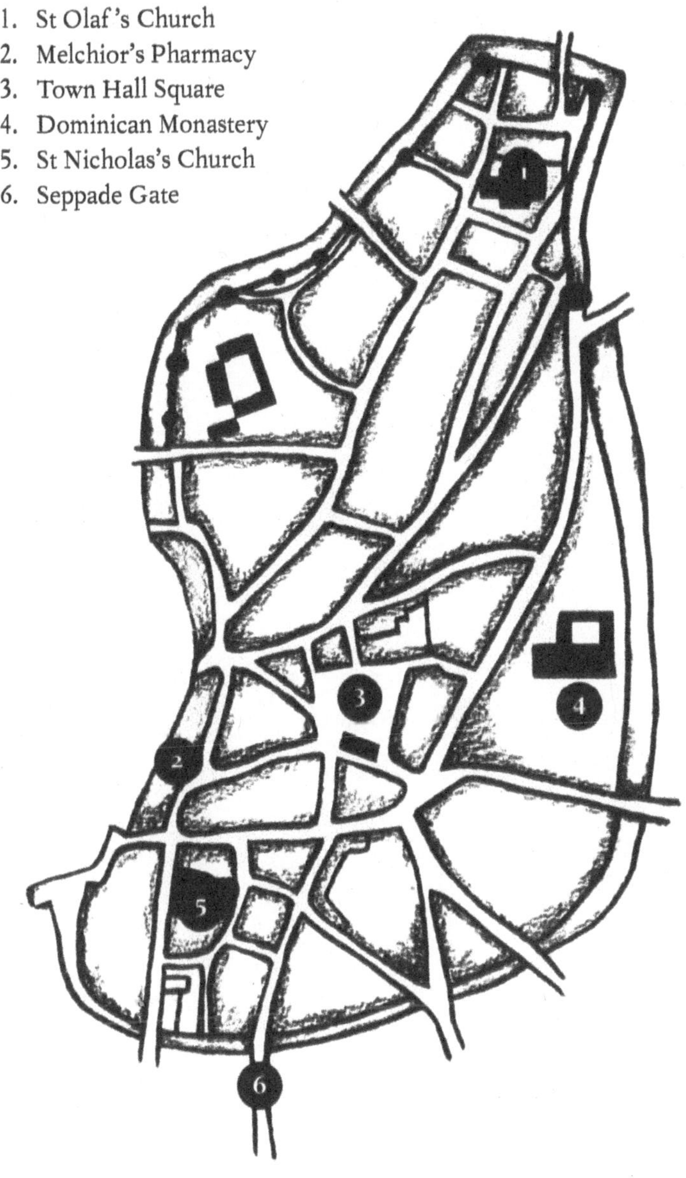

FOREWORD

Tallinn
1409

At no time, before or since, has Estonia been so closely connected with Western Europe as it was during the fifteenth century. It was a time when the Teutonic Order's power was finally consolidated in the region, when towns and bastions were constructed, when guilds and monasteries flourished. A constant influx of colonizers during what was the golden age of the Hanseatic League saw the sea traffic between Estonia and German and Scandinavian ports grow to unprecedented levels. Never before had Estonia been so closely involved in the wars waged by European rulers for dominance on the Baltic Sea. The Victual Brothers – a loosely organized band of pirates that grew powerful during the disputes between the German dukes and the Kingdom of Denmark – plundered the coast of Estonia mercilessly yet were also allies of the Tartu bishops in their internal quarrels with the Teutonic Order. The Victual Brothers conquered Visby in Gotland and made it their base until a fleet of the Teutonic Order, commanded by Ulrich von Jungingen, retook Gotland in 1398 and drove the Victual Brothers from the island. Visby was pillaged and lost its position in trading on the Baltic Sea. Every Victual Brother that had not managed to escape was executed in the same gruesome manner in which the pirates themselves had killed their prisoners. The Teutonic Order sold the island back to the Danish King in 1409.

A year later the Order was dealt a crushing blow by the Poles near Tannenberg.

Tallinn during the year 1409 in no way resembled what we might imagine, based on the current appearance of its Old Town. Tallinn was just being built. A town plan was indeed in place – the street pattern had been laid and plots divided out, and the Town Hall had been built, but the wall, the towers and churches were not yet complete. Nevertheless, the streets were paved, the Order's castle on the hill known as Toompea was one of the mightiest in Northern Europe and Tallinn's sewage system – comprising a canal dug from Lake Ülemiste, a moat and three mills – was a massive, groundbreaking engineering achievement for its time. The town's distinct architectural style was still in development, and a great many foreign master builders walked the streets. Tallinn was becoming one of the Teutonic Order's most important harbours, supplying Livonia with goods and trade. While the wealth of Tallinn and Livonia certainly could not be compared with that of towns in Germany or the Low Countries, the town nevertheless grew and moved forward.

Tallinn was surrounded by suburbs and a wider administrative region where the laws of the city of Lübeck were enforced; power was thus held by the citizens – that is, the merchants. The Teutonic Order's laws and land rights were enforced from Toompea Castle, and its authority was represented there by a commander. Relations between the town and the Order were often complicated, but one could not survive without the other. The Order guaranteed peace in the region of which Tallinn was the centre of economic activity.

Surviving records of Tallinn's Town Council inform us that in 1409 a high-ranking Knight of the Teutonic Order, travelling from Gotland to the Order capital of Marienburg, was murdered on Toompea in mysterious circumstances. But this was not the only murder to shock the residents of Tallinn that fine spring. Both the Order and the Council searched for the Toompea Murderer yet failed to apprehend the killer, and the reasons behind these acts of bloodshed remained a mystery.

Nevertheless, Tallinn's court records show that an apothecary by the name of Melchior entered the Town Hall one day and announced that he knew the identity of this mysterious murderer and why the crimes had been committed. The Town Council did not grant him an audience and sent him away – although not empty-handed. Melchior was given ten marks for his troubles. Was this fee paid for his silence? Was the apothecary's story just too sensitive and so the Council preferred not to jeopardize relations between the town merchants, the Order, the clergy and foreign wielders of power? We do not know, and we never will. Nor will we ever know what drove a Council secretary to inscribe the words that, to this very day, have remained a puzzle to all who research these records:

> The Lord's peace be with those who have wished good upon our town.
>
> They, who lived before us, have been closer to the Lord. May their graves remain undisturbed and that which is supreme endure.

We do not know whom Melchior accused or what became of the apothecary himself. Apothecary Melchior is never mentioned again in the Council records.

1

Toompea
15 May, Late Evening

H ENNING VON CLINGENSTAIN, former Commander of the Teutonic Order in Gotland, was roaring drunk. Truth be told, he was roaring drunk for the fifth day in a row, and if the local commander had not fed him generously – food had been brought out from the kitchen of Toompea Small Castle from morning to evening – he would already have collapsed from a beer-induced stupor and blacked out long ago. Yet Tallinn appeared to be a prosperous and good-natured town, not like Visby. Here people enjoyed eating and drinking. It was customary in Tallinn to make merry just as the people in Clingenstain's home town of Warendorf once had. And Spanheim, the local commander, seemed to be this town's king of merrymaking. For five consecutive days and nights the table had been groaning under the weight of beer, wine and more of the town's best and finest. It would have been a sin to turn it all down, just as it was actually a sin to quaff and gorge it all down – but Clingenstain had already taken care of that earlier in the day by having his confession heard by the Dominican Prior. Needless to say, forgiveness had been bestowed for his overeating and excessive drinking. Naturally.

Clingenstain now felt, however, that he might have had enough – his innards churned, his head buzzed and his thoughts were muddled.

Only now did he begin to make sense of what was reality and what was just an intoxicated illusion, now that, after a few blunders, he finally found the side portal from the northern wing of the castle that passed above the moat, straight from one fortress to the other – from the Small Castle of the Order to the Great Castle, or Toompea, as it was also known. Some attendant opened the door for him, and the Knight staggered towards his lodgings. Curses, I am seeing devils, he thought. A soldier of Christ shouldn't see devils.

He stepped out into the mild May night and filled his lungs with fresh air. The darkly glimmering walls of Toompea resembled shadows of a palace of darkness closing in around him. The jolly songs of the Commander's musicians still sounded in his ears, and, truth be told, the festivities at the castle were probably still under way. The cobblestones, however, rose up from the ground and scuffed against his foot. He stumbled and fell. If he wished to reach his dwelling without incident he would require assistance.

'Jochen, you son of a whore,' he roared. Where was his squire now? He should be at his master's side like a loyal dog, not doing the town in the company of wenches.

'Jochen,' he bellowed again, 'I am blind drunk, and you have climbed up into an attic with some washerwoman. Jochen, you knave!'

The page did not appear. Commander Clingenstain stood in the middle of Toompea, alone except for some attendants of the Teutonic Order who were tending a fire near the stables on the other side of the moat. The walls of St Mary's Cathedral, the Dome Church, loomed over the castle.

'I'll have you skinned tomorrow,' vowed Clingenstain, and he lurched ahead. Pages be damned. He wasn't so helpless at all; he could make it by himself. He definitely remembered where he was lodged; it was not far from here, a house that butted up against the stronghold wall. He could do it alone.

The Commander did not notice a solitary figure breaking away from the dark castle wall, trailing him stealthily as he stumbled towards his residence. He did not notice that the dark form followed him up to the door of the house, carefully keeping to the shadows. He did not even notice that the figure stood beside him when he, after several clumsy attempts, at last managed to unbolt the main door. The dark figure held the door open with his foot after Clingenstain had made his way inside. Clingenstain stood in the spacious entry hall and squinted against the light. Someone, probably Jochen, had lit the candles on the candelabra, and the bright light almost blinded him at first. He leaned against the mantelpiece and picked the candelabra up from the table. There should be a door here somewhere that led to the bedroom, if he remembered correctly, and in that room was a bed. He attempted to shrug off his coat but became entangled and almost fell. If only that slave were here to help him undress.

'Jochen,' he yelled again. 'Aha, there you are, you lout.'

He glimpsed hazily from the corner of his eye that someone had entered through the front door. It had to be Jochen, of course – who else? – but his eyes were not yet accustomed to the light.

'I'll slice your ears off from your head next time. Where've you been, dog?'

The dark figure approached the Commander, who, squinting, had just managed to form the thought that Jochen should really be of shorter stature and did not usually wear such a coat. Yet this was all he had time to think before the stranger grabbed him suddenly by his shirt and shoved him with great force. Clingenstain fell, as if he had been struck by a bolt of lightning.

'Thief, burglar,' he sputtered. 'How dare you, you dog. I am a Knight of the Teutonic Order.'

The stranger kicked him in the chest, and the Commander

doubled over from the pain. The intruder pulled out a sword from beneath his coat.

Clingenstain felt that he was incapable of standing up and much less of fighting, but the abrupt sense of danger and pain sobered him up instantly. He could almost make out the features of the stranger's face from beneath his hood.

'Who ... who are you?' he demanded.

'Someone who has prayed that he might take your filthy soul,' the stranger replied.

'Jochen! Help!' Clingenstain tried to shout, but the cry came out weakly and could not be heard in the street through the thick stone walls.

With his sword in one hand the stranger again grabbed the Commander by his shirt and heaved him on to the table. The Knight tried to struggle and fight, but he was no match for the intruder.

'What do you want?' Clingenstain finally managed to say.

'Justice,' came the reply. The unknown man forced him against the table with one hand and clenched his sword more steadily with the other. 'This is precisely how it must unfold – with you writhing on the ground, terrified and crying for help. You will die without making peace with the Lord, and all your sins will go with you to the grave. It is the road straight to hell, Clingenstain.'

Death? Is this really my death? The thought flashed through the Commander's mind. Such a death, and in Tallinn not on the battlefield; not holding a sword in his hand but here in some burgher's house in Tallinn, drunk, and by the blade of a thief. Virgin Mary, it was not supposed to happen this way. Not here and not now. I do not deserve this. His thoughts were sober but his body unresponsive.

'Who are you?' he enquired again.

Instead of replying the stranger raised something up before Clingenstain's eyes. He could not make out what it was at first, but his eyes finally focused. He also saw the stranger push the hood back from his face. That face … that face … and that object in his hand, that was … It was impossible. He recognized that face. Yes, now he recognized it.

Yet Clingenstain's time was up. He understood this unequivocally. He perceived it clearly through his weakness and his helplessness. For an instant he even saw in his mind's eye the saints looking down at him from the heavens with pity and indifference. Yes, said the saints' gaze, here and now, Henning von Clingenstain, right here and right now your end has come, and we cannot prevent it.

A strong hand seized Clingenstain by the jaw and forced his mouth open. One more powerful burst of pain shot through the Commander's body as the stranger stuffed the item that had been held before his eyes into his mouth.

'This is exactly how it will unfold,' said the man. 'Even begging for mercy will not do you any good. Until we meet in hell.'

He rammed the Knight's head against the table, raised his sword with both hands and slashed downwards.

Henning von Clingenstain felt how the sword ground against his neck. He even felt how the strong blow sliced through his spine. It was painful, unbearably painful, but that pain was nothing compared with what awaited him.

2

Melchior's Pharmacy, Rataskaevu Street
16 May, Morning

M ELCHIOR WAKENSTEDE, Apothecary of the town of Tallinn, had just risen from the breakfast table where his dear Keterlyn had stuffed him full of freshly baked bread and a generous slice of rich lard and entered the front room of his living quarters – Tallinn's pharmacy – where the most ordinary of workdays should await him. He would hear about the townspeople's recent illnesses and old pains; he would hear dozens of rumours; and he would sell some medicinal treatments and sweets and a few flagons of his own fine pharmaceutical elixir. He would see ailments and diseases; he would also see the healthy and the strong, who would step into the pharmacy simply to gossip and swap news, purchase strong elixirs and chew on sweet cakes or aniseed sweets. He would fulfil his duties and be satisfied and happy in doing so, just as he probably still should be, on the threshold of his thirty-first year of life, by the blessing of his patron saint and to the joy of his noble father – may he rest in peace at the right hand of the Virgin Mary.

Melchior Wakenstede was born in the city of Lübeck, whence his father had relocated to Tallinn more than twenty years ago. Melchior the Elder came to this new land where everything was being built, to a land that had not long ago been won from the grip of pagans and which had been dedicated to the Virgin Mary. Melchior even remembered from his boyhood the stories of those old warriors who had entered his father's pharmacy from time to time to buy ointments for their aching joints. They spoke of how they had battled against the local pagans when their forces surrounded Tallinn. This all seemed hard to believe now, because the grandchildren of many of these so-called pagans visited his pharmacy each and every day. Even his beloved wife Keterlyn was of the same lineage, descended from the tribes that had lived here since ancient times, and, no matter that they did not bake bread or brew beer as it was done in Thuringia or Westphalia, these people now went to church every Sunday, as did all proper Christians.

Melchior Wakenstede considered Tallinn to be his home, as he could barely remember Lübeck. He was the town's sole apothecary, just as his father had been. Melchior loved Tallinn. He had grown up here and vowed to treat the populace with his medications, to help those who suffered and to ease their afflictions. People referred to his profession as being simply that of a doctor's cook, but it was actually much more than that. Melchior was equal to merchants in status, on a par with clergy or city officials in education, was a respected man in the town and was regarded highly by town councilmen, nobles and knights alike.

Now, on this fine spring morning, he passed from the kitchen into the pharmacy, thrust the front door open wide and let in the fresh sea air. His house was small, but it was the only one his father had had the means to purchase. In the entryway on the ground floor in the entry hall of the building was the pharmacy, comparable to a merchant's shop, and to the rear of this were his living quarters. A small passageway led from there to the kitchen, which his father had rebuilt into a pharmacist's 'witch's kitchen', as people called it. Around the fireplace stood levered presses and burners: this was where Melchior boiled and brewed his potions. On the upper floor were storage rooms filled with wooden crates in which he stored dried medicinal herbs. In the pharmacy were a large table and shelves along the walls bearing extracts, oils and mixtures in glass vessels as well as mortars and pestles. Since every apothecary needed to appear slightly mysterious and display his countenance to the townspeople, Melchior had hung a small stuffed crocodile from the ceiling above his table. It had cost ten marks and, as the sly merchant assured him, was supposed to be a genuine Egyptian crocodile. Whether true or not the townspeople seemed to believe it was.

Melchior was a fair-skinned man of shorter stature, was rather thin and had an angular build and a slight stagger to his step. His sparse, pale hair held close to his head, even when he grew his locks out below his ears. His grey eyes always had a twinkle and appeared full of mirth. Melchior loved to laugh loudly at others' jokes, and his laugh was childlike and trusting. To many it seemed that he was always cheerful and in good spirits – an apothecary cannot be dour and off-hand – yet some had also caught those moments when it seemed that a grim shadow flashed across his shy face. Those were the moments when Melchior believed that no one was watching him, and a profound agony could then show in his eyes, an almost insane depth, a difficult and painful terror. Nevertheless, Melchior would then drive these feelings away and once again be the cheery Tallinn apothecary, a friend to all and a trustworthy aide.

It was still early, and the town was just beginning to stir. Melchior sat down and reviewed the notes of those who were due to come for their medications that day. Here were his bottles and mortars, his mixtures and dried remedies; here was his world from which he could never escape – should he ever have wanted to. Melchior opened a small pouch of dried-garlic chips and took down a vessel of hard spirits from a shelf, setting both before him. Today this would become throat medicine for the baker's wife, although he could make a much greater profit from other remedies, one example being charred wheat mixed with herbs and poured into a flagon to counter a stomach ache suffered by his good friend the Magistrate, Court Vogt Wentzel Dorn.

Yet, just as Melchior sprinkled the garlic chips into the mortar, the sound of bright music reached his ears. He peered out from the open door on to the street and saw that Kilian Rechpergerin – a boarder at the house across the road owned by Mertin Tweffell – was outside, sitting on the edge of the well and playing his lute.

The young man was barely seventeen, but Melchior understood that he had studied the choral arts in several foreign cities and arrived in Tallinn at the behest of his father, since the old merchant Tweffell happened to be a relative of the Nuremberg Rechpergerin family. Kilian had been boarding in the Great Guild Alderman's house since the previous summer. He would sing at various festivities in the town and could often be seen near the Guild of the Brotherhood of Blackheads, where of late not a single meal went by without Kilian being present to sing his playful verses. He tended to introduce himself as a *Schulfreund*, as this was how journeyman musicians who roamed to far-off lands to study the art of music were titled at the Nuremberg Guild of Meistersingers. Melchior had to admit he did indeed enjoy Kilian's music – it carried a sense of the spirit of warm southern lands, a melodic lilt and techniques unfamiliar to Tallinn musicians. The young man's voice was clear and pure, warm and resounding. Which, of course, has not gone unnoticed by many a young Tallinn damsel, Melchior mused.

While continuing to concoct the cough remedy Melchior saw the door of the house opposite open and Gerdrud, the young wife of the Master Merchant Tweffell, step out into the street. It appeared to the Apothecary that the young singer had been waiting for this very moment. Melchior grasped his mortar and positioned himself slightly closer to the open door. Curiosity is the vice of all apothecaries.

The young Mistress Gerdrud – who may well have been only a year or two older than Kilian yet was younger than her husband by forty years or more – carried a basket under her arm and nodded pleasantly in greeting to the musician. The young man, in response, jumped from the rim of the well and bowed to her.

'Good morning, Mistress Merchant,' he exclaimed cheerfully. 'A fine spring morning to you. Can you see what a beautiful, blessed day has been given to us? It would be nothing short of a sin if it were not greeted with a splendid melody.'

Gerdrud stopped and replied brusquely, 'Good morning, Kilian Rechpergerin. Alas, this day is beautiful only to those who are able to pass it by with song and music. It is exactly the same as all other days for honest townsfolk, full of work and many chores to do.'

Kilian picked a swift, incredibly complex melody and called in reply, 'Ah, Mistress Gerdrud, do you think then that the arts of song and of music are gifts of the Lord and that one does not have to work hard to do them well?'

'All is born of the Lord's grace,' the young woman replied. 'I can sing also, but no one will complete my work and my tasks. The day is given to some for playing tunes and to others it is for earning their daily bread.'

'Old Uncle Mertin is wealthy enough by now that his young bride should not have to busy herself every day in the manner of a washerwoman. You have Ludke and the old maid in your household ...' Kilian said pointedly, but Gerdrud cut him off in a somewhat irritated manner.

'Stop your prattling, Kilian Rechpergerin. It is not for you to say how the master should arrange his household affairs. You are merely our boarder.'

'A boarder has eyes as well. I certainly see how things are in Tallinn compared with how they are in Nuremberg; how my great-uncle's nephew burdens his fine young bride and demands of her work and chores for which three servant girls would be necessary and for the employment of which the old churl should have sufficient funds indeed.'

What an insolent boy, thought Melchior, eavesdropping on the exchange below the window. Insolent, but he does dare to speak the truth. No one would have accused Great Guild Alderman Tweffell of excessive spending or revelry. His young wife – in addition to the fact that she was a joy to the old man's eye in his twilight years – unquestionably did more housekeeping work than the mistress of any other wealthy merchant in this town. The servant Ludke and the old maid were the only servants employed in his household.

Gerdrud exclaimed, now even more heatedly, 'Silence yourself, Kilian. Cease your mindless nonsense at once. If Ludke could hear you he would tell Sire Mertin straight away.'

Kilian stepped closer towards the young woman, cocked his head and asked slyly, 'But you will not say anything, Mistress Gerdrud?'

Gerdrud faltered. 'I … I must go. I am in a hurry,' she said.

Kilian paid this no heed. 'But maybe you will listen to just one tune?' he asked. 'Or, even better, if, as you just told me, you are able to sing as well … Surely a spring morning like this brings a melody to your tongue? So, I will play the lute, and you will sing.'

The girl shook her head. 'As if I would sing right here in the middle of town. That isn't going to happen. I really must go.'

Kilian insisted, 'Just one song. Allow me to sing to you.'

'No, Kilian. No. Not one song.'

'Do you really not want to hear one of the Nuremberg Meistersingers' best melodies? I know several of them. Just now I remembered one about an old tanner who wed a woman fifty years younger than he and became the laughing stock of the entire town, and then …'

Gerdrud emitted a muffled cry and said quickly, 'Silence, Kilian, and please do not shame me in public. I am leaving this minute.'

'But wait. Maybe some other song? How about an old song of the Minnesingers? All of our Meistersingers study old Minnesingers' songs. Should I sing to you of how Tannhäuser or Konrad von Würzburg yearned for their darling lovers? Do you wish me to?'

'No, Kilian. No. Goodbye. I have things to do in the town, and I do not wish to stand and talk to you any longer.' Gerdrud determinately wedged the basket under her arm and made to leave.

But Kilian would not give up. He flicked his fingers across the strings of his lute and said in a low voice, 'Or maybe some song of Tallinn instead, Mistress Gerdrud? Yet these are so doleful that they do not suit a fine spring morning. Oh, but I can still recall one happier song. Maybe you would like this ditty about jolly sailors?' And without waiting for a reply, Kilian began to sing:

> 'I've seventeen brothers and seventeen vessels
> I've seventeen harbours, all full of fine wenches
> My brothers dread neither death nor Heaven …'

But Gerdrud promptly shrieked, and even Melchior winced with indignation. The young woman darted over to Kilian and covered his mouth with her petite hand.

'Don't *ever* sing that song in Tallinn unless you want to be run out of town,' she cried, stunned. 'Are you insane? The Victual Brothers have done us so much harm, those raiders and murderers from the sea … Whoever sings their songs in Tallinn must be mad.'

Kilian slowly removed Gerdrud's hand from his mouth and said, so softly that Melchior could barely hear, 'Perhaps I am mad.'

'Be what you may, but you must not sing such songs in Tallinn if you don't wish to be stoned to death,' the girl said resolutely.

'Fair enough, but then tell me what sort of song you would like to hear on this morn?'

'Not a single one. I must go. Not a single song of the Meistersingers, nor of the Minnesingers; not of spring or of the sea – none at all. I … I really must hurry. You, too, should go your own way now.'

Kilian smiled dejectedly. 'Your life might become empty and sorrowful without song. Such a life has neither joy nor solace, only things to tend to and work to be done, worries and toil. Goodbye then, Mistress Gerdrud, until tonight. I also have matters to attend at the House of the Brotherhood of Blackheads. Where are you going? Maybe we are headed along the same path?'

'Me? Only here to the pharmacy and then to the harbour and the market.'

'To the pharmacy? Is Ludke unable to fetch salves and medicines for his master?'

'Master Mertin sent Ludke away somewhere last evening, and I have not seen him today. Goodbye, Kilian. I am going now.' She turned away determinedly.

Kilian laughed, waved to her and began to stride along Rataskaevu Street towards the Pikk Mäe Gate. Melchior followed the boy with his gaze and shook his head sadly. It isn't right. It isn't right that an old merchant takes such a young wife, and it isn't right that a young, handsome boarder lives under that same roof. Melchior quickly moved away from the window and settled behind the counter.

That day Mistress Gerdrud wanted a bone salve for her husband's aching joints. Melchior had readied the ointment according to the town doctor's recipe, even though he was quite certain that it would not make the old man's bones and joints a great deal less painful.

Gerdrud was still lightly flushed when she stepped into the pharmacy and greeted Melchior.

'Mistress Gerdrud, our dear neighbour,' he exclaimed. 'What a pleasure it is to see you in such a good mood on this lovely morning.'

'You are always in such a good mood that I rue the fact I happen over here as rarely as I do,' said the young woman meekly.

'Well then, come by more often. It does even a young healthy person no harm at all to down some rather spirited remedy,' Melchior advised. 'Ah yes, your bone salve. Here it is, good and ready. As ever, it should be smeared over the aching bones while offering a prayer to the Virgin Mary – it will work best that way. Or at least it will ease the troubles of old age. I expected Ludke instead of you …'

'Master Mertin sent him somewhere yesterday. I have not seen him since then,' Gerdrud replied.

'And your husband?'

'He rushed off to the harbour at dawn to trade. Thank you for the ointment.'

'Rushed?' Melchior pronounced thoughtfully. 'You know, I am not an actual physician, of course, but even I know a thing or two about illnesses, and rushing is no longer proper at Master Mertin's age. That I say for certain. A calm, quiet life, fatty foods, not fasting too zealously during Lent – yes? – proper bloodletting and, once in a while, applying ointment to aching areas and, last but not least, taking hot baths. There is no other treatment than that to recommend.'

The girl was not yet twenty years of age. She had blonde hair and blue eyes, and her young, innocent face could be seen beneath her headdress. Did her carefree expression hide those troubled feelings that a young girl must have when her husband is fifty years older than her and infirm?

'He has prayers said for his well-being at St Nicholas's Church and pays for masses,' said the girl, sighing.

Not by any means generously, or so I've heard, Melchior mused silently, although he nodded enthusiastically.

The girl fell silent. Gerdrud observed Melchior with growing seriousness then asked abruptly, 'But tell me, Sire Melchior, will all this be of no help to him? His aches and pains show no sign at all of going away.'

'My dear neighbour, just as time has been given to one, so it, too, must pass, but maybe it can be prolonged a little through a mixture of the right treatment, prayer and bloodletting. If blood is let properly and his aching bones and joints are rubbed with ointment then Master Mertin will certainly not be in the shadow of death just yet. I told him this myself. He might live for another ten years or more.'

'Does your star chart say so?'

'My star chart?' asked Melchior. He leaned down and removed a folded star chart from beneath the counter. The item was the work of masters in Bruges and had been handed down to him by his father. The method for reading a star chart was one secret known to apothecaries' *zünfte*.

'No, not a star chart, rather my intuition and experience. Your husband's joints are ill and his bones ache, but his vitality is still strong. A star chart tells me when is the very best day to let blood, and, as I can see here, that would be …' His fingers glided quickly across the star chart's symbols and he murmured, 'We must look for the position of Sagittarius to counter Master Tweffell's hip pain. His legs are here in Capricorn, and his ailing knees are in Aquarius … and, as we see now that the moon is in Capricorn the evening after tomorrow, then I would say it would benefit your husband to let blood at the barber's in the morning two days from now, and after that he should be treated with ointment at once, then his leg pain should certainly subside.'

'I will pass word along to him. A thousand thanks to you, Apothecary Melchior, and farewell.' Gerdrud sighed once more and turned to leave.

Melchior nodded to her. 'Yes, yes, it is an old science taught to us by Saliceto Wilhelmus and Cremona Gerardus and all of those other famed healers of times past. Surely advise your beloved husband to let blood appropriately, and you will definitely see, my dear neighbour, that he will remain in excellently good health.'

'By the Lord's grace,' Gerdrud murmured and left. Melchior watched her as she departed and stood lost in thought.

'Poor girl.' A woman's voice sounded from behind him. The Apothecary had not heard his precious wife Keterlyn enter the pharmacy.

3

Tallinn Town Hall
16 May, Morning

THE MAGISTRATE of Tallinn Town Council, Wentzel Dorn, was standing before Councilman Bockhorst and an attendant of the Teutonic Order and in his mind was running through all the positions he would much rather hold than the cursed and detestable office of magistrate, or vogt. The first that came to mind was the honourable occupation of brewer, for two reasons: first, a brewer always has fresh beer close by; and, second, a brewer is never hounded out of bed early in the morning nor ordered to appear urgently at the Town Hall where awaiting him was – oh merciful Lord – the personal attendant to the Commander of the Teutonic Order in Tallinn bearing the sort of news that should cause one's hair to fall out.

Yet, here Dorn was, thoroughly lacking a good night's rest and with his stomach starting to rumble just as it always did when he heard bad news. Very bad news.

'Today at midday,' the attendant stated, and the Councilman nodded.

'What at midday?' asked Dorn.

The attendant glared at Dorn with unveiled animosity. 'The esteemed Commander awaits your presence before him at midday,' he said.

'Well, of course,' the Magistrate responded nervously. 'And are the other councilmen expected as well or only the Magistrate?'

'The councilmen have mass at the Church of the Holy Ghost at midday,' Councilman Bockhorst declared quickly. 'However, the Magistrate will most certainly be at Toompea this midday. He is the most familiar with all legal provisions, and all in all ...'

'All in all and most certainly,' Dorn grumbled to himself. The Commander is searching for a murderer from the town, and the Magistrate is the pre-eminent expert of local law. He looked out through an open window, and his gaze fell upon a beer-seller in the market with a large tankard of his wares. The Magistrate swallowed dryly. It wouldn't be a poor choice to call upon my friend Melchior prior to going to Toompea. Even more so if the Commander has very bad news. Unpleasant news should not be heard when sober.

This whole affair carried a hint of something from which the Magistrate tended to shy away. The high-ranking Knight that had been killed had come from Gotland, and Gotland was often in conflict with towns to which Tallinn needed to remain on good terms — or at least that was how the Magistrate understood the situation. The Council had been bickering with Novgorod and Vyborg and even Tartu in recent years. Until recently the Magistrate would have been required to throw all Russian merchants who arrived in Tallinn into the prison tower because Tartu demanded it — but what would then have become of Tallinn's merchants at the Hanseatic office in Novgorod? Dorn had no patience with affairs that might be connected to powerful overlords and foreign lands, and the killing of this Knight gave off a whiff of just that kind of matter. Dorn must maintain peace in Tallinn according to his oath of office, and the Council had enacted its own laws for that very purpose. These were simple and clear: traders on the market square who weighed goods improperly were to be shackled; journeyman tanners who fought with knives during designated night-time hours were to be fined. Dorn believed this was the most important work associated with the post of magistrate. He was capable of performing such tasks with absolute precision and according to his conscience because he knew the town would benefit from such acts. Tracking down the murderers of high-ranking Knights of the Order from distant lands, that he would gladly have left to someone else.

'What a frightful tale,' sighed Councilman Bockhorst, shivering. 'However, we are lucky to have such a fine magistrate in our town as Sire Wentzel Dorn, who will search both high and low to track this murderer down.'

Or else it will be his head that is next impaled on a hook, thought the Magistrate Wentzel Dorn.

'Indeed, the Order hopes the murderer will be found quickly,' the courier remarked ominously. 'However, the Commander will likely go into this in greater detail. This must not be spoken of in the town before the Commander has stated his wishes. If rumours get out it won't help.'

Oh, come now, Dorn thought. A town with a market hardly needs a crier – people find things out anyway.

As he descended the steps of the Town Hall with the attendant, Dorn asked whether the Commander had spoken of a bounty.

'The town must likely set one itself,' the attendant replied. 'It's not as if we have the right to carry out any affairs on town lands.'

'A terrible story, so it is,' sighed Dorn.

'It is a terrible story, yes,' the attendant agreed and sighed himself. 'There was chaos on Toompea the whole night. However, what is absolutely clear is that the Commander does not want to send a message to the Grand Master informing him that a high-ranking knight has had his head taken off, that a coin was stuffed into his mouth and that the murderer then escaped to the Lower Town and hasn't yet been found. No, certainly not …'

'Coin? What coin?' Dorn asked in surprise.

'I don't know what coin it was, but it rolled out of Clingenstain's mouth when his head was removed from the hook. The head was driven on to a *hook*, you know?'

'Oh, that murderer truly did a thorough job,' Dorn growled.

The attendant stopped suddenly in front of the Town Hall door, turned towards Dorn hesitantly and said carefully, 'Well, yes … Actually, the Commander did say not to mention the coin, so perhaps the Magistrate will fail to recall this until such time as the Commander himself speaks about everything himself in greater detail.'

'Agreed,' Dorn grunted and bade the attendant farewell. He then, however, made his mind up to call upon Melchior, as he could certainly use a proper drop of strongly spiced spirits to soothe his stomach ache, and – as he was well aware – his friend the Apothecary had quite a nose for finding murderers. If Melchior had not worked out who had strangled that Flemish heretic to death the previous spring the killer would still be walking about Tallinn like a dignified and respectable townswoman. The Town Council would definitely agree to Dorn employing Melchior as his sub-magistrate.

4

Goldsmith Casendorpe's Workshop, Kuninga Street
16 May, Morning

GOLDSMITH AND ALDERMAN of St Canute's Guild Burckhart Casendorpe was not accustomed to hearing shocking news from his daughter's mouth. He was usually informed of such developments by journeymen at the smithy or other masters at the guildhall, and this only as often as shocking news passed through the town of Tallinn at all. Master Casendorpe could not be regarded as being curious by nature: the profession of goldsmith was too important and dignified for much time to be left to discuss town affairs or pass the time gossiping. As Alderman of St Canute's Guild Casendorpe already far too much to do – whether it be tending to the guild altars, convening meetings of the trade, collecting dues, speaking for the masters and numerous other matters. Throughout the forty years of his life – thirty of which he had spent in Tallinn – Master Casendorpe had, above all else, wanted to work with gold and silver. Gold will always persevere, and no war, famine nor plague could change that fact. Gold nourishes. Gold is the essence of wealth and power everywhere in the world. Rich men will always desire golden ornaments. If wealthy men do not have gold of which to boast and to hang around their necks then no one considers them rich or important. And for that reason alone a goldsmith was always an esteemed master. Thus, when Burckhart Casendorpe was chosen to be Alderman of St Canute's Guild, he was forced, to his dismay, to start handling matters that were not so close to his heart. Yet, on the other hand, it made him an important – a *very* important – townsperson, just as it made his only daughter Hedwig one of Tallinn's most sought-after maidens.

On this occasion, however, the eighteen-year-old Hedwig was standing beneath the window of his workshop in Kuninga Street and delivering some shocking news. 'And that knight was chopped into pieces right there on Toompea. All of his arms and legs severed from his body. Cut into pieces.'

Hedwig had been to the market with her mother, which meant she had heard the day's news.

'Hush, girl, hush,' Casendorpe murmured and cast an irritated glance behind him to where his journeymen were trying to look busy and as if they were not listening to the shocking news that the young girl had brought. It was not usual for young maidens to speak of such things.

'Father, it is completely unbelievable, absolutely astounding,' Hedwig exclaimed.

'Yes,' the Goldsmith concurred, 'I believe it is indeed.' He adjusted his spectacles and wrinkled his brow. A goldsmith's work had to be visible to the townspeople so that the artisan might not compromise the quality of the precious metals, and the Town Council therefore required the goldsmith's workshop to have a large window that faced the street and from which the interior could be seen. Casendorpe serviced his regular clients through an open window that yawned above a table. Affixed to the wall next to the table was a shelf that held items certifying that the Goldsmith was an important, esteemed and wealthy man devoted to all kinds of arcane arts. On this shelf Casendorpe had placed items such as shark teeth, coconut cream, coral, peacock feathers, a lump of amber, parrot feathers, a dried crab and other articles that exuded meaning and power, brought to the town from far-off lands and purchased from wandering merchants in exchange for bulging purses full of coins. One did not need to fear growing cold while bartering at the open window during winter. The Goldsmith's workshop contained a large hearth and a forge that an apprentice tended when work was under way.

Hedwig stood below the window and shouted so loudly that even the journeymen turned their heads. 'But, Father, it is that very same knight to whom you sold a chain collar yesterday. Imagine – oh heavenly grace – you saw that man just a short time before he was chopped into pieces …'

Casendorpe raised his head slowly. 'Was that spoken of at the market as well?' he asked in a muted tone and peered around nervously.

'No, not that, but you yourself said that his name was Clingenstain – that Knight of Gotland – and now, in the market, they are saying it was he who was chopped into bits.'

'Into *pieces*?' the Goldsmith mumbled, then asked with growing seriousness, 'You didn't say anything to anyone about how I sold a collar to that knight, now, did you, Hedwig?'

'No, Father, I didn't say a thing,' the girl asserted.

Casendorpe pushed aside the guild's book of accounts into which he had been making notes while standing at the table. 'We could go for a short stroll about the town, Hedwig,' he said, 'perhaps around the market and the pharmacy.'

'Ah, so you want to hear the news as well. But, Father, I am telling you, he was chopped up into pieces and –'

'Hush now, please,' the Goldsmith rebuked his daughter. 'This is not a thing of which young maidens should speak. Wait for me at the doorstep. I shall get myself ready.'

Rumours, market tittle-tattle — these things were so dangerous that it was better to hear them straight away. Especially when they concern a man who wore a golden collar made by your own hands around his neck. A man who was now dead.

Thank heavens, he is dead.

5

Tallinn Market Square
16 May, Morning

MERCHANT CLAWES FREISINGER, Alderman of the Brotherhood of Blackheads, had also heard of Commander Clingenstain's murder in the market while he and two attendants were purchasing the finest foods to offer at that evening's beer-sampling festivity. The Toompea milkman's uncle told the fish trader's daughter … someone had seen, someone had heard … a head was chopped off … what a dreadful thing … oh, those Knights of the Order can't even manage to keep sober … that very same Clingenstain, yes, the one who had made merry for several days and who the Town Council had fed and plied with drink … a terrible shame on the entire town of Tallinn …

Freisinger pricked up his ears; rumours are only rumours. One thing was clear, though; there had apparently been a great deal of blood.

Unlike Master Goldsmith Casendorpe, Freisinger the Blackhead was a man of great curiosity. No rumour was too insignificant in the merchant's profession – knowledge of the town's affairs, troubles and misfortunes, joys and festivities are always of some use to a trader. A merchant – and especially one who hailed from a foreign land – must know more about town affairs than even the town's

Chief Councilman. Freisinger listened carefully, but the rumours and counter-rumours were overwhelming. One thing they all agreed on, however, was that there had been a great deal of blood.

He needed to find out more. Freisinger started to make his way towards the pharmacy but then, in the distance, spotted Casendorpe approaching arm-in-arm with his daughter Hedwig. Freisinger's heart leaped with joy. His future father-in-law and his fiancée drew nearer, and stories of dreadful bloodshed on Toompea were briefly pushed aside in his mind.

Hedwig was Clawes Freisinger's ticket into the circle of Tallinn's wealthy and respected citizens. She was the finest maiden in the town, not just because she was as beautiful as St Ursula but she was as rich as … as Master Goldsmith Casendorpe himself. Hedwig was Freisinger's passport into the Great Guild and his farewell to the status as a Blackhead. There were, of course, many in Tallinn who regarded the Master Blackhead as very best groom available. No one could say that he was poor – Clawes Freisinger always saw to that. His coats and cloaks were tailored from the most expensive cloth and his caps were as grand and feathered as those of any baron. Freisinger had not been shy about acquiring chains and rings: a silver clasp always adorned his collar, and even in winter he hung gold-encrusted ornaments from his fur cloak, which was cut from the highest-priced material.

And no one could say he lacked skill when it came to handling arms. He rode as gallantly as some knights, his arrows flew to their mark as accurately as those of an English archer, and when the Council ordered the Blackheads' war party to display its arms these were always in a commendable condition: the men's armour glistened with oil, and their battle axes were as sharp as butchers' blades. When the city guilds organized war games Freisinger set for the Blackheads the honourable goal of winning the highest number of prizes and to be declared the most valiant men on the field.

Members of the Brotherhood of Blackheads were, of course, only merchants – and most were foreigners at that – but taking part in a tournament allowed a townsman to feel like a nobleman, if only for a moment. Furthermore, Freisinger could not say for certain that neither he nor any other fine Blackhead would fail to unhorse any Harju vassal with his lance.

Clawes Freisinger had resided in Tallinn for five years and gave himself credit for the fact that the Brotherhood of Blackheads, which before had sunk into the deepest of comas, was now famed throughout the town.

The eligible bachelor Freisinger was a much-sought-after groom in Tallinn. He had become accustomed to merchants' wives stealing glances at him, and he had never needed to pay a girl for her company. This was without question no secret from Maiden Hedwig either, certainly not.

Clawes Freisinger stood and waited patiently until Hedwig noticed him. He then nodded discreetly and motioned with his head towards the western end of the market square. No doubt they would manage to cross paths there behind some well-concealed corner and once again vow to one another the very thing they had professed in secret for the last year.

To his surprise Clawes Freisinger had come to the conclusion that he deeply and passionately loved the Maiden Hedwig Casendorpe and that he was prepared to pay the price of forfeiting his Blackhead status if only so he could carry that figure – which he could only imagine from the silhouette beneath her clothing – to his bed as his lawful wife.

I should resist this temptation with greater fortitude, Freisinger thought as he ran after the Maiden Hedwig like some shepherd boy.

6

The Dominican Monastery
16 May, Morning

DOMINICAN PRIOR BALTAZAR ECKELL had been feeling under the weather for some time. He was afflicted by aches, heartburn and sharp stinging pains; his appetite had disappeared, his head spun, the world swam before his eyes, and on some occasions, when his condition was acute, the Prior believed he could hear the voice of the Archangel Michael calling out to him, letting him know that he was expected. Maybe his time on this earth was indeed coming to an end, although he still had so much to do … Alas, one man's time had reached its end just yesterday. He had heard this just now from the monastery *cellarius* Hinricus, who himself heard the news from the cook, who in his turn had learned of it at the market.

Henning von Clingenstain had been killed on Toompea. His head had been chopped off. Lord have mercy on his soul.

Prior Eckell was sitting with the young *cellarius* in the monastery scriptorium. The chapter meeting had just ended. For some years now the Prior had, without fail, come to the scriptorium at this time of day to contemplate heavenly and not-so-heavenly matters. The monks who were not in town preaching or handling other monastery affairs worked during this hour before their lunch. The Prior felt a strong need to sit and ruminate on this day because he had already

40

prayed. He could not even remember whether or not he had slept the previous night. Prayer is an art. Genuine prayer, a beseeching force bursting from within a person that makes its way up to God, this must be learned and learned diligently. Prior Eckell had learned to pray before falling asleep in a way that his prayers remained with him for the entire night, sustained throughout his dreams. Eckell relived these orisons in his dreams; they spiralled around his thoughts, and he even heard himself speaking with the angels and saints to whom he prayed. He had cultivated this skill as a young man in order to find refuge from the night-time visions of a twenty-year-old monk. And Eckell had kept up this skill, this art. Sin stalks a person with every step. A monk's thoughts must be like a town defended by a sturdy wall, but sleep is a time when the town gates are opened wide and the watchmen have vanished with the keys. It was for this precise reason that the young Baltazar learned to battle his dreams ceaselessly, so that night-time temptations might not poison his daytime thoughts.

He had experienced a profound need for this skill the previous night.

'Father, was that member of the Order the very same who took confession from you yesterday on Toompea?' the *cellarius* Hinricus enquired, agitated.

'Yes, none other,' Eckell replied wearily.

'Then it is as if it occurred according to some heavenly prophecy, is it not? He went to confession during the day, and a few hours later ... he is executed by the sword. As if he had foreseen the event ...'

Eckell did not reply. He did not tell Hinricus that Commander Clingenstain had no reason to believe he would meet his death on that night on Toompea. The saints charge a prior to keep young monks away from worldly horrors – they do not yet know death, they do not know its smell, they do not *remember* death as a prior does. And he, Baltazar Eckell, remembered a great many kinds of death; he could recall every colour, every smell and sound. No, Clingenstain was certainly not expecting his death would be the lustrous red colour of blood glistening on grey slate or that it would reek of beer.

'Should I have the infirmarer prepare for you an infusion for your aching bones?' Hinricus asked with a hint of concern. 'You are pale, Father.'

'I am pale because my blood has already gone as white as my hair,' the Prior replied. 'No, the infirmarer is not required. Do you know where Wunbaldus is?'

'He was in the brewery earlier tasting his bock – the very same that will be judged today at the Brotherhood of Blackheads. Should I have him summoned?'

'Yes … or, that is, no,' the Prior mumbled. 'I must think.' I must *calm myself* and *think*. 'Please have my chessboard taken to Wunbaldus's chambers and …' He fell silent. Hinricus waited patiently. The old man breathed deeply, his hand resting on a closed book and his gaze fixed on the window, as if he had just glimpsed St Catherine there. Only birdsong came from outside, penetrating the absolute silence that reigned within the dank walls of the scriptorium. Eckell felt his present train of thought slip from his grasp, melting like snow in springtime.

'Does the snow still fall, Hinricus?' the Prior asked without warning, his gaze still trained on the window through which the monastery's budding orchard trees were visible.

'No, Father, it does not,' Hinricus replied quietly. Snow has not fallen for two months. Virgin Mary have mercy on us.

'Then the snowfall has passed,' the Prior whispered. 'That is good, Hinricus. Praised be the Lord, that is very good.'

7

Melchior's Pharmacy
16 May, Morning

'POOR GIRL,' Keterlyn repeated as she stood next to her husband and watched Gerdrud as she left the house and came out on to the street.

'Everything else but that, my lovely wife,' Melchior said and chuckled. 'Gerdrud may be unhappy, but she is far from poor because Sire Mertin is one of the richest men in Tallinn.'

'Yet what good are riches if you do not see a single penny of them and every day you must rub lotion on your ailing husband's swollen legs like some almshouse healer?' Keterlyn replied. 'I still remember Gerdrud from when we played together in a meadow outside the town – she was so full of joy, such a spirited young thing, but look at her now.'

Melchior shrugged. 'Of course, Gerdrud's parents did not care enough for their daughter to have paired her with some young, skilled apothecary, but if you consider the dowry that old Mertin bequeathed to Gerdrud's father and mother and then at what I had to hand over to yours ...'

'My father was not of German descent, merely a simple stonecutter and, what's more, from the country,' Keterlyn said pointedly.

'Well, yes, I suppose I did get a good deal. I looked for the most splendid young lass for whom the tiniest dowry had to be offered ...'

Keterlyn erupted into laughter. 'What a greedy fox you are.'

'I complain not. Come now, the thought never crossed my mind. The money was not great – but *such* a lass. Furthermore, I took a look at my star chart earlier to find what has been promised for witty apothecaries today, and there was something quite gladdening there,' Melchior declared, winking slyly at his wife.

Keterlyn caught his eyes roving across her body and asked with feigned severity, 'Interesting. What was it, I wonder?'

Melchior winked again and spread his star chart out upon the table. 'But come closer, my lovely wife, and see for yourself.'

'All that astrological hocus-pocus is plain nonsense, and I do not believe in it. What am I to see from this?'

If Keterlyn held a serious belief in anything then it was her womanly intuition, which carried a mixture of ancient ancestral Vironian wisdom and contemporary townswoman caution. All the same, Melchior chuckled and bent over his star chart. An apothecary's wife is not an apothecary, he mused.

'If I understand correctly, then Sagittarius shows with great precision that this morning one fine and intrepid apothecary will – right here and post haste – receive a sweet kiss from his lovely young beauty,' he said. Melchior spun around quickly and drew Keterlyn into his embrace. If she made any show of resistance then it was only for appearance. Her suggestion that someone could walk in at any moment fell upon deaf ears. Melchior thrust her gently against the pharmacy counter, pressed his lips against hers, slipped his hand down along her dress and caressed her gently arched thigh.

'You see, my love. It happened just as Sagittarius promised: one sweet kiss to begin the day. Hence, it is for naught that you do not believe in star charts,' he whispered into Keterlyn's ear after a few moments.

And it was only after Keterlyn had readily accepted the star chart's divination that Melchior Wakenstede heard the news that a high-ranking Knight of the Order had been killed the previous day on Toompea. Keterlyn had gone to the market in the morning, and, as Melchior often noted, the market was the only place in the town where news could be heard earlier than at the pharmacy.

'Have the knights let a bit of each other's blood?' he asked inquisitively – apothecaries are very inquisitive.

'I know not. Clingenstain or something like that. They say his head was chopped off as he slept.'

'Holy Christ on the cross,' Melchior exclaimed. 'What dreadful games our noble knights play. Who, then, was the slayer?'

'Oh, there are all sorts of tales, but no one knows for certain. Neither does the Commander. No one witnessed the act. His head was chopped off, and that's all we know. The murderer was not to be found. Some knights' pages were seen this morning near the Town Hall, and they were properly bad-tempered and irritable. Tell me, Melchior, what has our world come to when members of the Order squabble amongst themselves and carry out atrocious murders?'

'I know not,' Melchior conceded, staring out the window. 'And I know not whether I even *want* to know – yet I think we will hear of this in greater detail very soon because here comes our dear Magistrate.'

The town had awoken, and the daily throng was bustling along Rataskaevu Street, but from the sea of familiar faces Melchior could easily pick out that of his good friend Wentzel Dorn, Magistrate of the town of Tallinn. Melchior knew what sorts of messages his friend would bring even before Dorn stepped into the pharmacy. The Magistrate appeared morose and ill-tempered; he had forgotten his livery collar and was itching for a couple of cups of elixir and good advice.

This is not the first time, Melchior said to himself. The Magistrate might have a thorough knowledge of Lübeck law and able assistants, yet when he was in need of good advice then the pharmacy was the first place he came to seek it. Melchior had come to the Council's aid in solving murders on three previous occasions. The last time, the summer before, when Melchior worked out who had choked that Flemish heretic to death, the two men had discovered that they very much enjoyed spending time in one another's company discussing world affairs and drinking beer. And that is perhaps what most call friendship.

Dorn was nearly ten years older than the Apothecary. He was a stout, robust man with red hair and a slight limp in his right leg. The hobble came from an old injury that Dorn had sustained in his youth when fighting the Lithuanians as a member of the town's army. Wentzel Dorn, who was a native of Tallinn, had been Court Magistrate for six years already. He was one of the fourteen town councilmen – although, in truth, the position of Magistrate was also referred to as the 'little councilman', since he lacked a strong voice in the town's affairs. The Magistrate's task was to seek out criminals and punish them for lesser crimes according to Lübeck law. He was in charge of overseeing craftsmen to ensure they fulfilled the Council's dictates and did not swindle the townsfolk. The full Council – all of the councilmen together – presided over trials for more serious crimes. Melchior believed Wentzel Dorn to be a good magistrate and a good judge, as his heart was in the right place. As it was written in Lübeck law, a judge must not allow himself to be influenced by anger, favour or bribery, nor may he fear anyone other than the Lord God – and Wentzel Dorn was that sort of man. When it was necessary to torture someone, then Dorn ordered that the person be tortured.

When a case involved justice and judgement, then Dorn was neither exceedingly strict nor cruel. He would hear out each side's account and impose a fine that the accused was capable of paying and which did not render the individual's family destitute. Yet, when a clever mind was needed or a criminal had to be tracked or if a thief denied everything and no one testified against him, then Dorn sometimes fell short on ingenuity. But that is what friends are for.

Yes, this was not the first time Melchior would provide his friend Dorn with good advice. He entered the pharmacy with the exact sort of furrowed brow that he usually displayed on such occasions. The Magistrate greeted Keterlyn politely and flopped heavily into a chair.

'The Lord's peace be with you, Sire Wentzel,' said Keterlyn.

'Things are far from peaceful,' the Magistrate retorted gloomily.

'Then I will not begin to enquire at length,' said Melchior, 'as to the state of the Magistrate's stomach this morning. Better I pour him a curative spiced wine straight away.'

'Oh,' Keterlyn exclaimed, feigning surprise. 'Is the Magistrate's stomach grumbling again? Just as *every* morning?'

'A small curative drink would do no harm, no. Something is grinding and cramping up inside,' Dorn growled.

Melchior already had the clay bottle ready. 'And I can see the Magistrate's stomach pains are absolutely frightful this morning, as he has even forgotten his livery collar,' he remarked as he poured the drink. 'Good health to you.'

'Obliged, Melchior, and good health.' The Magistrate downed the goblet of spiced pharmacy wine in a single gulp then exhaled. Keterlyn watched him and giggled furtively. The Magistrate, as she was well aware, was plagued somehow too frequently by stiff stomach pains, and a stronger sort of elixir seemed to be the only thing that helped.

Dorn groaned meanwhile, 'Like old Beelzebub himself, just churning and churning. As for my livery collar, well, yes … I likely won't be holding that much longer. But, Melchior, if by any chance you have not yet heard …'

'There is a good chance I have, as my dear wife has already managed to visit the market this morning,' said Melchior.

'In that case, you already know more than I,' Dorn speculated.

Melchior fell silent for a moment and then spoke in a more serious tone, 'Only a little more, Magistrate. Only that yesterday eventide the former Commander of the Order in Gotland was decapitated on Toompea and that the murderer escaped to the Lower Town.'

'To the town?' Keterlyn gasped. 'That was certainly not said at the market. How do you know this?'

'Well, it is not at all difficult to work out that if bloodshed has taken place on Toompea and no one has yet been put into chains then the murderer will have fled. And if the murderer fled and members of the Order were seen near the Town Hall in the morning, and the Magistrate is very grim afterwards, then it is obvious that the killer escaped to the Lower Town.'

Dorn nodded and took another swig from the goblet that Melchior had already refilled.

'The murderer is in the town? Oh great heavens, Melchior, the murderer is in the *town*? I dare not go out on the streets now,' Keterlyn moaned.

'All the better,' said Melchior. 'I told you earlier what the star chart promised fine apothecaries for the morning hours, although now that I think about it there was also a thing or two written about the noon hours, thus it is surely best that you do not go out into town.'

'Melchior, have some shame,' Keterlyn said, blushing.

Dorn wondered aloud what the star chart had in mind for magistrates that day.

'Three steins of spiced wine to treat stomach troubles,' Melchior replied and nodded cheerfully. Keterlyn, however, bade Dorn good day, as she did not wish to hear any further dreadful talk about murder.

It was a serious matter that the killer of such an elevated member of the Order had escaped below into town jurisdiction. The Order would certainly demand the culprit be handed over to Toompea, and the Council would certainly give him up, yet what then followed would depend on *who* the killer was and *why* the act had been committed. Members of the Order were not permitted to enter the town of Tallinn to exercise their supremacy. Melchior loved Tallinn; it was his town. He wanted Tallinn to be healthy, that sickness not spread here, that life be secure and that the town might be a safe place for his children to grow up. Tallinn was built on lands that belonged to the Teutonic Order, but Lübeck law prevailed within its boundaries, and the Order could not dictate town affairs. If, however, the Commander's murderer was a citizen of Tallinn then the Order's revenge could beset the entire town. No one from Tallinn had ever chopped off the head of a knight before. It was unheard of. It was appalling …

'Did anyone see the murderer?' Melchior asked suddenly. 'Did any member of the Order see who did it?'

'I know not what or whom they saw there. The Knights' eyes can still barely discern anything at all – they have been downing tankards with the men from Gotland for a number of days,' the Magistrate snorted.

'Yes, yes. Now that I think of it, then was that Clingenstain – may he rest in peace, of course – not the very same Henning von Clingenstain of Gotland who commanded the Order's forces under the honourable Grand Master von Jungingen when they took Gotland and drove the Victual Brothers from the island?' Melchior asked.

'One and the same,' Dorn confirmed. 'As the Council was informed, members of the Order are travelling from Gotland through Tallinn back to Marienburg to appear before the Grand Master now that the Teutonic Order has conceded Gotland to the Danish Crown.'

'That very same Clingenstain – the Butcher of Gotland, as he was called. It is said that Knights of the Order burned the Victual Brothers alive in Gotland, chopped off their hands and left them on the beach to die. Some were skinned alive, and the victors made themselves gloves out of their skin. Rivers of blood flowed there.'

'And rightfully so,' the Magistrate sputtered. 'Did the Victual Brothers show mercy to anyone? Did they not once rob every ship, whether Hanseatic, Danish or Swedish? Were they not the greatest scourge of the North Sea, a band of scoundrels and tempestuous raiders, accursed slaughterers and beasts detested by God himself? All those names, such as Störtebecker, Gödeke Michels and Magister Wigbold and who else have you …?'

Yes, Melchior knew those names, just as every citizen of every seaport on the Baltic Sea probably did. These were the names from his youth that had elicited fear and horror. The Victual Brothers showed mercy to none, and none showed them mercy. Victual Brothers who were taken prisoner were brought to land and executed publicly. Melchior had personally witnessed one of those events nearly ten years earlier. Three Victual Brothers were decapitated in Tallinn's harbour and their heads nailed to mooring posts. Hundreds and hundreds of men perished during those wars, and the Victual Brothers even carried out raids in Livonia. They sacked Haapsalu and burned the town to its very foundations. The Teutonic Order had put an end to all that. Melchior thought back on these tales, listened to the Magistrate's expostulations and gazed out the window from time to time. He noticed amongst the regular townsfolk

Master Blackhead Clawes Freisinger and the Maiden Hedwig passing beneath the window and whispering secretively. He saw Pastor Rode of the Church of the Holy Ghost stroll past. Then there was the cobbler's apprentice and other familiar faces who evidently had no idea that the Toompea Murderer might be walking alongside them.

'Did they not nail prisoners into herring barrels and cast them into the sea?' the Magistrate continued angrily. 'And did they not take my son-in-law captive, and then, after we paid the ransom, we received no reply? Only later did we hear he had already been impaled long before on the beaches at Stralsund. Curses, it was as if the town of Tallinn were under siege because of them. Not one honest captain braved going to sea without soldiers on board, and even *they* sometimes lost their nerve and sold the ship to the Victual Brothers. It was like a blessing from Heaven when the Order drove them from Gotland, Melchior.'

'A blessing from Heaven, that it was,' Melchior concurred. 'The air at sea is truly purer now, although piracy will continue for as long as goods are carried by ship. As I've heard, the Vogts in Vyborg and Turku still allow the men along their coasts to take hold of vessels from Tallinn. All the same, it is odd that Clingenstain met his end now, just after he left Gotland.'

'What do you mean by that, my friend?'

'Nothing more than that it is odd. He was alive and well for as long as he was overlord of Gotland, and it was after he became free from that post is when he met his maker. And, what's more, it happened in Tallinn, where Clingenstain probably never stepped foot previously and where no one could have borne enmity against him.'

The Magistrate sighed deeply. 'Right here in Tallinn, yes. You rub salt deeper into the wound.'

'I suppose it is an apothecary's responsibility to rub remedies on all types of wounds. Not that I would wish to jest at your expense, my dear friend, but I do say that if I can in any way help you pass between the boulders of the Order and the Council so that they might not grind you into dust –'

Melchior was interrupted by a high-pitched screech from outside. He turned to look and saw that it had apparently been the Maiden Hedwig Casendorpe, who, upon hearing Master Freisinger's words, had become thoroughly exhilarated and had then nearly run into Pastor Rode. The Blackhead Freisinger was now attempting to explain something apologetically to the priest while Hedwig joyfully flitted off back towards the market.

'What is it?'

'Nothing at all,' Melchior replied. 'Only the Master Blackhead and his bride-to-be. They just bade one another farewell rather sweetly. What a wonder. The Master Blackhead even has time to involve himself in affairs of the heart before such an important evening.'

'Evening? What evening?' Dorn asked.

'My good friend, today is the first day of the beer-tasting festival at the Brotherhood of Blackheads, to which both the Sire Apothecary and the Magistrate have been warmly invited. Yesterday I saw those casks of spring brew being rolled from the Dominican Monastery straight towards the Blackheads' guildhall.'

'Oh, devils,' Dorn cursed. 'How could I have forgotten? You don't suppose the festivities will be cancelled, now that …?'

'A murderer is running about the town? We can ask Master Freisinger right now.'

Melchior poked his head out the window and shouted down to Freisinger, who was standing with his gaze fixed longingly on the Maiden Hedwig.

'And a fine day to you, Master Blackhead. Don't just stand there in my doorway. Come into the pharmacy, seeing as you are in this part of town.'

'With pleasure,' the merchant answered from below. He glanced towards the Town Hall, his eyes following the bounding Hedwig, and then blinked rapidly. Freisinger opened the pharmacy door wide and stepped in; Melchior was already pouring him a tall cup of elixir.

'And the Magistrate here as well … A good morning to you,' Freisinger said, nodding.

Melchior would not say that Freisinger was a friend, exactly – the men were too different in character and in their spheres of operation – but the Apothecary did regard this lofty, tawny man with respect and not only because Melchior, as town apothecary, was invited to sessions of food and drink at the Brotherhood of Blackheads. Indeed not. Melchior believed Clawes Freisinger was a just-minded fellow with a grand and knightly air that somehow seemed to lift him above the level of the other town merchants. Freisinger encompassed an inexplicable dignity, as if he were nobleman or chivalrous trader. The Alderman of the Brotherhood of Blackheads also had a touch of mystery and an enigmatic force to him that Melchior had never quite pinned down.

Melchior filled a small stein of elixir while the Magistrate expressed his interest in who had just shouted out there on the street.

'The Maiden Hedwig Casendorpe almost ran down Pastor Rode of the Church of the Holy Ghost,' Freisinger replied.

'Ah, so it was the Maiden Hedwig. Then it is quite clear why she nearly knocked the Pastor down,' Dorn said, erupting into laughter.

'I know not. For what reason then?' Freisinger replied frostily.

'Now then, Sire Blackhead, the whole town is aware that you and the Maiden Hedwig will soon require the services of the Pastor, who will stand in front of the altar and by the power vested in him …' the Magistrate intoned knowingly and winked. 'Tell us rather, Master Blackhead, when will old Casendorpe arrange an engagement party?'

Freisinger was apparently not amused by this sort of discussion. 'That you should certainly ask of Master Casendorpe,' he marked curtly.

Melchior patted the Magistrate's shoulder and chuckled. 'Our town is small, and it is not as if anything goes unnoticed – and women also tend to gossip up a storm when a wedding seems to be imminent. Well, I, too, have heard that Master Freisinger is rumoured soon to be putting aside his merry life with the Blackheads and taking on the role of a married citizen of the town – but stories are come in all shapes and sizes, and once they have been let loose then they reach the pharmacy in time, so do not be irritated by our curiosity, Master Blackhead.'

'I hold it not against you, Melchior,' the merchant replied. 'Surely you, as a married man, know that you say one thing, although is understood otherwise, and all the while third parties hear it in a third manner and pass it along differently to a fourth.'

'Such it is, Master Blackhead,' Melchior assented. 'However, maybe you will have a sweet pharmacy elixir to counter the throat ache that ailed you last week? I still have some left, and by your expression I would say the pain has not quite passed yet.'

'It would be an absolute sin to not take a drink now that I am here. A thousand thanks. I shall, I presume, be treating you in return this evening.'

'Oh, of course, the beer-tasting festivity,' Dorn remarked. 'Do tell, it will not be cancelled, will it?'

'When has any festivity at the Brotherhood of Blackheads been called off before? No matter if a hundred enemies surround the town there will always be a fest at the Blackheads. Word has gone out and the beers brewed.'

'If you say so, Master Blackhead, if you say so ... I do not recall the Blackheads having held such grand festivities here in the past. There was really nothing to be heard of your guild when I was young,' Melchior remarked with a nod. It was said that the Brotherhood of Blackheads had been in Tallinn for a few hundred years, long before the other guilds, but the Blackheads themselves were the only party to assert this, and, in truth, Melchior could not remember having heard much about the Brotherhood before Master Freisinger arrived in town. Nevertheless, Freisinger did come to Tallinn, and the Blackheads' fame rose in no time. The young merchant invited the sons of Great Guild merchants and other foreign traders to join, and in the three years since the cheerful and easy-going Blackheads had been acclaimed across the town for their mighty festivities and drinking sessions, their hastiludes and tournaments. Before Freisinger arrived there had been only three old unmarried merchants in Tallinn who called themselves Blackheads, but they were so aged and frail that the Guild of the Brotherhood of Blackheads would have gone to the grave with them.

Freisinger sipped the elixir, saying it indeed did his throat well. 'I suppose the Blackheads are different in every town,' he said in reply to Melchior. 'Not that our brotherhoods are many in number either. But you enquired before as to whether the festivity would be called off. For what cause should it be cancelled? Has something happened?'

'Has the Master Blackhead then not heard about Toompea?' Dorn asked.

'I was at the market just before coming here, and I did over-hear something concerning Toompea, but I did not investigate the matter. What is it then? Has war broken out? Speak up, Melchior. No doubt these stories have also reached the pharmacy,' Freisinger probed merrily.

'What I know', Melchior began slowly, 'is that the former Commander of the Order in Gotland, Henning von Clingenstain, is said to have been divested of his head yesterday evening on Toompea.'

'Gracious Lord. That Clingenstain?' the Blackhead cried. 'So it is true then. Heavenly grace. Who would commit such a dreadful deed?'

'They say the murderer escaped to the Lower Town,' the Magistrate grunted, vexed. 'But who that person is, that I do not know.'

The men clinked their glasses together and drank, as is always done in Tallinn when bad news is heard from Toompea.

'Do you know whether Commander Spanheim has already set a bounty?' Freisinger asked after a pause.

'I know not what our Commander has or has not done, but no doubt I will hear of it soon enough because I am on my way straight to Toompea from here – once my stomach problems abate somewhat,' Dorn said. 'No, the members of the Order said nothing about a bounty. They only mentioned that some sort of coin had been stuffed into poor Clingenstain's mouth and that his head was nailed to a wall ...'

'A coin stuffed into his mouth,' Melchior exclaimed, astounded.

'So they said. That it rolled out of his mouth when the head was moved. I don't even want to think about such a grisly thing.'

'Dreadful,' Freisinger said musingly. 'The quicker the murderer is apprehended the better, or the Commander will be furious, and should his wrath fall upon the town ... That would not be good for merchants. When you are up on Toompea will you remind the Commander that we are expecting him as a guest of honour today and the day after tomorrow? By the way, what does the honourable Town Council think of the case? Will it set a bounty as well?'

'The honourable Council has not yet discussed anything,' said Dorn. 'The honourable Council is in repose or is handling its own trade affairs, and the Magistrate must now head to Toompea with a horrible backache. A foul tale, it is. No matter which way you look at it. Foul.'

Melchior chuckled. The Magistrate had spoken earlier of a stomach ache. Freisinger bade the men good day and asserted once more that as long as the Council did not forbid it then an event as important as *Smeckeldach* would certainly not be called off. And that, according to custom, the Commander, as the land's overlord, was also warmly welcome. Freisinger then tipped his cap and left. Melchior thought he glimpsed the face of Goldsmith Casendorpe flash amongst the crowd outside just a moment earlier, which in turn led him to the thought that he would certainly lament when the town lost such a resolute Blackhead, the most valiant in the guild's history.

It was written in the Great Rights of the Brotherhood of Blackheads that no citizen of the town or married man may belong to the guild. When a Blackhead takes a wife – and, given the direction from which the winds currently blew, Master Freisinger seemed to be sailing towards that very harbour – he must resign from the post of Blackhead Alderman. The individual then becomes a town citizen and a married man; he is accepted into the Great Guild, and the Blackheads must search for a new alderman. It was a somewhat strange rule, but all matters associated with the Blackheads *were* peculiar. They had certainly been in Tallinn since the earliest days, but no one had really seen or heard about them. There were some two or three old greybeards who had not taken wives, but they always looked for newly arrived foreign merchants to appoint as their successors. And no one knew what affairs were run by the guild itself. Yet, now that the Brotherhood had struck an accord with the sons of the Great Guild masters and with merchants' foreign journeymen, no jollier group could be found in the town. Who knows, maybe I would have become a Blackhead as well, Melchior pondered.

'Very well,' he said to the Magistrate. 'As I understand it we must now undertake an important trip to Toompea. I will quickly weigh out some remedies so that Keterlyn might make do on her own while I am out.'

The Magistrate scratched the back of his neck and acknowledged that he had indeed come with that request on behalf of the Town Council.

'Look, Melchior, if you do not oppose, then …' he began haltingly, 'then just as last time the Council would employ you as assistant to the Magistrate … Well, yes, and perhaps that story of a backache was actually something of a false pretence, or what have you …'

'That stomach-ache story? Very likely,' Melchior corrected, chuckling. 'Anyway, I consent gladly. And I have just recalled that I recently sent the Commander a unique drink that I concoct out of sweet mead and a few curative herbs and which drives exhaustion out from the bones following several days of revelry. As if by wizardry. This is my town and my pharmacy, and I want to know what goes on. Let us go to the back room. I will speak to my wife and then must search for my cap and clean the dust off it.'

'Away, away, my friend. Let us speak to your cap and clean the dust off your wife and then off to Toompea,' Wentzel Dorn exclaimed, springing to his feet.

8

Near St Nicholas's Church
16 May, Before Midday

KILIAN RECHPERGERIN enjoyed strolling through the gardens of Tallinn and practising melodies in the cool shade amongst the bushes. He had several favourite spots, one of which was in the orchard between Seppade Street and Mäealuse Street, where the poorer folk lived and where Ludke would not find him. Kilian was frequently irritated by the fact that the master's servant would tag along after him around town if Old Man Mertin had not given the boy any other jobs to do. But a boarder may not be surly; a boarder must show humility and gratitude. After Ludke located the garden Kilian began to pass the time somewhat closer to home in the cool shade of St Nicholas's churchyard at the foot of the hill. Below lay the courtyards of the houses on Seppade Street; above was St Nicholas's, and it was surrounded by trees. It was a shady, secure spot, and Ludke had not yet found it. There was a good sitting stone near the northern edge of the churchyard directly across the street from the town mint; it was enclosed by dense foliage, and from there Kilian could get a good view of whoever was passing by.

There, beneath the blossoming apple trees and lindens, was where Kilian had composed his most beautiful melodies in Tallinn, and it was in this place that he recalled the words of his friend Giuseppe that the best music truly springs forth in gardens, there, where the greenery enfolds you and where life blooms. Unlike Milan, Tallinn was not known for its gardens … Kilian's heart ached whenever he recalled his days in Milan. Oh, why, he often thought, could there not be such gardens in Tallinn – such sun and warmth, such a joy of living, such royal courts, grandeur and magnificence? However, something dear to the heart and pleasing to the eye could also be found in Tallinn. Yes, also in Tallinn. Here it was cold and bleak, the summers were brief and spring felt monotonous. The snow would melt, but the weather would not warm up, the grass would not burst forth from the ground and the trees would not unfurl their leaves. It felt as if nature no longer knew whether it was alive or dead after the long winter. Kilian loathed springtime in Tallinn the most – it was a spring quite different from that at home in Nuremberg or in Milan, where he had spent the most magnificent time of his life. It was spring, not winter, that was the time of death in Tallinn. Winter was even pretty in its cold, glassy essence, its glowing hearths and cosy evenings. Spring, on the contrary, wounds a person through its very absence, with its cold, filth and muck. That was when it was most painful to live here. Eastertide in Tallinn was filled with inertia, mourning and distress – not like in Milan. Now, in mid-May, it seemed as if even the trees and bushes prompted him to remember that the time of death was past.

The apple trees in St Nicholas's churchyard had broken out in bloom today.

Kilian Rechpergerin sat on his rock, freshly warmed by the spring sun, and played his lute while two girls sat at his feet and listened. Both of the girls, Katrine and Birgitta, were pretty, and proud town maidens at that, the daughters of town citizens. Alas, they were so young, and love was not even a game to them yet. Their hearts were certainly full of good cheer, and the prospect of betrothal was no longer too far off, but love remained a somewhat amusing and foreign land to them, a thing of delight. They were not aware that love must hurt and that true love means pain.

Kilian sang:

> 'Lo, the tavern lies there at the crossroads
> Close to Dorrenstamm
> And Satan himself runs the bar …'

It was an old song that he had heard a couple of years ago at a roadside inn in autumn while on his way from Nuremberg to Milan. The song spoke of a tavern where Satan led travellers astray, coaxed them into casting dice and forced them to sell their souls to cover their debts. Kilian had once felt that selling one's soul was an empty and unnecessary act. Bishops sometimes spoke of it, and travelling monks preached about it. Yet a person could not actually sell their soul; it was just fable.

Now he knew better. Now he understood that song.

A man can sell his soul. It is possible to tempt a person on to the road to sin. Sin lies in thoughts, in a look … sin lies in coveting. It is a mortal sin. It was not without cause that Kilian had chosen that very churchyard for his noontime idling. It was past this spot that Gerdrud walked every day at midday on her way to visit the mill beyond Harju Gate.

'Listen, you, Sire Meistersinger of Nuremberg, do you know any happier songs as well?' Katrine asked, giggling. The freckles on her brow flickered in the rays of sunlight – she was a pretty red-haired girl with mirthful green eyes.

'Yes, the kind of songs that are also suitable for young, chaste girls and not only those about dice and Satan,' Birgitta urged.

'Or do you believe that all songs should speak of men's merrymaking?'

'Sire Meistersinger Kilian Rechpergerin of Nuremberg has likely lost his tongue completely because of his great master-singing?'

The questions rained down upon Kilian; the girls giggled, but the singer could now see Gerdrud approaching in the distance. The young woman carried a basket under her arm. She noticed Kilian – and she also noticed the two girls listening to his music. If Kilian had been alone then Gerdrud might possibly have walked closer and chided him for wasting the day in this manner – singing along to melodies strummed on his lute – but this time she did not draw near. This time she did not even nod. She averted her gaze as if she had not seen Kilian. As if he were not even there.

This hurt him – however, it hurt him sweetly, filling his heart with painful joy.

'Not in the least, lovely maidens,' he said, raking his fingers across the strings of the instrument. 'However, I am not yet an actual Meistersinger, I am only a *Schulfreund*, a wandering journeyman. But, in spite that of that, I wish to sing to you. There is a song for everyone, be they young or old, fat or thin, beautiful or ugly, man or woman, robber or cleric.'

'And who are we, in your opinion? Young or old? Fat or thin?' Birgitta asked. 'Beautiful or ugly, robbers or clergy?'

'Women or men?' Katrine said through a fit of giggles.

'Who you are, lovely maidens, is for you to decide, for you to choose and for you to find out. I have already chosen my own path, and I walk it with song. You know, in our guild it is understood that in order for a man to become a true Meistersinger he must be able to create a song in an instant from thin air, from nothing at all, a song that has never before existed.' Kilian spoke with enthusiasm.

Gerdrud was now quite close, although she still did not turn her head to acknowledge him.

'And can you perform that art, Kilian Rechpergerin?' Katrine enquired.

'As I said, I am merely a travelling journeyman. My skill is not yet that of a true Meistersinger.'

'Do not be so modest, Kilian. We heard how you sang just now.'

'Then tell us, would you be able to conjure up your own song out of thin air just now?'

'Or one about something that you see and which is pleasing to you?'

'Oh, but do I not always sing of what pleases me and of what is dear to my heart? Can one ever sing of anything else?' Kilian asked wistfully.

But the girls pushed him further. Kilian only feigned resistance; he was simply waiting.

'Then sing, Kilian. You are supposed to wander and sing to everyone,' Birgitta commanded.

'Very well, I will sing,' the boy retorted. 'But of what?'

'Sing about something – no, sing rather of nothing at all. Yes, exactly, sing your own new song about nothing at all,' the girls clamoured.

'Of nothing at all? Fine, then I will sing,' Kilian acquiesced. Gerdrud was very close now and had to be within earshot. Kilian did not see that Melchior and Dorn had stopped for a moment at the foot of the hill. Dorn was still explaining some matter to his assistants, but Melchior had started up the hill. He raised his hand to Kilian in greeting and stopped to hear the song.

'Here is a song about nothing at all
It speaks not of I nor of any other

Not of love, nor of youth
Or of anything else, of nothing at all
It materialized before me while I slept
Galloping on its horse in solitude
I have no inkling of when I was born
I am neither happy nor angry
I am not a stranger here
And I have no place here
I am I to do
A mountain fairy cursed me like this
I do not know whether I sleep or I wake
My heart is nearly broken, I'm in such despair
Yet I care for this not, not with half of my finger
I have fallen in love with someone, I know not who she is
Because I have never seen her
Never in all of eternity has she made me glad or dejected
And I care not for this
I have never seen her, yet I love her so deeply
She has done for me not what she should nor what is forbidden
When I do not see her I am happy
I do not care for her in the least
For I know someone who is kinder and finer and richer as well
I know not where she lives
Whether above in the mountains or on flat plains
It would be too painful to tell her how she tortures me
And also too painful to remain
Hence I will depart
Here is my song
I know not what it concerns
I send it off to someone
Who will send it with someone else to someone in Nuremberg

Perhaps this person can send me a key from my small chest with which I might solve this puzzle.'

Gerdrud passed Kilian as if the boy were not even there. Melchior, however, listened to the end with interest and then cantered off after the Magistrate.

9

Toompea, Small Castle of the Order
16 May, Midday

MELCHIOR WAITED near the Town Hall briefly while Dorn tracked down the court servants, the assistant scribe and the town advocate, berated them all and then ordered them to head to Toompea. There were two roads that led from Lower Town up to Toompea. The larger, grander road, used by draft horses and livestock, was called Pikk Mägi or Long Hill. This started at the end of Rataskaevu Street close to the Town Hall and passed through a gate tower built during Melchior's youth. The other, Väike Mägi, or Short Hill, had a wooden gate with a narrow entry way at the base of the hill. The town watchmen locked both gates every evening and took the keys to the Town Hall. There was little chance of getting up Short Hill in spring, as it was too steep and slippery with mud. Many men had broken bones attempting the climb, and recently one Order attendant had fallen and broken his neck.

Reaching Toompea by way of Long Hill was no easy task in the month of May either, as the road was muddy and covered in manure, pitted by large potholes and was so narrow in places so that carts could barely squeeze through. Rocks and rubble constantly tumbled down on to the road from the cliff above, on top of which meandered the Great Castle's curtain wall.

One had to pass through two gates to reach Toompea. Melchior knew the way well because one winter he had attended school near the Dome Church. The road went straight as they passed through the stone tower at the base of Long Hill. The rocky base of the cliff loomed to their right, as if it were a protective barrier built by nature itself. To the left yawned a gorge – if anyone were to slip here they would reach the town with ease and very rapidly. Even Melchior's house and rear courtyard were clearly visible from there. At one stage the Town Council had ordered the construction of a railing alongside the road, but it had been damaged a couple of winters ago and no longer provided any security for those scaling the hill. The small, rectangular Short Hill gate tower stood a couple hundred paces above and marked the town's limits. Anyone ascending the hill was at that point forced to leave behind the free town air and Lübeck law because then they would cross into the dominion of Toompea where the Commander ruled and laws of the Teutonic Order held sway. In front of the timber tower was a heavy double gate constructed from oak, which the Council watchmen locked at sundown. No one could enter Order territory from the town at night-time or vice versa.

The group walked – rather stumbled – up the slope until the men finally reached the point at which the Short Hill Gate intersected with Long Hill. Melchior mused that it felt as if the stretch between the two gates had been put there for the sole purpose of allowing a citizen a chance to decide whether he really wished to pass beyond the castle walls and hand himself over to Order law; whether he really had the will to abandon his secure town rights and the protection of the Council and step into the stronghold of his country's overlords.

They were now within the outer bailey of Toompea, which had a courtyard enclosed by a low wall ringed by a moat. By passing through the bailey one could either go north through Bell Tower Gate to the bishop's residence or through the main gate leading to the Commander's grand keep, which loomed a few hundred steps away. Either way the party of town citizens was now on Toompea in the domain of wind, rocks and power.

The first thing that struck anyone arriving from the town was the sheer might of the walls and towers. Although the Lower Town wall was continually being built higher and stronger and new towers were erected all the time, it did not appear that way when viewed from the heights of Toompea. Melchior walked this path quite frequently, as Toompea did not have its own pharmacy, but he always felt a twinge of isolation and dread when he saw those cold walls and towers rising in front of him. The Order was the Order, and the more time passed the more divergent were the lives in Order castles and the towns that surrounded them. Despite this, the present Commander of the Order in Tallinn, Ruprecht von Spanheim, was a simpler and more gracious man than many of his predecessors and had even called the town's apothecary his friend a couple of times.

The streets of Toompea were not paved as they were in Lower Town, and there was a great deal of mud. The drab outer bailey was no exception. The men traipsed ahead through the muck towards the main gate of the keep. On their right was a moat in front of the wall that split Toompea in half, along with the Bell Tower, also known as Dome Gate. Were they to walk through that passageway and head straight along Piiskopi Street they would reach the Dome Church, the octagonal tower of which could be seen rising above the wall.

Toompea Small Castle – the Commander's residence – was immediately in front of them, as was Pikk Hermann Tower, which stood as a symbol to the townsfolk of the Teutonic Order's power and might. The stronghold had been built by soldiers of the Danish Crown, and the Order had further fortified it, piling the castle walls higher and erecting four tall towers at each corner that were visible far out to sea along with the spire of St Olaf's Church.

Although Toompea did not have its own pharmacy, the Commander had a personal physician who sometimes mixed remedies for his lord. Over recent years, however, the doctor's vision had grown dim along with – Melchior suspected – his mind. It was for this reason that the town apothecary did not mix the Commander's medicines according to the physician's recipes but rather used his own intuition or followed instructions given by the town doctor. He had not, of course, gone before the Tallinn Council and mentioned anything about how the town's apothecary would sometimes also mix remedies for their overlord on Toompea because one or other of the councilmen might well get a malicious idea when considering this fact. Melchior Wakenstede was an apothecary by permission of the town and practised on town land and was required to mix those medications passed down to him by the town doctor. Tallinn did not need to get involved in treating the lords of Toompea. But Ruprecht von Spanheim had a somewhat different disposition from previous commanders. He was rumoured to come from a very poor noble family in Germany, a family so low in fortune that it had long been unable to find the means to maintain its status. Ruprecht von Spanheim was the fourth son of a destitute knight who did not even have sufficient means to place his son in a monastery, and thus young Ruprecht was said to have entered the Teutonic Order as young boy to make ends meet on his own as a penniless warrior-monk. By this time, however, the man had become commander of the most important town in Livonia, purely as a result of his valour in battle. Ruprecht von Spanheim had fought bravely against the Poles, the Lithuanians, the Russians, the bishops and the Swedes, and this had gained him many supporters within the Order. Yet Commander Spanheim remained a man of even temperament who regarded Tallinn's town affairs with benevolence and understanding. Playing a large part in this was certainly the beer that Toompea received from Lower

Town and towards which the Commander had never shown much restraint. Quite the opposite, in fact, Melchior had deduced, given the frequency with which the Commander dispatched his attendant to the pharmacy to fetch a certain elixir. Melchior mixed this potion from herbs, apple juice and mead topped off with a raw egg, and it was because of this drink that the Commander had labelled Melchior his friend on more than one occasion.

The townsmen now reached the main gate of the *castrum minus*, the Small Castle. They stepped meekly through the portal, where, naturally, no one stood guard at this time and entered the castle's inner courtyard. They were now at the heart of Order power, a heart that gave off the pungent stench of slurry because the Order's barns, stables, sheds and coops were situated in the space. Hens strutted across the grounds, and a pair of swine wallowed in the shade.

Dorn looked around for an attendant who would inform the Commander of their arrival. This proved unnecessary, however, as the Commander himself stood near a well in a corner of the castle courtyard and ...

Commander Ruprecht von Spanheim roared.

He roared in such a way that the court attendants ducked and the Magistrate jumped in surprise.

In truth, this roar had nothing to do at all with the appearance of the Council envoys. The esteemed Commander had just doused his body in a bucketful of cold water. When he spotted the townsmen Spanheim issued a guttural grunt, kicked over a second full pail of water and gestured towards the door to the castle hold. An attendant directed the Council entourage across the courtyard towards the southern wing of the castle where the Commander's personal quarters were to be found. The group had to wait there for some time while Spanheim dried himself and dressed in fresh clothing. The court attendants were silent, the town advocate pursed his lips worriedly and Dorn inspected, with great interest, the view from an arrow-slit that looked down upon Toompea's grazing lands and Tõnismägi Hill.

The Commander finally entered and ordered them into his reception hall. When he saw Melchior amongst the other faces he guffawed cheerily.

'Melchior, you old wizard. Who allowed you up here?'

Melchior bowed cordially and handed a clay bottle to the Commander without a word.

'By the Holy Virgin, your miracle remedy,' Spanheim exclaimed and laughed. He snatched the bottle, guzzled it and then ordered the court attendants and Town Advocate to make themselves scarce because, as he said, 'Toompea is no fairground.' By the time, a little while later, he entered the starkly furnished reception hall mantled by a low-vaulted ceiling the Commander was glowing. He praised Melchior. 'No, do not protest. I affirm it is a miracle remedy …'

'I must hastily state that it is, nevertheless, a most ordinary pharmacy elixir, nothing more,' Melchior replied modestly.

'Oh, hell and demons, Melchior, do not argue with the Commander,' Spanheim snapped. His surly mood seemed to have passed as it always did when he had sampled Melchior's mellow beverage after several days of intense merrymaking. They stood in the Commander's reception hall, where there was really nothing more than a coal brazier, a writing stand and a faded Order tapestry.

'Do not argue,' the Commander repeated. 'On the battlefield, thank you for asking, I can hold my own – I sliced entire companies of Poles into tiny pieces in my younger days, that I did. At a feast I can drink Fellin's entire joker-filled castle under the table, where they would remain if only the dogs did not come to lick the crumbs from their beards. Even Tallinn washerwomen can hold more beer than that Commander of Fellin, whose name causes kittens to laugh and to keep laughing until someone steps on their tails.'

Dorn forced out a hollow laugh, and Melchior confirmed that the honourable Town Council and pharmacy held the general belief that they were, without question, absolutely certain that not a soul in Fellin could match Tallinn's Commander in matters of beer drinking.

'That's just how it is,' the Commander barked. 'I've drunk the lot of them under the table, and I'll carry on drinking and go to bed with my head held high and my back straight, and then I'll screw ten whores before daybreak if I choose to do so, and that happens to me quite often, I can tell you ...'

'And I, too, have always held the conviction that no one can compare with our Commander when it comes to laying whores and drinking beer. The whole of the honourable Town Council knows that ...' Dorn began to elaborate, but Melchior quickly stepped on the Magistrate's foot and coughed. Dorn fell mute, startled.

Spanheim paid this no heed. 'So it is,' he said, sighed and approached his writing stand.

'Come closer, Magistrate,' he commanded. 'I want to show you something.'

What the Commander had to show made both Dorn and Melchior reel. The Commander seized a human head from a chest on the stand and held it up before them.

'Knight von Clingenstain's head is here, but his body will rest in the chapel until it is entombed at Dome Church for his eternal rest,' Spanheim declared.

'Holy Mary and the heavenly host,' Dorn mumbled in shock. The head had belonged to a man of about forty years of age, and it had been drained of blood. A head becomes much smaller when the blood has been drained from it, Melchior noted. The face shrivels and the skin takes on a light-yellowish tone ...

'Back to the matter in hand,' the Commander said with greater seriousness. 'Yesterday evening someone decapitated Knight von Clingenstain and escaped down to the town. Magistrate, before I sent an attendant to the Town Hall this morning I dispatched my page to the Grand Master of the Order with these sorrowful words. Such an outrageous crime is a stain on the entire town of Tallinn. It is unprecedented for a high-ranking Knight of the Order to be heinously murdered in the town.'

On Toompea, Melchior thought, murdered on Toompea.

'And now it is Tallinn's solemn duty to put the murderer in chains and bring him to Toompea so that a tribunal of knights may sentence him to death. He will be staked to Pikk Hermann and tortured, as is just and righteous,' Spanheim continued. 'A decree stating this will be sent to the town, but this command has been made known to you in advance, here and now in this very place.' Dorn bowed and wished to say something, but the Commander continued, 'And when I send the next page to visit the Grand Master of the Order I want to be able to inform him that the murderer has already been strung up on Pikk Hermann and that Tallinn's Town Council has displayed the honour and respect to the Order that it is obliged to show. Magistrate, do you understand that I do not wish to send a message to the Grand Master to the effect that the murderer is still at large in Tallinn and that the Council has not yet apprehended the man? I do not want matters to take the same course as the last time that the Council and Toompea were at odds for more than two months over the surrender of a thief, who, during the course of that time, fled by ship. Your Lübeck law there in Lower Town is fair and just, by the Grand Master's good grace, but it denies me the authority to put the murderer in chains and drag him up to Toompea myself.'

Dorn collected his wits and asked, 'But could the esteemed Commander then state who this murderer is so that I may make his name known to the honourable Town Council and so that the Council might give permission to –'

'Torture him and so forth, as is just and righteous. Of course, I would tell you, damn it, but I do not know who it is. I have already interrogated every attendant, artisan and servant on Toompea, yet they neither saw nor heard a thing. Even that Jochen, the servant of our departed brother, Henning, was lying with some washerwoman at the time and has nothing to tell me.'

'But who, then, must I incarcerate?' Dorn asked, bemused.

'Holy thunder and Jacob's bones,' blasted the Commander. '*You* are the Magistrate. Does every killer there in Lower Town have a sign around his neck showing whom he has dispatched to the netherworld? Does every crook paint his name upon the church wall so that you might apprehend him accordingly?'

'But according to law Toompea must demand the town produce a criminal by name and then, and then a Council trial … But who then must the Council trial find guilty, shackle and bring here?'

'My dear Magistrate Dorn, *you* are the man who will establish the identity of Clingenstain's murderer, and then *you* will pass this information along to *me*, and *I* will issue a demand for him from the Council. It is exceptionally simple.'

'Esteemed Commander,' Melchior intervened, 'the Magistrate merely wishes to say that it would be of great assistance to him were Toompea able to provide him with advice and direction. For example, it would be very useful to know at what hour this dreadful murder became known and who found the corpse, whether there may have been things at the scene that could disclose anything about the murderer and how we know for certain that the killer fled down to the town.'

Spanheim glared momentarily at the Apothecary. 'Now, Melchior, what are you doing sticking your nose into this affair?

There are afflicted and diseased folk in the town. Go and mix medicines for them, and the Magistrate will act on his own by the Council's authority. If it is necessary, then take along an executioner to bend some bones, and certainly someone will ultimately confess,' said the Commander. 'I permitted you to enter here only because you brought me that miracle elixir.'

Dorn coughed and said, 'An executioner would definitely be of use to the town, but Melchior is also of great assistance to the Council, for where other than the pharmacy do the townsfolk go to gossip? Every person – no matter merchant or councilman, mason or cobbler, beer peddler or minter – has affairs at the pharmacy at some time or another. And it is there, you see, that the honest Melchior fills up tankards for men to wet their whistles and speak of all they have seen and heard.'

'And at greater length and with more pleasure than in the executioner's chamber,' Melchior added. 'The executioner, I might add, is my good friend and sometimes visits the pharmacy himself to request medicine for his aching bones.'

'And this is not the first time that Melchior has been of help to the Council Court,' the Magistrate continued. 'Last year, you recall –'

'Fine. Very well,' Spanheim interrupted. 'In the end it is none of my business to say how the Council apprehends the murderer, and if you and your pharmacy are indeed of benefit, then ...' He took another swig of elixir and began to relate what had happened.

Henning von Clingenstain stayed on Toompea for five days at a house belonging to a Viru vassal who was away at his manor, as most vassals generally are in springtime. Commander Clingenstain was travelling from Gotland to Marienburg, but certain obligations required that he pass through Tallinn on his way. There were eight men of Gotland on Toompea altogether, the others all being lower-ranking brothers that the Commander had housed in the castle dormitory. Clingenstain had spent the majority of his time in Tallinn within the dining-hall located at the eastern edge of the castle, because, as Commander Spanheim had said, 'something *had* to be done with those four casks of beer, that barrel of herring and heap of salted pork that the Council sent for the purpose of entertaining the esteemed guest'. In addition to Clingenstain, the Knight's squire Jochen was also staying at the vassal's house; he had now been shackled and beaten to a pulp. Clingenstain had only gone back the house to sleep. Last evening the Knight had set out for his lodgings at close to eight o'clock. He was alone – a couple of Order attendants had spotted him stumbling about near the stables, looking for the right path and shouting for his servant. Clingenstain reached his lodging through a side portal at the northern wing of the keep, via the gate where the road crossed the moat directly into the bishop's residence, without having to make a wide arc through the outer bailey and Dome Gate. Jochen found Clingenstain's decapitated corpse one hour later and ran into the castle shouting hysterically. Commander Spanheim had immediately ordered the alarm bell be sounded, yet for whom and for what was Toompea to be searched? The Commander personally interrogated every knight, attendant and squire for half the night, but no one had witnessed anything further.

'Eight o'clock …' Melchior murmured when the Commander had finished. 'So we can therefore say for certain that the murderer fled to the town.'

'Why are you conjecturing already?' Spanheim asked. 'You cannot infer anything, because it was only at dawn that we found the sword and a trail of blood.'

'The sword?' Melchior asked.

'Yes, the murder weapon, the one used to kill Clingenstain. It was an Order attendant's sword. The killer had stolen it from the castle smithy. The blacksmith was blind drunk, of course, and I have already had him shackled. The sword, though, we found at dawn in the moat near the Short Hill guard tower. Then we spotted a trail of blood on the wall of the Dome Gate as well as on the cobblestones leading from the vassal's house up to the gate. The murderer had cast the sword aside, but the blade caught the morning sun, and we found it. Now, I would like to know, how have you already deduced what we came to know only later?'

'The gates are secured at sundown, and no one can reach Lower Town from Toompea after that,' Melchior replied respectfully.

'And so?' queried the Commander.

'The murderer rushed to carry out the murder before the gates were closed. If the killer resided on Toompea it would have been simpler and more logical to wait until the dead of night when no one is moving about the streets and both Clingenstain and Jochen would have been asleep. But no, he committed his crime before nightfall so that it would still have been possible to slip out through the town gate.'

'That's what I thought,' the Commander replied. 'He had to exit the gate just moments before the guards arrived and secured it.'

Melchior continued, on a roll now, 'He likely cloaked the sword in his cape and brought it with him to the gate so that he would have something with which to defend himself had the murder been dis-covered immediately. We can conclude from this that he has been a soldier or has, at least, been involved in combat. The killer then went through the Dome Gate and cast the sword aside near Short Hill Gate because he would already have crossed into the town jurisdiction by this time. He felt more confident then, as he knew that members of the Order could not pursue him there. Hence the murderer almost certainly entered the town.'

The Commander stared at Melchior in surprise. Dorn remained silent, opening and closing his mouth like a beached fish.

'We can then say right away that he also came *from* the town,' Spanheim said after a pause. 'There is no doubt of that. No one from the castle trailed Clingenstain through the side portal – a guard is stationed there. The vassal's home is right next to the moat and by the wall, near the Dome Gate. It was the act of a stranger, a wretched, shameless stranger, who snuck up from the town to wait for the right moment. Oh, fiery demons, I know every man on Toompea and can swear that not a single vassal or anyone aspiring to become one bore such enmity against Clingenstain, the Lord's peace be with him. No one had even seen him before. The vassals are not even present on Toompea at this time of year, and the Great Castle is only populated by members of the bishop's household along with bakers and attendants – and I had every last one of them interrogated throughout the entire night. No one is missing.'

Dorn, who had been silent for a long while, now dared to speak up. 'Yet there is not a soul in Lower Town who might have borne animosity against that particular high-ranking knight. Rather the opposite. We in the town of Tallinn are all *grateful* towards the Order, thankful that they freed us of the Victual Brothers' accursed misdeeds.'

The Commander furrowed his brow. 'You say that, but, Magistrate, someone from that same grateful town still chopped off his head.'

'Which is indeed strange,' Melchior interjected. 'Is it then possible to slip up to Toompea and steal a sword and lie in wait for the proper moment for murder to unfold? Just as the honourable Commander himself just stated, no one either saw or heard anything suspicious. My thoughts therefore lean towards the possibility that the person who committed this dreadful crime might have been someone who knows Toompea quite well, well enough to have been able to conceal himself and steal a sword, someone whose presence could have been a daily occurrence. Not any random captain or cabin boy from a foreign land whose ship is docked in the harbour ends up on Toompea by mere chance.'

'We drive all vagrants away without delay,' Spanheim snapped.

That they do, Melchior mused. People from Lower Town did not simply turn up on Toompea and wander about. All unfamiliar faces attracted attention there.

'Although one vagabond did pass through here yesterday,' the Commander recalled. 'That musician from the town. He sang rather well; it was a thrill to hear him. That boy from Nuremberg.'

Melchior was taken aback. Kilian on Toompea?

'Is the Commander thinking of Kilian Rechpergerin who boards at Sire Tweffell's?' he asked.

'The very same, yes. He wandered up herewith Tweffell. Wanted some kind of attestation.'

'So, Sire Tweffell also visited Toompea? The Alderman of the Great Guild?'

'Indeed,' Spanheim affirmed. 'He paid a call here, yes. He had some kind of trading matter to handle with Clingenstain. As far as I can recall he wished to speak of some ship and then left here in a proper huff. Although, that was already close to noontime, immediately after the goldsmith Clingenstain had invited stopped by ...'

The Commander informed Melchior that the goldsmith had been none other than Burckhart Casendorpe, Alderman of St Canute's Guild. Quite a number of people had called upon Clingenstain at Toompea yesterday. He had wanted to purchase a gift to take to the Grand Master in Marienburg. Gotland's goldsmiths were said to be crude and miserly, but Tallinn-made jewellery was always of high quality and renowned in every land around the Baltic. Clingenstain had corresponded with Casendorpe by letter and bought a collar lavishly encrusted in gold from the master artisan. It seems to have been an exceptionally expensive piece, and Clingenstain even sent Jochen back to his ship for more money as his coffer had been emptied.

'Thus three persons from Lower Town called upon Clingenstain,' Melchior pronounced thoughtfully. Not one person for five days and then several in succession on the very same day that he was slain.

'And if Tweffell was here then his servant Ludke was certainly in his company, as the old merchant does not venture anywhere without him, not even to church or the Town Hall. Ludke sometimes even carries him up the stairs,' Dorn said.

'True, the servant was also present. A strong and sturdy man down to his very bones – even taller than our Grand Master of the Order himself to whom no men of comparable stature can be found. Hand a poleaxe to the likes of him and send him into battle, and he will hack through opponents with the might of three men. Why would a lad like that take a position as a servant?'

Melchior was forced to admit that he did not know. Alderman Tweffell and Ludke seemed inseparable, although he had rarely been able to coax the latter into conversation. Ludke, who was not of German descent, was not exactly the most talkative servant in Tallinn. He had a somewhat childish disposition but was on par with Goliath in terms of might. Melchior tried to think whether he had ever heard Tweffell mention his acquaintance with the Commander of the Order in Gotland. True, Melchior dimly remembered hearing something about an argument involving Gotland and of a vessel, but the Apothecary could not recall it in any greater detail. Melchior's ears suddenly pricked up at the Commander mentioning Prior Eckell.

'Baltazar Eckell, Prior of the Dominican Order?' Melchior asked in surprise.

'Damn it all, that's what I just said,' Spanheim snapped curtly. 'He came to express his reverence, and Clingenstain – the devout,

God-fearing knight that he was – requested that he hear confession. Clingenstain thus received forgiveness for his sins right there in Dome Church on the same day that he perished. But all this, Melchior, has not even the slightest connection to his murder.'

'In the name of St Andrew, that I hope,' Melchior murmured.

'What are you mumbling about?' the Commander demanded.

'Nothing at all, nothing at all … But is it not strange that he requested the Dominican Prior hear his confession and not the Pastor of the Dome Church?'

'It is not at all strange. The Teutonic Order has favoured the holy Dominicans for a very long time – Clingenstain used to hear the brothers' sermons at St Nicholas's Church in Visby. As I recall, Prior Eckell had also been at the monastery there – and, what is more, Melchior, it was the Dominicans who built the Dome Church.'

So it is indeed said, Melchior recollected. Many years ago, when the Dominican Order first arrived in Tallinn, they settled on Toompea and built their first church on the very spot that the Dome Church now stood. It was also on this plot of land that horrendous bloodshed unfolded between the Danes and Knights of the Order. The Danes were hacked to pieces within the church and stacked their corpses on the altar … And was that not the very same time that the Order drove the Dominicans out from Toompea? Yet nearly two hundred years had passed since that time, and this knowledge would not help to find Clingenstain's killer.

'Five townsmen of Tallinn …' Melchior spoke. 'We have five men who came into contact with Clingenstain yesterday. No more townsfolk walked about Toompea, perchance?'

'Well, some miller's journeyman or a cobbler's apprentice could have been here, of course,' the Commander huffed impatiently, 'but I do not recall any of them having had dealings with Clingenstain. Oh yes, before the Prior's arrival that lay brother from the Dominican Monastery was on Toompea collecting alms, as you would expect – but then he walks through here all the time.'

'Ah, Brother Wunbaldus?'

'That's likely his name. That hunchbacked lay brother.'

'That is he, Brother Wunbaldus,' Melchior confirmed. 'A hunch-backed, poor and devout brother who visits my pharmacy from time to time and always consents to recite prayers for me in exchange for medicines. He is said to be a fantastic brewer. The Dominicans' beer has acquired a wholly new character since Brother Wunbaldus's arrival. The Commander did not happen to notice whether Brother Wunbaldus also had any contact with Clingenstain?'

'Ha, he exchanges words with everyone he happens upon when making rounds with his alms basket. Clingenstain no doubt dropped something in it for him, too. Yes, I'm quite certain that he gave alms.'

The Commander remembered one other matter just before he finally ordered the men to depart. He asked Dorn what Tallinn's executioner would take for a hanging.

'The fee was once four silver coins and a cask of beer, although it was some time ago that we last had to arrange a hanging,' the Magistrate replied.

'Four? That's daylight robbery.'

Several days earlier the Commander had allowed Toompea's own executioner to return to Wesenberg, where his father – a farmer in a village near the castle – was said to have fallen gravely ill, and his son wished to see him one last time. It was a sorrowful tale indeed, and it meant that Toompea did not have its own executioner at present. The Commander reckoned that Tallinn would have to loan its own man to torture the murderer and hang or quarter him, depending on the court's ruling.

'Quartering costs more,' was all Dorn could say. 'For a quartering the executioner must be paid six silver coins and two casks of beer on the spot.'

'That executioner of yours is a downright extortionary Jew,' the Commander fumed. 'If I received six silver coins for every head on the battlefield then I'd buy Toompea outright for myself.'

'Cutting off a head is apt to be difficult work – not something any shepherd boy could do,' Melchior said.

'A shepherd boy,' Spanheim grunted. 'You know, Magistrate, the Grand Master would be more pleased if Clingenstain's killer turned out *not* to be someone – hmm, how should I put it? – the sort of man who is closely connected to the town, a dignified and moneyed man … you understand. Neither I on Toompea nor the councilmen below in Lower Town need any kind of dispute between the Order and the town. The murderer was certainly some ordinary vagabond or a thief, the kind that sometimes dock at our harbour. Some foreigner. Catch him quickly, lend us your executioner and let us resolve this matter straight away, just as we have managed to resolve all previous matters between the town and Toompea.'

'Let it be so, and may St Victor aid us in this task,' Dorn quickly agreed.

They were already making their way out of the reception hall when one more detail came to Melchior's mind. He bowed. 'If the Commander will allow, then I seem to recall hearing that some kind of coin was said to be stuffed into the late Clingenstain's mouth …'

Spanheim raised his eyebrows. 'Where did you hear that?'

'That man of the Order who came to find me in the town this morning. I also let slip a few words of it to Melchior,' Dorn admitted.

'Cursed blabbermouths. They might as well have gone to the market and proclaimed it there. Jochen found the coin in his lord's mouth when he removed Clingenstain's head from the hook. That murderer is a corpse defiler, a profaner and a despicable desecrator. He drove Clingenstain's head on to the wall and stuffed that coin into his mouth. When Jochen found the head the coin dropped out. And I told those attendants not to gossip carelessly. Why should the town know how a brave warrior's corpse was defiled?'

'The Commander might not, perchance, have laid the coin aside somewhere?' Melchior asked.

Spanheim walked back to his writing stand and removed a coin from the chest.

'It's a Gotland coin, an old Gotland ørtug,' Melchior noted with surprise. 'It is extremely rare for these to be seen in Tallinn.' He thought for a moment and added, 'If the Commander would allow once more, then I would say this is not exactly the behaviour of an ordinary thief – this man kills to give money *to* the victim. Robbers and thieves customarily relieve their prey of gold's heavy burden. Our killer here has, on the contrary, made his victim wealthier. Was anything else of value stolen from Clingenstain? What, for example, became of that gold collar that Clingenstain purchased from Casendorpe?'

'Do I look like his steward, Apothecary?' the Commander shot back in reply. 'He strutted around with that collar after Casendorpe delivered it, wore it around his neck for half the day and later said that he returned it to his chambers before taking confession. No doubt it is somewhere there locked in a chest … or, no, wait, I remember. He wanted it taken back to his ship.'

'So the Grand Master's gift is safely under lock and key on the Clingenstain's vessel?'

'Oh, hell and brimstone, Melchior, no doubt it is. You don't actually think that the murderer …' the Commander's words trailed off. 'No, how could the killer have known that Clingenstain had the collar? Absolutely not. He definitely had it taken to the ship,' Spanheim murmured unconvincingly.

'Then we are also sure that the Grand Master's gift is in a safe place. This is good to hear, if the Commander asserts it is so,' Melchior reasoned.

'I will ask Jochen. Yes, I'll certainly ask,' the Commander vowed. 'Now, however, my time is up, Magistrate. The Toompea councilmen await me. I repeat – I want the town to apprehend the murderer as quickly as possible, and it would be best were he some useless vagabond so that good relations between the town and the Order will not suffer.'

10

Rataskaevu Street
16 May, Afternoon

MELCHIOR AND DORN parted ways before the Town Hall. The Magistrate had to rush to meet the Council and pass on the news. Then he was further required to inform the town and harbour watchmen that they were tasked with searching for a murderer. Thus the Magistrate was very surprised when Melchior insisted that they meet at the Dominican Monastery that afternoon.

'We have to start somewhere,' Melchior explained, 'and we will begin by speaking to every townsman that saw Clingenstain yesterday.'

'You do not truly believe that the Goldsmith, the Prior, Sire Tweffell or that Meistersinger might have dispatched Clingenstain, do you?' Dorn objected.

'I am unable to believe anything at this stage. I only *know* that each one of these men might have something useful to say or know something that we do not.'

'So you think they might have spotted a vagrant?'

'Vagrants cannot gain access to Toompea; they are expelled immediately. No, Magistrate, the murderer could not have been a vagabond or an ordinary thief because, as we both know, such men do not wander through Tallinn very often.'

'And it could not have been any honest townsman,' Dorn said resolutely.

'Actually, Magistrate, it could have been absolutely anyone – and just as likely a resident of Toompea or any Order attendant who bore a grudge against Clingenstain for some reason unbeknownst to us and who was confident and audacious enough to shift the blame on to the town.'

Dorn snorted and made a brusque, dismissive hand gesture. To perturb him just a little bit more Melchior remarked that, in truth, they knew nothing at all. They could not even be sure that the head once rested upon Clingenstain's shoulders because neither had ever seen the man.

'Have you gone completely mad?' Dorn grunted crossly.

'Worry not, my friend. My thoughts are clearer than ever before,' Melchior said cheerfully. 'See here, we actually know exceedingly little; only as much as the Commander told us. He stressed that it would be best if the murderer were some thief that happened upon the town by chance. I agree with him entirely, and that would be the most fortunate outcome for both the Order and the town. But we do not know whether perhaps a bit of bloodletting might have taken place on Toompea during the night amidst the heavy drinking, whether perhaps some honourable knight had freed Clingenstain of his head while their minds were awash with beer froth ...'

'No, you must be mad if you do not believe the words of our esteemed Commander,' Dorn said.

'I have not said I do not believe them. I simply cannot say with complete certainty that the events did not unfold as such, and yet if they had then it would indeed be most favourable for the town to drag some thief up to Toompea, who, upon being subjected to torture, would confess that he killed Clingenstain, the Pope and even the Holy Roman Emperor. What I wish to say is that we know not whether it might have been some vassal or Knight of the Order who wished to give the misleading impression that the murderer escaped to Lower

Town. Anyone could have thrown a sword near Short Hill Gate – if indeed it was there in the first place – and it is likewise no difficult task to leave a false trail of blood. Nevertheless, I admit that the Commander's version seems to carry the most weight. The murderer cast the sword aside when he reached land under the town's jurisdiction, having no further need for the blade nor anywhere to take it.'

Dorn's temper dampened somewhat upon hearing this response, and he turned to leave. 'We do not have the right to doubt what the esteemed Commander tells us,' he said.

'Oh no, of course we don't,' Melchior mumbled, distracted in thought, 'so we *must* look for the murderer within the town. We *must* look for some foreign vagabond, whose capture would not jeopardize relations between the Order and the town, all of which would be agreeable to the Grand Master. Or we – and you in particular, Magistrate – must protect the innocent foreign vagrants who have not killed Clingenstain yet who might apparently have done so with great zeal according to the preferences of some lofty overlord.'

Melchior stood in front of the Town Hall, pondered a bit then decided that he would not visit a brewer – the business he would otherwise have had today, requiring, as he did, half a dozen tankards of beer – but would instead track Kilian down. Melchior held faith in the fact that he would find Kilian at the place where he usually idled at this hour – sitting in front of Tweffell's residence on the edge of the well, strumming his lute and doing his best to attract the attention of the lady of the house. Melchior furrowed his brow at this thought then turned to head towards home.

Artisans' lunch hour had just ended, the town pulsed with a sea of faces, and Melchior recognized the majority of those bobbing along on the tide. Tallinn is growing, he thought. Tallinn is becoming bigger and more important, wealthier and more beautiful; but there are still not so many living here, and one of them, a face that I would likely recognize, one of them murdered a high-ranking Knight of the Teutonic Order yesterday. The market square and the grandiose new town hall that bordered it were the very heart of the town. All of Tallinn's arterial streets came together in this spot, and it was the most protected area of Lower Town. If an enemy were to get past the moats and walls of Tallinn then the streets would be piled high with stones and Town Hall Square would be fortified – and no enemy could conquer Toompea. The square before the Town Hall was an important place. A market was run here during the day, tournaments were organized in the open space during holidays when merchants might, even for a fleeting moment, compare themselves with the nobility; Council declarations were made and festivities held here when the town was visited by some person of elevated status. Trials were sometimes held there, and a criminal might be executed or, more likely, chained to the pillory.

Before Melchior moved off, however, he cast a glance across the square towards the north-west corner. Several small houses stood there behind the pillory with their rear walls facing the Church of the Holy Ghost. One of these was home to the town weighing-house, another belonged to the Church of the Holy Ghost and the third – a snug two-storey building of modest appearance – was currently without a tenant. A Danish merchant named Lovenkrands had ordered the house to be built nearly ten years before but had died before he could to undertake the journey to Tallinn. Lovenkrands' descendants now wanted either to rent it or sell it off. The house was empty. Is it worth it, Melchior? thought the Apothecary. All that you do, all is worth doing. Help the Town Council apprehend a murderer and you are one step closer towards your dream. It is one thing to be an apothecary by permission of the Council; it is quite another matter when your pharmacy stands on the market square across from the new Town Hall with its regal tower and bears the name 'Town

Hall Pharmacy'. No one is forbidden to dream. Melchior's father had purchased a small building in Tallinn when he arrived because he knew that the town had no pharmacy at that time. He had taught his son that nothing is more rewarding for an apothecary than to be a *Council* apothecary, to practise through a council's endorsement and contract. You must become so essential to the Council and stand out so boldly for your extraordinary work that the Council will purchase a house for the pharmacy and rent it to you. Such was the case in many towns in Germany, and Melchior's father had wished for it to be so in Tallinn as well.

Having briefly admired his dream home Melchior turned and began to make his way home. Rataskaevu Street, which was still called Mäealuse Street when Melchior was a boy, had acquired its new name in reference to the roofed well with a wooden frame and a windlass that had been built around the time that Melchior's family had relocated from Lübeck. Mäealuse Street had been much shorter in those days and was flanked by fewer buildings, yet the more the town grew and accumulated wealth the more important Rataskaevu Street became and the more townspeople took up residence there. Many merchants, a few councilmen, as well as the Pastor of St Nicholas's Church, lived on this street, and there was even one house said to be haunted. Alas, the building bought by Melchior's father was becoming too small to hold his growing business. The Apothecary's workshop was slowly drowning amongst the buildings owned by eminent merchants. The place for a building as important as a pharmacy in a town the likes of Tallinn should be the Town Hall Square.

Melchior strolled down the street alongside the aqueduct – a long pipe fashioned from oak casks – until the sound of Kilian's melodies began to reach his ear. On this occasion, however, the song was more woeful than usual, even more so than when Melchior had listened to the boy in St Nicholas's churchyard that morning.

Kilian had been living in that house for nearly a year already, yet the Apothecary had to admit the boy had become even more incomprehensible than he had been initially. Oh, there was certainly much more to him – with his tall, cocked cap – than a mere wandering minstrel; of this Melchior was certain. To regular townspeople Kilian might appear to be a carefree drifter; Melchior sometimes felt that since his arrival in Tallinn the boy had been working on a devious plan. He sensed an avaricious devil hiding behind the suave joker. Yet Melchior sincerely hoped that these seeds of thought only germinated when he was gripped by depression and exhaustion from life's toils, when gripped by that demon that haunted him on occasion.

Melchior now found Kilian sitting in his usual place, plucking mournfully at the strings of his lute, and he asked why Tallinn's merry singing journeyman should be so glum on this fine spring day, why he was not off somewhere playfully flirting with the girls through his songs.

'Apparently you have formed an impression of me as being overly lighthearted, Sire Melchior,' Kilian responded. 'I sing not to titillate anyone at all.'

'Ah, but of course. You are a Meistersinger.'

'Only a travelling journeyman for now, although I practise my art of song in order to heap praise upon myself and to cheer others. I have just composed a new tune and was searching for the right words to accompany it.'

'You know, Kilian,' Melchior said decisively, 'it seems to me that all this singing has weighed heavily on your heart. Come, I will treat you to a cup of elixir – and please also allow Keterlyn to hear your new tune. Come, come, step inside. I entreat you. Otherwise you will squat here alone singing to the birds and the beasts like St Francis.'

In no time Melchior had poured Kilian a cup of sweet elixir and offered him a cake, and it seemed that Kilian's mood had begun to lift.

The boy is educated, Melchior noted when their conversation turned towards the saints, one of the Apothecary's favoured topics. Kilian informed him that St Andrew was the patron saint of the Nuremberg Guild of Singers.

'St Andrew, well, well,' Melchior spoke cheerfully. 'And you bear the name of a saint yourself. However, Andrew is a worthy saint in every respect, and your guild is fortunate to have only a single patron. Last year I wanted to hang a handsome sign next to the pharmacy designating it as "St Cosmas's Pharmacy"; alas it turned out not a single church in Tallinn has a statue of St Cosmas to whom I wished to light a candle and from whom I would receive a blessing for my business. And you know what, Kilian? When I went to take counsel from Prior Eckell at the Dominican Monastery we ended up having a heated debate. As the Father already knew – and who am I to argue with him? – pharmacists are also guarded by the patron saints Nicholas, Damianus and two Jacobs and, to top it all, the Archangel Rafael and Mary, the Mother of God. And I, fool that I am, thought St Cosmas was alone in his task.'

'I do not believe I have even heard of him,' Kilian said uncertainly.

'Many have not,' Melchior nodded, 'although my father, who also ran a pharmacy in the town of Lübeck, taught me that St Cosmas is the protector and guardian of all who concoct medicines. Ah, but here is your elixir, Kilian. Drink it down. It might not help to counter all the troubles of the soul, but it should certainly lighten your mood and help to overcome a sad state of mind. It is called burned spirits, and I have made it all the more fiery by adding ginger and pepper. Drink, drink. It will cheer you up.'

Kilian drank and began to cough profusely. Tears streamed from his eyes, and his precious lute nearly slipped from his grasp. Melchior gave him a few manly claps on the back while he caught his breath.

'Oh, hairy devil,' the boy cursed between coughs. 'And what then became of your saint? You still do not have that sign of St Cosmas here.'

'What happened was that I continued to attend St Nicholas's Church – which I had done previously – to express my gratitude to St Nicholas in my faith and am joyful that he has given his blessing to the success of my business. And I issue medicines for no charge to all in need of them on St Nicholas's Day, the 6th of December. Naturally, I also donate to St Nicholas's Church so that they might proclaim the eternal love and care that he bestows,' Melchior said warmly.

'Then I have only gladness for you,' Kilian reasoned.

'Another small stein?'

'Praise St Andrew. Bring it forth, Sire Apothecary.'

'Here you are. And since St Andrew also protects fishermen, without whom life in Tallinn would be exceptionally hungry, I will also pour for myself an honest ginger spirit. To your health, Kilian, and to the blessing of your gift for song.'

The two clinked their glasses together, drank, coughed, drank some more, and before long the heavy atmosphere that had surrounded Kilian had indeed been lightened. That is, until Melchior informed the boy in confidence that he had just come from the Town Hall. And, if his intuition was not wrong, that the Council's court attendants were presently searching for a murderer who had escaped from Toompea to the town after chopping off the head of Commander of the Teutonic Order Henning von Clingenstain the previous day.

Kilian's hand froze suddenly, still clutching the cup of elixir. The boy turned pale. His shock was genuine. Melchior did not doubt it.

'Lord Jesus,' Kilian exclaimed. 'Escaped to the town? I must tell this to old Tweffell straight away. Who was this murderer? Is his identity known?'

'Not yet, but the Magistrate will find him,' Melchior replied. 'The Council will no doubt offer a bounty, too.'

'Good Christ, *I* was on Toompea yesterday,' Kilian said, his voice faltering.

'I know,' Melchior replied. 'The Magistrate will certainly come to ask you what you saw and heard there. And, as I have given him my solemn vow and am the Magistrate's sworn assistant, it would be best if you spoke to me about what you saw there yesterday. If it helps us pick up the killer's trail then ...'

'We can claim the bounty for ourselves?' Kilian prompted.

'I know not,' Melchior said slyly. 'Did you then see anyone or hear anything?'

'No one – or, well, yes, actually. I saw the Dominican Prior, who turned up just at the moment that the Knight Clingenstain was to write me an attestation that said that I had sung in a castle of the Order. However, I did not see anyone running around with a bloody battleaxe.'

'You could not have because Clingenstain was killed much later than your visit. You went there together with Sire Tweffell and Ludke, did you not?'

The boy nodded.

'Tell me rather of this attestation. What was it, and why did you need it?'

'It was for our guild in Nuremberg, the Guild of Meistersingers.'

'And Clingenstain was prepared to write it for you?'

'Oh yes. He enjoyed my singing very much. I requested the attestation, and he agreed, but then the Prior arrived, and the Knight forgot about me,' Kilian said with regret.

The boy took a sip of elixir and began to talk about his guild. The best singers to have ever walked this earth, by the Lord's blessing, Kilian said, were twelve German poets: Wolfram von Eschenbach,

Heinrich Frauenloeb and Konrad von Würzburg, to name but three. These men invited young singers into their company and instructed them in the high art of how to praise womanly beauty and the power of heavenly love in such a way that the song might hold power. These German poets had founded schools in towns along the River Rhine until the art of the Meistersinger reached Nuremberg. Kilian's father was one of the men who possessed this skill and also founded the Guild of Meistersingers in Nuremberg, which took its place amongst the other fine groups of artisans in the town. Just as in every guild the Meistersinger passed through the stages of apprentice-ship, journeymanship and several levels of mastership. Kilian was a journeyman and – as the guild's statutes prescribed – was required to travel for four years to receive training from other masters scat-tered in far-off places and to sing, just as the Minnesingers once had, in noble courts, at fairs, tournaments, festivities and in castles, all the while extolling the virtues possessed by the damsel of his heart's desire. He must learn how to spin songs himself as well as how to sing those composed by masters in the lands through which he has travelled. After the four years have passed the journeyman must appear before the guild to prove that he has truly become a Meistersinger. It was for that reason that Kilian requested that the Knight issue him an attestation that he had sung before the high lords of the land and had pleased them with his art.

Melchior listened and then mused, 'What a merry life … But what am I doing here sitting around in my pharmacy, eh? Had apothecaries a guild and such rules then I suppose I would long ago have travelled to faraway lands long ago, gathering knowledge and extolling the virtues of the damsel of my heart's desire – although I have, by my good fortune, already wed that very damsel.'

Kilian's tongue had been loosened somewhat by the elixir, and he rambled on. His father was a merchant and had friends across the Hanseatic League. When Kilian had reached fifteen years of age his father handed him letters of recommendation and sent him to Milan, where he spent his first year as a journeyman. For Kilian, Lombardy was an incredible land, a true paradise on earth. Such girls, such wines, such music … what a love the people had for beauty. Alas, Kilian was forced to leave Lombardy when his time there was up. A stay in such an earthly paradise cannot be forever. He had tears in his eyes while he spoke; it was evidently painful for him to talk about, and Melchior sensed that the singing journeyman did not wish to disclose everything concerning his departure from Italy. Kilian's father had then sent him here to Tallinn, to the very edge of the Christian world, to new lands where his relative Mertin Tweffell just happened to live and ply his trade shipping goods even as far as Nuremberg by way of Lübeck. Sire Tweffell had graciously accepted Kilian as his boarder for as long as the boy studied his art of song and … and here his feet had now come to rest.

'Isn't your second year as a journeyman now complete, though?' Melchior enquired.

'I am indeed drawing up plans to depart. I have considered Bruges and Burgundy where my father also has close friends, but …'

'But you still have much more to learn in Tallinn?'

The boy seemed momentarily at a loss for words then continued, 'I like it here. It is definitely not Milan, but people here are kind and the prices low. I am able to send wax and furs from here to my father via Lübeck, and I also have an opportunity to study the merchant's profession. Meistersingers perform for honour and for the song itself; we all still practise the work of some artisan, whether as a cobbler or a hop merchant. A family cannot survive on song alone.'

'And it is good learning a trade at Sire Tweffell's side?' the Apothecary asked.

'Oh yes, he is very kind and has helped me greatly. Sire Tweffell helps me to select furs, and my father sends him paper and glass at a good price in return. I believe it is a high honour to study under the Great Guild Alderman. What is more, I am also allowed to sing at the Brotherhood of Blackheads and learn a profession.'

Especially as Tweffell has no children of his own – and will not have any either. Kilian is indeed an handsome lad, though, Melchior thought. 'Doubtlessly your father has already picked out a bride for you in Nuremberg?'

'I wrote to him to say that he need not rush in that matter,' Kilian replied somewhat hastily. Melchior did not enquire further and instead turned the conversation back to Clingenstain.

'What happened was that Sire Mertin had the Knight informed of his coming ahead of time. He sent a letter but did not receive a reply. So he decided to call upon Clingenstain in person, and I was lucky enough to tag along,' Kilian explained. 'The Knight was already well soused – a feast was under way – and they said ... that is, I did not hear it, but I knew what it was about. Sire Tweffell was demanding compensation for a shipment of goods that the Order had seized in Gotland last spring. I stood at a distance, close to the door, but I witnessed everything. Clingenstain was already so drunk that he probably couldn't make out much of what was going on around him. He pushed a beer towards Sire Tweffell and evidently had no understanding of the matter in hand. They did not speak for long.'

Kilian then managed to ask the Commander whether he could sing for the company, and Spanheim agreed readily. Kilian sang for about an hour, but when he came to request a letter of accreditation – of course, Clingenstain was already so befuddled that he would not have been capable of writing clearly – the Prior's arrival was announced, and the journeyman was turned out.

'So you left alone?' Melchior asked.

'Yes, but not straight away,' the boy replied. 'When I left the castle there were a few Order attendants standing near the gate who had also taken part in the feast. They paid me an artig to sing for them and treated me to beer. We passed through the Dome Gate to rest in the shade beneath the trees, and I played to them for some time.'

'Was it there in the churchyard where the lindens grow?' Melchior asked promptly. 'Did you see anyone there from Lower Town?'

'No one except Prior Eckell, who came out of the castle and entered the Dome Church. Ah … Brother Wunbaldus came over and rebuked us, saying that excessive drinking is a sin and then scolded me for singing songs that are too spirited. The Order attendants gave him a couple of pennies and a tankard of beer, and then he left. I saw no one else.'

'And then you went back down to Lower Town?'

'Well, the Order chaps went to the castle, and I continued to drink the beer, and when they came back I sang another song for them because they believed Brother Wunbaldus had gone by that time … I finished by singing that song about a maiden who at the beginning is still rather chaste and maiden-like but by the end is no longer either …'

Wunbaldus, of course, Melchior recalled. The Apothecary had almost forgotten about that hunchbacked Dominican lay brother. He, too, was wandering around Toompea yesterday, just as he often did while gathering alms. A monk, for sure, but he possessed a brute strength and also knew Toompea well.

'You didn't see anyone else from the town on Toompea? Master Casendorpe, perhaps?' Melchior asked. 'He visited Toompea yesterday. Sold Clingenstain a golden collar, which he was wearing at the table when you sang for them.'

Kilian fell silent for a moment. A kind of elusive glint flashed in his eyes.

'No, I did not see Master Casendorpe,' Kilian said with a slight shiver. 'But that collar was around Clingenstain's neck later.'

'The collar?' Melchior asked, startled. 'The gold collar? Wait – when did you see him?'

Kilian seemed confused. He sipped the elixir and plucked uneasily at his lute. 'I saw him just as I began to walk back to the town. Later, more towards eventide. When I passed the guardsmen. He came from the opposite direction.'

'Which direction did he come from? From the castle or the Dome Church?'

'Yes, he came, er, from the other direction … so, probably from the direction of the church, yes …' The boy appeared somewhat uncertain of his words.

Melchior thought for a moment. 'Listen, Kilian, don't tell me that you didn't have the courage to go up and ask him for that attestation?'

'In truth, I merely bowed to him and wished him a fine evening – not that he really took any notice of me. No, I did not work up the courage to ask him for an attestation again. Had I known he would be dispatched that very same evening no doubt I would have.'

'You could not have known that.'

'Indeed. I simply bowed to him.'

'That was probably about the time that he returned from taking confession at the Dome Church. And that gold collar was still around his neck then?'

'Clingenstain was wearing the collar when I saw him, absolutely,' the boy said looking straight into Melchior's eyes. The Apothecary wanted to ask more about the collar, but at that moment the back door opened and Keterlyn stepped into the pharmacy.

'I heard voices from upstairs and thought someone had come to buy medicines,' Keterlyn said. 'Oh, hello, Kilian,' she remarked when she noticed the journeyman.

Melchior started when his wife entered. He turned around so suddenly and awkwardly that he knocked over a mortar, a couple of tankards and some silver spoons in the process. He swore softly and hastened to greet his wife.

'You see? Every time I am in your company my hands start to shake like jellied meat, and I cannot hold a single thing in my grasp,' he exclaimed, clasping Keterlyn in an embrace and kissing her cheek. She feigned resistance. Out of the corner of his eye Melchior saw that Kilian had kneeled down to pick up the items he had knocked down.

'Melchior, you act as if you have not seen me for several weeks. If seeing womenfolk has such an effect on you then maybe you should choose some other profession?' Keterlyn protested, wriggling playfully in her husband's embrace.

'With the aid of St Nicholas and by disciplining myself into an evermore pious state I have driven away any last thoughts of monastic life,' Melchior said. 'But thank you, Kilian, thank you. It is plain that I am a clumsy oaf.'

'Think nothing of it,' the boy murmured, placing the mortar, tankards and spoons back on the table. Kilian then bowed to Keterlyn politely.

'Did you know, wife,' Melchior spoke with a chuckle, 'that our good neighbour Kilian has come up with a new song, and he wanted to perform it for me? I told him that you must hear it as well. Thus, if the song is fine and pleases the Mistress Apothecary then we will not take a fee from him for our pharmacy's medicine. So, Kilian, let's hear it.'

'For medicine? Is Kilian ill? He was warbling like a lark this morning,' Keterlyn spoke with amazement.

'His body and bones are certainly healthy, but he seems to be afflicted occasionally by a dreadful case of mournfulness. And one – or better two – cups of ginger elixir always help to counter such an ailment.'

'A case of mournfulness?' Keterlyn asked in wonder. 'Is that truly possible? I would never have believed it.'

'Oh no,' Kilian rushed to affirm, 'I came up with a song just the same, and …'

'Kilian is saddened by how all of Tallinn's young damsels run away from him and how no one wants to hear his singing,' said Melchior, laughing.

'Now, that certainly cannot be true,' Keterlyn replied. 'Go and stand on the square and sing for a spell, then you will see how the town's prettiest girls flock together right away, as if someone had lured them there with an orange boiled in sugar.'

'You jest, Mistress Keterlyn,' Kilian stammered.

'Not at all, not at all,' the woman exclaimed. '*I* should certainly know, Kilian. If you look carefully then you will see I am not yet so old that I should have no young girls in the town to call friends, and no doubt I am already aware of whom and what they speak when there are not too many ears around to hear.'

'So it is, exactly. And now let your song come forth, and we will listen,' Melchior commanded, and Kilian began to sing. His song was, however, truly melancholy:

> There is not a single living soul in this world
> Who might grasp my pain and understand me
> My torture, so harsh, which flays my soul
> I know not how I can stand it
> No joy nor consolation nor hope have I
> The lone knight is defeated, ground into dust …

11

Munga Street
16 May, After Vespers

THAT AFTERNOON Melchior walked along Pikk Street, where work on the main building of the Great Guild was under way. He strolled past the rear of the Church of the Holy Ghost and then down Munga Street, which led to the Dominican Monastery and their new church dedicated to St Catherine. The Dominicans were to be found in a quieter part of the town, edged up against the wall and at a slight remove from the daily bustle and clamour of the busier streets, yet still close enough so that they could easily make their way out to preach amongst the townsfolk.

Tallinn will no longer be recognizable in a few years, Melchior mused. Sire Dorn was right. There was construction work everywhere: here, members of the Great Guild were building themselves a structure nearly as grand as the Town Hall; there, St Olaf's Church was being raised to evermore lofty heights; along the wall St Catherine's Church had been completed just a few years ago, but the Dominicans were already putting up new buildings within the monastery walls. Work was in full swing everywhere, and the Magistrate should actually be pleased by that fact. A town that does not continue to build is marked by death, and Tallinn's endless expansion meant that it was attracting greater wealth. New faces arrived from

Germany every summer, not to mention those from even more distant parts of the Holy Roman Empire. A merchant from Burgundy had even purchased a residence behind the weighing-house, and the number of people from Bruges and elsewhere was growing as well.

Today, however, the mood in the town was agitated, as court servants walking through the streets proclaimed in their clear, shrill and commanding voices that the Town Council was pursuing a murderer. One crier walked past Melchior at the corner of Munga Street, proclaiming, 'And, therefore, all citizens allegiant to the town of Tallinn who have become aware of the location in which this very murderer doth conceal himself, or of his name, must appear at once before the Tallinn Council and declare these facts and confirm this statement with a vow that they have not lied. Hear ye, hear ye, citizens of Tallinn and all others …'

Yes, this was how things ran under Dorn's authority. All tower guards, town watchmen and boatmen had been warned to keep an eye on any and all suspicious persons, and Council servants declared the news about the town. However, if the murderer was cunning and no one had witnessed his act then the effort might be for naught. The criers had made similar rounds last spring following the fatal stabbing of a Stralsund skipper in a tavern beyond the town walls – although the killer was not found on that occasion. Even Sire Rinus Götzer was unable to give Melchior a lead … It actually wouldn't be a bad idea to look for old Götzer now, he thought. The former skipper and almsman possessed more knowledge of matters in the town and harbour than all the councilmen put together.

Vespers had just finished at the Dominican Monastery, and a current of townspeople exited the gates. Several guilds finished their daily work just as the church bells began sounding the call to evening prayers, and the Dominicans – who were quite talented in their preaching – attracted a greater congregation to their sermons than the town's pastors. Melchior had heard that complaints had even made their way to the Council that the Dominicans preached too much – and too well, Melchior thought – and were taking followers away from the Church of the Holy Ghost and St Nicholas's. Yet, the fact was that the Dominicans, as an itinerant order who moved from one monastery to the next in any number of faraway lands, were well versed in exciting tales and received extensive instruction in both the Scriptures and worldly life – hence they knew how to talk to ordinary people about matters that brought both care to their souls and stimulated their minds. And, of course, keeping in with the Dominicans was definitely beneficial to the townsfolk at times. The monastery of nearly fifty brothers functioned as one big crafts-men's guild, producing goods for sale and also purchasing items, both for their own use and in order to resell, making a profit in the process. The Dominicans' beer was famed throughout Harju and Viru and had been spoken of even much further abroad since the Lay Brother Wunbaldus had become involved in the brewing. Oh, the Dominicans have certainly brought much honour and renown to Tallinn, Melchior thought, and all by the Lord's blessing. Even the Blackheads, who were now so very active in Tallinn under the direction of Sire Freisinger, had their own altar consecrated right within the Dominican Monastery, and –

Melchior's train of thought was cut off by the appearance of Magistrate Dorn. The man elbowed his way through the crowd of churchgoers, protesting that even the church bells couldn't be heard through the masons' pounding – although by Melchior's calculations the evening service had already ended.

The Apothecary agreed with Dorn's grumblings when the latter came closer. The pair reckoned they should wait until the crowd had dispersed then send word of their arrival to the Prior. People were presently making their way out through the wall gate where Brother

Hinricus stood holding his donation basket amongst all the cripples and tramps who were begging there as usual.

'Forgive me, esteemed Magistrate – you are indeed the Magistrate, are you not?' A voice bearing a hint of a foreign accent sounded from behind the Apothecary. Melchior turned to see its source. A cloaked man who looked like a mason had stepped up to them, and Melchior thought he vaguely recognized the figure.

'I and none other,' Dorn grumbled and eyed the man up. 'And you are …?'

'Caspar Gallenreutter, from Westphalia,' said the man. 'Your humble servant, a master mason by trade.'

'Right, right. You're the one building that chapel there next to St Olaf's. We have certainly met before, but my ageing head no longer desires to hold its memories so well,' Dorn said.

Gallenreutter laughed, albeit in a somewhat forced manner. 'It was at the Brotherhood of Blackheads that we met, at the penny-beer drinking to which I was invited last month. However, it was a very merry time, and it is no wonder that you do not remember me.' He turned towards Melchior. 'And you are our town apothecary, are you not?'

Melchior bowed slightly. 'By the grace of St Nicholas, I am. Whether you be afflicted by stomach flu or some other health ailment begs to be healed, you are most welcome to stop by, and we will certainly find a cure.'

It turned out, however, that the Master Mason Gallenreutter did not want to talk to the men about his health. He began to speak then broke off, appeared to search for the right words and then asked, 'The thing is, my good sirs, I wished to ask whether it is true – what they said in church – that Commander of the Order Henning von Clingenstain met his end in a dreadful manner yesterday on Toompea.'

'Unfortunately it is true,' Dorn said gloomily. 'His head was chopped off in a single blow and –'

Melchior jabbed Dorn with his finger. The Magistrate was inclined to ramble on instead of listening.

'It is indeed so, Master Mason,' Melchior continued in Dorn's stead. 'His head was chopped off.'

'How could such a thing have happened? Did the knights go on a rampage amongst themselves, or …?' Gallenreutter asked, prying.

'No one can say for certain yet,' Melchior replied. 'But the murderer will certainly be captured.'

'And at roughly what time did this happen?'

'If you will allow me to enquire, why should this be of such interest to a foreign master mason?' Melchior questioned.

'Why should it be of interest?' Gallenreutter peered about nervously. 'When I heard about that dreadful bloodshed then I started to fear that maybe *I* was on Toompea at that very hour and that maybe –'

'You visited Toompea yesterday?' Melchior interrupted. He now observed the Master Mason more closely. Gallenreutter looked to be around forty years of age and was a strong man with soft facial features and saffron-coloured hair; his shoulders were broad and his face tempered by the wind. He had clever eyes, but his awkwardness and agitation did not seem to be affected. Yes, Melchior now reckoned that he had seen Gallenreutter at the Brotherhood of Blackheads, although they had not been drawn into conversation.

'Yes, I was on Toompea yesterday,' Gallenreutter confirmed. 'About what time did that killing take place?'

'It happened shortly before the Long Hill gates were shut, at around half-past eight in the evening,' Melchior replied slowly, studying the man closely.

'And what business did *you* have on Toompea?' Dorn prodded, perhaps in a harsher tone than was necessary, as the Master Mason drew into himself even further.

'I wanted to call upon Clingenstain, but I was not admitted into the castle. And just now, when I heard that he had been killed yesterday, then I thought suddenly that I … that maybe I was on Toompea at the same time. Oh, what a horrible, horrible tale … Although if it was at half-past eight then it certainly could not have occurred when I was there.'

'Tell us, Master Gallenreutter, at what time *were* you there? This is the first time I've heard that you also went to call upon Clingenstain,' Dorn asked.

'I did not speak to him because I was not allowed to enter,' the Master Mason reiterated.

'Master Gallenreutter, this is a very important matter. I ask you – and the Magistrate asks as well – please, tell us in greater detail about your visit. You see, thus far not one person has mentioned you being on Toompea yesterday. So, at what time did you attempt to call upon Clingenstain?' Gallenreutter breathed in deeply, cracked his knuckles nervously and spoke. 'It was in the afternoon, shortly after I had lunched near St Olaf's. They wouldn't allow me through the castle gates. They said the Knight was not present and I should make myself scarce.'

'And what business did you have with the Commander of Gotland in the first place?' Dorn enquired. 'Was he an acquaintance?'

'Oh no, not at all. You see, he was born near the town of Warendorf, where the roots of my family tree extend as well, so I wanted to visit him to pay my respects and tell him that my father built his uncle's house, and to say that if the Grand Master of the Order knows of any wall that needs to be constructed somewhere or of any church someone desires to be built, then my skills and hands would always be at his service. We both come from Westphalia, and in these times, when masters mason are multiplying everywhere, such ties are increasingly important.'

'And you were not permitted to say this to Clingenstain?' Melchior asked.

'Curses, no. I was turned back at the gate. It was all quite odd up there. Not a soul to be seen, only some singing and the telltale sounds of beer-drinking under the trees in the direction of the Dome churchyard. There was one watchman at the gate, but he was fast asleep and snoring. I woke him up, and he went to call the other watchmen, who were having a singsong elsewhere at the time. Two Order attendants then came and asked who the devil I was and what I wanted. I waited while they went into the castle, and when they came back they said Clingenstain wasn't there and that I should clear off. Which I did.'

'Intriguing,' Melchior murmured. 'Did you see who was singing?'

'No, I did not, but it was some very muddled song, a song about nothing at all – something about a horse and some kind of puzzle. I made no attempt to look closer. In any case, I was sent away and not even allowed to leave a message for the Knight.'

'And you, Master Mason, did you leave then? You saw no one else?'

'I went back to St Olaf's, yes, seeing as the chapel needs to be built. And today, when I heard that Clingenstain had been killed, I wondered … Lord have mercy, might that have been at the very time that I was there …'

'No, it occurred much later,' Melchior replied, 'at least we must believe that to be so.'

'It occurred later,' the Master Mason repeated in a more confident tone. And the fact that you are searching for this murderer here in the town, does that mean … is he a townsman? Is his identity known with any certainty?'

Dorn started to reply, but their conversation was interrupted by a piercing but gravelly voice. Melchior glimpsed Great Guild Alderman Mertin Tweffell approaching. The merchant's young bride Gerdrud was on his arm, and his loyal servant Ludke plodded in his master's wake.

'Hear, Magistrate,' Tweffell bellowed. 'Stop right there, in the name of the saints.'

Gallenreutter bade them farewell. He bowed quickly, wished them luck in their search and said that – if the Lord willed it – they would see each other that evening at the Brotherhood of Blackheads. Old Tweffell marched directly towards the Magistrate, while Melchior turned and caught up with the Master Mason of Westphalia to ask him to wait a minute.

'You heard the sound of singing coming from the churchyard,' Melchior said. 'Tell me, did you happen to see a Dominican lay brother or Prior Eckell himself walking in that direction?'

Gallenreutter shook his head quickly and said he saw no one there other than the drunken guardsmen. The mason then left, and Melchior walked back to Dorn. Alderman Tweffell was presently demanding that the man inform him of the latest news.

'Yes, someone from the town,' Dorn was saying, 'although whether it was some unknown rogue or a town citizen I do not know. When we apprehend him we will drag him up to Toompea where a tribunal of knights will condemn him to death by hanging at the very least – that is certain, yes.'

Gerdrud stood obediently, arm-in-arm with her husband, and if one were to observe them carefully it would have been evident that the young woman was not simply standing but was actually support-ing her husband. The woman did so deftly, however, to minimize any chance that a passer-by might notice. Ludke towered a few steps away, a behemoth, a flaxen-haired Estonian whose brawny wrists were like oak stumps. Gerdrud blushed lightly, and Melchior could not blame her for doing so. The young woman always looked abashed when she accompanied her husband about town. Stories, Melchior thought, nasty and spiteful stories. Oh, Gerdrud has certainly caught wind of those. Merchants' journeymen and apprentices, wagon haulers and other townsfolk of the sort — Melchior had even half overheard, while sipping beer at the master carpenter's workshop, how the men there made fun of the Alderman's marriage. No doubt they took pleasure in discussing how the young maiden wet her husband's dried-up old sausage and rubbed it with oils just so that it might have even the slightest trace of vitality. Nevertheless, Melchior felt that Tweffell himself was guilty by dint of the fact that such a young girl had become the object of such derision. He pricked up his ears, however, as Master Tweffell was speaking about Clingenstain.

'Yes, indeed, I knew him,' Tweffell spoke emphatically, 'quite well enough to say that he was a greedy scoundrel, a thief and a crook from head to toe, who only wore a monk's cloak to hide his dreadful avarice and impudence.'

'Those are strong words,' Melchior noted softly as he nodded to the Alderman in greeting.

'Aha, Melchior,' Tweffell exclaimed upon seeing the Apothecary, 'my good neighbour and lifesaver. The Council has employed you once again as its spy, eh? Well, I know not whether the words are strong, but they are true, that I swear. If you are searching for someone in Tallinn who bore enmity against Clingenstain then such a man stands before you.'

Dorn started and waved his hand in the air feverishly. 'Master Merchant, *Master Merchant,* have some discretion.'

Tweffell appeared not to possess such discretion, however. 'There is nothing to hide here. Each and every merchant of the Great Guild knows that whoever does business with the Commander of Gotland will be swindled *if he is lucky*, and it would only be by good fortune that he would not be robbed of the very clothes he stands up in. That deceased Commander was an absolute lout,' Tweffell sputtered.

'Then perhaps you know someone who may have borne such great enmity towards Clingenstain that he would go so far as to dispatch him from this world?' Melchior asked.

The merchant scowled at Melchior for a moment and then harrumphed. He lowered his voice and leaned in closer to the Apothecary and the Magistrate.

'Hear, let me tell you something,' he said. 'The Order is our overlord, is it not? As are the bishops, who are ordained by the Lord's great love to maintain order and justice by the word of God or by sword and to beseech the Almighty for our happiness and blessing. Yet not a single Order castle nor bishop's stronghold will stand if it has not food to eat nor clothes to wear nor silver dishes and fine wines from foreign lands, tools and everything else that their farm boys do not craft on their own. No. They receive only grain and meat from their lands, and they produce a great deal more grain than they or their farmers are capable of consuming themselves. Thus they have grain but have no cloth or silverware and cannot grow salt on their fields either. And therefore they require merchants to transform their grain into gold and to bring back expensive English broadcloth, Burgundy wines and silver dishes for them. In order for a merchant to do this he must also receive his own profit to feed his family and maintain his household, to put something aside for his later years and to have masses said for his salvation. For a merchant's salvation is jeopardized by engaging in trade; there is no escape from that, as otherwise you would be neither a merchant nor anything else. And so his coins must also be donated on occasion to a church that will pray for the happiness and for the soul of each one of us. Yes, that is how such things must be. The Order provides us with land, with Lübeck law and the entitlement to exercise this right by counsel and by force when anyone violates it. The town of Tallinn is the Order's harbour. The Order cannot survive without merchants, and merchants cannot survive without the Order. So it has been, and so it must remain. We must believe in and trust the Order and they us in return, as there is not one without the other.'

Dorn listened and nodded. 'That is the truth, sire, the truth.'

'Of course it bloody well is,' Tweffell barked. 'I myself know it. Yet what comes to pass when one Knight of the Teutonic Order is a liar, a thief and a crook? What happens then? What happens is that a merchant no longer desires to purchase any goods from the Order nor sell it anything in return. A merchant will buy furs from Novgorod, purchase grain from an Order vassal and sell it to Lübeck; then he will receive the money and procure from Lübeck silver plates, English broadcloth and a few casks of sweet Rhineland wine. No longer will he sell anything to the Teutonic Order. A merchant is a town citizen; he has his rights, and so does the town. Tell me what will become of the Order then.'

'The entire Order cannot become so steeped in lies and robbery that merchants will no longer purchase its goods,' Melchior pointed out.

'Not the *entire* Order, not yet, but one drop of tar can ruin a barrelful of honey. If you ask me whether or not I am glad that Clingenstain is deceased, then I will tell you that, no, I am not, because now my ship and my gold will never be returned. However, if you ask me whether he deserved such a death, then I would answer yes, without question he did.'

Gerdrud let slip a muffled exclamation. 'But, my dear husband, how can you say such things in front of a place of worship?'

'Truth is truth in all places, whether in front of a place of worship or in a tavern,' Tweffell snapped. 'Go home, woman, if you do not wish to hear the truth.'

'So it was for that reason that you went to speak to the Knight yesterday, to tell him all this?' Melchior asked.

'Yes and no. Last spring one of my ships did not return from Gotland because the local commander – Clingenstain – had picked it clean from bow to stern. The reason given was that its cargo had been bought from Erengisel, the Vogt of Vyborg, who was apparently in debt to Gotland. In debt he may have been, but from the very moment that I bought those wares from that fox-faced Erengisel they were *my* wares, and I owed Gotland not a single penny. Gotland may war directly with Vyborg for its debt – or with the King of Sweden himself, for all I care – yet not with the Order's loyal subjects, with Tallinn's merchants. I had stated all of this in my *tenth* letter to Clingenstain, and he was aware of the matter already. What I went to tell him was that the Great Guild would not allow itself to be ridiculed and worked over like some ignorant peasant girl and that we have a great many friends in Lübeck. If Clingenstain did not pay off his debt then the Great Guild would write to Lübeck and to the Grand Master in Marienburg.'

'And what did Clingenstain make of all this?'

'Ha!' Tweffell barked. 'He made of it what he had since last springtime: absolutely nothing. He was already so drunk that he could not tell up from down, boasting about that golden collar – which he had bought from Casendorpe with *my gold* – and thrust towards me a tankard of beer brought to him as a gift from the Council. He did not wish to hear anything about a stolen ship. And I'll tell you one more thing, Magistrate. The town of Tallinn might be home to a number of merchants that the Commander of Gotland has robbed, and such men might be found in all towns lining the shores of the sea, but, as sure as I am the Alderman of the Great Guild, this I tell you, Magistrate Dorn, if you search for your murderer amongst merchants then you are looking in the wrong place.'

'I certainly do not believe that any merchant committed such an act. Absolutely not,' Dorn rushed to avow.

'That I would certainly hope,' Tweffell growled. 'Tallinn's merchants are not the sort of men who would slink off to remove heads like a thieves in the night, no. Tallinn's merchants behave like baptized Christians, with justice and good counsel. They allow neither the Order nor the town to overstep their boundaries. They write to Lübeck's Town Council and, when necessary, to the Grand Master of the Order himself. They demand fair trial be held over all thieves. It is time that the Order also came to understand that merchants are now a force. With each passing day they demand evermore justice in the name of the Lord, as well as the status, the treatment and the respect of which they are worthy. But I digress. I wish you fine health, good Magistrate, Sire Apothecary – and my gratitude for your salve. Wife, Ludke, let us depart.'

The Alderman and his entourage began to move off towards the centre of town along Munga Street, Gerdrud subtly supporting her master and the loyal Ludke trailing after them.

12

The Dominican Monastery
16 May, Before Evening Mass

BROTHER HINRICUS greeted Melchior and Dorn before the main portal, left them waiting for a short time and then reappeared to announce that, yes, the Prior would receive them. Hinricus stated that the Prior did not feel too well, but he was in a better state than he had been that morning and would take their company. The Prior was in the dormitory, and Hinricus would show them the way.

Melchior was aware that Hinricus was the *cellarius* of the preaching brothers. The monk was still a young man and apparently of Estonian descent: tall in stature, gaunt and gangly, somewhat bow-legged, yet with sinewy-strong forearms. His face was rather crudely formed, as if etched in stone or densely compressed, and his eyes were too close to the bridge of his nose. He is probably not regarded as a handsome man, Melchior mused. Hinricus was, however, a devout Dominican and had been promoted to the rank of *cellarius* only recently, no doubt as a result of his upstanding religious work.

They stepped through the sharply arched portal, which was adorned with painted symbols of the Dominican Order: a dog, a lily, a rosette, a vine and an oak-leaf garland. Melchior's father had once explained the meanings of these symbols to him, which he had learned through his education at a Dominican monastery school: the dog symbolized a monk; the lily the Virgin Mary and St Dominic; the rosette St Catherine; the winding grapevine Jesus Christ, our saviour; and the oak-leaf garland the Virgin Mother. Also painted on the arch were lions, snakes and dragons. There had been snakes and lions painted on the doorway of the monastery in Lübeck, too, a detail Melchior remembered. He had been four years old when he had visited the monastery with his father for the first time. Melchior the Elder had sought the monks' help to cure his son's sickness. Or *was* it a sickness? His father had been unsure. Was it a wrathful spirit, a demon? The Wakenstede line had suffered this curse for several hundred years ... The old half-blind infirmarer's wrinkled hands had groped their way across Melchior's entire body, and the only medication he recommended was to say ten Our Fathers. Melchior's father, though, was already perfectly aware that this would be of no help.

Melchior drove those terrible memories from his mind. The Wakenstedes' curse had not beset him for a whole year. Perhaps his guardian saints had helped.

Melchior always sensed a kind of transition when he entered the monastery. He breathed a different sort of air – it was not the air of a church, it was more ... sacred? The thick walls of the monastery instilled a feeling of having stepped closer to God, that one was now in a place where fifty men served Him from morning to night, praying for the salvation and happiness of all who lived in the town. Every monastery had its walls, and once inside you were in a separate world.

Hinricus led them through the gates and up to the newly erected St Catherine's Church. The church had been completed only a few years ago, but the building work never seemed to draw to a close in the realm of the Dominicans. Immediately in front of the men stood the dormitory that had been constructed from the monastery's old church; wooden scaffolding and unfinished walls were already rising next to it. A new, larger refectory was being built on the north side of the complex, and a second dormitory was taking shape behind that. At the south wing, alongside the new church, the passageway into which Hinricus now led them was being fashioned from the older, smaller church. The men walked in absolute silence behind the *cellarius* and breathed in the monastery air, which, in truth, smelled rather earthy – more specifically, of baked fish; the brothers had taken a small meal following vespers. Melchior gazed through the windows of the passageway out on to the courtyard, which was dotted with a few quaint plant beds, and there was a small well next to which an older lay brother garbed in a white robe was washing a pile of laundry. Masons had apparently just demolished the old church's last remaining face, the north, and were now putting up the wall of the western passageway. A poor monastery does not build, Melchior said to himself, and a poor monastery is of no use to anyone.

Hinricus warned the guests about the piles of stones that were scattered around. The new passageway was only half completed, and there were building materials everywhere. The floor in some places was still simply packed soil, and large holes yawned along those stretches. Hinricus directed them towards the lay brothers' dormitory. It was a long structure that squatted between the northern nave of the new church and the unfinished dormitory that was still under construction bordering the western wall of the passageway. Half of its wall was still unfinished. Melchior glimpsed hay-stuffed sacks used as mattresses that were lined up side by side, a modest table and a jug for water alongside each. The lay brothers lived a truly humble life, but then they had entered the monastery penniless, looking to work. They were not schooled in the Scriptures nor could they ever be ordained as full brothers; they were simple souls who found in the monastery that which had eluded them in the world outside.

Hinricus guided them through the lay brothers' dormitory and finally came to a stop in front of the door to a small chamber.

'The Prior is currently with Brother Wunbaldus,' Hinricus said softly. 'He felt unwell, and Wunbaldus mixed him a therapeutic drink.'

He then bowed, opened the door and disappeared without a sound.

Melchior and Dorn entered the small chamber and crossed themselves devoutly. The room had no windows, but a soft evening light spilled in through a gap in the unfinished passageway wall. The chamber contained a sleeping-mat, a chair and a low table with a shelf bearing four small silver relics. Brother Wunbaldus sat behind the table and was apparently busying himself with cleaning the relics using a small brush and vinegar, causing a pungent, sour odour to permeate the room. Prior Eckell sat on the mat, holding a cup. Between the two Dominicans was a bench, on top of which was a chessboard lined with black and white squares. They were evidently in the middle of a game, as the chess-pieces were spread across the board. True, many of the figures were no longer in play, and the majority of pieces had already been cast on to the floor. Only a few lone combatants were left in position. Prior Eckell rose immediately to greet the Magistrate and the Apothecary. The two men kneeled before the holy Dominican Father.

Prior Eckell was ill. Melchior could tell that immediately. Even the smell of vinegar could not mask the foul odour of sickness that seeped through his clothing. The old Prior trembled slightly. He was as pale as a skull, and red spots flashed in the whites of his eyes. Both men wore the Dominicans' white tunic, which signified the purity of their souls, Melchior recalled. However, while the Prior was dressed completely in white and wore a cream-coloured scapular around his neck, Wunbaldus's scapular was black in the tradition of the lay brothers. The room was warm, and consequently the brothers were not wearing the Dominicans' traditional black hooded cloak over their shoulders.

Wunbaldus must have been about twenty years younger than the Prior, but strife and work had moulded his once proud and noble face into a wan and emotionless landscape. Melchior could not remember, if he had ever known, where Wunbaldus might have come from – but then he did not possess that knowledge about most of the monks. Based on the lay brother's speech, which the Apothecary had heard only rarely, he might have been born somewhere near Lübeck. A hump on the man's back forced him to walk bent over – Wunbaldus's tall figure in his lay brother's habit was always easy to recognize.

Dorn kissed the Prior's hand and said they had come on the Town Council's behalf to request a blessing for their difficult task – to find the Toompea Murderer from the town. The Prior nodded, wheezing slightly, and recited a barely audible prayer. Then he spoke. 'If you wish for the Lord's blessing for your just charge, Magistrate, you have received it from both myself and the monastery – but, believe me, a blessing falls short in a task of this nature. If such matters could be solved by a blessing alone then would any criminal still walk about this earth freely?'

Dorn moved to reply, but Melchior got in first.

'Consequently we indeed dare to enquire whether anything that might bring us closer to this murderer might have stood out to the holy Dominican Father that day on Toompea,' he said. 'You did visit Toompea yesterday, and perhaps he saw or heard something there?'

The Prior eyed them for a moment and then motioned that they should stand.

'What stood out?' His hoarse voice trembled. 'Do you mean *aside* from that life of revelry and filth that knights lead when warfare is not presently under way? No, nothing stood out. However, I have seen and lived quite enough in this world to know that knights with alcohol in their veins tend to forget who and where their rightful enemy is.'

'The merciful Prior does not mean to suggest that some other knight ...?' Dorn enquired haltingly.

'The Prior does not wish to say anything he has not seen with his own eyes, Magistrate,' Eckell replied. 'I went to Toompea to fulfil my duty as the head of Tallinn's oldest monastery. It is my task to bow before our protector and overlord, the Teutonic Order and to thank its knights for all the good they have done for Livonia. As I did. What I observed on Toompea was excessive eating and excessive drinking, revelry and a life of depravity that a monk's oath should, in truth, prevent our knights from living yet does not.'

'As we heard, Clingenstain wished to take confession,' Melchior spoke.

'Which I should have refused,' the Prior replied sharply. 'Only a person who is in their full and absolute senses may take confession, not one whose mouth only fumes beer and who cannot issue a single clear word from between his lips.'

'Yet you did *not* refuse,' Brother Wunbaldus spoke from behind his table. Melchior sensed something in the Lay Brother's tone on which ... on which he could not quite put his finger. It wasn't criticism but rather – remorse?

The Prior sighed. 'By the guidance of St Catherine I thus administered this sacrament correctly in my pity, so the Knight Clingenstain was able to die with his sins absolved.'

Before Melchior could open his mouth Eckell continued, 'Yes, I know what you want to ask, Sire Apothecary. You are aware that I took his confession, and you came to enquire whether anything he disclosed might help the Council find the murderer's trail.'

'Oh, I could not even have imagined such a thing,' Melchior interjected quickly.

'Is it not so that our Grand Master of the Dominican Order and keeper of canon law, the Pope's own chaplain, Raymond of Penyafort, has written that the sanctity of the confessional might no longer hold when it involves unjust absolution for the confessor when a man is no longer able to stand for his good name?' Wunbaldus asked in a soft voice.

'So it has been written,' Prior Eckell confirmed. 'And the deceased Commander of the Order would certainly wish for his killer to be found and executed.' He sighed heavily, glanced briefly towards Wunbaldus and nodded. 'Yes, it is so. However, I fear that it cannot help you … not even by Clingenstain's own desire. His burden of sin will not lead you closer to finding his murderer.'

The Prior took a sip from his cup and placed it on the floor. Melchior noticed that Eckell had difficulty speaking.

'Not all have been given the ability to see and recognize their sins,' the Prior continued. 'The more frequently a Christian takes confession the more he will cultivate an understanding of where his sins can be found. There are men who confess to infidelity in their thoughts yet who forget to confess stealing a last mouthful of bread from the poor. There are men who confess to killing their enemies too clemently yet who do not regard the killing of dozens of innocents to be a sin. But let us speak of this no more. Clingenstain was too intoxicated to produce a clear word from his mouth. He was also absolved of those sins which I believed he wished to confess.'

'Given all of the good that he has done for the Dominican Order …' Wunbaldus said. Again – that tone, Melchior thought. He cast his gaze for a moment over the state of the unfinished chess game. Melchior's father had once shown him the game and probably even taught him how to play. He sometimes heard people speak of chess, but not many of Tallinn's townspeople played. In any case, Melchior had forgotten how the pieces moved across the board and the significance they held. He did, however, remember that each figure had a unique meaning, which many people believed mirrored earthly life.

'Yes, Wunbaldus, I was unable to let go of the fact that Clingenstain has not always only wreaked havoc upon wine and beer but also upon the enemies of the Church and of honest men,' the Prior retorted then fell silent.

'Commander Spanheim did indeed mention that you had come into contact with Clingenstain before, in Gotland,' said Dorn.

'In days long past, yes,' said the Prior. 'It has been almost ten years since that time. I was then the *cellarius* of our monastery in Visby. You see, Sire Apothecary, we Dominicans are a very transient group; we are not tied to a single monastery until the end of our days but instead roam from one place to another. This is, in fact, my seventh monastery. We travel around and proclaim the Word of God in every place to every person. We come and we go, but the Word does not change. People are born and they die, yet the Word of God remains …'

The Prior suddenly broke off before he could finish his sentence. He grabbed his chest, wheezed and began coughing intensely.

'Are you ill, Father?' Wunbaldus exclaimed quickly. 'Quick, hand him his cup.' Wunbaldus sprang up and supported the Prior, helping him to sit. In doing so the Lay Brother knocked over the chessboard, and the pieces scattered across the floor. Dorn grabbed the cup from the floor and pressed it into the Prior's trembling hands. The old man shook like the last leaf of autumn and was breathing with difficulty, but his condition began to improve after a short time. He leaned back against the wall and reassured the others with a nod.

'The Prior's health has not been in a commendable state for quite some time,' Wunbaldus said with a hint of rebuke.

'And what is the opinion of the monastery's infirmarer?' Melchior asked.

'Our infirmarer is in his twilight years and unable to suggest anything other than to let blood,' Wunbaldus replied.

'It is said', the Magistrate chipped in, 'that letting blood aids all ailments except the plague.'

Wunbaldus stared at Dorn expressionlessly and spoke slowly. 'We pray for the Prior's health and hope that the relics will help him also. Nevertheless, I have a few salves and medicines here that I have mixed according to the old instructions of our Dominican Order; no doubt they will aid him as well. This, of course, does not mean that we doubt the power of our relics.'

'Ah yes, those famed heads of yours …' Melchior murmured and turned his gaze to the relics lined up on the shelf. The monastery's relics – said to be the heads of saints – were the very objects that pilgrims made their way to Tallinn to see and for which the town's Dominicans were renowned throughout all lands around the sea. Aside from their beer, of course. Melchior took note with some surprise that the Lay Brother Wunbaldus had been entrusted with the job of caring for the relics. Lay brothers typically performed simpler tasks at monasteries. Much simpler tasks. Silverwork was the dominion of goldsmiths.

Wunbaldus handed the Prior his elixir and dabbed his brow. Whatever was in the tankard seemed truly to relieve the old main's ailments – or perhaps it was the power of the relics. The manner in which the hulking, hunchbacked Lay Brother cared for the old Prior was somehow moving, Melchior thought. Eckell looked like a dwarf alongside Wunbaldus. The Lay Brother was certainly his junior by some decades, but the pair seemed to be very close despite this. It was perhaps surprising that they found the Prior – who, furthermore, appeared to be suffering from a grave illness – right here in the tiny workshop of a lay brother.

'The Prior should rest a great deal more,' said Wunbaldus, and Melchior grunted in agreement.

'I am already better,' Eckell said in a whisper. 'The Almighty wishes to remind me of the fact that I am no longer young. I am already better. Thank you, Wunbaldus.'

'You should indeed rest more, Father,' Melchior spoke up. 'And, of course, I would dare to recommend a salve, rub or treatment mixed according to Council Doctor Grawertz's instructions, if I only knew your ailments in greater detail.'

'Old age is the name of those ailments,' Eckell sighed. 'Wunbaldus's salves and medications bring me respite only for a moment. The Almighty wishes to give me a sign that the time will soon come when He calls me unto Himself.'

'Come now, you are not at all that advanced in your years. Just as Sire Dorn said, fine old remedies such as bloodletting – or, for example, Melchior's pharmacy elixir – always help in all cases short of the plague,' Melchior said with a smile.

'So far Wunbaldus's elixir has brought me more relief than absolutely any other kind of doctors' wisdom from Lübeck or Rostock,' Eckell replied. He smiled for a moment then turned serious. 'Regarding the plague … I presume neither of you have witnessed plague, have you?' he asked.

'Thanks be to God, no great plague has yet befallen Tallinn,' Dorn said. 'Alas, I have heard, oh yes, I have heard of what devastation it wreaks in German towns. It is a dreadful disease, dreadful. Scourge and punishment for sins.'

'I am indeed unable to offer medicine that counters the plague,' Melchior reflected. 'Have you seen plague, Father?'

The old man sighed heavily. It was difficult for him to speak, but he had a strong desire to do so. 'I have seen two plagues during my lifetime. That called the Black Death when I was just a small boy in Fleckenberg and then later in Flanders. The Lord spared me, although I did not regard myself worthy of such a blessing. I lost my parents and my teachers; I saw distress, destitution and despair, the likes of which one cannot begin to imagine. However, it was at that very time that I made the decision to dedicate my life to serving the Almighty.' He turned towards Dorn suddenly. 'And if you, Magistrate, say with such certainty that plague is a scourge sent by God for sins then I ask, how have those saintly, God-fearing and pious men and women whom that sickness has snuffed out in their countless thousands across the entire Christian world, how have they sinned?'

Dorn shifted uncomfortably. Theological debate was not exactly his forte. He grunted something about whether not all in the world is born of the Lord's grace and looked towards Melchior imploringly.

'*All* in the world?' Eckell retorted sharply. 'Do heretics then also exist by the Lord's grace?'

Dorn shot back. 'Heretics? They are followers of false teachings, those who misread the Word of the Lord …'

'No, not all in this world is born of the Lord's grace, and plague has *certainly* not descended upon the land by His mercy,' the Prior stated with confidence. 'It is through God's grace that we are given a head and intelligence, that we are able to determine both right and wrong, that which is just and that which is unfair. We have been given free will and intelligence, and if we use the latter correctly then we are also capable of seeing that plague spreads first throughout places where there is filth and mire, where people care not for their health. If we have wit then we eat fresh foods and drink pure water, and if we have even greater wit then we are also able to protect ourselves against the plague by using other means.'

'Do you then know of some other medicines against the plague, Father?' Melchior asked with interest. 'I have read one or two books, and –'

'Oh yes, Melchior is a well-educated man. He has four entire books at his home,' Dorn interrupted.

'Three, actually,' Melchior corrected. 'However, are there then other medications to ward off the plague?'

'Certainly,' Eckell replied. 'Certainly. Man can help himself in fighting this epidemic, although there is not yet a definitive treatment known in the world. But if you are indeed a learned man, Melchior, then tell me, do you also believe that plague has been sent by the Lord as punishment for sin?'

'If I were *truly* an educated man then I would believe that if the Lord had unleashed upon the world a plague that lays waste to all people irrespectively – be they sinful miscreants or devout men of God – then this act would be no more sensible than poisoning the town well,' Melchior replied. 'Plague is no different from the other sicknesses and sickness-causing poisons that surround us, and when a person's body becomes frailer – through ageing, for example – then it also falls ill more easily. I believe that the holy Father is correct. A person receives their salvation from the Lord, but the causes of sickness must be sought elsewhere. Where illness is found so can be found its cure.'

The Prior coughed and nodded. 'I have seen heartless miscreants and murderers untouched by the plague while the bodies of loving mothers and God-fearing holy men were carted one after another by death wagons unto the bonfires. It was at that very moment, as if through a vision, that I came to understand that as long as there is so much strife and poverty in this world, so long do we also have need for assuagement, faith and love to make a stand against such troubles. It was during those days of plague that I, as a young boy, joined our Dominican Order.'

'Praise the Lord,' Wunbaldus declared loudly.

'Oh yes, let us,' agreed the Prior. 'And let us learn to perceive the world through His words, because they hold truth and recognition. May we see truth and justice, love and mercy in every place, and forgiveness, because it is not here, not in this world, that each one of us will face our last trial and judgement.'

Melchior was not exactly sure whether he correctly understood the Prior's point, but the word judgement reminded him of why they had come to the monastery in the first place. He said, 'Nevertheless, the Lord has charged us with judgement here on this earth. In truth, it is for this very reason that the Magistrate and I came to enquire whether the honourable Prior might be able to help bring us closer to the truth.'

'You do see that the holy Father is ill,' Wunbaldus spoke with warning in his voice.

Eckell shook his head. 'No, I am better, already much better. I always feel more fit here when I am near St Rochus,' said the Prior, gesturing with his eyes towards the relics.

'St Rochus? Ah, the holy Father means the relics,' Melchior remarked.

'Yes, here they are. I requested that Wunbaldus clean our silver relics. He once practised as a goldsmith ... amongst all his other trades.'

'This, before the Lord allowed me to reach my epiphany to which I must dedicate my life without end or reservation,' Wunbaldus recited.

'Did the Prior have these same relics in mind when he said earlier that the Lord also sent a medicine to ward against plague in the world?' Melchior asked.

Eckell looked him sharply in the eye and then said with a slight chuckle, 'You are a very curious man, Melchior.'

'I confess my vice. All apothecaries are this way. Our profession is to find medicines that work to counter the sicknesses of man. Yet, if you will allow, I wish to ask once more, are they indeed those famed heads that help to cure diseases? I have heard people speak of the relics, but I do not believe I have seen them before with my own eyes.'

'Very few have seen them, Melchior. We never expose the relics. Yet here they are: the head of St Rochus, who guards against plague and was sent to us by our brothers in Arles; the head of St Walburg, patron saint of those afflicted by dreadful coughing; the head of Erhardus of Regensburg, patron of those with poor eyes and of the blind; then we have the head of St Wolfgangus, who, when prayed to, helps those –'

'Who suffer from stomach pains,' Melchior interrupted excitedly. 'I know of one good, bitter remedy that is also called Erhard's Cure.'

'You know the saints well,' the Prior commended.

'All Wakenstedes study the lives of the saints diligently. My father insisted that I research everything I could about them and I have made every effort to follow his teachings,' Melchior replied modestly.

The relic that Wunbaldus was cleaning was presently uncovered. Melchior glimpsed a round head and blackened, wrinkled skin. So this would be the head of St Rochus, whose brain was removed and boiled, Melchior contemplated. He wanted to enquire about the object, but the chamber was suddenly flooded with the sound of beautiful, powerful, clear voices. It was the Dominican Brothers singing before evening mass, although the sound seemed almost to be coming from the room next door.

'*Ecco virgo concipiet*', Eckell pronounced. 'Forgive us, Magistrate. Our brothers are already singing, and the evening service is near.

We must leave. Wunbaldus, please assist me. We have many more duties before setting out for the Brotherhood of Blackheads.'

'The holy Father is not really considering ...' Melchior began with hesitation, but Eckell chuckled.

'Of course he is. I may be old and frail, yet now that the casks have already been taken to the Blackheads' guildhall the Dominican Prior really cannot be absent from the event. Do not believe that word of the fine taste of the beer made by Tallinn's Dominicans will only be heard within Tallinn and Livonia. News of our beer's victory is awaited by all of the monasteries, even as far away as Augsburg. By the way, I sent two casks of beer brewed at Wunbaldus's hands to our brothers in Magdeburg, and now they are demanding our Lay Brother for themselves.'

'However, I have given my vow never to leave the town of Tallinn, again,' said Wunbaldus with assurance.

'Thus the Magdeburg brothers must make do with their own. I could indeed free Wunbaldus from his oath, but I will never do so, absolutely not. I can say to you that we had never had beer with so fine a flavour brewed here as we have since the day that Wunbaldus arrived at our monastery five years ago.'

Wunbaldus placed his arm beneath the Prior's and helped him to stand. Mass for the Blackheads and then the evening service awaited the pious brothers. A black head in a reliquary and the Blackheads. The thought dawned upon Melchior in a flash. It was odd that he had never before made this connection. Now that he had thought of it the Apothecary realized he did not know how the Blackheads had come to be given their name. However, Melchior now believed he saw an obvious connection – the Dominicans' black head and the Blackheads' association with the Dominicans. This was all very well and interesting, but it could not help solve Clingenstain's murder.

Melchior addressed Wunbaldus, 'So, Wunbaldus, you should stop by the pharmacy more often. Perhaps we have things to teach one another. You can train me in the secrets of your brewing, and I will demonstrate how to make a few stronger-tasting elixirs, perhaps the kind that will help the holy Prior Eckell with his ailments.'

'Absolutely,' the Lay Brother agreed. 'However, I have many tasks to fulfil here at the monastery and gather alms three days each week. Nevertheless, I will certainly stop by.'

'And the Magistrate and I will no doubt be busying ourselves with catching a murderer,' Melchior mused.

'It is unfortunate that I cannot help you with your pursuits in any way other than giving a blessing,' said the Prior. 'I have already told you everything I know. Hinricus and I reached Toompea when Clingenstain had drunk himself to the point of senselessness, and it was difficult to make out a word he said. He wished to confess, more down to the emotions that surfaced because of his drunken state than in the manner of a holy, God-fearing man. I went to the Dome Church, and he followed a short time later. Wunbaldus and I returned to the town after his confession.'

'If I may ask, Father, was Clingenstain wearing his new gold collar when he came to confession?'

'You mean the one that he purchased from the Goldsmith? Yes, I saw it around his neck at the feast table in the Great Hall of the castle — I was told that Clingenstain had purchased it that very morning — but he was no longer wearing it when he came to confession. At least he had enough sense to appear before the Lord unadorned with jewellery.'

The singing from the church was coming to an end, and it was time for Melchior and Dorn to depart — but Melchior had one more question for Wunbaldus. The Apothecary recalled that Wunbaldus had scolded Kilian in the churchyard. Yes, said the Lay Brother, yes, of course, he had also been on Toompea yesterday.

'It is my duty to gather alms for the brothers on Toompea. The knights and vassals are usually quite generous, especially so when any merrymaking is under way. But that young minstrel was singing some extraordinarily improper verses, which, while it did please the guards immensely, I deemed it improper and impious – especially so given that our holy Prior was on Toompea at the time.'

'*Good* Wunbaldus,' the Prior said sharply. 'I can tell you that even when I was a young lad wandering minstrels sang all sorts of vulgar songs to gladden commoners. So it has been, and so it shall remain. A Christian land is made no weaker by this.'

'None the less, it is still painful for my ears to hear the Holy Mother of God maltreated in such a manner,' said Wunbaldus assertively.

'As I heard, a tankard of beer and a couple of pennies cooled your justified ill-temper,' Melchior remarked.

'The beer was of no great consequence, but those pennies go towards the good of the monastery and our brothers. What can you do? It is not difficult for me to be led into temptation, but at least I succeeded in putting an end to that profanity.'

'Be not distressed, Wunbaldus,' said Melchior. 'Our Kilian actually has a lovely voice and does not sing badly at all. He has committed himself to becoming a member of some Meistersingers' guild, which means that he must travel the land and lighten people's hearts with his art – even those of guards of the Teutonic Order. Not all are able to appreciate the kind of singing that I hear from your brothers now.'

Dorn, who had been unable to get a word in for quite some time, now said, 'Yes, just as your brothers might sing right here within the monastery walls – although your church is right across the courtyard, is it not?'

'Doubtless it is so clear because the new passageway is just being built,' Melchior suggested.

'Precisely,' said the Prior. 'The north end of the church had to be demolished for its construction – from where the Blackheads' side altar is up to the garden. Since the eastern wall of the passageway was the first section to be built, every sound coming from the north nave can be heard in the lay brothers' dormitory.'

'And when the pious Brother Wunbaldus came down from Toompea, he saw no one?' Dorn asked.

The Lay Brother shook his head slowly. 'Nothing unusual. I arrived back amongst our holy brothers prior to the evening service when the bells tolled seven times.'

'So it was indeed, just as our rules stipulate,' the Prior confirmed. 'Time can be kept accurately according to Wunbaldus's comings and goings.'

'If you will allow, and just so that matters might be crystal clear to the Magistrate,' Melchior interposed quickly, 'then, as I understand it, the esteemed Prior arrived back from Toompea at …?'

'About six o'clock,' Eckell answered.

'And Wunbaldus came back at seven?'

'Slightly earlier. The Blackheads' mass had just ended. Prior Eckell was serving the Blackheads at their altar while I came here to my chambers to count the day's alms. The esteemed Prior then stopped by my room, and afterwards I took the alms to our *cellarius* and reached the church in time for the start of the evening service.'

'Yes,' Eckell verified. 'I remained before the Blackheads' altar for a moment to speak to Freisinger then bade him farewell and came to Wunbaldus's chamber to assist him in counting the alms. Go now in the peace of God, and may our great saviour be with you.'

Melchior and Dorn kneeled before the Prior.

Brother Hinricus led the pair back through St Catherine's Church where the Dominicans were gathering for their evening service. They crossed themselves before the main altar and also glimpsed the Brotherhood of Blackhead's side altar, which was consecrated to St Mary, along with its new retable.

Afternoon had slipped into evening, and the hour had now come when Melchior and Dorn had to set off for the Blackheads' guildhall.

13

The Guildhall of the Brotherhood of Blackheads
16 May, Evening

T HE CUSTOM OF HOLDING a Smeckeldach competition was said to have been around as long as Tallinn's guilds themselves, and each guild regarded it an honour to offer the very best brew that had been chosen at their own drinking festivities. Melchior could not remember whether it had been the Great Guild, St Olaf's or St Canute's that had been the first to hold such beer-tastings, but a number of such events had now become established throughout the year. The most important, however, was held under the roof of the Brotherhood of Blackheads. The men attending these events were chosen with care – only those whose judgement was deemed the very best were selected, and it was nothing to do with an invitee's profession. When, a few years back, the Commander of the Order had heard that such a competition was being held in Lower Town he had the guild informed that their members had forgotten to invite their local lord. Spanheim, whose origins were less lofty than some previous commanders, would happily sit at the same table as the townsfolk – particularly when the Blackheads arranged such a hearty feast to go with it. Master Freisinger believed the Blackheads' feast table to be crucial to the success of the event, and no expense was spared to make sure that everything was of the highest quality. It was highly unlikely that anyone besides himself and the other hosts would be able to count the number of boars, lambs, ducks or swans that had been heaped upon the table. The Town Council's cook had been working at the guild for several days to assemble such an opulent feast, and, as Melchior was aware, Freisinger had personally visited each and every butcher in town and picked out only the finest cuts of meat.

The rules of *Smeckeldach* stipulated that guilds compete over two separate days with a day off in between for rest and recovery and to allow the samplers' thirst to be properly restored. On the first day the Dominicans and members of the Great Guild would each present four types of beer that had been brewed at locations around the town or, as the Dominicans did, had been brewed by themselves. All competing beers were to be produced according to old German traditions, and if anyone loudly criticized any of the beers then not one of the four could be declared winner.

Melchior counted about fifty men gathered at the Brotherhood of Blackheads' guildhall that evening, the most esteemed amongst them being the Commander of the Order, the Dominican Prior and the Tallinn Town Councilmen. The rules of *Smeckeldach* also prescribed that there could not be two guests of honour at any one time; this distinction could not be shared. Thus Commander Spanheim – as the chief judge – sat slightly apart from the long table in his place of honour, and Freisinger himself assumed the duty of serving the Knight. The Blackhead hosts and the devout Brother Wunbaldus attended to the other guests' beer steins.

Melchior could not enjoy the beer particularly that evening. Of course, he was not the only man there somewhat perturbed by Clingenstain's murder, but he felt a black emotion rising up from the depths of his soul, could sense the pain it imparted even before it arrived. Melchior had visited the Dominican Monastery, he had seen the chessboard, and his father's face once again appeared from Heaven in his mind's eye, causing him pain, even though he tried with all his might to push it as far away as he could. But the stabs of pain bursting from his soul would not pass. Melchior was of Wakenstede descent, and there was no escape from the curse. The symptoms that signalled his pain were seemingly insignificant – merely flashes of memory, different each time. Sometimes they came by day, sometimes by night.

But despite this approaching sense of dread Melchior sipped every brew placed before him out of duty and called his decision out to Spanheim in a loud voice when it was asked of him. So far he had had to praise all of them truthfully and with enthusiasm: the Great Guild's mark beer, the Hamburg-style brew, Tallinn beer and the six-veering beer. Nevertheless, Melchior shouted with even greater resonance when Wunbaldus began to tap the Dominicans' spring brews, including a laurel beer and his bock, which now stood triumphantly like a flag-bearing knight atop his enemy's tower. The pious Wunbaldus himself kept modestly to the shadows behind the Prior and Brother Hinricus, while words of praise were aimed in his direction.

Melchior also noted Master Goldsmith Casendorpe, Merchant Tweffell and Gallenreutter, the Master Mason of Westphalia, sitting at the table. Even Kilian was present and rotating through the acts of playing his lute, voraciously devouring the feast and knocking back beer. Every man who had come into contact with the unfortunate Clingenstain on Toompea yesterday was at the feast, and Melchior observed each one of them closely. He watched their faces and strove to read their thoughts; when they spoke tried to catch what they were saying. Melchior had come to the conclusion that if Clingenstain had had some kind of arcane connection to the town then these same men must hold the key to it – or if not a key then at least a map to someone who knew where this key was hidden.

He watched these men and tried to guess what was going on in their minds because it was in this way that he strove to dispel his own dreadful secret. It was in this way that he resisted the curse – by directing his mind elsewhere. The profession of apothecary was both the Wakenstedes' joy and their despair – the key to breaking their hex. Yet perhaps this was also wrong, as thus far not one single afflicted Wakenstede apothecary had found the cure to their dreadful torment.

Goldsmith Casendorpe appeared to be in a particularly good mood that evening – entering into conversation with their host Freisinger and patting him on the shoulder at every opportunity – which Melchior put down to the impending wedding. Melchior was sitting next to Pastor Mathias Rode of the Church of the Holy Ghost. The Pastor was a quiet and dignified man even at an event such as this – even though, as most people in the town were aware, beer could occasionally so unfurl the sails of the clergyman's tongue that even sailors would wince in embarrassment. Master Mason Gallenreutter of Westphalia had, on the other hand, already drained several tankards of beer, and his banter seemed to know no bounds. He did his best to rattle off all sorts of tales to any open ear within range and make his presence known in other ways, often in a more thunderous tone than was customary in Tallinn. Melchior detected, though, that when Gallenreutter was not actually talking in a brash voice then he instantly switched to looking completely sober, his gaze darting around the table as if searching for the best person to whom to tell his next story.

The *Smeckeldach* had reached the point at which no one had any further doubts over the evening's best beer. Commander Spanheim arose from his seat and proclaimed, 'The damn truth, it is, devil knows – pay me no heed, Father – and may all the saints bear my witness, that – and now definitely pay attention, Father – that the Dominicans' beer, this bock, is certainly the best to my liking and to everyone else's, too, it seems. Satan's steaming grandmother, do tell, where did you find such a brewer?'

The question was meant for the Prior, who had difficulty making himself heard over the hubbub. The esteemed head of the Dominican Order still had a tired and beleaguered air about him, although he was drinking the beer like a much younger man.

'That brewer is none other than our Lay Brother Wunbaldus. He genuinely possesses a gift for many practices that are essential to our poor brothers,' the Prior spoke, and shouts of praise trumpeted from dozens of mouths around the table. Merchant Tweffell was also forced to acknowledge that the Dominicans had triumphed over the Great Guild that evening. While Wunbaldus refilled the men's flagons Master Blackhead Freisinger officially declared the Dominicans' bock to be the very best, as such was the opinion and the will of all present. The men naturally began to demand that Wunbaldus reveal where he had learned this art, and Master Mason Gallenreutter entreated him to do so at characteristic volume.

'Tallinn might sit at the edge of the world when you look from Westphalia, but when it comes to beer, this town … well, it tastes like that made by the Warendorf Town Council's Master Brewer,' he declared. 'Or no, wait, the flavour even seems to remind me of one particular English brew that I tried once in London. Where have you studied this art, Wunbaldus?'

'Here and there,' the Lay Brother replied self-effacingly. 'I have roamed much through this wide world.'

'We Dominicans have a wandering way of life, Master Mason,' Eckell also affirmed. 'It is our duty to bring all that is good in one place with us to another – and to proclaim the Word of the Lord at the same time.'

Gallenreutter, who was sitting on Melchior's other side, nudged him playfully and chuckled, 'Yes, the devout brothers do not only surpass all others at trading herring and selling indulgences.'

Freisinger overheard the mason and shouted in response, 'Hey, do not mock our holy brothers. A poor monastery would be a scourge to all – to our overlord, to the merchants, to the bishop and to the farmers who should all support the brothers' work. Such a monastery would benefit no one.'

The men drank and lavished compliments upon Wunbaldus and the Dominicans while the Blackheads served dried salted cod, white sausages, garlic ham and baked pastries to accompany the copious amounts of beer. Melchior sampled these morsels and had to admit that no one else in the town could compare with the Council's cook.

He had noticed that none of the guests dared talk of the murder on Toompea until it was brought up by Spanheim. The Commander's tongue had now loosened, though, and the ghastly event very soon became the subject of every conversation.

Gallenreutter spoke loudly at Melchior's side. 'So, just when I had wished to speak to the Knight, to bow before him and declare myself his most loyal and humble of servants – because we both hail from the same area, you see – he was snuffed out. Like a heavenly scourge, am I right?'

'You, Master Mason, wished to speak with Clingenstain?' Melchior heard the Commander enquire from his own table with astonishment.

'That I did,' Gallenreutter confirmed. 'However, your guards-men sent me away. I am a stranger, and they know me not. I am indeed a foreigner here in Tallinn, but Clingenstain and I are both from the same place, and I do declare that this fine beer would have been very much to his liking also …'

Many then turned towards Magistrate Dorn to demand news of how the Council's hunt for the murderer was progressing. Who is he? Is he from Tallinn? Where is he in hiding? Why did he slay a Knight of the Order? Gallenreutter likewise asked how the man was being sought and who it might be.

Dorn could do little more than proclaim loudly, 'Tallinn's Council has given the Order its word. This man will not escape, as that would bring shame upon the entire town. The court servants and guards are searching for him at this very moment, and he will soon be in chains and so forth, and then to trial on Toompea.'

Sire Tweffell bleated in laughter, 'Hear, but tell us, if you know not who this man is then how are you searching for him? Are the court servants asking every townsperson, "Good sir, it was not you perchance who deprived our Knight of his head?"'

'The Council certainly knows how the Council will search,' Dorn retorted. 'It's not as if this is the first time. Murderers of an even more horrendous character have been apprehended before. We already know quite a good deal about him …'

'What exactly does the Council know?' Tweffell demanded. The councilmen at the table shook their heads and averted their gaze. Dorn looked pleadingly towards Melchior for a moment.

'Well, that he came from the town and what not,' the Magistrate slowly stammered, 'that … with a sword and off with his head … and then back to the town and …'

Melchior sipped his beer, coughed loudly then rose from his chair and began to speak commandingly.

'What do we know about the murderer? Esteemed Alderman and honourable Commander, we know quite a great deal. We know that he must be a strong and robust man capable of wielding a sword, one for whom chopping off a head poses no great difficulty. We know he had to have come into contact with the Knight somewhere before and that the killer bore enmity against him. We know that it must have been someone familiar with both the town of Tallinn and with Toompea, meaning that he is not a stranger. No one could have thought the man's presence there unusual, and he has to be as bold and brutal as Satan himself. If he had been discovered then he would have fought back with the same sword. It is someone who was not where he was meant to be yesterday evening at eight o'clock. How will the Council catch this murderer? I answer: with the Lord's aid and by its own wit.'

The room was silent. Spanheim finally nodded approvingly. 'Those are righteous words, Melchior,' he said. 'This devil must be seized and dragged to Toompea. Certainly we will then hang him and desecrate his corpse in the same way he did Clingenstain's. We will chop off his head and drive it on to a stake for all to see.'

'On to a stake?' someone exclaimed. The Commander dismissed this with a gesture and did not bother to respond.

Tweffell shrugged and mumbled just loud enough to be heard, 'I still do not comprehend how you will ensnare him if you do not know who he is.'

Before Melchior could open his mouth to reply Gallenreutter spoke up.

'If you will, then please allow me to tell you all a tale from my home town of Warendorf, where I built a church a few years ago, when a councilman was treacherously murdered in the dead of night. The killer slipped in through the window and choked the council-man in his sleep.'

'Do tell, Master Gallenreutter. It sounds exciting,' someone called out, and several others voiced their approval.

Gallenreutter rose to his feet and continued. 'As one might suppose every councilman has many mortal enemies, yet how can the right one be found when all swear they did not commit the act and there was no witness? It's not as if a town council would dare to put a single wealthy merchant on the rack or send him before the Lord's judgement based on suspicion alone. Luckily there was a very clever magistrate in the town of Warendorf, a smart and able man, who began to investigate more closely how the murderer had broken into the councilman's home late at night. And what did he do? He found the locksmith who had crafted the lock on the councilman's door, and they tried together to see how to break the lock in the way the killer had done. Next, the magistrate went to look for the ropemaker who had woven the rope with which the councilman was strangled. Third, he took note of the fact that rain fell on the night of the killing; there was mud and patches of filth in front of the councilman's home at the time, but the entry hall was clean and no trail of mud led from the door to the councilman's chamber. Fourth, the magistrate started considering who would benefit most from the councilman's death. And what became clear? It turned out that –'

Before Gallenreutter could continue Melchior butted in, 'If I may interrupt you, Master Mason, then I would deduce what became clear.'

'By all means. Have at it, Sire Melchior.'

'I would say that, as you have already mentioned these circumstances, it is not difficult to conclude that the door's lock could only have been broken in that particular manner from within, a similar rope was found inside the councilman's house and his wife would enjoy the greatest benefit from his death …'

'Indeed, Melchior …' Gallenreutter exclaimed in surprise.

'Yes,' the Apothecary continued, 'and would I be mistaken if I also postulated that the household had a major-domo? The murderer did not enter from outside; he came from within the house.'

Gallenreutter seemed somewhat disappointed but acknowledged that Melchior was correct in his guesses. 'No, Melchior, you err not. That very same major-domo had recently purchased an identical hemp rope and, after he had been tortured for a short time, confessed that he and the councilman's wife had been staining the master's sheets probably since the very day the councilman brought the young man into his house.'

'Have some clemency, Master Gallenreutter,' the listeners shouted upon hearing this. 'What a dreadful tale.'

Even Pastor Rode stood up angrily and proclaimed, 'Womenfolk! Temptresses! Serpents! Even St Augustine said they must be kept away from holy men.'

'I hope that whore was stoned to death,' the Commander grunted.

'Oh no. She was buried alive,' Gallenreutter replied. 'The major-domo was hanged, although he had admitted on the rack that the woman had bewitched him and seduced him into murdering her husband. They had planned to sell off the councilman's assets after his death and continue to live their life of sin in some other town. However, what I wanted to say through this story was that even when there are no witnesses to a murder, some clever man can always be found.'

'As can such a magistrate ...' Melchior quipped.

'Yes, and our magistrate is – as we know now – a sharp and clever chap. But some astute man able to read the signs a criminal leaves behind must always be found; a man who can track down witnesses even when it seems at first as if there is none. Even the most impossible of crimes can be deciphered and the guilty parties served their just punishment.'

Then the festivities continued, as no one wished to hear any more such horrifying tales. Melchior visited the rear courtyard to relieve himself and afterwards moved around the room from one conversation to another. Prior Eckell and Master Goldsmith Casendorpe had begun to talk business. The Prior may have been gravely ill, but the management of monastery affairs did not seem too far from his mind even at the beer-sampling table. He assured the artisan that no one paid as good a price for the craftsman's gold as the Dominicans.

'Our brothers sold so much good oily herring to the vassals over the last fasting that our money will rust if we do not get rid of it quickly. We can also count the free masses and prayers said for all of your deceased family members as payments in kind,' Eckell assured the Goldsmith, who still seemed doubtful.

'Gold is in short supply, Father,' Casendorpe reasoned. 'Gold is expensive, as you well know, and it is rising in price. The last ship that was supposed to bring me gold from Bruges either sank or was ransacked by that Vogt of Turku ...'

Melchior could tell the Goldsmith had already made his final decision and was simply pushing the price up. He will, without question, make that precious golden chalice for the Dominicans' altar – of that Melchior was certain.

Sire Tweffell was positioned near Kilian at the beer table and instructing the minstrel in the principles of shrewd business. Kilian sat listening attentively, seeming to pay not the slightest heed to Freisinger's repeated demands for him to play his lute. He was much more interested in what he was being told about wax trading.

The evening's fine beer had unbound Tweffell's tongue. 'Buy wax from the Russians in winter,' he tutored, 'and drive the price down so far that they start to shout with rage – and don't even think of speaking about this to anyone before St George's Day either. Don't bother selling it in Livonia; everyone here is poor. Sell it instead to Bruges where there are moneyed monasteries – and a large number of them at that. When they start dipping candles they do it till their fingers bleed – and they do not sleep for weeks on end; all they do is make candles.'

'I will remember that, dear uncle,' Kilian promised obediently.

'Of course you'll remember it. When I am under the ground who else will instruct you? No man has ever become rich by playing tunes either. Now, where was I? Ah, so, if you want to buy felt and fabric from Bruges, then, you know, I've heard that those damned Victual Brothers, of whom our sea is now much clearer, have – at least as many of the demons there are left since their chief's head was chopped off – now based themselves near Zeeland and continue to pirate merchant ships from there. And I'll say, too, that the Teutonic Order may have trounced them on Gotland, yet who pays for all of those war-going galleys that purify the sea of this scourge? *Hanseatic merchants* pay for them. It is the merchants not the Order or any other overlord. *We* pay. We pay for our own laws and rights and all else. Tell me, boy, what good would these barons and *Fürsten* be without merchants? Where would they obtain their fine clothing and silver plates? My eyes will not see such a time, but yours might look out on a world when barons bow before traders.'

To his surprise Melchior noticed that Spanheim had left his table of honour in order to hear the Master Mason of Westphalia spin his tales. The Apothecary slipped in amongst the men while Gallenreutter rambled on about how constructing a castle, a church and a house are completely different art forms. The most difficult of these was, of course, a church.

'A church does not merely have to be pleasing to the eye,' he continued, 'it must be visible from afar. A church is not built by one single master, because a man needs to know so much and has to consult others who also possess great knowledge – and not just about sacred matters. A master must have knowledge of the town, of its people and its history. Just as in the construction of any building, a church begins first and foremost with digging. You dig at the site of the future church in order to build strong foundations. You root and sift through the layers of mixed earth; you dig deeper and you see what stood on that place before and all that there is within the folds of the earth. Alas, time has no other path – the old must always make way for the new.'

Several others were listening to Gallenreutter, Pastor Rode and even Kilian amongst them – since Sire Tweffell had pulled some councilmen aside in the meantime to complain about the shoddy work done by the Tallinn Mint. Gallenreutter's narrative rippled smoothly from church construction to the Guild of Stonemasons, the membership of which included many Estonians that spoke German oh-so poorly and who occasionally even conducted affairs in some strange tongue amongst themselves as if they were not baptized Christians at all.

'Estonians? Yes, they are good stonecutters,' the Commander grunted, elbowing his way into the conversation. 'Brutish, burly men. Fine warriors. None can contend with them when it comes to swinging a battleaxe. Devil's dawn – they've the brawn of many men put together.'

'One evening,' Gallenreutter continued, 'I made merry with them beyond the town walls, although they did not understand my manner of speaking very well nor I theirs ...'

'That language of theirs is devilish, yes, such that the God of Christians certainly did not come up with it,' the Commander affirmed. Although you hand them a battleaxe, send them against the Russians and they will chop and chop and chop.'

'But their songs,' continued the Master Mason, 'I didn't understand their songs nor they mine.'

Kilian and a couple of Blackheads immediately began pressing Gallenreutter to state whether he was a singing man. The Westphalian Master maintained that his mouth worked better with food and beer than it did singing and that he certainly was not blessed with the gift of music.

'A mason's trowel, that is my instrument. With a trowel I can truly conjure incredible and godly tunes. However, if a whistle happens into my hands then even stray dogs try to flee my presence,' Gallenreutter exclaimed raucously. Still, Melchior noted again that the Westphalian Master was in no way as drunk as he seemed to want to pretend.

'So what you are saying is that you still *occasionally* sing, Sire Gallenreutter,' Kilian persisted.

'Ah, what singing, really? I stirred up a racket there in the tavern, singing a song I thought that the masters of Tallinn's guilds should know, but, alas, they had never heard of it,' Gallenreutter hollered in return.

'No matter. You sing,' Kilian exclaimed and positioned his lute. 'Sing for us, Master Mason, sing, and I will play. So, how goes that song? Worry not, sire. I've travelled across half the world and know more tunes than I would be able to perform over the entire forty days of Lent.'

An even larger crowd had now collected around Gallenreutter, amongst them Sire Casendorpe, who asked what song it was which all Tallinn guildsmen should supposedly know. He himself was unaware of any such thing.

'Ah, it is an old song said to have originated in Tallinn itself, composed by the very first guild to make its way to these parts,' Gallenreutter declared.

Casendorpe erupted into laughter. 'Well then, ask the Master Blackhead, as they believe themselves to be the very oldest here in Tallinn. Ha! The oldest ... what rubbish. Our Guild of St Canute was already famed across the entire Hanseatic League *and* the Holy Roman Empire before anyone had even *heard* of the Blackheads.'

Freisinger immediately bustled over to the group of men upon overhearing Casendorpe's boast. 'What is this I hear? Is someone casting aspersions on the age of our guild?' he enquired good-naturedly.

'I cast nothing. I simply stated that you are not nearly as old as Jesus Christ or the city of Rome,' the Goldsmith declared loudly.

'I remember now how that old song went,' Gallenreutter exclaimed. 'I cannot sing well, but I can recall a few verses. I think it is in a very old dialect. Kilian, play.'

The Master Mason truly lacked skills in the art of singing. None the less, his voice rang clear and strong as he followed Kilian's melody, reciting loudly and articulately:

Come, for daybreak is nigh and light gleams from the east
oh, my friend, our seven brothers await thee at the crossroads
nonpareil the Lord's temple, to which they'll show ye the way
radial compass and trowels, they hold
aid them to drink the light that glimmers at the grave
their oaths as ancient as Solomon's wisdom
unto the seven masters, their shields extended
solemn Death drapes in his cloak he who is afore all
Favete linguis et memento mori
relic calls afar for its blood
elegiac yesterday is closer to Christ's blood which floweth down
    the walls.

Gallenreutter gave a powerful performance, and all the men seated at the table fell silent and listened. When Gallenreutter had finished Kilian put down his lute and sighed heavily. The song had not been all that special after all.

'Master Gallenreutter, I certainly have no knowledge of such a song. It isn't even much like a song but rather some kind of riddle,' Kilian said glumly.

'Truly, Gallenreutter, that may be some kind of ditty or riddle of the masons, but never in my lifetime have I heard that in our Guild of St Canute,' said Casendorpe. 'And if the guildsmen of St Olaf's are unaware of it, then ...' He turned to address members of the other guilds. 'Hey, Sire Tweffell and you others. Listen, do you know any song about seven brothers, Solomon, a trowel and walls and death that covers something with its cloak ... or how did that go again?'

'What in the name of St Victor are you asking now, Master Goldsmith?' Tweffell barked hoarsely, pulling himself away from a conversation with the councilmen. 'My old ears did not hear.'

'Our guest from the town of Warendorf wishes to know whether men of the Great Guild know a song about seven brothers who, at dawn, show someone the way somewhere, and there's the temple of the Lord and some sort of trowel?'

'Holy Christ, you've had far too much beer, Master Goldsmith, and I cannot understand a word you're saying,' Tweffell huffed in irritation. 'What seven brothers? What trowel?'

Casendorpe shrugged and turned back towards Gallenreutter. 'You see, no one knows a thing about such a song. No doubt you recall it incorrectly.'

'It is not really a song but rather a riddle,' Kilian repeated. 'I have never heard it before.'

'If it is a riddle then it must also have an answer, but I have no idea what it is meant to mean,' said the Goldsmith. 'Ask our pastors; maybe they know. If they do not, then they do not, and the mystery of your riddle will remain a mystery to us.'

'No doubt every town has its secrets,' Gallenreutter replied – but just at that moment, some men on the other side of the table were demanding that more beer be poured, as Ulm the merchant had knocked his tankard over. Freisinger rushed over to see whether the man could mop up the spill with his sleeve or whether a fine was to be paid. The latter instance would not, of course, mean that he would not receive a new stein of beer, but the Dominicans' bock was already starting to run out, to the great disappointment of all. Freisinger proclaimed that this was of no consequence, as the Blackheads' own five-veering beer could now be tapped. The Master Blackhead had purchased several casks of the brew today and now commanded the servants to roll them into the hall. Hearing this the Pastor of the Church of the Holy Ghost remarked that the Blackheads appeared to have a treasury comparable with that of the King of England.

'Don't you worry, Pastor,' Freisinger laughed. 'The Blackheads have enough wealth to maintain an altar at the Dominican Monastery, and if they so wished could also have one at your church, were it deemed necessary.'

'What I have heard,' Gallenreutter exclaimed, sitting next to Melchior, 'what I heard when I began my journey to Tallinn ... what is said everywhere is that this is a poor town and there are no great coffers or piles of wealth to be found.'

'That is false talk,' Freisinger said to the mason. 'Tallinn is a prosperous town, and a peril such as a shortage of coins has never nipped at the Brotherhood of Blackheads' heels. We Blackheads have always had quite sufficient funds for maintaining our dignity and significance, as ours is the oldest guild in Tallinn – no matter what the men of St Canute's and St Olaf's may believe.'

Just then Dorn tapped Melchior on the shoulder and quipped that Pastor Rode seemed once again to have some exceedingly jolly stories to tell. At the other end of the table several men were leaning close to the Pastor as he spun some yarn and then broke out into fits of laughter. Melchior nodded and raised his eyebrows. Pastor

Rode was not a tongue-tied man and was actually a very skilled storyteller, yet when one mentioned women to him while he was in a beer-infused state it was not unheard of for his speech to be peppered with words that would certainly not be fitting if proclaimed from his pulpit. Several Tallinn guildsmen were, however, quite adept at stirring the Pastor up with their tales during his drinking bouts, so that by the end of the evening he would give a sermon that would provoke laughter around the town months afterwards.

While some had already begun to goad the Pastor, saying they wished to hear again whatever it was that had caused the others to laugh so much, Melchior listened as Freisinger related to Gallenreutter the many virtues of the Blackheads.

'The Brotherhood of Blackheads was already in this town when one still had to fight the pagans for every square foot of land. They helped to dedicate this town's holy sanctuaries to the Lord Christ, and the fortunes both of Tallinn and the Blackheads have grown since then. When death dances around the town it is the Blackheads who are the first to reach for their arms.'

'Are the Blackheads then so warlike that they go for their weapons straight away? If they are so wealthy that –' Gallenreutter marvelled.

'*Absolutely* correct, Master Mason, absolutely correct,' the Blackhead's Alderman agreed with gusto. 'The good Lord has bestowed great wealth upon the Blackheads. One often accomplishes more with good counsel and a barrel of silver Riga marks than with a halberd.'

At the other end of the table the men were demanding, with increasing volume, that the Pastor give his enlightening sermon about a nun at the Heisterbach Abbey, which all had heard was quite a diverting tale. Only Prior Eckell protested, angrily cautioning against giving a homily in such a place and at such a time. Rode reared up from his seat in spite of this, knocking over a tankard of beer in the process, and not even Freisinger insisted that the Pastor measure the spot with his sleeve – the customary way to determine the amount of the offender's fine.

'Good friends, "The Sermon of Heisterbach Abbey". No one tells it better than the honourable Pastor Rode,' Freisinger announced. Rode had already started to slur his words a little, but he spoke so expressively and with such emphasis that all fell silent to listen.

'I wish to tell you a holy and illuminating story that took place at the abbey at Heisterbach, and it is a tale as true as that fact that I am standing here before you. A young maiden named Beatrixa lived amongst all the other pious womenfolk at Heisterbach, and this young maiden had a figure that was very – how should I put it? – pleasing to the eye. However, Beatrixa was also devout in her beliefs and faithfully served the Holy Mother of God, before whose altar she prayed whenever she had any time – and after she became the oratory supervisor she prayed there even more. Now, there was also a cleric at the abbey, and he observed the devout Beatrixa, admiring her figure, and this man began to covet the pious maiden and lead her into temptation, may the Lord have mercy on her. The more this man spun his carnal seductions to her the more that she rejected his advances, but the evil words had already done their work, and the old serpent – the very same that led Eve on to the path of sin – had already begun to coil around the maiden's chest so tightly that she could no longer resist, and …'

Rode paused, sipped the beer a servant had just placed before him and then continued, as the men were shouting, demanding to know what happened next.

'So then Beatrixa went before the altar to St Mary, the Mother of God, and said this, "Oh, benevolent queen, I have served you in truth and in spirit and with deep belief, but look, I now place my keys before you because I am no longer able to withstand the temptations of the flesh." Saying this, Beatrixa put her gate keys on the altar and went after that man who had tempted her on to the path of sin, because the minds of womankind are weak. And then that man took her back to his own home, ordered her to take off her nun's habit, and then ...'

Rode faltered as the rolling thunder of laughter burst from the guildsmen's mouths.

Even the Commander shouted, 'Yes, what did that man do then?'

'Do not hide the facts, Pastor. Tell us everything just as it happened,' other voices also insisted.

Rode inhaled deeply, and fumbling for support with his hand on the table, blurted out, 'And then that unholy man tempted heron to the path to sin and had his way with her.'

Laughter detonated like a cannon shot again, and someone shouted, 'But I don't understand. What did that man do with her then?'

'That man deflowered her,' Rode proclaimed even more loudly.

The crowd of guildsmen was not satisfied with this response, however, and continued to demand the Pastor articulate in detail what had come about there.

'That cleric performed a carnal sin with the dishonoured woman, just as men do with women –'

'Oh, come now, Pastor,' Casendorpe's voice could be heard through the laughter, 'that was not the word you used before. If you truly recall what happened there, then say it as such.'

'That man lay down with her –' Rode began again, but even this did not satisfy the guildsmen, who knew very well the kind of words that the Pastor loved to use when as soused as a herring. The men banged their tankards on the table, stamped their feet and shouted, 'Pastor, don't hold back. We don't understand.'

Rode took a drop of courage from his beer stein once again and declared, 'The plague take you all. That man fucked that woman –'

Deafening laughter cut the Pastor off mid-sentence, and he shouted even louder, 'Fucked her in a way that no man had ever fucked anything before. And then he fucked, and he banged –'

None could contain his laughter any longer – some men lay flat on the table with their faces lodged in the meat platter; others thumped their tankards and howled. Only Prior Eckell shook his head.

'Fucked our devout maiden for a full day,' Rode roared, 'and then he fucked her a second day, and then a third, just for good measure. But then, when his filthy itch had been satisfied and he no longer cared for the woman, then he deserted Beatrixa and threw her out into the street.' The Pastor then calmed somewhat, sipped his beer and continued, 'Since Beatrixa no longer had anywhere to live and had no money and was too ashamed to return to the other pious sisters, she became a whore on the town's streets – for fifteen years. Beatrixa prostituted herself for fifteen years, screwing men and performing all kinds of sins with them. And then one day after fifteen years had passed she went back to the door of the abbey, dressed in her lay habit and asked the doorkeeper, "Did you know Beatrixa who was the oratory supervisor here some time ago?" The doorkeeper replied, "Indeed I know her very well, as she is an honest and holy woman who has lived here entirely free from sin since she was a child." When Beatrixa heard this she was confused and made to leave in a hurry. But the Mother of God herself then appeared before her, saying, "For the fifteen years you have been away I have undertaken your duties in your own guise and clothing, and now you may return to your place and repent your sins, as not a soul knows that you have been away." The Holy Mother of God herself had taken Beatrixa's place in the abbey for that entire time, taking on

Beatrixa's own form. This very same Beatrixa went back straight away and prayed before a statue of the Virgin Mary, and only during confession did she reveal the miracle that had happened to her.'

The men demanded another sermon from Rode, but Melchior did not stay to listen. He wanted to go home, where Keterlyn was waiting. He left the guildhall along with Prior Eckell, Hinricus and Wunbaldus somewhat before midnight.

14

Beyond the Town Walls, Süstermaye Tavern
17 May, Late Morning

MELCHIOR HAD a splitting headache the following morning, so he concocted a strong, bitter drink made from spirits, herbs, currant juice, mead and raw egg, according to a recipe his father had passed on to him. He drank the mixture and left the pharmacy in the care of his wife.

When he stepped outside Melchior saw that, even at this early hour of the day, he was far from being the first person to have overcome his exhaustion from the previous night's merriment. Kilian sat on the rim of the well, playing a dirge-like tune on his lute and from time to time toying with a loose stone at the base of the wall. The clanging of blacksmiths' hammers and whinnying of horses already sounded from the workshops at the town stables, which were located just a couple buildings down from the pharmacy. Thick soot rose from the town mint's chimney, and men at the arsenal were arguing loudly over some cannon.

On this day of the week Melchior usually went out of the town, beyond the Seppade Gate windmill to St Barbara's Chapel where his father had purchased a small plot of land for the pharmacy garden. There Melchior grew medicinal plants according to his father's teachings, plants that did not grow wild in Estonia's fields and forests. The Apothecary and his wife planted the seeds together in spring and weeded and watered the plants throughout the summer. Melchior would normally tend for the sprouting vegetation for the better part of the day, but he limited himself to a short visit just to see if the tiny green buds – mallow, celery, cress, camomile, valerian, endive and others – had duteously reared themselves up out of the earth. His garden was set alongside the main road leading south. On one side stretched the farmlands that bordered the suburbs and on the other one could see the town gallows looming beyond Tõnismägi. Melchior quite often had business to conduct at the town's execution site, as his father had bought permission from the Council to be the first to be allowed to cut open the corpses of executed criminals to acquire body parts that might be used for medicines.

Melchior had been ten years old the first time his father had taken him to Võllamägi; an apothecary must become accustomed to death. Moreover, there are many parts of a dead person's body that help to heal the living. On that first occasion the condemned had been some young, strong man – a fisherman from near the village of Viimsi – who had stolen from the Town Council. A body's organs still function for some time after he or she suffers a sudden death, and parts can be cut from it to be used for medicinal remedies. For example, human fat can be boiled to produce an effective salve for aching bones, and a young maiden's kidney is a good antidote to poisoning from forest berries. Or when thin fillets are cut from the muscles in a young man's thighs, are spiced with myrrh and aloe, soaked in wine, hung in a dry, dark place and finally bathed in the light of a full moon, they can become a remedy for sicknesses of the liver. Melchior's father had also received permission from the Council to dig beneath the gallows to search for mandrake root, which holds great power. When a person is hanged all the liquids once contained within the body flow out and into the ground, including a man's sperm, which germinates into a mandrake root in the soil. This tuber resembles the shape of a human body and helps with a number of sicknesses when ground into a fine powder, and it also restores virility when boiled and the liquid is drunk. Tallinn's town doctor had prescribed very few such medicines as of late, however, and it had been over a year since Melchior had last cut the liver out from a fisherman's corpse on Võllamägi.

Melchior watered the rows of plants, exchanged a few words with the beadle of St Barbara's Chapel and then turned back towards the town. His route led him west along the cart road leading to Karja Mill, near Karja Gate, and past the cluster of shacks that formed the village of Pleekmae. The south road was lined with goods-laden carts, herds of livestock and wagons transporting logs and broken slate. Tallinn was growing so fast; with every passing year the wall was built higher and thicker. There was always some new tower or a gate being widened somewhere. Tallinn was stunningly beautiful when approaching from the south: the grey stripe of the wall, the windmills spinning lazily, the drawbridges and gates cast against a green backdrop, the steeple of St Olaf's Church and Toompea Castle cutting across the line that marked where sea and sky met. The air carried a fresh scent, and a warm sea breeze carried moisture inland. The weather was gorgeous, and Melchior decided to take a circuit around the town to clear his head a bit and think.

He strolled from the Karja Gate weir onwards in the direction of Savi Gate, from which both the sea and the port could be seen. Water was channelled along an aqueduct from Lake Ülemiste, Härjapea River and smaller brooks into the moat that surrounded the wall, which was then dammed into small ponds. The weirs thereby created pools before three of the town's gates, pools that were also enclosed by defensive embankments. One had to climb a flight of steps and then cross a bridge in order to reach the mill and the gate. If an enemy were to attack from the south they would find it so difficult to negotiate that even if they did reach the gate the crossbowmen, cannons and harquebuses would have already sent half the marauders on their way to the next world. There was a place for watering horses near the weir from which the water flowed out towards the sea. The banks along the channel were good for fishing, which was another skill that Melchior's father had taught him. The pair had come there to catch food appropriate for the fasting table only a short time before his father's death ...

But Melchior did not wish to think about that now. He forced his thoughts away from memories of his father and back towards more everyday affairs, quickening his pace along the shoreline. The town wall now ran directly towards the north and edged along the rocky coast. The path diverged close to Väike Rannavärav Gate. One of the paths crossed the Council's woodyard and wound down towards the harbour, but Melchior took the other fork and began walking towards the suburbs of Süstermaye and Köismäe. These glorified villages held a great number of taverns in which seamen whiled away the hours. He needed to find the almsman and former ship's captain Rinus Götzer.

Götzer was a fine man who had once captained a warship that had hounded the Victual Brothers. The brave Götzer had lost all his property as well as his hand in fighting them – although he had survived a period of imprisonment by the pirates – and was now under the care of the almshouse of the Church of the Holy Ghost. He spent the greater part of his time wandering from tavern to tavern in the villages near Tallinn where there was always someone willing to buy the old skipper beer in exchange for a good story. Melchior could not think of another person in town who knew more about the ships docked at the harbour and their crews or of anything to do with the sea. It was said that merchants would regularly send an attendant armed with a couple of pennies to visit Götzer and hear whether there might be any truth behind the banter of guildsmen at the beer tables as well as more general information about what was going on at the harbour and what snippets of information some merchants might be keeping from the others. Melchior remembered this man from his boyhood when he used to visit the harbour with his father to watch the ships. Now only a poor cripple was left of that once proud skipper.

Having made his way through two or three establishments Melchior finally found the old sea dog in a tavern near Grusbeke and Epping towers where he had gone to buy a couple of tankards of its cheapest beer with the money he had collected in alms that morning. The small tavern was nestled amongst other identical rickety wooden shacks, where fishermen of mostly non-German descent resided. Melchior slipped Götzer a handful of aniseed sweets, which brought a tear to the withered old man's eye. They were the sort of sweets eaten by councilmen and nobles, and such delicacies rarely appeared on an almsman's table. Melchior said he had come to the harbour on business but thought to quench his thirst a bit beforehand because the weather today was hot, and he had already walked far.

The old man devoured the sweets, washed them down with a swig of beer but did not get a chance to thank Melchior for the indulgence before the Apothecary spoke.

'There is absolutely no need for thanks, Sire Skipper,' he said after himself taking a sip of the tavern's beer, which definitely packed a punch. 'You have done so much good for the town of Tallinn that now is the time when the town of Tallinn repays you. I myself would not dare set sail to hunt pirates down, but my business would soon fail were those thieves to seize the goods that I have ordered.'

'So it is, perhaps,' Götzer sighed. 'They rob and they murder at sea and will carry on robbing and murdering. Nothing will change by the Lord's grace alone.'

'No doubt, although it is now more peaceful out there,' Melchior reasoned. 'The Victual Brothers are no more and … ah, well, you, Sire Götzer, know better than I. You did command a Hanseatic warship.'

'I sailed the sea my entire life, and there is no harbour, no bay where I haven't been with my ship, sheltering from a storm or trading. I know the sea as I do my own pockets – where there's no longer been even half a grosz since I fell into the hands of the Victual Brothers with my few valuables,' Götzer sighed.

Melchior shook his head in sympathy. 'Allow me to buy you another drink. That is a truly awful tale. Hey, beer to this table,' he called out.

'Thank you, Melchior, my gratitude,' said the Skipper, and the pair again clanked their cups.

'A cripple I may be,' Götzer soon began, 'but I complain not of it. The sea teaches you not to complain; the sea teaches you humility. It teaches you much more than you will ever learn from pastors. Be as devout as you like and abide by the Scriptures and so forth, but no seaman can help it if he sometimes thinks that the sea is God and God is the sea. Everything that fate does with you, everything that you are a part of, springs from the sea, and you are at the sea's mercy when are a sailor. You may be a wealthy merchant, buy a chapel and an altar for yourself, give money to the monastery and to the poor and have masses held for you from morning to night, but when a storm be on the horizon and it carries you towards some bay … And then you see that yonder are beacon fires, you thank the Lord again and say your prayers as you've been led safely to shore. At daybreak you see that three swift ships are there at anchor, ships that have been in wait for the very moment that someone entered the bay led by their false beacons. Yes, that was what those Victual Brothers did, may the plague take them and Satan skin them alive.'

'I'm with you completely on that,' Melchior declared firmly. He downed a hearty swig of beer and ordered the innkeeper to bring bread so that their feet might not feel lighter than their heads. 'Yet you, Sire Götzer, kept your vitality, did you not?'

'For this I've praised the Lord God for many a year but at the same time wondered what indeed his plans were when I was forced to watch as Gödeke Michels gouged my crewmen's eyes out with his own fingers before stuffing the men into empty herring barrels and throwing them overboard so that those who did reach the shore would be dashed against the cliffs.' The Skipper spoke with sadness. They had no barrel left for me, so they speared me in the chest and threw me overboard all the same. I know not to whom I prayed, Melchior, whether it was the Lord God or St Joost or whoever, nevertheless, I was picked up by a Rostock herring boat, and I made my way back to Tallinn without a penny, poor as a church mouse.'

'You are alive, Sire Rinus, and your crew is dead. God has his own plans for everyone ...'

'And we must humbly accept them. Yes, so it is said. So it is said by the Dominicans and at the Church of the Holy Ghost and at every church along the Baltic Sea. Melchior, I do not complain about these events. Everything that the Lord has allowed me to have a part in, that I will humbly accept, yet I ask these pastors why it is that God does not hear the prayers of those thousands of men that have been murdered at sea like rats during the plague.'

'You are posing questions that are either too difficult or too simple. No doubt men of faith will reply that those who have robbed at sea will never enter the Kingdom of Heaven ... Sire Götzer, will you allow me to ask, did you ever reach Gotland on that warship of yours?'

'Gotland? *Gotland,* you say?' the Skipper barked. 'Ha! I lost my hand off the coast of Gotland. Some Dane wounded it so badly that the hand began to rot and was cut off at the Dominican infirmary in the town of Visby, otherwise I would have gone straight to the Creator's flock. No, I do not complain and I do not grumble. Few men that have sailed the seas live to such an age as I have, and the Guild of the Holy Flesh cares well for us all at the almshouse.'

'Honour and praise to them,' Melchior affirmed.

'And, well, as the town also has such a generous apothecary, then …' The Skipper dried his eyes once again.

'My father told me that no one who served as an apothecary can become as rich as a merchant, but neither can anyone harbour hatred against an apothecary in the way that one might hate a merchant,' Melchior recited.

'In the name of St Victor, Melchior, your father spoke the absolute truth, may he rest in peace,' declared the Skipper.

'Yes,' Melchior mumbled, 'yes, he died in peace, here in this very town and just at the time that the Teutonic Order's ships set sail for Gotland to wipe the Victual Brothers out.'

'An honest and fine man he was, Melchior, an honest and fine man,' Götzer sighed. 'But you asked something about Gotland …'

'Oh, indeed. I wished to enquire whether you ever happened to come into contact with Prior Eckell of our pious Dominicans on Gotland?' Melchior questioned.

'No, I did not. Eckell I do not remember. Not that I generally recall much of that time; I was unconscious for the greater part of it. I may well have asked God to send us on the path to find Gödeke Michels so that *I* might gouge *his* eyes out, just as he had done to honest sailors, but I never had the chance. I tell you, Melchior, we often numbered three ships full of soldiers escorting Tallinn merchants' vessels, and, well, there were also Knights of the Order on board the ships, as the Order usually had its own section of every boat that carried goods, and, well, my eyes, alas, did not see for themselves the Order battering the Victual Brothers off the coast of Gotland, because at the time we were engaged in battle somewhere near Bornholm and merely heard of the victory, you see – of how Order Knights skinned Victual Brothers alive and strung their corpses along the walls of Visby, chopped off their heads and drove them on to the ends of mooring posts, and … Melchior, I would have wished to have been there in person and to tear Gödeke Michels into quarters with my own bare hands.'

'What about the rumour that he escaped?' asked Melchior.

'Ha! All their chiefs escaped the Order on Gotland,' Götzer was spitting with anger. 'Gödeke, Klaus Störtebecker himself and that treacherous Magister Wigbold as well. They were all later captured near Zeeland and then beheaded on Hamburg's Isle of Grasbrook, or at least so it's said …'

'To punish them for all their crimes, each of their heads should doubtlessly have been chopped off a number of times – and even that wouldn't have been enough,' Melchior said. 'Please, carry on while I rest my legs and listen.'

'I could carry on all the way through to next Christmastime. At that, well … where'd I leave off?'

'You left off with how the Victual Brothers were beheaded on the Isle of Grasbrook.'

'Well, not that I witnessed it with my own eyes, but I suppose I know well what people say,' the old man said, leaning back to spin his tale. 'So, yes, the Hanseatic League finally caught them – Störtebecker first and then Magister Wigbold and Gödeke a year later, too, and the executions began at the cock's crow and lasted until night-time, so that blood flowed up to your knees, and the crowd still cried out in great joy when the next head was removed. But the man that took them captive was no other than Simon of Utrecht himself with his famed ship the *Bunte Kuh*. It was a huge vessel, a true warship with cannons on deck and a downright ... I've seen it once in my life. Well, of course there were other ships there also, so – since the towns paid captains according to how many thieves were captured – they branded every Victual Brother with a hot iron so that there wouldn't be any dispute afterwards over who caught how many men. Störtebecker himself, right, their highest chief and the most terrible seafaring murderer this world has ever seen, that Störtebecker's knees buckled in front of the killing platform and he pleaded for his life, promising to gift the town of Hamburg a gold chain so long that it could be wound around the church. Naturally he was shown no mercy, as there was not a single man or woman there whose family had not been harmed by Störtebecker's men. Ha! Then another tale runs that Störtebecker said, "No matter – if you don't let me live, then at least have mercy on my men, and on as many men as the number of steps I take after you've beheaded me."'

'I seem to recall having heard that story as well,' Melchior grunted.

'They say he took thirteen full steps after his head had been removed, and only then did he fall to the ground. His head was nailed on to a post. However, mercy was not shown to thirteen men or anyone else. All were made shorter by a head's length, yes. And so Magister Wigbold and Gödeke were also snared after another year, although no one dared to believe this for some time because Wigbold's cunning was so great that he had escaped every previous trap set for him ...'

The Skipper broke off his story, as the tavern door suddenly banged open and there stood none other than Magistrate Dorn himself. The innkeeper started upon seeing him and even spilled a three-legged clay pot of sprat soup on to the floor, since the appearance of any court official had never heralded anything good during the decades he had run the tavern. It usually meant the law had come to issue him a fine for selling beer that was too light or for serving too late. However, on this occasion Dorn did not pay any attention to the innkeeper and marched straight towards Melchior.

'Ah, our magistrate is here as well and already on his feet so early in the day,' Melchior exclaimed cheerfully.

'Rounding you up like a sheepdog,' Dorn growled. 'They said at Rannavärav Gate that you were looking for Sire Götzer.' Dorn then noticed the old captain and nodded to him respectfully. 'And our good Skipper here as well. Listen, Melchior, I have heard something of consequence.'

'Maybe the Magistrate will wait for just a short time, as the Skipper and I were in the middle of talking,' Melchior replied.

'No, no. I don't want to hold you up. I haven't got anything important to say,' Götzer said.

'I would still ask the Skipper to kindly finish his tale. It is of interest to me', Melchior reiterated, adding with emphasis, 'and of *great* interest to the Magistrate.' The Apothecary then turned and winked at Dorn, who, naturally, did not notice.

'But, Melchior, someone just came to tell me ...' the Magistrate began, but Melchior patted him on the shoulder and asked whether he wouldn't like to take a seat and order a beer.

'Beer? What blasted beer?' Dorn sputtered, then abruptly fell silent and blinked. '*Beer?*' he asked, astounded.

'If the esteemed Magistrate does not decline then we are offering a strong beer brewed behind the Lurenburg Tower,' the innkeeper called over, trying to win Dorn's favour. 'And, naturally, we would not take any money from our esteemed Councilman ...'

'*Silence*, you gallows lout,' Dorn snarled. The Magistrate then considered for a moment and said, 'Yes, bring your beer, although I cannot take it for free. According to my oath of office I am not allowed to take anything from those who will be summoned to a Council trial before long.'

The innkeeper did as he was told and, saying nothing, brought Dorn a tankard filled with strong mark beer then disappeared into the backroom. Götzer seemed to be somewhat confused by the Magistrate turning up, but Melchior assured him that both he and Dorn wanted to hear the Skipper's story right to the end.

'I should tell the Magistrate that it is a *very* interesting tale,' Melchior added.

'What's interesting is the news the Commander's squire just brought me,' Dorn replied, but he sipped his beer compliantly.

'Did the Commander's squire bring word of a certain golden collar? Yes, I thought as much. However, Sire Götzer was halfway through telling me how the Victual Brothers' high-ranking men met their end. We had just got to the execution of Gödeke Michels. The Magistrate and I would very much like to hear about this.'

Götzer needed no further encouragement. 'Gödeke, yes, he was captured later, you see, after a dreadful sea battle far off near Frisia, in which nearly a hundred men went to their watery graves. They also say that Magister Wigbold was captured at that time, and he and his men were tortured with pliers on Simon of Utrecht's ship in the hope that one of the rats might give away where their treasure and Störtebecker's might be hidden. Alas, not one said a word, only that everything was shared equally and they wouldn't give it back to pepper sacks such as them.'

'But they were still beheaded?' Melchior asked.

'So the Hamburg Council confirms and so it swears – although seamen tell all sorts of tales. Gödeke was said to have been seen years later somewhere near Bergen, and Magister Wigbold – the Master of Seven Arts, as he was called; he who was so clever that no one could trap him until that day – well, they say that his face was not known in Hamburg and that four men came forth on separate occasions to claim that they were the him and that all laughed manically when they were beheaded.'

'Because it is said that God himself was so tired of their piracy.'

'Satan more like …' the Skipper sputtered. 'And, speaking of God, was it not that same man they called Magister Wigbold – because no one knows his true name – who once lived in a monastery? While there he studied various arts, which is why he was called the Master of Seven Arts. Well, he was expelled from the monastery for theft or some such sin, after which he studied at some town in England whose name I know not – it is because of this that he was also called "Magistrate". They say he was the most clever and cunning of the Victual Brothers and that on many occasions he had to knock some sense into Gödeke and Störtebecker, which is why they left some seafarers alive. Yet it was Master Wigbold himself who devised their most effective raids. When they needed to parley, then it was done according to Wigbold's counsel. They say he was a clever merchant, too, and that because he had been a monk he would never allow Störtebecker or Gödeke to sack monasteries or kill monks. Not that Gödeke would always listen, of course. He was known to have tortured seafarers simply for pleasure and used their bodies for archery practice, ripped their tongues from their mouths and gouged out their eyes.'

'Thank God those pirates are all dead,' grunted Dorn.

'Well, Magistrate, that I could not say for certain unless I saw Gödeke's head. And could I still gouge out his eyes after his death, then that I would do, may I be damned,' he raged, banging his empty tankard on the table. 'But now a good day to you, gracious

Sire Apothecary and Sire Magistrate. This cripple is away to meet some other cripples. May the Almighty grace you with good health.'

Götzer bowed awkwardly and stumbled out of the tavern. Dorn immediately leaned over the table towards Melchior and said, 'In the name of St Victor, Melchior.'

Melchior chuckled, 'May he be praised.'

'In every sense and every weather, as our honourable Prior Eckell says. But, tell me now, why were you so keen to hear that rambling nonsense when I come bringing word that –'

'That the golden collar that belonged to the honourable Knight of the Order Von Clingenstain has disappeared and that Toompea wants the town to find it.'

'*Precisely so,* although I cannot see how you already know this. The Commander sent word that the collar was nowhere to be found. He had Clingenstain's servant – that Jochen – shackled and tweaked with red-hot pliers, yet Jochen swears to the Lord most high that he knows nothing of the collar, that Clingenstain did not ask him to take it to the ship and that he has never even set eyes upon it.'

'And the Commander believes the man who cut Clingenstain down a notch also took the collar,' Melchior mumbled.

'That is precisely what he believes.'

Melchior thought for a moment and then spoke. 'Well, this is an odd thief then indeed – a man who takes with one hand and gives with the other. The world has never before seen the like.'

'What the bloody hell are you saying now?' Dorn demanded.

'Simply that strange affairs are wound around this collar. Clingenstain buys the collar to give as a gift to the Grand Master of the Order and wears it around his neck to show it off for half a day. Before he goes to confession Clingenstain says he is taking it home so that Jochen can put it under lock and key on the ship. Now I hear he did no such thing.'

'And what is so strange about all that? The murderer chopped off his head and stuffed the collar into his own pocket.'

'Only that he stuffed a coin into Clingenstain's mouth. You see, Magistrate, the man who dispatched Clingenstain must have hated him deeply, and it would therefore be very strange if the murderer chopped off the Knight's head, forced a coin into his mouth and then stole his collar.'

'Why? That was quite a good trade-off, was it not?'

'Yes, it would have been, but you don't make deals with a man you abhor. Nothing about that golden collar seemed to fit even before, and I believed from the off that the Order Knights would not find it.'

Dorn sipped his beer and said, 'Listen, Melchior, if you know anything about this collar now then say at once because Spanheim is full of holy rage. I have to tell the councilmen *something* about this collar.'

'Tell them that you will, of course, apprehend the murderer and that the Order will get the collar back if it is in his possession,' Melchior replied.

Dorn glared at the Apothecary for a moment and then shrugged. Melchior always had odd thoughts and spoke in a puzzling way. Nevertheless, the Magistrate was reassured by the fact that the Apothecary did not seem concerned about the golden collar.

'A strange matter it is, but I suppose that's just what I'll say,' the Magistrate sighed in the end. 'And what happens now?'

'Now? Now I should very much like to talk to Master Casendorpe, and there is no better way for me to do that than to visit his workshop on Kuninga Street, which is what I intend to do. For our magistrate, however, I cannot recommend a better course of action than for him to keep his eyes and ears open and to ask around as to whether anyone has seen any old Visby coins recently. I receive money from townspeople every day, but I certainly do not recall anyone having paid with that old Gotland coin.'

Melchior winked slyly. The Magistrate sighed again and left – but before doing so barked at the 'swindling' innkeeper that he should start counting up his veerings for payment of a fine.

15

Melchior's Pharmacy, Rataskaevu Street
17 May, Afternoon

M ELCHIOR STOPPED by the pharmacy to find out from Keterlyn how many ailing townspeople had been in and how business had been going. She was not permitted to sell prescribed medicines herself nor was she allowed to make up any of Melchior's recipes, but she had picked up a great deal of pharmacy wisdom while working at her husband's side, so if the person in need was a good friend who would not tell the Council or the town doctor she would be prepared to sell some simpler medicines. She was allowed to sell elixir – which was what most customers actually came to sample – aniseed sweets or spiced cakes; the Council had no say in such transactions.

Melchior should, by that time, have already taken on an apprentice or even a journeyman, a boy to whom he could pass on his wisdom, but he had not. Melchior's father had not taken one either, he had instructed his own son, just as Melchior's grandfather had taken *his* firstborn son as an apprentice – all of whom, as tradition demanded in the Wakenstede clan, were given the name Melchior. As with all artisans, an apothecary could not call himself such until he had completed his years as apprentice and journeyman and before he had proved his competency by demonstrating his skills in front of the town doctor and a senior apothecary.

As his father's apprentice Melchior the Younger had not had it any easier than would an apprentice from outside the family. His father demanded discipline and that he study hard. He had been strict, and if Melchior did something poorly he was sent to the attic to kneel on dried peas and recite the apprentice's virtues. Melchior's father had been a harsh yet just man, and he had never raised his voice against his son without reason, and never in his life had the boy felt a rod on his back … never.

Melchior's mother Rosamunde had died when Melchior was just four, and he barely remembered her. His father never remarried – a Wakenstede must always take the *right* wife – and Melchior the Elder never found another like Rosamunde, although not through want of trying.

Melchior had received his early schooling at Lübeck's monastery school and later as his father's apprentice in Tallinn. In Tallinn he also made his way up Long Hill to the Dome Church School for one winter, but the boy was beaten so harshly while there that his father went along to make a few things clear to the Dome School teacher – although no good had come of it, of course. At twelve Melchior ceremoniously gave his father his journeyman's vows, promising always to mix medicines exactly and quickly according to the recipes, never to deceive anyone in anyway concerning these remedies, to place all money in the pharmacy coffer and not to sell poisonous medicines to anyone without the correct doctor's order. He vowed to help anyone requiring something from the pharmacy, no matter what time of day or night, and to administer his skills faithfully and diligently with the grace of God. He vowed this in the manner of a true Christian and in the name of the saints. Melchior served for two years as his father's journeyman until the time came for him to travel to learn his trade from others, taking with him an attestation issued by a master. Melchior's father sent him to study with an acquaintance, a pharmacist in Riga, whom he trusted and who was aware of the Wakenstedes' curse – Melchior the Elder did not dare send him further abroad to board with strangers. It was in Riga where, in a cold and unheated chamber, Melchior was first struck by his line's eternal scourge. His father had warned him, and he was prepared. He had expected it. He believed he could learn to live with it.

Melchior walked up to the Short Hill gatepost and turned on to Niguliste Street at the corner of the sacristy, passed by the churchyard, the well and the town mint and then reached the corner of Seppade and Kuninga Streets. Master Casendorpe's building could be seen from there, a two-storey limestone construction with the goldsmiths' insignia – a small, gold-encrusted hammer – hanging above the doorway. Not all that many people were on the streets at this time, as the craft guilds were still working, the market had finished for the day and the evening church services had not yet begun. Because it was so quiet he noticed a young couple turning from Seppade Street on to Kuninga Street, recognizing them as Sire Freisinger and the Maiden Hedwig Casendorpe. Melchior quickened his pace to greet them. They stopped in front of the Casendorpe house. The Blackhead had escorted his future bride home, no doubt after the pair had been out for a leisurely stroll … However, as Melchior drew nearer, he realized that they weren't discussing details of a wedding feast – no, they were arguing. Hedwig seemed to be pleading for something and was not satisfied with Freisinger's explanations. The young woman then shouted shrilly and abruptly, shoving the Blackhead away from her.

'You and your promises. The devil take them,' the Maiden Hedwig shouted, bursting into tears. Freisinger tried to catch her hand and comfort the girl, but she pulled away too fast and dashed through the open doorway. Freisinger stood helplessly in front of the entrance until he noticed Melchior and nodded to him.

Melchior bowed lightly in return. Perhaps this might not be the best time to visit Master Casendorpe after all. There he would find a sobbing girl and her bewildered parents, who would probably not be in a position to discuss matters with a curious apothecary.

'Sire Blackhead,' Melchior greeted the merchant. 'What a beautiful evening – although it sounded as if someone shouted of the devil, at least from what I heard.'

The Blackhead appeared out of sorts. 'Oh no. That was merely the Maiden Hedwig.'

'Ah, your future bride?'

Freisinger shrugged and mumbled in a cracked voice, 'As for that, well, as they say, as the Lord giveth …'

'You know what,' Melchior said decisively, 'perhaps the Sire Blackhead has enough time to make a short visit to the pharmacy so that he may take a strong, potent drop of elixir in return for the mighty generosity showed towards our town's esteemed men yesterday; one that will clear the senses and raise his spirits?'

'Heavenly grace, I am in a rush – however, I could never turn down such an offer,' Freisinger said with a laugh, his dignified air restored.

'Then it is settled,' said Melchior. 'Let us make for the pharmacy', and in no time Melchior was already topping up a cup of his celebrated drink for Freisinger.

'To the Sire Blackhead, in gratitude for yesterday's lavish feast – and for beer that was not the poorest.'

'You should thank our Brother Wunbaldus for the beer. I visited the monastery this morning, and he already has a new brew fermenting. As for the feast, as long as the Blackheads' prosperity lasts so will they treat their honest friends, as is right and proper,' Freisinger vowed.

The two men drank, coughed and ate cakes to wash the elixir down.

Melchior spoke first. 'This is an old recipe that was passed to me by my father. He came from Lübeck, but it was taught to him by the squire of some Franconian knight and was popular even in the royal courts.'

'One may imagine.' Freisinger nodded then frowned. 'Listen, Melchior, perhaps you would teach this recipe to the Blackheads as well?'

'Aha,' Melchior exclaimed. 'Alas, I cannot. A trade secret. The Blackheads should understand this well indeed, as they are also men with secrets.'

'Ah, come now. We are simple and merry merchants.'

'However, you are the type of simple and merry merchants that claim their guild has been in this town since its very foundation – although no one can recall any particular details. As you said yourself yesterday, "The Brotherhood of Blackheads was already in this town when one still had to fight the pagans for every square foot of land. They helped to dedicate this town's holy sanctuaries to the Lord Christ."'

Freisinger took a sip of elixir and tried to deflect the comment. 'Ah, well, we all tend to exaggerate somewhat when we have beer on our breaths. It is true, though, that the first in Tallinn to call himself a Blackhead was a Strasburg man who arrived during Danish rule – even so, the Blackheads have not gained as much respect here as the Canutes.'

'Nevertheless, with your arrival, and especially after coaxing all of the unmarried sons of Great Guild merchants to join together … But I cannot remember now. Where did you come from?'

'From Cologne, and our guild ordained me there as well. My father had been a member and his father before him. I tried my luck over the years trading goods in various places until I finally reached Tallinn by way of Rostock.'

Melchior had not known this before. The Apothecary knew a lot about many of the townsmen – where they were born and where they had been before – but it was increasingly hard to keep up, as the pace of new arrivals to the town accelerated. Clawes Freisinger may be the most fashionably dressed of Tallinn's merchants and wear the finest clothes, but Melchior had not known much about his origins until now.

'You must descend from an old and dignified line of merchants then, Sire Freisinger,' said Melchior.

'My great-grandfather was a master mason by trade. He built the cathedral in Cologne and was also likely a member of one of the first guilds in the town. Our guild is not titled the Brotherhood of Blackheads in every place, Melchior; it bears different names in different towns. His father had carried the cross fighting for Jerusalem in the Holy Land. I, on the other hand, have made my way here over time … This land pleases me.'

'Then we have had similar fates,' Melchior mused. 'I, too, am from a long line in which the eldest sons have always been apothecaries, and now I have reached this place, which I enjoy greatly. Shall I pour you another cup?'

'Bring it forth. But Livonia … why do I like it here?' Freisinger was becoming more talkative. 'It is a new land, a land just recently brought under the Holy Roman Empire. There may not be as much wealth here as in other places, yet there is a kind of freshness and vivacity. Things that already exist elsewhere are just being built and established here. We are at the edge of the Christian world, Melchior. After this it is just philistines and barbarians, and if the Lord blesses the weapons of the Order then we shall continue eastwards from here. That war has not yet been fought.'

'If the Lord wills it … Although, He might first give the bishops and the Order a Christian mind for conciliation, as they fight amongst themselves more than with the Russians, or so it seems to me.'

'Money, Melchior, it is always money that comes between wealthy men and stops them from behaving like true Christians. The Order wishes to become greater and richer, as do the bishops. In the end only the Russians will benefit as long so these wars between Christian peoples so exhaust us.'

'You are absolutely right. The fact that we trade with them does not mean that they are proper Christians yet, and this we see each and every day.'

'Exactly. We live at the edge of the world and so must defend our saints and the word of God that much more resiliently. The Blackheads and the Dominicans have been called here and tasked with bearing the Word of the Lord and holding high the flag of the Holy Cross.'

The pair spoke further of Order affairs and of politics involving lords of high status and then raised another cup, after which Freisinger announced he should take his leave, as he had business to conduct at the weighing-house and would then head off to the guild's altar at the Dominican Monastery. He promised as he left that tomorrow's festivities would be no less handsome than that of the previous day, as the Blackheads had selected some formidable beers.

As he left Freisinger bumped into Sire Tweffell's servant Ludke, who had been lurking in front of the pharmacy door in his slightly asinine, boorish manner. Ludke stepped into the room guardedly after the Blackhead had gone.

'And what bodily ailment is troubling you today, Ludke?' Melchior exclaimed jovially, welcoming him in. Ludke was not exactly a regular visitor; Tweffell did not allow him to spend time away from the house to drink beer. Ludke was probably not much of a drinker anyway – in fact, Melchior had never seen him intoxicated, which was something the Apothecary could not say for the majority of the town's lower classes. Ludke had the brute force of a bear, a hulking presence with fair hair and blue eyes. He was quiet and seemingly a touch simple yet was utterly devoted to the old merchant. No matter where Tweffell went he always took Ludke with him — it was rumoured that the boy even carried his master up the stairs at home. Ludke was a boy of very few words, but he *was* one of the townspeople who had visited Toompea the previous day – and had disappeared afterwards, Melchior now recalled.

'Not one bodily ailment,' the boy replied. 'Not a thing troubles me. Sire Tweffell sent me.'

'Of course, how foolish of me,' Melchior boomed. 'How could any bodily ailment ever trouble such a behemoth of a man? The Town Hall's tower will collapse before you start to suffer from aching bones. So, what can I do for our merchant?'

'He requested you send the very same salve as yesterday – and then another bottle to counter fatigue.'

'I think I know which bottle he has in mind,' Melchior laughed. 'It is that one and only Melchior's famous elixir that has been especially pleasing to the entire town of Tallinn this very morning following yesterday's festivities at the Brotherhood of Blackheads.'

'No doubt it is,' Ludke said flatly and fell silent, waiting. Melchior already had the ingredients prepared, but he did not rush. He slowly poured ground herbs from a small sack into his mortar, pounded them together, added oil and spirits and then set to sorting out bottles. He needed to get the boy talking. Melchior enquired after Sire Tweffell's health and cheerfully gossiped about events in the town. Ludke stood quietly and waited, clutching a couple of pennies between his fingers.

'Always the very same. Melchior's famous elixir. What else? I can sell it without the town doctor's prescription. Yet I tell you this,

Ludke, our Sire Merchant must continue to let blood with care at the barber's; going without that won't do, not at all. It would be even better for him to place leeches on his skin occasionally – but where can you find good leeches these days, eh?'

He finally finished the drink and went to hand it across the counter to Ludke, who had not said a word the entire time.

Melchior took the coins from the servant's hand, stared at the boy for a few seconds and then asked, 'So, tell me. How is Sire Tweffell's health, *really*? Has it perhaps suddenly become much worse? You are strangely silent about this.'

'Bone aches and backaches and sharp pains in his side. Sire says he no longer has much time,' Ludke mumbled, as if grudgingly. He snatched the bottle and turned to leave.

'Wait one moment, Ludke,' Melchior said. 'Tell me, did not the trip to Toompea exhaust Sire Tweffell? I am now worried about him. You were there also, yes? Did, by chance, bad news tire the merchant out?'

'I know nothing of these things,' the boy said bluntly.

Still you must know something, thought Melchior. He scooped up a handful of cakes from a basket on the table and held them out towards Ludke. 'In case I forget, these are samples for Mistress Gerdrud. If they are to her liking then she can always acquire more from Melchior's pharmacy. And you may also try them, Ludke.'

'My gratitude,' the boy mumbled, stuffing them into his pocket.

'Hearing unpleasant news at an age such as his may indeed make a person hurt all over. I'm thinking of that story of a ship that the Knight Clingenstain was said to have seized for himself in Gotland,' Melchior pressed further.

'Ask that of Sire Tweffell. Why do you ask me?' the boy retorted gruffly.

'Of course, of course … Perhaps I shall. Although, I would still ask you whether you happened to notice anyone strange lurking on Toompea the day before yesterday? You do know that I have promised to help the Magistrate find and seize the murderer?'

'I saw no one there.'

'So when you've been down to the harbour and chatted with the other attendants and servants … you haven't heard any such talk?'

'No. I do not speak to strangers, nor do I gossip. I wasn't even in the town yesterday,' said Ludke, his eyes boring a hole into the table.

'Oh, come now, you are a serious man who says little. Oh yes, that's right. You weren't in town and Mistress Gerdrud had to come for the medicine herself. Of course.'

'Yes. I wasn't in the town at all yesterday,' the boy affirmed in a monotone.

'Right, yes. You were sent somewhere to handle affairs …'

'I went to a village outside the town to call in a debt,' the boy burst out suddenly, 'and … and to bring back leeches as well. Just as Master ordered. I brought leeches for Sire Tweffell, and Mistress Gerdrud will place them on his back today when he bathes.'

'A real manly conversation, Ludke,' Melchior exclaimed following the boy's oration. 'I haven't heard you utter such a long sentence for many years. Did you get the money?'

'I always get the money.'

'And never will that man fall into debt again,' Melchior mused and peered closer at Ludke. The servant shrugged and made to leave once more.

Melchior waited until he had reached the door and then called out, 'Listen, hold on. I cannot recall at the moment … How many years have you been at Sire Tweffell's?'

'Four years,' came the reply.

'Ah, yes.' Melchior nodded. 'And before that you were – if my memory does not fail me, as you always tend to say, St Cosmas – a sailor?'

The Apothecary did not expect the boy to reply, but he did. 'Only on one voyage. The ship ran aground, and the people along the shores of Arensburg made off with all the cargo. I later ended up in Tallinn and was a soldier for the Council here.'

Melchior now peered at the boy with genuine interest.

'Well, Ludke, you should request an evening free from your service sometime and come tell these tales to the Apothecary. Townspeople make their way through here, and men do enjoy dashing tales of battle and the sea. Eh, what do you think, Ludke?'

The servant shrugged. 'I'm no storyteller. Not that there is anything to say in any case. We were sent to wage war against Novgorod, and so we went.'

'And what happened there? You were handed swords and axes and ...'

'A halberd. I was given a halberd.'

'Oh, how exciting. And what did you do with that?'

'I chopped the Russians in half. But I really must leave now. Sire Tweffell has already been waiting too long, and I need to visit the horse trader beyond the city walls to buy a new horse –'

'A horse? What happened to that sturdy draft horse that Tweffell purchased last spring?' Melchior asked in surprise.

'It died this morning. Yesterday it was still healthy and had no ailments at all, but today it convulsed and then died. Right there in the stables near Köismäe where we kept it.'

'This is a strange matter,' Melchior muttered.

'Sire Tweffell was as raging mad as the devil himself. Promised to have anyone who had fed his horse any kind of shit hanged. But I myself gave the horse oats and water yesterday – and drank some myself, too. It's as if someone had put the evil eye upon it during the night and cursed it. I'm going now.'

Melchior closed the pharmacy earlier than usual. He sat and looked into the distance absentmindedly for a time but then decided to stir up his courage and see what the Master Goldsmith might make of an inquisitive apothecary in the evening.

Melchior took along a small bottle of lavender oil, just in case.

16

Kuninga Street
17 May, After Sunset

B URCKHART CASENDORPE had already closed his workshop
for the evening and left his seat at the window. He stalked the
spacious room, growling at the journeymen because he had found
a pinch of silver dust on the floor, just as he had been assailed with
harsh words for such a thing during his own years as a journeyman,
in his turn he aimed such curses at his own subordinates. They
were supposed to wear leather aprons and hold their legs spread
wide when working, so that every minuscule scrap of metal would
be caught by the apron if dropped. But if, however, anything was
found on the floor it meant that the journeymen were lazy, negligent
scoundrels and that, instead of becoming goldsmiths, they would
end up as cobblers or something even worse. It was possible that the
boys were tongue-lashed even more than usual that day, as it had
not exactly been a good one for Casendorpe.

Melchior's face appeared at the window just as Casendorpe
was concluding one such tirade. The Apothecary winked slyly and
announced he had important news for the Goldsmith. Melchior was
allowed in, and Casendorpe released the journeymen with a few
final profanities. His intuition told him that the Apothecary's messages would probably not be welcome news. Melchior nonchalantly

inspected the Goldsmith's shelf above the sales table, which was meant to catch the eye of every regular customer and inform him that this goldsmith was a master amongst masters and chosen to possess the secrets of faraway lands. The Apothecary grunted a few compliments about the exhibits, saying they were indeed extraordinary and that if he had something similar in place of his shrivelled-up stuffed crocodile, then no doubt business would be better. Both Apothecary and Goldsmith were required to demonstrate their exceptional status to the people of the town, and there was no better way to do so than to hang something exotic and mysterious from the ceiling.

'My father', Melchior began, 'taught me people believed these teeth here are supposed to tell you when the body has been poisoned. Did you know that, Master Goldsmith? They are called "serpent's tongue", you see, and they change colour when placed upon poisoned skin. And if you drink an elixir made from coconut shell then it should remove poison. Do you know what else my father taught me? That one should not always believe such things. He told me never to sell a medicine that people tell you about but which has never been tried out. Take bezoar or witch's root, for example. There are all sorts of fairy-tales that speak of these, but we know for a fact that they help the afflicted because they have been tried on innumerable occasions.'

'No doubt it is so,' Casendorpe barked impatiently. 'But I understood that you had something important to tell me.'

'Yes, indeed so,' Melchior answered. 'I didn't come just to chat, of course ...' He abruptly fell silent, squinted and went down on one knee. 'Ah, look here. It appears as if there is some gold dust or something of that sort between the flagstones ...'

'Halfwits,' Casendorpe seethed. The Goldsmith set his spectacles firmly on his nose and leaned over to peer at the floor. 'There is. Damnation. The plague take those lazy dogs.'

Casendorpe searched for a brush and a tiny pan and set to gathering up the dust while Melchior looked inquisitively around the Master's workshop, as it was not somewhere he visited very often. There was a large workbench that ran from the window into the room, positioned so that the light would shine directly on to it. Only daylight is suitable for a goldsmith's work, so in order to catch the light when the sun begins to go down Casendorpe's workshop, like that of all goldsmiths, had a rounded mirror – sometimes called a witch's mirror, the type used by Flemish masters – resting on a table in the back of the room that was used to reflect light back into the room and on to the bench. Melchior had no idea if it helped all that much. A large forge with a hearth, in which that day's fire had already begun to die down, was built into the western wall of the room. The walls were covered with shelves and pegs that supported a large number of goldsmith's tools of every size and shape: tongs, hammers, chisels, files, saws, knives, pokers, tweezers, burins, drills as well as rabbit paws of various sizes used for sweeping up gold dust. In the east corner of the room was a small altar dedicated to St Eligius, above which was another shelf holding three absolutely identical metal jugs – in order to attest to his mastery a goldsmith must show that he is capable of faultlessly crafting items identical to one another.

Casendorpe finished sweeping up the gold. Melchior had been talking about the incredible medicinal properties of rubies and sapphires but then said, 'And seeing as our conversation has turned towards precious items, well, what I came to tell you, Master Goldsmith, was that, you see, that very same collar you sold to the Knight on Toompea two days ago has vanished. The Order sent word of this to the Town Council today, and since I am now at the Council's services, or something of the sort, that is what I came to say. The Commander's order was to apprehend the murderer and the collar along with him because they believe that the murderer took the collar.'

Casendorpe removed his glasses, scratched his cheek and then positioned them back on his nose.

'So his head was cut off for that collar?' he asked numbly. 'For *my* collar?'

'No head – and no collar to be found,' said Melchior regretfully and shrugged. 'So how did the transaction go on Toompea?'

Casendorpe snorted and shook his head. 'Just as they often do with the Order.' Casendorpe told Melchior how he had received the order from Gotland a couple months back. Apparently the local goldsmiths produced shoddy work, and Clingenstain wanted to take a piece by a Tallinn master along as a present for the Grand Master. Casendorpe wrote back, and they came to an agreement upon a price of sixty Riga marks. He should, of course, have demanded that a notary or the town scribe draw up the contract and given it a wax seal and an avowal because – as it turned out – the Commander of the Order on Gotland later paid no heed to the negotiated amount.

'You mean Tallinn's notary?' Melchior clarified.

'The very same,' Casendorpe rumbled and made a face. 'Oh, dung and the devil, I should have called upon him today. I wish to annul my will. That blasted Freisinger ...'

'Has something happened?' Melchior asked quickly. 'And all are talking about the great betrothal feast? Ah, and how did it slip my mind? I brought along a gift for Maiden Hedwig.' The Apothecary set the small bottle of lavender oil on the table.

'My great thanks to you for the present, Sire Apothecary. However, the betrothal festivities will be cancelled,' the Goldsmith said unsteadily – and at the same moment a sob sounded from the doorway and Hedwig stepped out into the room. Melchior figured she must have been listening in on the conversation. Hedwig was a very pretty girl, even when she was miserable and her eyes red from crying. Melchior bowed to her in greeting, and she nodded and emitted another sob.

'My dear maiden, please forgive me, but earlier I did see what appeared to be an argument between you and Sire Freisinger,' Melchior said. 'But that the betrothal festivities —'

'Cancelled,' Casendorpe interrupted him firmly.

'Oh, Father, but he *promised*,' Hedwig blubbered.

'Promised, promised,' imitated the Goldsmith crossly. 'A merchant's promise is worth about as much as a thief's. But, damn it, did I not scour the entire town for a decent and wealthy suitor for my daughter? I do care enough about my child not just to give her away to some old cripple. And did that Blackhead himself not come courting the girl like some fox after a hen, always pushing her —'

'Father,' shouted Hedwig.

'Not to worry, the whole town will know soon enough, and I will not allow myself to be made to look an idiot.'

'Alas, nothing in a small town remains a secret for long,' Melchior remarked. 'You are quite right about that. Not that I can understand why any man wouldn't wish to say his vows before the altar to such a fine and chaste maiden and one with such a dowry.'

'But he *did* wish it,' Hedwig said, choking through her tears. 'He said, too, that he was the happiest man in all Livonia, and he spoke such fine words, and Father had already arranged the dowry, and then *today* that Freisinger said he wants to wait a little longer before marriage and that … and that I had not quite understood —'

'Silence, girl,' the Goldsmith commanded. 'We will not discuss our affairs in front of others.'

'Everyone already knows that I have been spurned anyway.'

'Well, I would never have believed that someone could ever spurn such a fine maiden,' Melchior spoke soothingly. 'No doubt it is simply that – and just as I felt before going before the altar – that "farewell to thee, ye cheerful bachelor's life and joys of youth". Perhaps Sire Freisinger just needs to think about it for a while and hold some rousing feasts at the Brotherhood of Blackheads.'

The maiden looked up at him, smiled in a crestfallen way and wiped her eyes. 'There is no need for such kind words. You do not know everything that he vowed to me, the oaths he swore and the verses he read. But I have enough pride in the fact that I am the daughter of the Alderman of the Goldsmiths' Guild and daughter of the Alderman of the St Canute's Guild, and I will not allow myself to be treated in this way. It was an honest dowry that my father prepared, and with it we will find a suitor from the town of Lübeck for me – and then Freisinger will bitterly regret his behaviour.'

'Enough of such talk,' Casendorpe snapped, then thought for a moment before adding, 'However, the girl is quite right, in the name of St Victor. I will write to Lübeck, and so many suitors will arrive that their ships will not fit into Tallinn's docks, and then Freisinger may salt himself in a herring barrel. Oh, I'm sure I know what happened. He used his honey-sweet words to try to coax the girl into his sinful bed, but when –'

'Father,' Hedwig squealed, horrified. 'Father, before a *townsman*?'

'There's nothing to be ashamed of. May all know henceforth that some foreign Blackhead will not coax Burckhart Casendorpe's only daughter into his bed, and if he thinks to make a joke of courtship then he may do it with the horse trader's daughters.'

'And I,' said Hedwig, 'I will not even look in his direction. I would now rather become the wife of some foreign journeyman minstrel than of Freisinger.'

'Enough now, girl. And no minstrels either ... Fine, then, enough. Melchior, you asked something about that collar? And what are you doing lingering here, daughter? Go and cry your eyes out with your mother.'

Hedwig turned to leave, paused for a moment, turned back, came and took the small bottle of lavender oil from the table and then exited. Casendorpe continued to rant about merchants with sweet tongues and false promises, saying that none in the goldsmith's profession could ever be accused of behaving in such a manner, at which Melchior simply nodded.

'Precisely,' he said, ending Casendorpe's tirade. 'However, that same golden collar that you sold to Clingenstain – for the price of a man's soul, as the Commander said – what I wished to ask was, how did that exchange then take place?'

'Price of a man's soul. Ha!' Casendorpe huffed angrily. 'He was *supposed* to pay such a price. I tell you, he acquired that collar for next to nothing, and if it hadn't been meant as a gift for the Grand Master in Marienburg, well, then the proper price would have been twice as much again. I only received a lousy thirty Riga marks in silver. Even the Bishop of Tallinn would have paid the right price, at close to sixty.'

'And did you ask such a price at the very beginning?'

'Well, of course we *began* by discussing a price of sixty marks, as had been agreed, but he wanted to cast me out when we spoke of this two days ago and said he would purchase a collar from Riga instead. My sense of honour could tolerate no such a thing – Tallinn masterpieces are famed across the sea, and we do work that is fair, proper and certainly worth the price.'

'And at what was the price finally left?'

'Thirty measly marks,' Casendorpe bellowed. 'So it remained, and I only agreed to it to maintain the good name of Tallinn's masters within the Order. Curses, he didn't even have the full amount on his person, so he had to send his squire to the ship's coffers.'

'But in the end you received your thirty marks?'

'Nearly. As I weighed the coins up Clingenstain moaned that I was like some usurer Jew. First the Knight emptied his money sacks, which held probably around ten marks in Gotland ørtugs, and then his squire brought more from the ship. After weighing it all it came to about thirty Riga marks, well, actually, more like twenty-nine marks altogether.'

'And all of that money was in old ørtugs?'

'There was all manner of coins. I surveyed the lot and stacked them all separately for weighing according to the amount of silver they held – because I know the tricks those Order Knights pull. I am a master goldsmith, you see, and a goldsmith is not some rope-maker or stonecutter that the Order can order about as it pleases. I perform my art in the way it is done in the town of Lübeck and just as it once was by the famed goldsmiths along the Meuse. I will not be pushed around by the Order – nor by any infernal Blackheads,' Casendorpe declared.

After they had wished one another good health the Goldsmith thought for a moment then said that he would agree to purchase the collar back for thirty marks were Melchior to find it – although the Commander need not know that.

17

Rataskaevu Street
17 May, Late Evening

I T WAS ALREADY dusk by the time Melchior reached home. The church bells had struck nine times, and few people still wandered the streets – the only townsperson who passed him was a court crier at the corner of Mäealuse Street, still shouting out the same, 'Citizens allegiant to the town of Tallinn who have become aware of the location in which this very murderer doth conceal himself ...' The millstones of Town Council judgement grind on regardless, Melchior thought as he approached the steps to his door. The sound of a lute and the joyful giggles of young girls brushed his ear. He strained his eyes in the fading light and could make out three figures drawing closer from Lai Street, one of whom he recognized as Kilian. Melchior swiftly opened his door, stepped into the house and cracked open the window to listen in on the trio. Before he could do so, however, he briefly glimpsed the face of Mistress Gerdrud lit by candlelight in the window of her house. The candle was snuffed out as the sound of music grew nearer, but the window was left slightly ajar.

'You know, singing journeyman, you would be one of the richest men in the town of Tallinn if honours were bestowed for singing sad songs.' Melchior paired the cheerful voice with that of Katrine, the

192

daughter of a town merchant and one of the girls from the church-yard the previous day.

'Oh yes, Kilian, have you ever thought of becoming a monk? You know, they are similarly quiet and mournful fellows, and I sometimes wonder whether they still have their vitals at all …' The second voice apparently belonged to Birgitta, a councilman's daughter and the other girl from the day before. The girls were seriously laying into Kilian and pestering him spiritedly. The trio came to a halt next to the well. Kilian sat on its edge looking forlorn and jiggling the loose stone in the well wall with his toe.

'Kilian, why do you play your lute at all if you can only play melodies so gloomy that it makes me want to burst into tears? Look around you. A gorgeous spring is blossoming everywhere, and, as my mother says, youth is only given once and merely a pinch of it at that – although she doesn't say this to my sister, who has already pledged herself to the nuns at St Michael's.'

'Darling maidens, darling maidens,' Kilian lamented despond-ently. 'I cannot force my songs. I sing of joy when my mood is joyful and of sadness when my mood is sad. If a song does not emanate from the soul, then there is no point in singing at all.'

'What so plagues your young soul that it only wishes to sing of pain?' Birgitta demanded, laughing. 'You do not live like a monk in a monastery, so you are allowed to sing of happiness and cheer to young girls.'

'Of love and of spring,' Katrine piped up.

'Of flowers and of happiness, and of all the beauty in the world that makes the heart beat more rapidly and the soul cry out in jubilation.'

'You must know about such things, Kilian; you've travelled throughout half of the entire world and seen noblewomen and knights and heard all kinds of songs and stories.'

'And have seen the ways and manners of foreign lands. Surely you can sing the kinds of songs that are more attuned to the hearts of Tallinn's virtuous maidens than those that moan on about sorrow and heartbreak.'

Kilian seemed at a loss. 'Sorrow and heartbreak are the very elements that produce the greatest songs. You wish for me to sing of happiness and joy …' he sighed.

'Oh yes. Absolutely,' the girls squeaked.

'Of the heart's beating and the soul's cries?' Kilian questioned.

'More than anything in the world,' Katrine affirmed.

'Of foreign ways and noblewomen, of happiness, joy and of spring?'

'And of marital bliss, too, Kilian,' Birgitta exclaimed.

And of love, Kilian, and of love.'

'And of love?' Kilian echoed. 'Of noblewomen and love, the heart beating and spring … Yes, I will sing – although in a real song these go together with sadness and heartbreak, with separation and despair.'

He took up his lute, played a melancholic chord and began to sing slowly and quietly, yet still loud enough that his tune would carry through the open window of Sire Tweffell's house:

Bernard de Ventadorn lived in Limousin, in Ventadorn Castle
He was not of noble descent but the son of an attendant who
    tended the
castle bread ovens
And he grew up to become a fine, handsome man
And he was skilled at singing and at weaving beautiful songs
He learned the ways of the lords and was a friend to many
And the count, the ruler of Ventadorn, enjoyed his company
He certainly enjoyed his songs and verses and honoured the man
    highly

Yet the count had a wife, so beautiful and young, lovely and cheerful
And she, too, enjoyed Bernard's songs of love for her and her
    virtuousness
And their love lasted such that no one realized it, secretive and
        hushed
When the count perceived the truth he became enraged at Bernard
        and
locked his wife in the castle tower
And the woman denounced Bernard
And he went away, far from that land, alone in his sadness …

A window banged open somewhere along the street, and a man's voice roared out, shouting that he would start disembowelling the singer if that racket didn't stop immediately. The girls huddled together and whispered to one another then curtsied adoringly to Kilian and ran off. The boy sighed and then unhurriedly made his way through the courtyard door of Tweffell's house. Melchior spied the adjacent window being pulled shut as he did so.

It was a peaceful May evening, filled with the scent of lilac and with a light spring breeze. Melchior also closed the window and lit candles. He needed to think and to write. He located a scrap of parchment, ink and a quill, searched for his star chart and spread it out on to the table. Record everything, his father's words came back to him, an apothecary must remember so many things, and it is wiser to put it down on paper. If something troubles an apothecary, if something does not match up, then write it down. So Melchior wrote, becoming so engrossed in his task that he did not hear Keterlyn slowly open the rear door and steal into the room.

'Well, my dear husband, is catching a murderer harder than concocting witches' remedies? Your star chart is of no help in this task, it seems.'

Hearing Keterlyn's voice Melchior straightened up, smiled, rose and kissed his wife. 'A star chart tells us basic things. It tells us how people generally behave. Even a stealthy murderer is a person. The mixing of medicines is undertaken according to recipes that have been recorded by wise men who have studied the ways in which various remedies behave and how their properties interact with one another. All that has been will be again; there is nothing new under the heavens. Mix yarrow with peppermint and a strong, sweet wine, and it will take away whooping cough … Place the blind-drunk Butcher of Gotland into the same room as a man planning his revenge, and that man will chop the Knight's head off. But *who* was it, and *how* did he end up in that room?'

'And that does not lie within your star chart?'

'A star chart holds knowledge but not specifically of our contemporary Tallinn. A star chart contains the wisdom of hundreds of years; it is devised by men who understand people, their passions and their desires. A star chart never lies; it just has to be read correctly. It speaks of life, of people and the heavenly forces that influence them. Everything is interconnected, my darling wife. Just as the stars and planets affect one another in the skies, so do people influence others by way of their actions. All are held together with invisible threads: one tweaks another, and that one a third. Look.' Melchior pulled his wife down to sit at his side and pointed to the star chart. Aquarius wishes to tell me something that I still do not quite understand. Here is death. Death? Will the Apothecary see death today? It forces me to speculate, and I am incapable of solving this mystery.'

'Should not Sagittarius warn you that such things must be avoided?' Keterlyn asked, stroking her husband's hair.

'I may surely avoid them, but death will not stay away from the town of Tallinn. And if a murderer is on the loose here, then that means the town is sick and needs healing.'

'But, my darling Melchior, it's not as if you will ever guess who beheaded the Knight. You are not a seer.'

'I do not want to *guess*, I want to know. So, first I wrote down what I do know and then those things that bother me most about Clingenstain's murder.'

'So, tell me then. What *do* you know?'

'I know that Clingenstain arrived in Tallinn, having never been here before but having ties to a number of people in the town. For five days he made merry on Toompea, and then four townsmen visited him all in one day. A couple of hours later someone chopped his head off in a fearful rage. This someone ran from Toompea down to the town – this I also know for certain, as no one followed him from the Small Castle, a trail of blood led through Dome Gate towards Lower Town and he cast his murder weapon aside on town soil.'

'But this could have been someone from the parish who did so to put people off his trail,' Keterlyn suggested.

'There are no vassals in the Great Castle at the present, only clergy, a couple of dozen cobblers, bakers and other servant folk, and the Commander asserts it could not have been any of these because no one was missing. He knows them all, and he knows this as fact. I believe this also because even if it had been someone who resides in the Great Castle then he would have carried out this bloodshed in the dead of night when Clingenstain was asleep. After all, it's not the wisest move to run through Toompea and through two gates with a bloody cloak and a sword.'

'But neither could it have been any Tallinn townsperson.'

'Why not? Any one of those four men could have held a grudge against Clingenstain. He cheated Casendorpe over a golden collar, swore at him profusely and underpaid him. He had stolen a ship from Sire Tweffell, he did not give Kilian an attestation, and Prior Eckell –'

'Melchior, surely you truly do not believe that old Tweffell or the Prior might have cut his head off?' Keterlyn interrupted, taken aback.

'No. However, Tweffell is served by the loyal Ludke, and the Prior was once at the Dominican Monastery on Gotland. Clingenstain took confession with Eckell, my darling, and Eckell did not visit Toompea alone – he was accompanied by Brother Hinricus, and Brother Wunbaldus collected alms there that day. Both are young and strong.'

'You think then that what he confessed …' The woman fell silent and eyed her husband uneasily.

'I am still unable to think beyond the fact that four men called on the Knight during the day and later he was found dead. Anyway, I wrote three more things down that puzzle me. Take a look.'

Keterlyn looked closer and read, forming each letter with her lips. 'From what you have taught me of writing … I can make out something here about a coin, yes?'

'An old Gotland ørtug was stuffed into Clingenstain's mouth. Why? For what purpose? Is it a statement or message of some kind? If so, to whom and for what? The second point I recorded was that Kilian said Clingenstain wore the golden collar around his neck after having taken confession, yet the Commander and the esteemed Prior Eckell claim something quite different. How can this be? And third …'

Keterlyn read haltingly, 'The third point you have written here is … Freisinger's change of mind?' She raised her eyes in surprise.

'Yes,' said Melchior. 'Up until Clingenstain's death the Sire Blackhead wished fervently to take the Master Goldsmith's daughter as his bride and had already agreed upon a dowry at the notary. The entire town knows that the happiest of marriages would come of this union – not counting the Apothecary's own, of course – but then, straight after the murder, Freisinger changed his mind. Promptly and abruptly.'

'What then does this have to do with Clingenstain?'

'At first glance nothing more than the fact that it was Casendorpe who sold Clingenstain the now missing golden collar and that Freisinger suddenly dropped the most beautiful and wealthy maiden in Tallinn, just as the star chart states, everything is interconnected and everything influences everything else. Sire Freisinger must be an absolute dolt if he does not wish to become a citizen of Tallinn by marrying the highly honourable St Canute Guild Alderman's daughter – and with a good dowry at that – but he is manifestly *not* an absolute dolt.'

'No, doubtless he is not,' Keterlyn said tenderly, and kissed Melchior's forehead. 'However, I know of one absolute dolt who happens to be married already and who sits hunched over in his chair alone despite his own star chart's predictions. Sagittarius indeed promised the Apothecary a sweet kiss yesterday.'

'Ah, so you *do* still believe the star chart,' Melchior exclaimed triumphantly.

'Oh, how much of that nonsense do I believe?' Keterlyn said with a wave of her hand. 'No doubt it is a game, like chess perhaps, which someone can use to envision life and *people*, just like pieces on a chessboard, so are the zodiac signs *people* from a certain perspective, and –'

'Chess? You are right in a way – although you don't know how to play chess.'

'That is true, but Gerdrud does, and old Tweffell forces her to play with him when Ludke is off somewhere handling affairs, and –'

'Ludke plays chess?' Melchior raised his eyes in disbelief. Keterlyn answered that chess was the old merchant's sole passion, and he had taught every member of his household how to play with him, including Kilian and his wife – as if the game were an activity fitting for a young woman. Pastors could often be heard delivering sermons on the dangers posed by games that distract people's thoughts from heavenly matters.

Keterlyn was right. Melchior had also heard that chess is a mirror of life and of the world, that every piece has its own significance and role, just as people in the temporal world. He thought of the chess game that the Prior and Wunbaldus had been playing and which he had noticed while at the monastery and then again recalled his own father. Chess is probably the one thing Father taught me that I have forgotten.

Melchior asked Keterlyn to ask Gerdrud whether she would lend them a chess set in exchange, perhaps, for a therapeutic salve at half price, and Keterlyn reckoned she could easily do so.

I must remember how to play, Melchior reflected. It is not right that I have forgotten my father's teachings.

18

Melchior's Pharmacy, Rataskaevu Street
17–18 May, Night

M

Y FATHER IS DEAD. The thought seized Melchior Wakenstede in the night as he lay in bed; it pierced his thoughts with no warning, painful and deep as an executioner's searing-hot lance. Melchior had a dream in which he was walking on the rocks between the town wall and the sea; a woman approached him, crying, and said to him, 'Do you understand that your father is dead, Melchior? You are all alone.'

He is dead. He's gone. He died in my arms. All that remains of him is rotten earth in a decaying coffin deep under the ground in St Barbara's Graveyard. Never again will I smell his scent or watch his hands as he prepares medicines. Never again will I listen to his voice as he teaches me something. He loved me, and now he is dead.

To understand this was painful, as painful as it had been the first time Melchior really grasped it. His father fell ill when he had been back in Tallinn for two years following his journeymanship in Riga and was working with his father once more. Not with a simple sickness, the medicines to counter which he would have known himself, no – it was an ill-natured and onerous affliction that made him cough blood and confined him to his bed with a high fever. It was not the cough and the fever, however, not the periods of weakness or the sweating palms but rather his expression that spoke to Melchior and told him that the man would not rise from his bed on this occasion. His father's expression had no life, no love for life; it showed that he knew that this was the end and that he had submitted to God's will. An apothecary must be familiar with and understand death, and he must know when his own is coming.

Melchior's father died after eight days of suffering. He faded away and heeded the Lord's call, and Melchior knew that nothing, *nothing in this world*, could lead him off this path. The town doctor paid a visit and shook his head, said that he was powerless, that this man's life was in the hands of God alone. No earthly cure could be found for this disease, not any miracle remedy, no theriac, nor Mithridates' potion, nor bezoar, nothing at all. His father was beyond help, and all Melchior could do was to wait and watch as his father coughed blood, faded and eventually expired. Melchior would be left with only memories and teachings, with things his father had touched, this house in which he lived … nothing more.

Melchior screamed and writhed in his bed. *My father is dead.* His chest heaved from the torment, and there was no other thought in his mind. He felt nothing as he pounded his head against the stone wall; he did not feel the wetness after he knocked over a jug of water. Only the agony of loss churned within. He clawed at himself to relieve it and howled.

Three days before his death his father could no longer speak. His countenance, from which the life had already vanished, said it all. He loved his son and regretted his departure from this world, but this was how it had to unfold. And he would not be alone in the Kingdom of Heaven; his Rosamunde awaited him there. Melchior's mother visited his father in dreams, so his father had no fear; he knew he was expected. None the less, he felt grief. Just before drawing his last breath he managed to speak one final time. He had found the strength within at that moment to seize Melchior's hand in farewell and utter his departing words in a feeble voice, 'Take a good wife.' A Wakenstede must always marry the right woman. A Wakenstede is damned without a good woman. The scourge will devour the man's soul from within until he crawls naked in the dirt, screaming, flailing and tearing his hair from his skull, gnawing the flesh from his own bones, clawing his eyes from their sockets. Then Melchior's father had whispered these words, 'Saint, remember, fear.' He gripped his son's hand – he had wished to say so much more, but he was given no more time. Which saint was it that he must remember and fear? Melchior did not know, nor was he ever able to work out what his father had wanted to say, whether the words were a raving before death or something else. He was determined to find out one day.

Keterlyn was woken by her husband's howling.

So it is tonight, the woman thought with alarm. Tonight is that night. It had been over six months since the last time, and she had begun to hope the Wakenstedes' curse had released its grip on her husband, that her prayers before the altar to St Barbara and the candles that she lit there had helped, but no. She must be patient, she must believe, and hope, and love.

Keterlyn embraced her husband, but Melchior pulled free from her arms, curled up into a ball and howled.

This is the Wakenstedes' curse. The pain of the whole world descends upon them like a hundred demons, and they cannot find solace. Death and horror, inferno and plague haunt them. Not every Wakenstede is afflicted – but if one is free from it then his son will not be. It had never found its way into Wakenstede sisters and daughters; only the men were stalked by it, as if a malison had been placed on them for some unspeakable sin committed hundreds of years before, one that they must carry and suffer. They had read books by scholars and scrutinized the secrets of nature to find a cure, but no cure had yet been found. They learned about the lives of the saints to find one to help them – yet no saint, no pilgrimage, no relic had ever been of any succour. And a man taken over by the Wakenstedes' curse ultimately either perishes in the clutches of its pain – as if all the world's sins were heaped upon his shoulders – or finds the right woman to be at his side, a woman who loves the man and prays for him and with whose support he can venture out across this sea of torment. Yet the curse does not leave these women unscathed – Melchior's mother departed this world before her time because she had helped her husband to vanquish his pain, and in doing so had been punished herself.

Keterlyn took no notice. Keterlyn believed, hoped, loved.

Be it godly wrath, be it a demonic curse, be it a scourge for whatever sin, but Keterlyn was an honest Christian and would fulfil the oath she swore to God before the altar. Neither St Catherine nor St Gerdrud nor any other saint could stop her from doing so, as she had vowed to be at her husband's side in distress and in worry, in storms and in blizzards, in life and in death.

There was a drink that Melchior had mixed for himself for these occasions. It was so strong that it dried the moisture from his eyes and knocked the wind out of him, but Keterlyn did not dare to dash to the pharmacy to search for it at this stage. She was the wife of a Wakenstede and must do her duty. Melchior was unconscious, babbling. He shrieked, 'Father, Father', and when Keterlyn kissed him on the mouth she found that it was salty blood not sweat that now encrusted his lips.

Keterlyn cast the blanket off and gripped the man in her embrace. Melchior resisted, but she caressed his body with her lips. She straddled him, grazed his stomach with her breasts and buried his mouth in deep kisses so that his howling could no longer be heard. She squeezed his hips with her legs and ground her vulva against his penis and testicles, which did not yet seem to understand what was expected of them. Keterlyn was tough; she was no pampered town girl but rather descended from the ancient Viru elders in a line in which the women had always been known for their prowess in taking what they needed. Keterlyn rubbed herself against her husband's skin, covering his naked body with hers. Her tongue penetrated deeply into his mouth, and she finally sensed Melchior beginning to grow calmer and something twitching between his legs. She slowly slipped down along his body, brushing his staff gingerly with her lips. It was still small, but Keterlyn took it into her mouth and tickled along the length with her tongue. The towns-people called this 'the bishop's love' although the art had also been known in Viru since time immemorial. Melchior's senses were still not in their right place, but his body began to calm itself and follow the summoning of his wife's lips. Keterlyn continued to move her tongue around Melchior's penis and sucked the erect shaft straight in towards her throat until she felt her vagina moistening. Melchior groaned – and now no longer from pain. Keterlyn ran her hands along his stomach and chest while caressing below with her tongue until Melchior's cock was fully engorged with a manly force. She moved her tongue more rapidly and swallowed down more strongly, rubbing Melchior's cannonballs with one hand and his buttocks with the other. Melchior was still not yet aware of his surroundings, but the curse was retreating. When his cock began to throb with anticipation and his hips moved with his wife's rhythm Keterlyn released him from her mouth, straddled him again and worked Melchior's firm trunk inside her. She placed one of Melchior's hands on the curve of her buttock and the other against her firm breast, feeling how a wave of pleasure moved like molten iron upwards from between her legs through her abdomen. She moved her hips more rapidly and rocked her thighs backwards and forwards until Melchior's body loosened and he ejaculated. Keterlyn threw herself off of him and clutched her husband's quivering church tower as if it were an udder, milking it to the very last drop. And then, finally – thank St Catherine and all the saints; thank the ancient Viru shaman – she felt Melchior's hand groping her breast and the brush of his lips against them. She heard him whispering sultry words to her, and she knew that the curse had been broken for this time. And only when Melchior started to breathe regularly and slept did Keterlyn raise her naked body from his, slide off of the bed, sit on the cold floor and rub herself between her legs until *her* body, too, shook from pleasure.

Under the bed Keterlyn kept a stork's beak and a multicoloured cloth band knotted in Viru, which had been blessed by the shaman of linistagana – just in case St Catherine's blessing might not work. Keterlyn reminded herself she must send some beer and salted meat to linistagana. It would also be better if Melchior did not find out about the objects yet. There might be other medicines that counter the Wakenstedes' curse apart from the biographies of saints and the recipe books of Roman sages.

Keterlyn pulled on her nightshirt, covered Melchior with a blanket and snuggled up at his side. She fell asleep immediately to the sound of Melchior's peaceful breathing.

They both awoke earlier than usual. The clamour of marketgoers filled the room together with the first rays of dawn sunlight.

'Christ Almighty ... killed ... the Toompea Murderer ... his head chopped off, holy heavens, his head has been chopped off ... the Toompea Murderer has killed again.'

19

St Nicholas's Churchyard
18 May, Early Morning

MASTER MASON GALLENREUTTER's headless corpse lay in St Nicholas's churchyard. It was discovered in the mud near the lilac bushes behind St Matthew's Chapel next to a small path that ran to the sacristy. The spot was hidden from Mäealuse Street by a thick hedge. Headstones were dotted around the southern end of the cemetery, and the walls of houses on Seppade Street bordered it on the west. The Master Mason of Westphalia had been killed in a shadowy place, into the darkness of which curious eyes had not yet penetrated. His body was draped over an old Danish-period cross, and his head had been driven on to the branch of a pine tree, its eyes staring at those who had gathered to inspect the rest of the remains. The yellowy grass was covered in clotted pools of blood. Blood was sprayed over the cross and the lilac buds. Blood was everywhere. The morning warmth had not yet reached this dark corner; the sky was cloudy, and a half-hearted gust of wind stirred Gallenreutter's long, blood-soaked hair.

Dorn had managed to push back the crowd that had been gaping at the scene by the time Melchior arrived, and he was now arguing with the unhappy old Vicar of St Nicholas's – an old, skeletal man of Swedish descent who had been in the post for as long as Melchior

207

could remember. Another man was leaning over the body. Melchior recognized him as a foreign journeyman mason that had likely travelled with Gallenreutter to work on St Olaf's Church.

The Vicar was just telling Dorn that he had found the body of the unfortunate victim when crossing the churchyard first thing that morning. The man was complaining that holy ground had been desecrated, and they would now have to implore the bishop to bless it anew.

'The Toompea Murderer.' The journeyman was distraught. 'The one who escaped to the town. The Knight had his head chopped off, and our mason came from the very same town as that Knight of the Order. He said so himself.'

Gallenreutter, Melchior thought, Master Mason Caspar Gallenreutter from the town of Warendorf. The same who had wanted to call upon Clingenstain. Are only Warendorf men being killed in Tallinn now? Incredible. Melchior had run to the scene immediately on hearing the shouts and now stared dumbfounded at the corpse. He had still not fully shaken off the dreams of the night before and wanted to believe that this was all part of his nightmare. It had been a painful night, and he felt like someone who had just been taken off the torturer's rack. He always felt this way after a bout of the Wakenstedes' curse, and if it hadn't been for Keterlyn then he would now be half dead with anguish and pain ... Melchior shook these thoughts from his head and bent over the headless corpse.

'When will you capture this Toompea Murderer, Magistrate?' the Vicar demanded. 'He is a scourge to the entire town if he is now starting to kill within the walls of Tallinn.'

'As soon as I find him I will capture him,' Dorn snapped crossly. 'Although he is running out of time. What business did Gallenreutter have here at St Nicholas's?'

'He has not been here before. I don't even know him. I have no idea what business he may have had in our churchyard at night,' the Vicar replied in a snivelling voice.

Melchior touched the body and wiped some blood on to his fingertip. From what he knew this man must have been dead for many hours already. The slaughter had certainly not been carried out that morning. He reached into the breast pocket of the dead man's bloody doublet, and his finger brushed a piece of blood-encrusted paper. Gallenreutter's doublet was covered in blood, yet how had it found its way beneath the man's long jacket? Melchior untied the laces fastening the front of the doublet and inspected the victim.

Meanwhile Dorn was interrogating the journeyman mason. 'How did your master mason end up here? Did he have some business to conduct in the churchyard, eh?'

'In the name of St Victor, that I cannot guess,' said the latter in a daze. 'He left yesterday after work and did not return to the chapel this morning. That was when I went to look for him. He was boarding with some relative in a house not far from here. There were people running past me saying over and over that there had been a murder ... I said from the off that it wouldn't bring good fortune, and none did it.'

'What wouldn't bring good fortune?' Melchior called over from where he was still inspecting the body.

'That coffin or crate or whatever it was that we dug up. It contained some bones,' the boy explained, 'and it looked like it had been buried directly beneath the old walls and not within the graveyard, you see. And he said he would have a look to see what it contained and took it away. No good fortune did it bring. We should have got the Pastor to rebury those bones.'

'What bones were they then?' Melchior asked. He plucked the paper from Gallenreutter's breast pocket, smoothed it out and ran his eyes over it. The scrap held four lines of quickly scrawled writing. Melchior could not decipher much of the text initially, as the first letters of each row were covered in blood. He rose and approached the pine tree, peering with interest at the head of the unfortunate Gallenreutter, whose glazed eyes still showed fear and dread.

'May St Nicholas forgive me,' Melchior mumbled and prised Gallenreutter's mouth open. A clot of blood rolled off of the purplish tongue. Melchior stuck his fingers into the cavity and fished out a coin. Just as one would have guessed, he thought.

The journeyman mason was explaining that those at St Olaf's had no idea whose bones they were. 'Doubtless they were the bones of a man, right there where the old church once stood, but Master Gallenreutter took them away, and … I don't know.'

'Speak now, boy. Did anyone hold a grudge against him?' Dorn continued. 'Had anyone threatened him with a knife or vowed to do away with him? Speak honestly and with a pure heart.'

'I don't know,' the boy cried and drew into himself. 'I've not seen anyone draw a knife on him or anything. All we do is build the church – and who has ever heard of a man building a house of God having his head chopped off?'

'Lord cast thy mercy upon us. Lord cast thy mercy upon us,' the Vicar intoned.

Dorn ordered the mason to get moving and tell all the other journeymen that when a court servant arrived then they must all appear before the Magistrate and swear in the names of all the saints that they will only speak the truth about what they know of the killing.

'Magistrate, come over here,' Melchior called.

'He'll have to be buried now, and the Council will have to write to his relatives. Well, this is certainly something … Yes, Melchior?' Dorn fell silent and turned his head. The Vicar kneeled next to the corpse and began to pray.

Melchior wiped the coin clean on the grass and showed it to Dorn.

'Look what was stuffed into his mouth.'

'Jesus and Mary, another coin. So it really *was* the Toompea Murderer,' Dorn exclaimed.

'So it seems. But why did he do this to poor Gallenreutter? See, it's not a Gotland ørtug this time; it's a Tallinn artig.'

'An artig, yes. Damnation, Melchior, that is a great deal of money,' Dorn marvelled.

'Clingenstain came from Gotland and had an old Gotland ørtug in his mouth. However, Gallenreutter came from Westphalia ...' Melchior thought out loud.

'Well, yes, but what does this mean then?'

'Damned if I know. Gallenreutter and Clingenstain both hailed from the same region, although ... It's a muddled situation. And one more thing. Gallenreutter has a deep wound near his heart. It appears he was stabbed with a dagger.'

Dorn now stared at Melchior in bewilderment. 'Why did he need to stab him? Are you certain?'

'There is a deep wound to the heart.'

'What? The killer cut off his head and then stuck him with a knife just to make sure?'

'Well, perhaps it could have happened that way around, yes,' Melchior reasoned, 'although it is more likely that first the dagger was thrust into his heart and only then was he beheaded.'

'Actually, yes, that makes sense. But why? Why still chop his head off when a blade was already in his heart?'

'Evidently Gallenreutter would not agree to being deprived of his head while still alive. The murderer therefore dealt his death blow in advance and only then removed the head. He did not have the same problem with Clingenstain, as the Knight was so drunk that the killer didn't have to try very hard. However, I *still* do not comprehend why it was necessary to chop Gallenreutter's head off with an axe, attach it to a tree and leave this coin here for us to speculate over.'

'This murderer is not ungenerous, you have to admit. No doubt he'll tell all on the torturer's rack, why ...' The Magistrate suddenly fell silent and furrowed his brow. 'With an axe? You said "with an axe".'

Melchior nodded. 'The bloody axe is lying there beneath the lilac bush. A court servant could check to see if there are any distinguishing marks on it or whether anyone is aware of its origins. However, I doubt very much that the murderer will have taken it from his own home and then left it lying here.'

'That won't be necessary,' they heard the Vicar said wearily. 'It is the axe from our woodshed. A church servant complained yesterday that it had disappeared. It is usually kept next to the woodpile.'

'Yesterday?' Melchior repeated, amazed. 'Interesting. Poor Gallenreutter's fate had already been decided then, so it wasn't an argument that got out of hand or simple bloodlust.'

'Melchior,' the Magistrate shouted, his eyes bulging. 'Melchior, *this* man was from the town of Warendorf, just like Clingenstain.'

'Yes,' nodded the Apothecary. 'That we know, yes.'

'But do you recall what Gallenreutter said about Warendorf at the Brotherhood of Blackheads?'

'I certainly do,' Melchior replied and tried to call back the memory. 'He said that ...' The words died upon his lips. 'Well, I'll be damned,' he whispered.

'Precisely.' The Magistrate grabbed him by the sleeve and carried on at speed, 'You recall that he told a story about a murder in the town of Warendorf and then mentioned that even when there have not been witnesses to a murder a clever man can always be found who can decipher the clues left by a criminal and find witnesses even when at first it seems as if there is none. And that in this very manner even the most impossible crimes can be solved and the guilty brought to justice.'

'I'll be damned,' Melchior murmured again. 'Everything considered, his words were quite unusual.'

'Maybe they were meant for the ears of the murderer. And why did he feel obliged to say it, eh? Maybe because he *was* that clever man who knew something about the murderer and *was* able to decipher the clues …'

'And the murderer must have been at the Brotherhood of Blackheads,' Melchior concluded. 'I would prefer not to believe this, but you may be right. It is possible he did not yet know the murderer's exact identity, yet he believed that the man was at the beer-tasting and that he had some idea as to who it might be.'

'But, Melchior, it is truly not possible that the murderer could have been there. Every man there was known and of some position in town.'

'Why not?' Melchior replied gruffly. 'Every man who visited Clingenstain on Toompea was also there at the Brotherhood of Blackheads – Casendorpe, Tweffell, Ludke, Kilian, Eckell, Hinricus, Wunbaldus …'

'But, Melchior, none of them could be the Toompea Murderer.' The Magistrate seemed absolutely convinced of this. 'Of course, there were a couple of dozen other merchants and officials there, but they didn't go up to the castle. It's very confusing.'

'And it only gets more confusing. Look what I found in poor Gallenreutter's pocket.'

Melchior drew the bloody piece of parchment from his breast pocket and held it up to Dorn.

The Magistrate squinted. 'There is something written here. Some … some sort of verse. I can't make out what it says.'

'It is in very small handwriting, yes. I don't know what it is, but this is what is written:

'... ined angels will bring our town a protector, higher than us all
... istic death will dance a jig around their names
... n eternal secrecy be affirmed the first's oath of flesh
... umen, of the holy flesh, seven will have part.'

Dorn shook his head. 'Is it some kind of song, or a riddle?'

Melchior shrugged. 'I don't know. I don't understand it.'

'No doubt the Master Mason then constructed poems, too,' Dorn reasoned. 'Or is it some kind of sermon?'

'It is a strange verse, a very strange verse for a builder.' Melchior was about to say more, but he then looked up and from the corner of his eye glimpsed a figure in black approaching. Prior Eckell had appeared from around the side of the church with Brother Hinricus immediately behind him. The Prior approached at speed, although it was obvious, even from a distance, that his infirmity had not passed. He limped and wheezed, and Hinricus seemed poised to catch him if needed.

'Gallenreutter ... Gallenreutter has been killed?' the monk shouted in a tremulous voice as he approached. 'Is it true?'

'Yes, Father. The Toompea Murderer has made the Master Mason of St Olaf's shorter by the length of a head,' Dorn replied and bowed.

The Prior came closer, drew back in shock upon seeing the headless body and crossed himself. Hinricus stood behind him, deathly white, mumbling a prayer.

'By the Lord's will, this was not the only death in Tallinn last night,' Eckell spoke gravely, ashen-faced. His left eye twitched nervously as he looked up from the corpse. 'Magistrate, you have no power within our walls according to canon law, but I request that you accompany us to the monastery. Melchior, you, too, please.'

'Father, is there also ... in the *monastery* ...?' Melchior asked, horrified.

'Brother Wunbaldus,' Eckell replied. 'The Almighty has called him unto his own. I would like you to see him.'

'Brother Wunbaldus? Dead?' Dorn cried. 'Him, too?'

The Prior lowered his eyes and swayed.

Hinricus buttressed him and said, 'He did not come to morning prayers today, nor did he attend to his duties at the brewery. The esteemed Prior held morning mass for the Blackheads, and then we went to search for him. He died wracked by dreadful torments.'

20

The Dominican Monastery
18 May, Early Morning

THE DOMINICANS' black robe serves to remind us that we are all mortal and that everyone is equal in death, Melchior pondered as he stepped once more through the doorway to the monastery. Today it seemed quieter in the courtyard – death had breathed here, and death's breath brings silence and an icy chill. We avoid speaking loudly in the presence of death, as if the Grim Reaper has not yet departed, as if he is searching for his next victim and we might draw attention to ourselves. Perhaps death was lurking right here in the garden of the monastery, in the damp soil beneath the fruit trees, where Brother Wunbaldus used to busy himself; where medicinal herbs and vegetables grew in rows planted straight as rope; where the monk came to pick peppermint and cress to flavour the Dominicans' beer. Death's cloak was shrouding the monastery. One of their own had departed that day, but it had not been a natural departure, this Melchior sensed immediately, although the Prior and Hinricus had been quiet on the subject. There was mourning here but also anxiety blacker than the Dominican cloak, deeper than the knowledge that death will some day come for every one of us. There was something wrong about this passing, otherwise the Prior would not have requested the Magistrate's presence.

They moved in silence. Hinricus opened the creaking door to Wunbaldus's chamber. The Prior crossed himself, and Hinricus lowered his eyes. Dorn looked towards Melchior questioningly then ducked to pass through the low doorway and disappeared into the room. Melchior followed.

Everything in the room was almost as it had been the previous time – relics on the shelf, the half-built wall of the passageway through which a dull light seeped into the chamber, a chair and work desk, a pitcher of water, two beer tankards, a box of chess pieces and a mattress – but today Wunbaldus was lying on the latter. His soul had departed, and this must have happened in the throes of dreadful torments indeed. A stench hung in the room. The Dominicans had not yet washed and cleansed their departed brother.

Wunbaldus's stiffened body was curled up, his rigid fingers clasping at his chest as if he had tried to tear the source of his pain from his body. He lay with his head arched back, pain disfiguring his face, his chest covered in foul matter. Wunbaldus's white tunic … yes, it was blood, stained with brown spots both around his torso and on his sleeves.

Dorn had frozen in front of the corpse in shock.

'He … he's …?' he stammered, unable to finish his sentence.

'From as much as I know about the art of healing,' the Prior spoke in a cracked voice, 'and all Dominicans know a thing or two about that, he died last night not long after evening prayers. I did not see Wunbaldus there, but he had many jobs to do, so we did not search for him yesterday evening. I thought that he would be in his chamber.'

'And here he was, it seems,' Melchior said quietly. 'You realize, of course, that death arrived in a manner that points to some ghastly sickness.'

'As far as I know he was in good health. I am the one here whose soul teeters on the brink.' The Prior nodded to Melchior. He approached the body, squeezed Wunbaldus's joints lightly, forced open his eyelids, opened his mouth, sniffed, unfastened his tunic and inspected his body.

'Heavenly grace, Melchior,' Dorn mumbled.

'Did Wunbaldus complain about dizziness at all yesterday? Did he have any aches and pains?' Melchior enquired.

'No,' the Prior and Hinricus replied in unison. The *cellarius* then bowed and took a small step backwards.

'He did not complain of anything. No one heard him complain,' Eckell continued.

Melchior thought for a moment then said, 'Father, please tell us what he had been doing yesterday.'

'Wunbaldus? Everything that he always did. He was at the brewery in the morning, and I later saw him here in his chamber cleaning the relics while the brothers were reading from the Scriptures. He went to collect alms in the afternoon.'

'Do lay brothers not visit the scriptorium? I understood that Wunbaldus was well acquainted with the Scriptures.'

'Oh yes, he was able to read and write – Tallinn was not his first monastery – but he was merely a lay brother, and according to our rules they perform tasks separate from those of the brothers.'

'Although he knew the holy Scriptures well?'

Eckell did not respond immediately. His tone was hesitant. Melchior waited and attempted to bend the cadaver's stiffened fingers.

'He had a soul that was more attentive than that of many a brother,' the Prior finally replied.

'When did you last see him?'

'Yesterday evening following vespers. He came from the garden and walked towards the lay brothers' dormitory together with Sire Freisinger.'

'And he seemed in good health?'

'He seemed as healthy as ever. He did not look as if he was about to die in great pain. Believe me, I have spent a great deal of time in the company of the sick.'

'And our Sire Blackhead was here with him?'

'Wunbaldus likely assisted him with arranging something at their altar.'

Melchior nodded. Freisinger was a frequent visitor to the monastery. He then touched the Magistrate's wrist, as if to indicate that he now wished to say something of significance.

'Father,' he began, 'did you invite us here because you are unsure whether or not you may bury Wunbaldus in the Dominicans' cemetery ... in sacred soil?'

The chamber went very quiet. Eckell breathed with difficulty while Hinricus stared at the floor.

'I believe that he might have eaten something ... rotten,' the Prior said at last, his voice uncertain. 'However, he ate the very same food as the other lay brothers, and they are all fine.'

'The Almighty's ways are unforeseeable,' Hinricus whispered.

'They certainly are,' Melchior reasoned. 'Father and Magistrate, please come closer. I wish to show you something.'

When the pair stepped forward Melchior lifted up Wunbaldus's bloody habit and said, 'This man died in terrible pain, and that pain churned up his bowels. He vomited and released from his body everything that had collected within him over the course of the day. He died in convulsions, and as he died he was no longer able to swallow the vomit back down. His muscles no longer did his bidding. Yes, a man dies in this way when he has eaten something bad, something that already holds poison within. A man also dies in this way when he has consumed poison.'

Eckell crossed himself, and Hinricus turned away from the corpse.

'Holy indulgence,' Dorn grunted.

'Tell us, please, did none of the lay brothers hear anything?' the Apothecary questioned. 'When a person develops such dreadful pains he usually calls for help.'

Eckell remained silent, and Hinricus slowly shook his head.

Melchior continued, 'Yes, he would call for help – unless he did not want it, if he had brought this bane upon himself. This man did not call for help. He suffered alone in this very chamber until he died. The poison in his body had to be very strong, because death arrived with haste – in about half an hour, I believe. Most likely during compline. A poison as strong as this cannot be ingested from spoiled fish, for example, and if any such food should indeed reach a man's plate then he would have sense enough not to eat it. This man evidently swallowed the poison deliberately.'

The Dominicans already knew this, of course – or at least that is what they believed. No matter how old and frail their infirmarer was even *he* could recognize the effects of poison. All Dominicans are familiar with a few remedies – they have cared for the sick, have visited almshouses and administered confessions to the dying.

'Poison? Melchior, do you wish to say that Brother Wunbaldus consumed poison?' Dorn asked.

'Something very poisonous,' Melchior replied, nodding. '*Which* poison is impossible for me to say with absolute certainty, but I have at home *The Book of Poisons*, written by the greatly esteemed Magister de Ardoyn, and in that book it is written that a person who has ingested a very large dose of white arsenic has an appearance quite similar to this. That same poison, which ...'

The Prior sighed loudly, as if his heart was about to erupt from his breast. His voice trembled, and Melchior noticed that the Prior clasped his own chest while speaking, no doubt instinctively. 'The same poison which was discovered by Albertus Magnus one hundred and fifty years ago,' Eckell finished, his voice cracking.

'And who was, if my memory does not fail me, a Dominican. By the way, Dorn, it is said that arsenic is the poison of choice of high lords in the Papal States and Milan. It is impossible to detect in the human body, as it has no colour, no smell, no taste. It is simply a white powder, similar to flour. And it is deadly.'

'But we don't have that poison here in the monastery,' Hinricus exclaimed, horrified. 'We have no need for it.'

Melchior shrugged and pulled the tunic even further up Wunbaldus's body, revealing his entire chest.

'Look. Wunbaldus's tunic is indeed bloodied, yet there is not one fresh wound on his chest.'

'Unholy demons,' Dorn mumbled, drawing closer towards the corpse, 'that man had been pierced by swords from top to toe.'

'Yes. Whenever a person cannot speak for himself his body might offer many more clues,' Melchior replied. He inspected the body. Hinricus also came closer, but Prior Eckell turned and slumped into a chair and stared into the distance. Melchior turned poor Wunbaldus over on to his stomach with Hinricus's aid. The men saw the ugly, humped mass at the top of his back, looking almost as if some disfigured gnome was waiting to climb out from the man's body. Yet the scars … there were so many scars on the dead monk's body.

'Curses,' Dorn murmured softly. 'It appears that Brother Wunbaldus had been in more than ten battles.'

'If you look closely,' Melchior said, 'then there is an old scar on his back – here on his hump. I would venture to say that a blow from a battle axe injured him so badly that the hump grew as a result.'

'It is a wonder that he was still in one piece.'

'A wonder, true, but it is not the only wonder with this man. He is completely covered in scars, and his body was once healthy and strong, although he grew much thinner in recent years at the monastery. You are looking at the corpse of a soldier, Magistrate, a soldier who died horribly from poisoning.'

'And that wound on his shoulder, it must have been deep,' Dorn affirmed. He looked questioningly towards Hinricus, but the *cellarius* was distracted by voices in the passageway. He shook his head and left the chamber.

Melchior turned his attention back towards the body and traced his finger along the scar on Wunbaldus's hump. 'Deep indeed, so deep that the bones never again grew together properly.' His attention was then caught by something else, and he leaned in to look closer.

'Wait, Magistrate … It is dark in this room, but if I had a fine pair of glasses on my person as does our Master Goldsmith Casendorpe, then … But as far as I can make out it looks as if he has some sort of a mark here at the base of his neck.'

Dorn also looked closer. 'It is on the scar, as if some mark has been branded there – as they do with cattle. One letter looks like an E, and a K …'

Wunbaldus's skin was covered in scars, but it did appear that a mark of some kind had been branded on to his body. Across the letter E ran a deep scar. Melchior shivered. The mark looked almost like an apparition. And then there was what the Magistrate had just said.

'Cattle … of course,' Melchior murmured. 'See here. It's as if the scar cuts straight through the mark, here across the E.'

'It does, but what does it mean? I had no idea that monks were branded. And that's quite a blow he took there. It's a miracle that his soul remained within him.'

'It must have been a miraculous escape indeed – exceptionally miraculous. The poor man lied when he said he had been a hunchback since birth. No doubt he lied of this to you as well, Father?'

Eckell did not at first realize that he was being spoken to. He appeared as if roused suddenly from a dream, staring at Melchior with a faraway look.

'Yes, yes,' he then mumbled quickly. 'No doubt he misled us also ... Poison, you said, Melchior? Arsenic? White arsenic?'

'I cannot swear to that, nor could any doctor, but that would be my surmise. Every apothecary recognizes poisons and their effects.'

Hinricus appeared once more at the door, and, much to Melchior's surprise, he was accompanied by Pastor Rode of the Church of the Holy Ghost, who seemed alarmed and stuttered as he spoke. Hinricus immediately approached the Prior, whispered something into his ear and departed. Rode cast a distraught glance towards the Apothecary and the Magistrate and then noticed Wunbaldus's corpse lying face down behind them.

'Honourable Prior, Magistrate ...' Rode's words stuck in his mouth. Melchior could not remember ever having seen the man so agitated. The man could certainly spit fire and brimstone while preaching, and he could come out with profanities when proclaiming the Lord's mercy on a stomach full of beer, but Rode – barely forty years of age and, although underweight, a strong-willed and loyal servant to the Almighty – was terrified. Prior Eckell raised his eyes, but he remained somewhere distant, away with his thoughts. It seemed he even failed to notice that someone else had entered the room. Rode bowed awkwardly to the Prior and turned back to the corpse. His hands shook.

'I heard that Brother Wunbaldus is ...' he stuttered, searching for words. 'Is this ... is this Wunbaldus? Is he dead?'

Melchior grasped the cadaver by the arm, and with Dorn's help turned the lifeless body back over so that the man's face – frozen in rigor mortis – was towards Rode. The Pastor jumped.

'*He* is Wunbaldus? And that Master Mason of Westphalia as well? They say that the Toompea Murderer …'

Eckell now appeared to becoming out of his dream. He shook himself and stood up. 'What brings you here to our monastery, Pastor?' he asked.

'I came to … I heard that the Lay Brother Wunbaldus had … at night …' Rode was confused. He looked at the corpse and then again at the Prior. It seemed as if he had turned up at the monastery without really knowing precisely why or how.

'Yes, God has called his soul unto himself. We will pray for his salvation.'

'Is there blood?' Rode questioned.

'His cloak is bloody, although, as the Apothecary will confirm, he did not die of wounds –'

Melchior interrupted, 'He certainly did not die of wounds or loss of blood. More scars are found on his body than on that of many a knight's squire, yet these healed years ago. He died from poison.'

'Poison? Did he drink poison? He drank it himself?' Rode let loose a barrage of questions but could not bring himself to step closer to the body. Melchior eyed him attentively. This man was genuinely afraid of something.

'We cannot yet claim this for certain. We do not know any reason why he should have committed such an act,' said the Prior.

'And there is no poison kept here either,' Melchior noted softly.

'May the Lord Christ have mercy on his soul if it occurred in such a way. Father, you must have this wretch dragged by horses across the town to the gallows and hanged,' Rode said.

'Pastor, we do not yet know whether he took the poison himself,' Eckell replied sternly.

'Why should this unfortunate man have deliberately poisoned

himself?' Dorn snapped. 'And, Melchior, why is there so much blood on his habit?'

'Magistrate, I do not *know* why – at least, not just now. The only thing I am certain of is that it cannot be his own blood.'

'It cannot be *his* blood …' Eckell echoed and froze again.

It was an odd scene, Rode staring in terror at the corpse from a distance and the Prior slipping back into his world of heavenly thoughts.

Both of these men know something that I do not, Melchior suddenly realized. Dorn cast him a look. It seemed it was time for them to leave. Melchior nodded to him but first covered the body with a blanket. The living Wunbaldus – known as a brewer of distinction and an devout Dominican – who had he been? In death he presented puzzles and secrets that no one could have guessed at while he was alive.

'Who was Brother Wunbaldus, Father?' Melchior asked gently. 'Judging by his scars he must have been a warrior once.'

'Who was he?' Eckell repeated in a weak voice. 'A penitent. A lost soul.'

Melchior nodded. 'No doubt we all are.'

'According to the Lord's teachings such a soul can always find the right path,' Rode asserted.

'It may already be too late for some,' Melchior suggested.

'No, it was not yet too late for Brother Wunbaldus,' Eckell said in his defence.

'Did you know this man before he came to Tallinn?'

'This man? Did I know him? Yes and no. He came here to repent his sins, and his path of penitence had not yet reached its end.' The Prior looked around the chamber, at the whitewashed limestone walls, and it was as if he spoke to Melchior yet with someone else at the same time, possibly himself, as if thinking out loud, it could never have been completed in all eternity, and he knew this. He was humble and patient. He knew that he would never see the Kingdom of Heaven, but he believed he might come closer to it – only a small step, maybe, but still closer. Although he left a very long stretch of this path untravelled, because some people's lives are too short for such journeys, he nevertheless believed and repented. Did I know this man? Yes and no. God had punished his body but left him with a soul that he so yearned to save. Alas, perhaps this had not been ordained.'

'Did he die without taking confession? Here, alone in this chamber?' Rode said.

'Yes, and that much longer is his path now. Yes, he was in his chamber for the entire evening and died in terrible pain.'

'Why do you ask this, Pastor?' Melchior enquired.

The Pastor appeared to waver then came to a decision. 'This man, Brother Wunbaldus, was not in the monastery the entire evening. He came … he came … to the Church of the Holy Ghost, and …'

'He took confession,' Melchior exclaimed, finishing Rode's statement. This explained the Pastor's sudden appearance at the monastery. 'He went to the Church of the Holy Ghost and asked to take confession.'

'No, no. Impossible. That is impossible,' Eckell cried out.

'Why is it impossible if Sire Rode confirms it? You yourself said no one had looked for him yesterday evening, that you last saw him before mass but not afterwards. He *could* have left the monastery, could he not?'

'Regardless, it not possible that he would have gone to the Church of the Holy Ghost for confession.'

'I do confirm that he visited the church,' Rode stated.

'Wait now. Hold on,' demanded the Magistrate. 'Are you saying that Wunbaldus took confession at the Church of the Holy Ghost, returned to the monastery and then took poison?'

'He did not return immediately, he –'

Rode began to speak, but the Prior raised his hand and shouted, 'That is a secret of the confessional, Sire Rode, a secret of the holy sacrament.' This exclamation seemed to sap his last scrap of strength. The Prior struggled for air, sat upright, clutched at his throat and wheezed. Melchior and Dorn rushed to support him.

Rode shouted, 'The Prior is unwell. Call for help.'

Eckell's speech was restored, however. His brow was dripping with sweat as he rasped, 'I hold power over this – yes – I still do, and I can dismiss you from your post as can the Bishop of Tallinn. And *that I will do,* that I will do … Wunbaldus would never, in all eternity, have allowed his body to be dragged through the mud to the gallows. Never. He saved the lives of three holy men, and all Dominicans are for ever in his debt …'

The Prior's speech was muddled, and if he was trying to make a point then Melchior did not get it. Brother Hinricus dashed into the room together with two other monks and the infirmarer. The men supported the Prior and took him to the infirmary to let blood.

It was time for Melchior and Dorn to leave.

21

Between the Dominican Monastery
and Tallinn Town Hall
18 May, Before Midday

ELCHIOR AND DORN were walking from the monastery towards the market square. The wind had scattered the morning's clouds, and sunshine now warmed the cobblestones. A salty sea breeze scampered through the streets.

'This matter is becoming ever more muddled,' Dorn finally harrumphed glumly.

'This *matter*?' Melchior said.

'Of course. Don't deny it. You are thinking the same as me. It's as if Clingenstain unleashed some sort of killing machine into the town.'

'So you believe that these deaths are …'

'Linked? Certainly. Clingenstain brought a scourge to Tallinn.'

'So it seems.'

'Damned if I understand what is going on here, though,' said Dorn. 'Clingenstain comes and purchases a gold collar, bickers with Tweffell and confesses to the Prior. Then, after confession, someone lops off his head and two days later removes, in the very same manner, the head of that unfortunate master mason, who came from the same town as Clingenstain and who wished to speak to the

Knight about something. Now Wunbaldus is also dead – he was up there that day and might have heard or seen something.'

'You seem very sure about this connection,' Melchior grunted.

'True,' the Magistrate acknowledged. 'If you view the circumstances in this way, then I do indeed have some sort of an idea, but I am unable to tie it all together properly. Is it possible, Melchior, that Clingenstain confessed something to the Prior, which …?' He fell silent and looked directly at his friend.

Melchior shrugged. 'I understand what you say, but we are still missing several tiles from this mosaic, and it is for those that we must search.'

'And then there is Gallenreutter's tale of the clever man. It's like he talked himself into trouble.'

'The murderer set a trap for him the following day,' Melchior said pensively. 'He readied the axe and invited Gallenreutter to come to St Nicholas's in the evening. It is not hard to work out why he chose that place – it is safe from prying eyes. You could ask the town watchmen if they saw anyone around after nine o'clock – although I believe that the killing took place before nine because the murderer is very careful. No one takes a stroll behind St Nicholas's after nine o'clock when it is dark. But there are other hidden places, in courtyards and alongside the wall. After the murder he would have been covered in blood, so he then either cast the bloody clothes aside or, because he did not have to go far to go, he was able to avoid being seen.'

'Of course he would have been covered in blood,' Dorn agreed. 'Although, tell me now, how was it that poor Wunbaldus had so much blood on him if he had no new wounds?'

'One thing comes to mind, Magistrate, but it is not worth rushing to say anything out loud.'

'You wish to say that …'

Melchior touched the Magistrate's sleeve and shook his head. 'No, I do not want to say anything yet. Did you notice that there were two tankards in Wunbaldus's chamber?'

'You think he'd been drinking with someone else?'

'That's possible. Of course, it could have been one of the brothers, but Sire Freisinger also visited the monastery yesterday evening.'

'One of the Blackheads visits the monastery every day, Melchior, as if you didn't know. Freisinger seems not to have anything to do with this, though. He didn't set foot on Toompea that day.'

'He did not. Not that I'm saying that the murderer *has* to be someone who visited Toompea on the day in question. However, we are simply laying the groundwork by finding out who from the town had what to do with Clingenstain, and thus, step by step, we might find our way to the truth. Freisinger could not have been the Knight's killer, if only because he was at the Brotherhood of Blackheads when the murder took place. But the fact that Freisinger unexpectedly spurned the Goldsmith's daughter so soon afterwards makes me want to find out why. And, by the by, did you notice that there was no trace of blood anywhere else in Wunbaldus's chamber? Not on the floor or the walls or on the door or in the passageway but only on Wunbaldus's clothing.'

Dorn nodded. It was one conundrum out of many that had been laid before them.

Melchior continued, 'I believe we should step into the Church of the Holy Ghost for a moment and that we should also speak to the other masons at St Olaf's. That coffin is troubling me. And that scrap of paper I found on Gallenreutter, is it not an odd song to dig out of a mason's pocket?'

Melchior fished out the scrap of parchment and read it aloud again. Dorn listened and shook his head. It wasn't from the Scriptures; it was more like a riddle or a verse.

'Some angels will bring our town a protector, higher than us all,' Melchior spoke. 'A kind of death will dance a jig around their names ... the devil take me, were I only able to read those words that have been covered here by blood. Body affirming an oath ... have you ever heard anything like that before? Seven will have a part of the holy flesh.'

'Muddled and silly,' Dorn reasoned. 'Some kind of heretics' jest.'

'Heretics?' Melchior murmured. 'Interesting.'

'In any case, I am now driven to thirst,' the Magistrate said, 'and hunger is also upon me. I think I'll head for the tavern just outside the Savi Gate and ladle out a sinfully large bowl of sprat soup for myself, because no one cooks it better than the old Kiruna hag there. The beer there is terrible, though ... Our town has been left without its best brewer now that Wunbaldus is gone. Damned demons, where will we find another like him?'

'He was a fantastic brewer,' Melchior said. 'May he rest in peace, and may the brothers pray for his salvation – although they also have their work cut out in keeping their Prior fit and well.'

'What's wrong with him, Melchior? Eckell is quite sick, and it seems to me that not everything is quite right in his mind any more.'

Melchior shook his head gravely. 'He is indeed sick and appears at the end of his strength, but no doubt a bloodletting will help him back on his feet again. It seems to me that he is confused. He is worried about something; something troubles him dreadfully. That much is clear.'

'Which brings me back to the question of what it was the Commander of Gotland confessed to the Prior that has meant people have begun to die,' the Magistrate grumbled.

They stood at the side of the market square, where the everyday hustle and bustle was in full swing. Melchior bade farewell to Dorn, who trotted off to find his sprat soup. He decided to look in the market for the butcher who made the delicious barley sausages he liked, and he would ask Keterlyn to fry them up with sauerkraut for lunch. Yet Melchior's thoughts kept returning to Wunbaldus and Eckell and to the poison that had snuffed out poor Wunbaldus's candle of existence. Wunbaldus's agonized expression in death materialized before him – a face contorted with pain and asphyxiation and disbelief that he had to die in such a way. Why had Eckell called them to the monastery in the first place? The Prior had been shaken; that was certain. Seemingly he wanted a second opinion on what was already clear, that Wunbaldus was poisoned, and he wanted to show the Apothecary and the Magistrate something he did not dare put into words.

22

At the Chessboard
18 May, Mid-Afternoon

T HE TOWN COUNCIL often arranged meetings at the Church of the Holy Ghost, which is why it was also known as the Council Chapel. There was no session on that day, however. The councilmen had been to the church the previous week to decide what to write to the Vogt of Turku and to the trade office in Novgorod, as each accused the other of robbing ships. While it was true that the Victual Brothers had disappeared from the eastern Baltic, it was equally the case that greedy magistrates were likely to appropriate ships that had run aground and blame it on the pirates, whom they would then pursue yet somehow never find. As long as goods are transported by sea they will continue to be plundered.

So the Church of the Holy Ghost was currently empty. Melchior cracked open the squeaky door and stepped into the cool interior. Deacon Holte approached to ask what the Apothecary needed, and his eyes nearly popped out of his head when Melchior told him he wanted to inspect the confessional chair.

'The confessional chair?' the Deacon asked, baffled. 'Does the Sire Apothecary want to confess? He must await Pastor Dorn in that case.'

'No, no,' Melchior replied quickly. 'I merely want to have a quick look. Apparently someone came here to confess quite late last evening?'

'True,' he nodded. 'It was already dark. Who it was, I don't know. Sire Rode was here alone, and I was in the brewery.'

Melchior was then told that no one had confessed so far that day; no one had sat in that chair since the previous evening. Holte directed him to the booth, and he carefully examined the chair, the floor and the walls and grunted in amazement.

'No one has washed anything down in here?' he asked the deacon. 'Bloodstains, for example?'

'Bloodstains?' the poor deacon echoed in surprise. 'There has never been a single bloodstain here. This *is* a confessional chair, Sire Apothecary ...'

Afterwards Melchior walked to St Olaf's Church along Pikk Street, which led towards the harbour. There was a great mass of people at the church and even greater commotion at the southern end of the building behind the churchyard where construction on the new chapel was under way. Rocks had been hauled by wagon from the nearby quarries and wooden beams and boards had been brought to the site; however, the carpenters, masons, diggers, haulers, attendants and other craftsmen had no idea what to do with the materials because the Master Mason's head had been chopped off that morning, and the journeymen were unable to direct them. No doubt the Council would have to employ a new master mason, although it would have to be a brave man who took up such a position when the Toompea Murderer would promptly wield his axe. Melchior pricked up his ears. He overheard a journeyman blacksmith saying something about an old curse that befell every master mason at St Olaf's; one drayman knew of the exact place where one builder of St Olaf's tower fell to his death. Melchior jostled his way through the crowd and inspected the new chapel's foundations. He saw that the ground had been properly excavated around the site, the foundations and posts that once supported the old church had been broken up, loaded and stacked into piles. He finally glimpsed amongst the crowd the journeyman mason who had been present at St Nicholas's that morning. Melchior pulled the boy aside and asked him to point out where the coffin had been dug up. The boy willingly showed him the place. It was on the eastern edge of the old wall where rubble had already been piled high.

'There were bones there, yes,' the boy said, 'and maybe even a skull, too – not that I saw anything all that clearly myself. Someone suggested reburying it elsewhere, but Sire Gallenreutter said he would arrange the matter with the Pastor on his own and took the coffin away.'

After hunting around for some time Melchior managed to find the Pastor of St Olaf's amidst the chaos. The man was fractious and distracted, saying in an irritated voice that Gallenreutter had not shown him any kind of coffin nor told him about any bones, that burials had once been held there, and who knew how many battles had been fought on that soil; bones surfaced every time you put a spade into the ground.

Melchior stopped by the Köismäe stables and exchanged a few words with the stableman who had taken care of Tweffell's horse. The stables were very close to the monastery and had been built recently to take the strain off the old workshop stables at the foot of Toompea. The horses belonging to the town's cavalry and the guilds were kept at Köismäe, and Tweffell had ordered his to be stabled there because it was more peaceful. Two horses had recently broken their legs in the stables at the base of the hill. There was heavy work going on there from morning through dusk – cannons were cast and boards sawn in the workshops – and the merchant moved the horse for its own well-being. The days went by more calmly at Köismäe, said the stableman, and a healthy beast simply dropping dead for no reason had never happened there before. The horse had been in good health in the morning; however, just as if it had been hexed, it suddenly collapsed into spasms, foaming at the mouth, and the stableman took a hammer to its head with the Sire Merchant's permission in order to end its suffering. All the other animals were fine. They had eaten the same hay and drunk the same water but had no troubles at all.

Melchior did not go home immediately. He chatted with the stableman for a while longer, expressing an interest in anything else he might have heard, and as the day went on Melchior could be spotted at several establishments along the town walls where beer was sold; he could be seen stepping into the tanners' workshop, the stonecutters' shops, the cobblers' stands and ropemakers' work-places. He enquired about various goods and chewed the fat about trifling matters until the conversation led to the Toompea Murderer. Oh, there were stories of all sorts. Clingenstain, that high-ranking Knight of the Order, had been chopped into pieces on Toompea; his head, arms and legs sliced clean from his body. He had been hung upside down before his head was removed and driven on to a stake. Or the head had been impaled on a pike or thrown into the mud. And there were plenty of stories of a similar nature concerning what the Toompea Murderer had done with poor Gallenreutter's head. Rumours – yes, they were rumours. Someone knew someone who had heard from someone else who had seen it. Yet all of the rumours agreed on one thing: both of the heads had been removed and then placed somewhere for all to see. The insane Toompea Murderer was loose in the town and searching for his next victims.

When he arrived home he found that Keterlyn had left him copi-ous notes on the day's transactions, and he spent some time adding them to his ledger. Business had been good, but today this would not cheer him up. He drew columns on a piece of paper, entering numbers and shorthand notations about goods between the lines, just as his father had instructed him. He had been taught that there was no point writing things out in full, especially when there was no standard way in which a word should be written. Symbols and signs did the job just as well – and, besides, a stranger, should he happen across the notes, would be less likely to be able to work out what had been written. Everything in the ledger had to tally; money could not simply appear out of nowhere from God's good grace nor could it fall short without leaving a trace. Everything had its own cause, and all events influenced one another. Melchior saw his calculations matching up, and his mood began to lighten. When the recent deaths came to mind, however, his face became darker once again, and he gripped the quill so tightly that it scraped harshly on the paper. Those incidents were an entirely different matter – what had once seemed simple now became complicated, and things that had previously appeared to be absolutely impossible now felt incredibly simple.

Once Melchior had finished he noticed a small bag of chess pieces and a wooden chessboard on the table in the corner of the room. Keterlyn had borrowed the set from their neighbour. Melchior poured himself a beer and unpacked the set. Tracing his fingers over the wooden pieces brought back old memories. His father had taught him what the pieces were – king, queen, bishops, knights, rooks and pawns – and that to win the game one must trap the opponent's king into a position where it will be taken on the next move or all of the other pieces have been taken. Melchior stared at the black and white pieces and was reminded again of the Dominicans' habit – white symbolizing the Lord's grace and black reminding us of our mortality and obligations towards our souls. The Apothecary remembered exactly how the pieces had been positioned on the board at the

Dominican Monastery – not many had been left – and he now set the pieces up in this same way. Who was vanquishing whom? Was white defeating black, or was it the opposite? Wunbaldus the Prior, or the Prior the Lay Brother? Was it not an odd time to be playing chess – in the middle of the day, when both Eckell and Wunbaldus should have been run off their feet? Melchior was so engrossed in the state of the game that he did not notice the proud figure of Clawes Freisinger in his doorway.

'A thousand greetings to you,' Freisinger bellowed – evidently he had been standing there for some time before Melchior had taken notice. 'Is business not being done in the pharmacy today?'

'Sire Freisinger?' Melchior rose. 'Sire Blackhead.'

'I heard sad news, Melchior,' Freisinger spoke in a more serious tone. 'However, it concerns an ailment that medicine from a pharmacy is unlikely to able to counter.' He stepped in.

'Caspar Gallenreutter and Brother Wunbaldus in a single day … Is there anything I can do for the Sire Blackhead?'

'If only you could …' Freisinger sighed. 'I came to look for Kilian, who appears to have vanished. I would like him to be present this evening with his instruments because the minstrels we usually invite have gone off to some manor today along with Councilman Herberstein. Then I thought I would step into the pharmacy for a moment as well …' He broke off, shook his head and said in a tone that sounded as if he were angry with himself, 'Well, no, what tale am I spinning? I am indeed searching for Kilian, although I actually also wanted to hear better news in order to offset the bad. What is going on in Tallinn, Melchior? Has some kind of demented executioner been let loose upon the town?'

'I don't yet know whether I can say anything for certain,' Melchior replied. 'However, you mentioned this evening … Does that mean …?'

Freisinger nodded. 'Yes. At first even I thought that we should perhaps delay the beer-tasting now that the town's best brewer is dead. Nevertheless, the Prior himself sent word that nothing should be cancelled in the name of Wunbaldus's salvation, and everything must carry on as arranged. I was amazed, as you can imagine, because St Olaf's Guild ordered a mass to be said for Master Gallenreutter in the church, and it had all the appearance of a service during a time of plague. However, we cannot allow the Toompea Murderer to chop away at the town's good traditions, and what has been arranged should take place regardless.'

'Agreed,' Melchior murmured.

'I also heard from the monastery that you and the Magistrate went to inspect the body of the unfortunate Wunbaldus this morning. He now lies in the chapel awaiting the Prior's decision. There is word passing around through the monastery that Wunbaldus drank the poison himself. Melchior, do tell. What are we to make of such talk?'

'We should all act according to our best judgement and not hold as true that which has not been proven. We should concentrate on what we know for sure. Sire Freisinger, you were likely the last person to see Wunbaldus alive yesterday, were you not?' Melchior switched tack so abruptly that he surprised even himself. Freisinger might have taken his question as inappropriate, even impolite, but the merchant only nodded seriously; his eyes were crystal clear, and sadness flashed in their depths, the Apothecary noted.

'I do believe I was one of the last. I had matters to conduct at the monastery. Hinricus and I needed to tally our accounts because something had got mixed up somewhere. The Blackheads needed to buy candles for the guild's altar, but both of our calculations spoke a different tongue. We went down to the garden to count the candles, and Wunbaldus was standing right there busying himself with the grain measures, weighing out the correct amount for a new batch of beer.'

'So he had brewing on his mind and not the drinking of poison?'

'Holy heavens, I don't know what was on his mind. We spoke together briefly as we walked from the garden towards the dormitory. I joked about today's tasting and whether he would be greatly saddened if the Blackheads' beer triumphed over the monks', but he simply replied that that would perhaps be heavenly will.'

'Afterwards he took confession at the Church of the Holy Ghost,' said Melchior.

'So I heard – although he was heading off towards his own chamber after we said farewell.'

'And he did not seem to be overly serious or in any way ill?'

'Ill? Certainly not – although his demeanour was always serious. I never once saw him laugh – and our monks are not exactly reclusive souls once they get behind a tankard of beer.'

'Unquestionably.' Melchior nodded. 'One could never say that our Prior does not laugh raucously at times, although he has not done so of late. He appears to be quite sick.'

Freisinger concurred. Prior Eckell had grown more and more frail over the period that the Blackhead had been visiting the monastery. His gaze then fell upon the chessboard.

'Has the Sire Apothecary begun playing chess as well?' he asked. 'I suppose it is becoming ever more popular – I even heard that the Harju vassals play chess instead of rolling dice these days.'

'No, I don't really play,' Melchior answered. 'I was just trying to remember what my father taught me about the game.'

'That I can see,' Freisinger replied and concentrated for a moment on the state of play.

'Can the Sire Blackhead play chess?' Melchior asked.

'A little. Not that I would dare play against the Harju vassals for money, but sometimes I do for fun. Prior Eckell and I have waged a few battles.'

'Ah. Hm. And with Wunbaldus as well?'

'Oh, he was a true master – always routing the Prior,' the merchant spoke absentmindedly and squinted at the chessboard, studying the pieces. 'Now then, Melchior, there is something wrong here. This is a very unusual way for a game to have progressed.'

'How so?'

The merchant explained with enthusiasm. 'Well, first, how have the pawns ended up here? Second, the black pawn will take the white knight here on the next move. White will be left with only his king, queen and two rooks – see, these towers here. The white king will be defeated after a couple of moves, as the queen will not be able to come to his assistance in time – there would be two knights, a rook and a bishop attacking her. The white player's only chance is to bring a rook in to protect the king, but then his queen will most likely fall.'

Melchior stared at the board, and for a moment it was as if human faces had materialized on the black-and-white board in place of the pieces. The carved wooden figures were made human, and he now saw something completely different from Freisinger's explanation – but what exactly this was he did not yet understand. The thought flitted away from him, although for a brief instant it felt real enough for him to seize hold of it.

'That is very interesting,' Melchior murmured. 'Is there no way white can triumph?'

'Triumph? Only if black abandons all plans to win, and if this knight here and this rook and pawn are all sacrificed. Then, perhaps. As it is now white can only hope that the rook protects the king, meaning that the queen will fall and which will merely delay the white king's demise. Black would have to lay down its arms. Best case would be that the white king would remain under the protection of its rooks and without the queen will be left in a position where it can neither win nor lose. However, black would still have to play very foolishly for this to happen.'

'So white will be overpowered …'

'Whether the king submits to check and acknowledges its defeat or is protected by the rooks the queen will fall either way. Neither player would then win. And that would defeat the object of the game – it would be a failed match.'

Melchior studied the positions of the pieces excitedly. Once more, for a brief moment, living souls and faces appeared before him on the table; the key was so close … He recalled his father's words, 'The knight and bishops are weapons – they must be used for attack – pawns, although at first they seem weak and defenceless, may also be strong in attack. Whoever loses his weapons also loses the game.'

'Why did you say that this is such an unusual way for a game to progress?' Melchior asked animatedly.

The merchant shrugged. 'Games typically do not reach this point. White must have played very carelessly, and it would have been wiser to concede earlier and begin a new game. Would you like to start playing chess, Melchior?' It seemed that Freisinger had now lost interest in the topic.

'Possibly. It is said that chess is a metaphor for the natural arrangement of people's lives and of world affairs. And my father wished for me to understand the game, but I'm sorry to say I have forgotten what he taught me.'

'So it may be,' Freisinger nodded. 'However, one occasionally hears in sermons that chess is evil because it has no god and no faith – and nor can it, because a person may not rise to the status of God and start playing with Him as if with a chess piece.'

Melchior blinked rapidly. 'That depends on how you look at it …'

'True,' Freisinger conceded, 'because the holy brothers play it, and, well, it is just a game after all. And we, the Blackheads, enjoy all manner of games and feats of strength.'

The two bade one another good-day, and Melchior promised he would definitely be sampling beer in the Brotherhood of Blackheads' guildhall in a couple of hours, because ritual is ritual and it must be observed. After Freisinger had left the Apothecary immersed himself in the chess game once more. He stared at the board at length, and at last a sorrowful smile mixed with astonishment crept on to his face.

'Oh no,' he said to himself. 'I believe that God and faith *do* exist here. Oh, certainly they do. Oh heavenly grace.'

23

The Guildhall of the
Brotherhood of Blackheads
18 May, Evening

T HERE WERE FEWER present at the Blackheads' guildhall for the second evening of beer-tasting, and those there were more sombre to begin with than they had been two days before. All manner of stories had made their way through the town by this time, including ones claiming Wunbaldus had taken his own life, yet those passing on the rumours only dared speak this from friend to friend or from wife to husband – no doubt it was to do with immoral acts behind the monastery walls; no doubt it was over sin; no doubt it was over money. The Toompea Murderer is stalking through the town and looking to claim his next head; it's impossible that there won't be another victim. The stories going around were many and varied, and quite a number of them had accompanied the men to the guildhall. As time passed, however, the beer flowed and the servants served food, so the conversations perked up somewhat. As host, Freisinger declared the words that he needed to say and that tradition required. Even Prior Eckell, who had been revitalized by bloodletting, responded with the proper phrases, accepting the challenge on behalf of all the monks and permitting those who had gathered there to decide who had brewed the better beer; that all

244

must proclaim and laud this winning brew about the town and not lie about any particular beer's quality. Prior Eckell sat a few paces away from the long table at the place reserved for the guest of honour, and he was served food and drink by his own servant. Commander Spanheim – the second guest of honour – sat in a high chair at the end of the long table wearing a modest black scapular around his shoulders. In front of him were the other Blackheads, foreign naval captains and merchants and other guests, who, like Spanheim, were dressed somewhat less ostentatiously than before.

Melchior listened and observed. He caught fragments of conversations and glances and expressions. One can cloak feelings and genuine thoughts, and when someone is really angry, afraid, full of disdain, haughty or condescending towards someone or something the person will not openly demonstrate this fact. Tone of voice and words, a laugh and compliments – these may all be merely a ruse if one wishes to shroud one's true feelings. A listener cannot always judge a speaker based on his voice. But Melchior fully believed that a stealthily cast glance can say much more than any number of words.

Time passed, and the men became increasingly jovial, no longer fearing that they might accidentally let slip an unseemly word or touch upon an improper subject. When they had all sampled an ample amount of the beer brewed by the Blackheads and lavished it with praise – because it truly was a worthy beer – then they began to speak of Wunbaldus. The Blackheads' beer was good, but it could not compare with Wunbaldus's, that was the general opinion, and no doubt this was helped along by the fact that Wunbaldus was no longer in their company. To announce that Wunbaldus had been defeated by the Blackheads after his death would have seemed an affront to the Lay Brother's memory, and it appeared that Freisinger went along with this, too. Eventually the Commander stood up and proclaimed the words he was required to proclaim and which were expected of him, and everyone shouted back unanimously, and thus the Dominican beer was proclaimed the winner, and an oath was taken that everyone there would praise Wunbaldus's beer for the coming year, acknowledging its superiority over that of the Blackheads – and if anyone did the opposite then he would pay a fine of one mark. With that said, the men further complimented the beer selected by Sire Freisinger and admitted that its taste was not so poor either. The Commander even remarked that it might not be inappropriate if the Blackheads might perhaps have it rolled up the hill to the castle once in a while, especially given that the town's best brewer was now … in another world. The Commander then turned serious, looked at the faces around him all so full of questions and finally said, 'I'll be damned if I can make sense out of any of these rumours. It really can't be true that Wunbaldus drank poison of his own accord …'

A deadly silence fell over the hall for a moment, which was broken by Prior Eckell's rasping voice, saying, 'What is true and what is false is known only to the Almighty.'

'Doubtless,' the Commander agreed without hesitation. 'However, some portion of worldly truth should still become clear to mortals also.'

The Prior's gaze was fixed on the ceiling. His face was pale, although beads of sweat sparkled on his forehead. His tone was cautious, as when the truth can easily be guessed by all but actually saying it is too awful.

'Our brothers trained in the art of medicine inspected Wunbaldus's dead body. They said the very same as Melchior, that a person who dies in such a manner could have ingested poison. However, it might also have been a dreadful, sudden sickness, and that of which he perished is … is a mystery that may never become clear to us.'

Through the rising din Tweffell's husky voice could be heard fulminating that there had been too many deaths and too many riddles over the last few days for a small town. Since there were no councilmen other than Dorn present the men began demanding facts from the Magistrate.

'The Council is hard on his heels, and he will not evade justice for much longer. I spoke to the councilmen just this morning, and –' Dorn began to announce, but was interrupted by the Goldsmith Casendorpe.

'Precisely. You are on his heels, yet he is ahead of you with his sword and axe. Two days ago a Knight of the Order, today a church mason, tomorrow ... Who will it be tomorrow?'

The merchants complained in chorus that soon no one would dare bring their goods to such a town. It was Great Guild Alderman Tweffell who summed up the merchants' fears.

'If the town of Tallinn acquires the reputation that master builders are murdered here then no good can come of it. You must apprehend him quickly or trade will suffer. And when monks start drinking poison ...'

'You should not say such things about Wunbaldus. That pious man would never have taken his own life,' Eckell stated.

'I'm not saying anything of the sort,' Tweffell retorted. 'What I am saying is that if this is indeed so the monastery should make certain that word of this is not spread and that the poor Brother's body still be buried in the Dominican cemetery. We still do fine trade with you, and if the townspeople know that –'

At this point Pastor Rode's voice soared above the other exclamations. He even stood up from the table and declared that Sire Tweffell was blaspheming. The merchants became agitated, and Tweffell, seething, forced himself into a standing position with Ludke's assistance.

'I am only saying that which is good for the town of Tallinn. What is good for the town is good for merchants, and what is good for merchants is also good for the Order, for the townspeople and the church as well.'

'If that man indeed laid hand upon himself then his corpse should be dragged through the town by horses and hanged at the gallows,' Rode shouted.

'Only the Bishop of Tallinn and the Dominican Abbot in Denmark can make such a decree, Sire Rode,' Eckell replied. 'Brother Wunbaldus was a Dominican and not a citizen of the town.'

'However, he was a lay brother, and that is not the same as an ordained Dominican.'

The town's pastors and the Dominicans will always find something to fight about, Melchior mused. He stood up and saw Freisinger do the same.

'Sires, sires,' Freisinger cried out, raising his beer tankard. 'As host I ask that you do not bicker here within our guildhall – we want to avoid arguments and fights. We have not gathered here in order to pass judgement upon anyone.' He looked towards Melchior and added, 'Does the Sire Apothecary wish to say something?'

Melchior took a deep breath, sipped his beer and then addressed Rode. 'Esteemed Sire Rode, I wish to ask whether you know of any reason by which you can claim with conviction that Brother Wunbaldus's corpse may not be buried in the cemetery's blessed soil? If this reason does exist then speak up; if not then let us drink to ratify this so that truth might rise higher than rumour.'

Rode appeared uneasy. He spread his hands and looked around pleadingly, but everyone shouted, demanding a reply.

'Even if I did know …' he said, stammering. 'That is, if I were able, then I …'

'Sire Rode's tongue is bound by the holy secrecy of the confessional,' Prior Eckell declared.

'That is true,' Rode asserted. 'Brother Wunbaldus came to the Church of the Holy Ghost yesterday – that is fact; however, his confession is a secret of the holy sacrament, and I may not speak of it.'

This came as a surprise to most present, even to the Commander, Melchior noted. Yet Eckell then raised his hand, and the uproar slowly subsided.

'You may, Sire Rode, because I free you from your obligation to keep secret the holy sacrament,' the Prior said. 'I may do this under canon law. The abbot of my monastery in Lund has given me this right, and the Bishop of Tallinn is also subject to his word. I free you from your obligation to keep the confession secret.'

'I don't know whether here and now is the proper time and place, Prior?' the Commander exclaimed. 'Sire Blackhead?'

It was unheard of, shocking, that a pastor be freed from keeping the secrecy of the confessional in a guildhall. Melchior noticed Hinricus speedily approach the Prior and whisper in his ear, but the old Dominican merely shook his head. He was agitated and unsettled, but he was certain of his privilege and his rights.

Freisinger called for silence, consulted a pair of Blackheads and finally declared, 'In the name of the Brotherhood of Blackheads, I allow this to be done. And what is more, I demand it. If Wunbaldus can help us find a murderer from beyond the grave, then speak, Sire Rode, speak.'

Rode was still having doubts. He admitted that he was not that familiar with canon law and pointed out that the Council and the Bishop of Tallinn were his superiors.

Dorn reassured him. 'Fear not, Sire Rode. Even I have heard – and I believe that the esteemed Prior may confirm my words – that the secrecy of the confessional is not sacred when the confessor has taken his own life. He then no longer has a right to the divine sacraments. Is this not so?'

'That is true indeed,' the men rumbled in consent.

'Speak, Sire Rode, speak,' Eckell demanded, 'and do it quickly because I must soon ask Hinricus to lead me to our infirmary. Speak and fear not. I free you from secrecy. I hold myself responsible and assure you that God will soon allow light to be shed on the truth, and even you will understand. Speak.'

Rode prayed, and the Commander promised that Tallinn's bishop would confirm everything the Prior had said if needs be. Pastors had been freed of their obligations to secrecy on previous occasions.

A clear sense of relief could be heard in Rode's voice when he at last finished praying, squeezed his wooden cross tightly in his hands and rose with determination. He certainly seemed to doubt whether what he was doing was correct by canon law, but it evidently brought him some relief.

'I will speak, I will speak,' he sighed, and everyone around him fell silent. 'And may all the saints be my witnesses that I do this in the firm belief in the secrecy of the holy sacrament and in the confidence that the man to whom I administered confession yesterday is not worthy of it. Esteemed Commander, Prior, sires, last evening when I was locking the door to the Church of the Holy Ghost a man whom I recognized as the Dominican Lay Brother Wunbaldus stepped into the church. He called to me that he wished to confess and strode quickly towards the confessional bench. He went so quickly that when I caught up with him he was already sitting and saying that his burden of sin was grievous.'

Only the Prior's heavy breathing pierced the quiet. All eyes were fixed on Rode, as if he were about to relay to everyone the Pope's confession.

'He said that he had thrust the Word of God away from him and that greed had driven him to criminal acts. He did not allow me to speak or to question. He said that he had killed two people; he said that he had cut off their heads; he said that one of them was a high-ranked Knight of the Order and the other a master mason –'

Rode's words were buried in shouts of outrage. Everyone leaped up, knocking beer tankards flying, and a pair of mutts scampered out from beneath the table, howling and running to cower in the corner. Only Melchior remained seated as if he had not heard anything surprising, although only the more acutely did he thus observe the others.

The Commander's thunderous and enraged roar drowned out the other men. 'Wunbaldus? It was *Wunbaldus?* The *brewer?*'

Melchior noticed that Eckell wished to say something. He was waving his arms in the air wildly, but no one paid attention. Only Hinricus stood near him, supporting him and attempting to hold him back. However, the old monk ripped himself free of Hinricus's grasp. He wanted to speak, but it was as if his words were caught in his throat.

When Freisinger had succeeded in quietening the men, Rode continued, 'Yes, he said those very words. He said he had killed two men, that he had done what he had to do, although he also knew that these sins had ruined his life. He said he could no longer bear to live – he recognized that he no longer had the right to live. He would not hear me and said that he only had one step left to take. He was to drink from the cup that he had filled with his two murders.'

'Did that filthy miscreant say why he killed Clingenstain?' Spanheim shouted, incandescent with rage.

'No, he did not. He said nothing after stating that a cup of poison now awaited him ...'

A screech cut through Rode's speech. 'You poisoned … It is poison. You …' It was Prior Eckell whose frantic voice silenced everyone.

Hinricus had drawn a couple steps back from the Prior, but Eckell rose up and then almost immediately collapsed. Melchior initially thought that it was hysteria that had knocked him off his feet, although he realized in the next second that it must be something else. Everything happened very quickly and yet in slow motion. Eckell had shrieked these words, leaped up then lurched and collapsed over the long guild table a split second later. He was unable to breathe and tore his tunic open at the front with a flailing motion. He tore something from around his neck that flashed like silver, yanking it with such force that the leather cord snapped. The Prior threw it somewhere, at someone, towards the table. Melchior could not make sense of what was going on. The object fell between the benches.

Hinricus jumped up to support the Prior, but Eckell pulled himself out of his grasp, extended his hand towards the table and croaked, 'You knew. You …'

But there the man's words stopped as his breath reached its end. He fell to the floor, and, as he did so, grabbed at Commander Spanheim, who stood nearest to him. He seized the Commander's black scapular and tore at it like a madman. Everyone jumped to their feet and saw how the old monk – his eyes red with rage, fear, insanity or something else entirely and his face distorted into an anguished grimace – lashed his arms wildly around himself and brandished the Commander's scapular like a cross to drive out an evil spirit. Eckell pulled the cloth down over his head then slumped to the ground.

Melchior bolted to his side and held back the crowding men. He watched as the Prior thrashed and twitched convulsively, gurgling and inhuman groans of pain emerging from his throat as he then doubled over, vomiting and heaving. All his intestines burst forth in an instant, and the life in Eckell's eyes faded. If his eyes had indeed focused on a particular person during his moment of death, Melchior could not determine who.

'Father, Father,' Hinricus cried. Someone roared that the town doctor must be called. Another shouted, 'Poison? What poison?' 'Lord have mercy, he is dying,' someone cried, then suddenly – as if the Archangel Gabriel himself had commanded all to be silent for an instant so that the dying soul could spend its last earthly second in peace – everyone fell silent. They stood and stared at the old man twitching before them, the spark of life already extinguished in his eyes. Eckell's body lived for just one more inhalation of breath, and then out from between his vomit-covered lips slipped a final sigh. Prior Baltazar Eckell could no longer hear this himself, though. The Dominican Prior Baltazar Eckell was dead.

'He is dead. St Catherine and Mother of God, he is dead. Our beloved prior is dead,' Hinricus whispered, falling to his knees beside the body. He wept.

Everyone now grasped this fact.

The men backed away from the corpse haltingly, and only Hinricus remained at the old man's side, praying. Tears streamed down his young face from beneath his closed eyelids. Prior Eckell's dead body lay curled up in a puddle of his own purged innards, his frozen expression containing pain and … anger.

Anger? thought Melchior. Oh, it was anger all right. The Prior had grasped the truth in the final moment of his life, but he had taken it with him to the land of the dead.

'Poisoned,' someone whispered.

Poison? Absolutely. There could be no doubt of that. Melchior heard disquieted, frightened voices whispering around him, 'What did he say about poison?' 'Who poisoned him?' 'What did he actually say?' 'Has he been poisoned?' Everyone drew away from the body. The breath of poison could still be there.

'The Prior said someone poisoned him,' Hinricus said abruptly and loudly. His eyes remained shut and his face was wet with tears. He spoke to everyone at once and to no one at all. 'St Catherine, this truly *cannot be possible*. Then he, he ... grabbed the Commander ...'

'What now?' Spanheim sputtered. 'He fell on to me, he was in his death throes.'

'Yes, but he said that someone had poisoned him.'

'Send for the doctor,' someone shouted again.

But Freisinger's voice then sounded, 'There is nothing more the doctor can do here. Someone should send rather for the Dominicans, who might properly care for the Prior's body.'

The Blackhead pushed his way through the horrified guests and approached the corpse. He kneeled down next to Hinricus.

'Oh, heavenly grace, he believed he had been poisoned. He believed he had been poisoned at the Brotherhood of Blackheads.'

This fact now struck everyone. Poison was a dreadful, stealthy weapon. All knew of it, but people were only poisoned in foreign lands far away and never here in Tallinn. Poison had no place within the *safety* of the town walls. Poison had even less of a right to trespass into the rooms of the Blackheads' guildhall, on to the sacred *Smeckeldach* table, on to the trays filled with tankards of beer and plates groaning with meat. Every townsman present – merchants and masters alike – now stared with open mouths and frightened expressions at the plates and cups from which they had just eaten and drunk.

'He said that someone had poisoned him,' Freisinger echoed gravely. 'Sires, Commander, that is not possible.'

'I must run, I must ... I must take word to the brothers. I must inform them of this awful news, I must ...' Hinricus muttered, rising to his feet.

'Of course. Go, run, monk,' the Commander barked.

Hinricus now began to move quickly. He was suddenly overwhelmed by many thoughts and many words. 'Yes, I must go. To the monastery … Yes, I must tell the almsdealer that the Prior is dead and that he must now give out alms to the townspeople. Yes, I must leave at once …' He drew further away and at a faster pace with every step until he reached the door, by which time he was already running. No one watched him leave. It was Dorn, who, surrounded by the great disorder, finally proposed that someone should also inform the authorities.

'We don't know what message we should take,' Melchior reasoned.

'What do you mean, what message? He's dead, poisoned, just as he himself said,' the Magistrate huffed in bewilderment.

'Yes, but what did he say *precisely*?' The Apothecary's voice was loud enough that the other men fell quiet and pricked up their ears. 'He certainly wanted to speak – he wanted to say many things – but he was unable to get the words out.'

'I heard precisely,' Freisinger said. 'He said, "You poisoned."'

'Yet who did the Prior have in mind? Did he accuse anyone?' Melchior asked. No one replied. Melchior noticed that a few men cast glances towards the Commander, although Spanheim did not see this himself. The Apothecary then cleared a path through the crowd and bent down close to the Prior. His death had not been pretty; it had not been the death of a clergyman. Eckell had departed in fits of torment, and a lump even rose in Melchior's throat when taking in the disfigured body. He leaned over the corpse and inspected it carefully, lightly squeezing the dead man's joints, raising his limp hand, peering at his fingers and fingernails, parting the Prior's hair away from his temples and touching his face, sniffing at his mouth. As the minutes passed, a look of incredulity crept over the Apothecary's expression. Melchior stared at a clump of Eckell's grey hair in his palm, as if he could not believe what he was seeing. Others gathered around him, but no one dared step any closer to the body.

'The Prior believed he had been poisoned, but how could he know this?' Melchior murmured. 'He suffered pains, yet he was an old, sick man and had been no stranger to pain for quite some time. I fear that the monastery infirmarer is not the best bloodletter.'

'You are right, Melchior. How did the Prior work out that he had been poisoned?' Freisinger said suddenly. 'I can swear in the names of all the saints that he cannot have been poisoned. It is simply not possible. I can swear, I can swear that no one in our kitchen has mixed poison into –'

'That would be madness,' shouted one of the servants. 'I bought all of the meat and other foods personally.'

A shocking thought had surfaced in the Blackhead's mind. He walked over to the table at which the Prior had been seated and seized the dead man's beer tankard.

'We all ate the same food and drank the same beer,' he declared. 'It simply cannot be that only the Prior swallowed poison. You see, here is his plate on to which food was served from the same tray as ours. Here is his cup, and the beer is from the same cask.' Freisinger grabbed a bone from the Prior's plate from which the old man had gnawed the softer meat.

'Sire Blackhead, under no circumstance should you try ...' Melchior shouted, but Freisinger had already made up his mind.

'The good name and honour of the Brotherhood of Blackheads are as important to me as the Scriptures. In the name of truth and justice, you are all witnesses.' And with these words Freisinger bit from the shank of meat, drank every last drop of beer from Eckell's tankard to wash it down and stuffed a piece of gravy-soaked bread into his mouth.

Someone shouted out in fear.

'Do not dice with death, Freisinger,' came Tweffell's voice.

Nevertheless, Freisinger stood up and placed the empty tankard upside down on the table.

'You are all witness to the fact that no one is fed poison by the Brotherhood of Blackheads,' he declared. 'You see that the Prior's food was not poisoned, that his beer was not poisoned. I live and breathe, and, if the Lord wills it, I will still breathe tomorrow morning.'

'If that was arsenic, and I believe that it *was* arsenic, then the pains should begin after a few seconds. Arsenic does not take effect in a heartbeat but still with extreme swiftness,' Melchior spoke seriously.

'Arsenic? Arsenic, you say?' came Spanheim's voice.

'Yes, I said arsenic,' Melchior replied. 'I am familiar enough with apothecaries' wisdom to believe that it was arsenic by which Brother Wunbaldus perished and that arsenic also put an end to Prior Eckell's days.'

'Arsenic? That dreadful poison?' Kilian exclaimed.

'Yes. I believe this based on what Magister de Ardoyn wrote in his *Book of Poisons*. The knowledge contained in that book was passed down from the Berbers and the Romans. Every apothecary must recognize poisons, and there is likely no other poison in the world as fearful as arsenic. It has no colour, no scent, no taste. It is not bitter, not sweet, not sour, yet when it has made its way into your veins it causes hellish pain and kills quickly. There are few attributes by which an apothecary can say that a person has swallowed arsenic, and the majority of them – as Magister de Ardoyn writes – are similar to the signs of ordinary food poisoning or cholera. However, when I now look upon the unfortunate Prior's corpse, then –'

'Arsenic or not, here I stand alive and well because there could not have been a speck of arsenic in Prior Eckell's food or drink,'

Freisinger interrupted. 'And whoever says that the Prior was poisoned at the Brotherhood of Blackheads' is a liar.'

'You are a bold man, Freisinger,' grunted the Goldsmith. 'But are you not too bold, perhaps?'

'What in heavens do you see, Melchior?' Dorn asked, ending the exchange.

Melchior slowly raised his head. 'When I observe this body and recall what De Ardoyn wrote about arsenic then I would say with all certainty that this man died of arsenic poisoning. Look here, you can pull his hair out easily; and see, white lines have appeared on his fingernails. These are sure signs that the poison was arsenic, although ...'

'Although what, Melchior?' Dorn pressed.

'Yes, it was arsenic, but there is something odd about it. I do not understand it ... Hair that comes out in clumps, lines there on his fingernails, and then there is everything I know about Prior Eckell's last days. He complained of pains, he had difficulty digesting food, he breathed heavily and was short of breath, he had aching cramps. Sometimes he carried on strange conversations, as if all was not right in his head. These are all the effect of arsenic, but they are symptoms of *long-term* poisoning.'

No one understood what Melchior meant at first. They demanded that he explain, which he did. 'The hair does not start to fall out immediately, not after half an hour. White lines do not appear on a man's fingernails in minutes. De Ardoyn writes that all of these symptoms, along with weakness and pain, show that arsenic has worked its way into the body in small doses over a long period of time, as if he had swallowed a minuscule quantity each day. Arsenic poisons slowly and unnoticeably at first if it is fed to a person regularly, bit by bit over time. It is said that a compressed ball the size of a pea will kill a man quickly, but ... no, that is ridiculous. The light scent of garlic can be detected on the Prior's mouth, which is another characteristic of arsenic, yet ...'

'Has he been poisoned or not, Melchior?' 'What are you trying to say?' the men demanded.

'Oh yes, oh yes – it was arsenic.' Melchior nodded fervently. 'However, the Prior ingested it over some time. He certainly did not drink poison here, today, at the Blackheads' guildhall.'

'And that is as definite as an "amen" in a church,' exclaimed Freisinger. 'You see for yourselves. I am alive.'

'That is true. Just as the bold Sire Blackhead demonstrated to us, his food cannot have been poisoned,' Melchior concurred yet continued to look baffled.

'But how could the Prior have been poisoned then?' Kilian asked.

'It must have happened earlier, perhaps at the monastery?' Dorn suggested.

It was Pastor Rode who now spoke up. 'Wunbaldus. It must have been Wunbaldus who killed the Prior. That murderer ...'

'That is certainly possible, but why then did Wunbaldus only admit to killing two people during confession?' Melchior queried. 'Shouldn't poisoning the Prior have inflicted the greatest torture on his soul if he had elected to take his own life contrary to the Scriptures and to Christian duty? I do not understand it. Furthermore, how could arsenic have been there in the monastery? The Prior assured me that they kept none; the Magistrate heard this also. It is a mystery.'

Commander Spanheim put an end to the Apothecary's reasoning. He brusquely cleared a space for himself at the front of the crowd and announced that the Prior's death might be a mystery but at least they now knew who had killed Clingenstain and the Master Mason. And as soon as the Town Council informed him that Wunbaldus was indeed recognized as the murderer and the golden collar was returned to the Order then all may forget this unfortunate occasion and ask God that such criminals might no longer find their way into a monastery.

The Commander's words reminded Melchior of the Prior's last moments. Eckell had torn open his clothing, he had difficulty breathing, had ripped something from around his neck and thrown it … towards the table. While the other men gathered around the Commander and praised his words Melchior inspected the floor around and underneath the table. He got down on all fours, crawled across the floor and finally found what he was looking for. He held it up for the others to see.

'It looks like something made of silver, maybe in the form of a saint. It was probably choking him, and he broke free of its constraint …' someone suggested.

'Simply some amulet. I've seen many like it,' Kilian added.

'It is indeed made of silver, but it is the work of an ordinary apprentice. Nothing valuable,' Casendorpe remarked.

No one could comprehend Melchior's excitement as he showed them the silver amulet hanging from its leather string. But Melchior knew what it was, just as any apothecary would. Spanheim doubtlessly recognized the object as well, since his expression darkened as Melchior displayed his find. The amulet was in the shape of a small chest that could be opened from the side. Something was engraved on its surface, although the text was worn away. Melchior could make out a few words in Latin – it was apparently a phrase taken from a prayer. Many noblemen and other lords of high status wore such amulets; they were used as protection against evil and sometimes as a defence against poisoning. Items such as powdered dried snake scales or gems were placed into amulets of this kind to protect the wearer. But this did not protect against poisoning because the poison was there inside it. Melchior carefully opened the tiny box. It unlatched more easily than he expected.

'The Prior and I recently spoke about the plague,' Melchior said with passion. 'Prior Eckell said he believed there was a medicine that protected one from plague.'

'Of course,' Kilian exclaimed suddenly. 'I have seen others like it in Milan – the Black Death laid waste to that place terribly. Many in the town wore similar amulets.'

'Yes, and I am amazed that I only recalled this just now,' Melchior responded. 'Quite a number of doctors have written about the phenomenon. If a man wears a silver amulet that holds arsenic around his neck it is supposed to protect against plague.'

'Yes, I think I've heard something of the sort, too,' said the Commander.

The tiny chest contained a white powder. The others backed away from the Apothecary in horror, leaving him standing alone before the body.

'White powder,' Melchior uttered gravely. 'Just as I thought.'

'Yet that was around his neck, was it not?' Spanheim pointed out. 'How then did it penetrate his body?'

Melchior took a deep breath and closed the small box. His hands were shaking. 'Magister de Ardoyn writes that arsenic is such a strong poison that if a person spends sufficient time in its vicinity or inhales the substance then he will surely die. The death will be slow and painful; the man's hair will fall from his head; he will experience pains and addled thinking; and white lines will appear on his fingernails. It was Prior Eckell who poisoned his own body. It was the Prior himself and certainly not Wunbaldus – or whoever that man was.'

24

Melchior's Pharmacy, Rataskaevu Street
18 May, Around Midnight

MELCHIOR COULD NOT sleep that night; too much had happened. His head was spinning; there were too many questions to which he had no answer, which maybe he did not wish to answer. He had seen three violent deaths in a single day, and that was too much even for an apothecary. And perhaps he did not dare to fall asleep. He had managed to drive memories of the curse that had seized him the night before down into the depths of his soul, but the pain still remained. Just when he had secretly begun to hope that the prayers he and Keterlyn had recited might be helping, that the saints had heard his plea, that he was finally free from his bloodline's curse … No, he had not been freed. It had returned crueller than ever before, just as always with each new onslaught. This was known by all Wakenstedes: the curse never gets easier; it will only become more brutal.

Yesterday it had been the pain over his father's death that had tortured him. The time before it was sparked by a realization of his own mortality and over his sins – because he had never received any reassurance that they would ever be absolved. Tomorrow it could be the fear of a dark room – as it had been with his grandfather. The curse would appear in a different guise every time until the sufferer would be driven mad, until he became an inconsolable wretch who could no longer find solace in anything earthly. Over the centuries no amount of new blood, or pilgrimages, or donations to monasteries, or fasts, or confessions, or medicines ... nothing had been able to break its hold. Only an even greater descent into sinfulness could bring relief. *A Wakenstede must marry the right woman.* Only a woman could save the damned man's soul, although she would destroy her own in so doing. At some point, when the man's bouts began to become more frequent and painful, at some point the woman would break and lose the peace within her own soul; she would not be able to bear the strain any longer because for her it would also become more agonizing every time until she would be able to take no more. A loyal, strong Wakenstede wife would die before her husband; a weak wife would get herself to a nunnery because she could not love the man in whose eyes flickered the flames of madness. A Wakenstede man will either destroy his own soul or that of his wife; such is their fate.

The Wakenstedes had studied the art of healing and had been searching for a cure for generations. Alas, as Melchior's father had said, it is impossible to find a cure for an ailment if you don't know the cause, and if his father had ever learned the source then he had not had time to tell his son. The curse had not touched Melchior's father – he had been blessed – but it now troubled his son that much more acutely.

Melchior was now bent over his writing. Set before him on the table was a bottle filled with a concoction prepared according to Master de Ardoyn's instructions. The liquid's colour spoke in a clear tongue of what the deceased Prior Eckell had worn around his neck. It spoke in a clearer tongue than the old tomcat that sometimes padded around the front of the pharmacy and meowed for scraps of food.

Melchior jumped as he heard footsteps approaching from the doorway. He straightened and looked up, worried, at Keterlyn, who stood behind him holding a candle.

'Literacy is a curse to some,' she said softly. 'What are you doing still up so close to midnight? Still toiling away at your star chart? You are not trying to figure out who the Toompea Murderer was any more, are you? It was Wunbaldus – you know that.'

Melchior and Keterlyn had not spoken about the previous night – they never spoke about his episodes – but her eyes became darker after each one.

'Oh yes, yes, it was Wunbaldus, all right. I'd already came to that conclusion some time ago,' Melchior replied, stroking his wife's hand. 'Which does not mean that everything is clear to us concerning *all* of the murders.'

He showed Keterlyn the list he had written about things that left him puzzled, to which he had now added a few more entries.

Gotland coin stuffed into Clingenstain's mouth
Kilian says that Clingenstain wore the golden collar after
   confession
Clawes Freisinger's change of mind
Wunbaldus admitted at confession that he has killed two people
A Tallinn artig was in Gallenreutter's mouth
The Dominicans' habit is black and white
Everything from the northern nave of the church, where the
Blackhead's altar lies, is easily heard in the dormitory

Keterlyn read the list and shrugged.

'There is nothing particularly odd here, not as far as I can see. Wunbaldus confessed to killing two people, and two people have been killed.'

'Yes, that is true,' Melchior chuckled.

'So why are you still puzzled then?'

'Because things don't fit.'

'What things don't fit? Two men have had their heads chopped off. One of them was Clingenstain and the other was that foreign Master Mason from St Olaf's.'

'And he had a Tallinn artig stuffed into his mouth. That's on my list. Why would Wunbaldus have done that?'

'Why would a monk kill a mason building a church? *That* is against all reason. But I really don't understand why you're bothering with all this now; the man admitted to the crimes.'

'Precisely because there is no obvious reason for it,' Melchior exclaimed. 'Even if I do work out why he killed Clingenstain –'

'Wasn't it over that golden collar?'

'No, no.' Melchior waved the comment away. 'Certainly not. That collar was no longer in Clingenstain's chambers when the murderer arrived; it was already in the thief's pocket and on its way to where it rests now. Clingenstain was definitely not killed over the collar, and because of that it is curious that Gallenreutter was killed in the same manner but that a perfectly ordinary Tallinn coin was placed in *his* mouth.'

Keterlyn asked why he was killed in that case. Melchior spoke on. Why do some people kill? They kill from greed, fear, revenge, over money. They kill from treachery. Gallenreutter announced at the Brotherhood of Blackheads that, although an act of murder may not have a single witness, it is possible for a clever man to identify the criminal by interpreting the clues. Did Wunbaldus hear this and fear that Gallenreutter would reveal him as the killer? But why kill at all if the murderer afterwards takes confession, admits to the crime and then takes his own life?

Keterlyn shook her head, perplexed. There were many things that she did not comprehend either, such as why her husband troubled himself with such questions when he had a talent bequeathed by God for mixing medicines, had his own home and a successful business and when he was troubled by such a dreadful curse.

'You asked why people kill,' Melchior continued. 'I will tell you why they kill. They kill out of fear and foolishness. Darling wife, I watch what goes on at our neighbours' every day, and I pray that Sire Tweffell does not accidentally tumble down the stairs or that the troubles of his old age don't induce a stomach sickness that quickly leads him to the grave. I pray that when he dies he will do so in the full view of others and in the manner that old men perish.'

'Heavens have mercy. What are you saying?'

'I speak of that which only the blind do not see. Were old Tweffell to die and Gerdrud to marry Kilian ...'

'What sinful talk is that? Really, Melchior.'

'Kilian would then become a town citizen and inherit most of old Tweffell's assets thus allowing him to become a man of quite some status – and not to mention that he would also gain a young, pretty wife with whom he is already head over heels in love.'

'That's true enough, but would Gerdrud consider marrying Kilian?'

'Tell me, what does she think of then? Does she think of her old crippled husband's stiff limbs and rotting legs while Kilian bats his eyelashes and endlessly woos her with his songs?'

'Gerdrud is a faithful wife,' Keterlyn replied determinedly.

'And Kilian is a very astute young man. He stole a silver spoon from us, by the way, so slyly that I almost didn't spot it.'

'A spoon?' Keterlyn said, amazed.

'Yes, when I knocked them off of the table in feigned clumsiness. He sneakily slipped a spoon up his sleeve while he gathered them up. But Gerdrud? Yes, oh yes, of course she is chaste. What else would

she be? Yet when has chastity ever stopped a woman from considering children and her happiness in life? Old Tweffell – who is a fine
man and has done so much good for the town of Tallinn – simply
married her so that he could make his final days just that bit more
enjoyable. It is no accident that he boards that young relative in his
house. Only a very stupid man would invite Kilian to live under his
roof if he was married to Gerdrud. But Sire Tweffell is not a stupid
man, and he has ordered Ludke to keep an eye on him. And it is for
this reason that I say a small prayer every evening that old Tweffell
not stumble on the stairs by chance and that Kilian and Gerdrud
might have the wit to wait and be patient and humble. Patience is
wisdom's best companion, so said St Augustine. If my intuition does
not deceive me then Tweffell has already written his last will and
testament. However, my dear wife, people do kill over such things.
They have killed before and will kill in the future, regardless of how
innocent and chaste they may appear. Greed and carnal desire have
driven people to bloodshed since biblical times.'

'I cannot allow myself to believe that you think about Gerdrud
and Kilian like that,' Keterlyn whispered.

'I don't *think* anything. I simply watch what's going on. Our
magistrate is a fine man, but he often does not see the details, and he
does not understand people, not in the way that some apothecaries
can. He does not spot things that are right there in front of him –
although he is quite capable of making complicated matters very
simple. It was he, for example, who suggested that Gallenreutter
might have brought about his own demise with his allegory. Wentzel
Dorn is my friend, and I must help him. That is why I sit here and
think.'

'You are thinking about the fact that the Dominicans' habits are
black and white,' Keterlyn stated with a smirk after she had read
through Melchior's list again.

'Yes. I cannot help the feeling that the Dominicans' colours are somehow the key to this entire mystery. White, which symbolizes purity of the soul and the Lord's grace, and black, which stands for the death that awaits us all and reminds us that it is every mortal's duty to be prepared for it. These are also the colours on a chessboard. But what is significant is that, although the Dominicans wear a black cloak, Prior Eckell was not wearing one when he died this evening. Because it was warm he was only in his white tunic. Lay brothers wear almost the same clothing, although they have a black scapular instead of a white one. Aside from that they also wear a white tunic and a black cloak.'

'Everyone knows that, Melchior. It's hardly a secret.'

'Exactly, although our Magistrate hasn't spotted the significance.'

Keterlyn shook her head again slowly. 'Do you not have too many keys and too many riddles?'

'I do indeed. It seems to me that this entire affair is much simpler if viewed from the right angle, although I lack that one correct clue which explains all of the rest.'

'I *still* don't understand you.' Keterlyn gently ruffled her husband's hair and nipped at his ear. Melchior covered her hand with his and continued. Talking things through out loud helped him find the right path through the thicket of his thoughts, although the trail still seemed to lead nowhere.

'Every sound from the northern nave of the Dominican church, where the Blackheads have their altar, is clearly audible in the dormitory. Is this not an interesting fact that our Magistrate has failed to pick up on? That it's obvious that all the various strands of this affair appear to converge on the monastery?'

Keterlyn gave a weak smile. 'Well, then, it should all be quite obvious,' she replied. 'In addition to those things that are already known – that Wunbaldus killed Clingenstain, and because everything from the northern nave is clearly audible in the dormitory then that Master Mason from St Olaf's had his head cut off (and all builders of St Olaf's come to a sticky end), and Prior Eckell died from a poison that he wore in an amulet around his neck – then it *is* all clear, just as you said. But now, my dear husband, your candle is as good as burned out, and …'

She reached over to snuff the candle, but Melchior caught her hand.

'No, wait just a moment now. Hold on.' He pulled Keterlyn down on to his lap and kissed her on the cheek. When his wife turned her head to respond with her lips to his, however, Melchior had already continued speaking. 'That poison … it isn't poison.'

'That poison isn't poison,' Keterlyn echoed wearily.

'Indeed. What should have been poison isn't. The amulet the Prior wore around his neck was supposed to have contained arsenic. Some hold that arsenic protects against the plague. The Prior believed this and wore the amulet because, through experience, he dreaded the plague terribly.'

'But it isn't arsenic?'

'No. I think it's just flour. I did think it was poison at first, and it *should have* been, but it isn't. I gave some to the old tomcat that hangs around out front, and he is still very much alive. I performed a few experiments with the powder in the way that Magister de Ardoyn recommends in his book, because the properties of arsenic are well known. Albertus Magnus solved the puzzle of its nature and passed down a few tips to apothecaries, describing what happens when it is dissolved into a certain liquid and then heated. No, the powder that Prior Eckell wore around his neck was not arsenic. It was flour.'

'Flour? Really? How could the man die from flour?'

'There had been poison in it before. Someone substituted flour for arsenic, and I need to know exactly when that happened.'

Keterlyn thought for a moment then said, 'Melchior, my darling, I *still* do not understand what troubles you so. If Wunbaldus took poison to free himself from the guilt weighing upon his soul after the killings, then it had to be *him*.'

'I thought that, too, and it brings me right back to the fact that everything from the northern nave of the church is clearly audible in Wunbaldus's chamber. Wait, but you said something … something I …' Melchior looked at his wife with excitement in his eyes, taking her head between his hands with affection. He shook his head and squinted. Keterlyn recognized this expression – something was forming in his mind.

'Hang on. What did you just say?' he asked softly. 'Something about all builders of St Olaf's Church coming to sticky ends. Why did you say that?'

'Did I?' Keterlyn sounded surprised, not grasping why Melchior was asking. She thought for a moment and then remembered. 'Oh yes, I did say that. I mean the old myth about St Olaf's Church being cursed. You must know it, too. Not everyone believed it, but people used to say it was true. My father told me about it. Surely you've heard it.'

'I can't remember now. Tell me. It sounds interesting. There's usually a grain of truth in a myth, but whether we can pick out what that might be is another matter.'

'Come on. I will tell you about it in bed, not here.'

Melchior had to convince Keterlyn to stay, and she finally agreed, although her eyelids were heavy and her voice was weary. Her husband's embrace gave her strength, however, and she managed to rouse herself enough to tell him what her father – a Tallinn stone-cutter of Estonian descent – had once told her.

'This is the story of the master who built St Olaf's Church –' Keterlyn began, but her husband interrupted.

'But no one knows who that was, do they?'

'Exactly, and that is just what the legend tells us. And if you interrupt me one more time then I'm straight off to bed and taking you with me … by force, if I must.'

'Then do speak, my wife, speak.'

And Keterlyn spoke. 'It is said that once upon a time, when the town of Tallinn was still new and there were few churches within its walls, it was not well known abroad in the German lands, and merchants had difficulty finding the path to its gates because landmarks that showed the way were few and far between. The Town Council then came up with the idea of building a church consecrated to the Virgin Mary with a tall spire that would be clearly visible from a great distance, one that would have the tallest steeple of any church anywhere in this land or any surrounding lands. There were, of course, those who said that a church must be a house of God, that pride and hubris should not be the emotions that guide the building of a church but rather humility and reverence to the Lord. Yet those who said that it must become the tallest of them all prevailed, and then –'

She felt Melchior start. He reached across the table, scanned his notes and almost shouted, 'Angels. Illumined angels. *Illumined angels will bring our town a protector, higher than us all* … In the name of St Victor, keep talking.'

Keterlyn spoke of how, once the councilmen had decided that this new church must be the very tallest of all, they needed to find a master mason to undertake the job. They looked everywhere, from the surrounding lands and across the sea, and various masters came to Tallinn and laid the foundations and built the walls. But whenever work was attempted on the spire the master mason in charge at that time would have an accident and die. Every single one of them fell to their deaths, one after the other, like apples from a tree. There were many in the town that claimed that this was punishment for arrogance and that a house of God should only be built with a meek soul and a pure heart.

Yet, when hope was beginning to fade that this work would ever be completed, a foreigner arrived in the town and promised to finish the job, but only if no one were ever to find his name out. He would not tell anyone, and it was to remain a secret for all eternity. As long as his name remained a mystery the church he built would stand. But if his name were to be revealed, then cataclysms, fires, plagues and misfortunes would beset the town, the steeple would fall and Tallinn would never become the famous and wealthy town its people wished it to be.

Keterlyn enjoyed telling stories, tales that had been taught her by her parents and many of which dated back to the days when Estonian tribes still ruled the land and which spoke of things that she did not quite comprehend. Many of them would now be regarded as blasphemous. However, Keterlyn also knew the legends that the members of St Olaf's Guild – to which her father had belonged – told when drinking together, and this was one of those. Melchior listened attentively, his body erect and with a curious half-smile on his lips. Keterlyn could not remember any other old tale having had such an effect on her husband before.

'But', she continued, 'what the master also said was that if anyone *were*, despite his warnings, to find his name out regardless then he would not take any money for his work. And so, along with his foreign journeymen, he began to build, and the church spire climbed higher and higher and soon became visible from a great distance; sailors could sight it from a long way out at sea. People often saw the master mason in the company of a stranger wearing an unusual cloak, however, a man as old as clay who spoke with a nasty grating voice, and rumours soon started to spread that since the church builder had the skill to erect a spire as high as that of St Olaf's – in a way that none other could – then he must be in league with the devil. There were also many who, in their greed, believed that the man's name should be revealed in order to avoid paying him his ten binders of gold, and so a spy was sent to infiltrate the foreign builders' camp. But, even after hanging around the masons for several months, he hadn't managed to pick up a single clue. Finally, the spire was completed, and the only thing left for the master to do was place a weathercock on the top, as was customary. At this point the spy finally struck lucky. He overheard a conversation amongst the foreign journeymen, and –'

Melchior started and exclaimed suddenly, 'Yes, *now* I remember. Yes, of course. I've heard a part of this story – in a somewhat different form. The spy overheard that the master mason's name was said to be Olaf, and –'

'If you know that then I have not much more to tell. His name was indeed said to be Olaf, and when a crowd of townspeople started calling out his name while he was placing the weathercock then it was as if Satan himself had pulled the man down by his legs. He fell to his death, just as every master before him. They say a toad and a snake came from Olaf's mouth and that his body turned to dust almost immediately. The journeymen gathered up what was left of him, buried his remains in secret and disappeared, after which the cloaked man was seen one final time, laughing. Nevertheless, St Olaf's is still standing. Anyway, that's the story, Melchior, and if you do not come to bed this instant …'

However, the Apothecary did not allow Keterlyn to blow out the candle. She knew her husband well enough to understand that she was not now going to get what she wanted because the signs of tiredness had disappeared from Melchior's eyes. He started writing again, even more feverishly than before, and there was nothing else Keterlyn could do than to kiss him on the forehead and go to bed alone.

Once Melchior was alone he picked a sheet of paper up from the table and read again what he had written:

Come, for daybreak is nigh and light gleams from the east
oh, my friend, our seven brothers await thee at the crossroads
nonpareil the Lord's temple, to which they'll show ye the way
radial compass and trowels, they hold
aid them to drink the light that glimmers at the grave
their oaths as ancient as Solomon's wisdom
unto the seven masters, their shields extended
solemn Death drapes in his cloak he, who is afore all
Favete linguis et memento mori
relic calls afar for its blood
elegiac yesterday is closer to Christ's blood which floweth down
    the walls.

'An ancient tale, for sure, although all of them have their roots in *something*,' he muttered excitedly. Melchior took up his quill and added:

illumined angels will bring our town a protector, higher than us all

He laid the quill down and sat staring ahead for a moment, astonished.

'Lord have mercy. Saints Cosmas and Catherine, how did I not spot this straight away? The verse is one and the same; the mystery one and the same. I should have … Oh, heavenly mercy.'

There were only three more words to add; three words the first letters of which had been obscured by Gallenreutter's blood. It now made sense. Melchior's hands shook as he filled in the gaps. He read over the riddle once more and poured himself a goblet of strong elixir.

Sadistic death will dance a jig around their names
in eternal secrecy be affirmed the first's oath of flesh
numen lumen, of the holy flesh, seven will have part

Was it really so simple? Did he now know everything? Could he manage to grasp those causes that drive people to murder? Has not enough heavenly grace been given to the world to stop people from allowing madness to be done in their own names?

He drank the stiff drink down to the last drop and peered out of the window and into the street. It was dark, and the town watchmen were nowhere to be seen. He reached a decision. He blew out the candle and walked to the front door. Some matters still had to be arranged, some innocent souls were to be saved, and some just begged to be condemned to eternal damnation. He didn't have to do much – just arrange a single miracle. He just needed to creep over to the well, look for a golden collar that should be there beneath the loose stone at its base and then allow a miracle to take place in the town of Tallinn.

In the morning Melchior would have some matters to attend to at the Dominican Monastery.

25

Rataskaevu Street
19 May, Morning

KETERLYN WAS ALONE in the pharmacy. Sunlight streamed in through the open door and a warm spring breeze caressed the stone walls and floor, driving out the dank and musty air that had been trapped there over the long winter. Keterlyn had just finished cleaning and now set sweets and cakes on the counter while tidying up the mess left after Melchior's late-night meditations. In the morning her husband had not told her what had unsettled him so or why an old wives' tale about St Olaf's Church had seemed so important to him. Melchior had sped out of the house, leaving Keterlyn to handle the pharmacy affairs once more. But Keterlyn could manage by herself – she had learned a small amount of pharmacy wisdom at Melchior's side and was even able to concoct some simpler medicines that did not require the permission of the town doctor – not to mention the fact that her Viru ancestors knew a great deal about medicinal plants, certainly no less than any monastery herbalist. None the less, Keterlyn also knew when to mind her tongue and not irritate her betters with shows of excessive wisdom or arrogance. She just quietly slipped in the odd recommendation now and again, and Melchior probably never even noticed how his wife carried on practising the ancient wisdom of the Viru shamans here in the town.

Keterlyn sat on the doorstep in the sunshine after getting the pharmacy ready for customers. Not many people were passing along Rataskaevu Street; only Kilian was there, sat hunched on the wall of the well just as he was every morning. This morning, however, his face seemed sad and miserable; he had even put his lute down and sat stiffly, as if he had just received terrible news. Maybe he is still depressed over the Prior's dreadful death, thought Keterlyn, but maybe … She recalled what Melchior had said about Tweffell, about his wife and about Kilian and had to admit that, looking at things from a certain perspective, Melchior was probably right.

As Keterlyn mulled this over Mistress Gerdrud stepped out of the house with Ludke at her heels. The young woman waved to Keterlyn, and Keterlyn waved back. Gerdrud then shouted something to Kilian, but the boy took no notice.

Gerdrud shouted again. 'Kilian, good morning. You seem out of sorts, as if the strings on your lute had snapped. Or has something happened to your voice?' The boy turned and bowed to her, but his movements were stiff and formal.

Ludke stepped towards Keterlyn and asked whether the pharmacy was open, as Sire Tweffell urgently needed a salve for his aches.

'Melchior should be back soon,' Keterlyn spoke gaily. 'I am unable to give you the salve right now.'

Ludke seemed worried. 'Master is in great pain,' he mumbled.

'You can stay and wait for Melchior,' Gerdrud said to him. 'No doubt he has business to attend to elsewhere on occasion. I will head off to the market while you wait.'

Ludke seemed even more confused. He stared first at the pharmacy, then at Kilian and Gerdrud and wavered over what to do, looking uncomfortable. Then he grunted, 'But the Master said you're not allowed to go into town alone, that as long as that murderer is on the rampage and that sack of flour who calls himself a magistrate is unable to apprehend him –'

Gerdrud interrupted shrilly, 'Silence yourself, Ludke. Not everything that is said in the privacy of one's home is to be declared loudly in the street.'

'But what am I to do then? The Master is in great pain and needs medicine as soon as possible, and the Mistress is not allowed to walk about town alone.'

'It's not as if war has broken out,' Gerdrud retorted. 'But you're right, medicine is needed soon. Kilian. Hey, Kilian, maybe you could come with me to the market?' she suggested hopefully.

A more vigorous spirit now seemed to enter the boy, as he slowly stood up.

'Yes, I would gladly accompany you,' he returned.

At this Ludke appeared to descend into even greater uncertainty.

'That minstrel?' he sputtered. 'He'd be of no use if he had to protect you. Even a stray cat would get the better of him.'

'Listen here, servant, I have studied swordsmanship in Italy,' Kilian growled, but Gerdrud just laughed radiantly. 'Oh, Ludke, when will you learn that it is not polite to express all of your thoughts out loud,' she exclaimed.

Ludke muttered, no doubt to himself yet loud enough for Keterlyn to hear, 'Mistress has certainly learned this skill very well.'

'What are you going on about now?' Gerdrud put her hands on her hips and spoke in a tone reminding all in range just who the Mistress of Sire Tweffell's household was. 'Sire Mertin also knows very well that a merchant's wife is not to be argued with out in the street in broad daylight – not by the Toompea Murderer or anyone else. So, what will happen is this. You will remain here waiting for Melchior, and Kilian will escort me … if he has no other urgent matters at hand.'

Ludke did not like this, Keterlyn noted, but neither did he dare argue further.

Just as Gerdrud was about to head off towards the market square with the journeyman singer at her side, someone shouted, 'Kilian! Meistersinger! Have you heard the news? A miracle. A miracle has occurred …'

Keterlyn turned her head and saw Birgitta – one of the girls with whom Kilian often passed around the town – hurtling towards them from the direction of Long Hill Gate. She dashed towards them giddily, having nearly run into a couple of master armourers striding towards the stables. Birgitta noticed Gerdrud as she came closer and appeared to falter lightly, although she collected herself again quickly.

'Mistress Gerdrud, good morning to you. I saw, that is I … I saw Kilian in the distance and wished to tell him the news. They say that a genuine miracle has occurred near the Church of the Holy Ghost almshouse. A genuine miracle.'

Keterlyn rose and stepped closer in order to hear better. After all, it was not often that miracles took place in Tallinn.

Birgitta explained breathlessly and gestured wildly. 'It's such a miracle that when I heard the news and then saw Kilian, I thought, well, it's *just* the sort of thing that he might be able to compose a song about in an instant, just as he always does –'

'Well then, tell us about this miracle,' Keterlyn interrupted the girl, growing impatient herself.

'It's that alms-box – you know, where people can donate a penny or whatever. Apparently yesterday evening the chest was completely empty, but this morning it contained the most amazing golden collar you can imagine – the sort that noblemen wear around their necks, beautiful and worth a great deal of money.'

Keterlyn did not fail to notice that Kilian started, supporting himself against the well wall and nearly dropping his lute in the process.

'Collar? A golden collar,' he stammered.

'Exactly. One made of pure, shining gold. If it's sold then the poor almsmen can buy lots of food to eat and more clothing than they will ever need. They say it is a genuine miracle and that either the Holy Ghost or St Victor has allowed this to take place and that a mass of thanksgiving will be held in the Church of the Holy Ghost and that –'

No one seemed to notice Kilian's astonishment.

Gerdrud merely shrugged and broke off the girl's prattling. '*I have never heard of miracles happening just like that. If it is a collar then someone has placed it there, and may the heavens impart heaps of thanks upon the person for having a heart that aches for the poor and the crippled. However, Kilian and I were just about to go to the market. Were we not, Kilian?*'

Gerdrud's final sentence was pronounced in a tone that hushed Birgitta. The young girl bowed to Gerdrud, albeit in a somewhat forced and ostentatious manner. Kilian nodded quickly, and the pair began heading slowly towards Pikk Street while Birgitta ran off. Ludke remained standing stiff and immobile in front of the pharmacy waiting for Melchior.

Keterlyn sat back down on the doorstep and chuckled. She believed in miracles, of course – or, rather, she wanted to believe in them – yet to her knowledge such things only happened far away and a long time ago. The idea that some saint had visited Tallinn and dropped off a gold-encrusted collar for the almshouse ... oh no, that she did not believe, especially given the fact that her husband had slipped away somewhere during the night believing that she had not heard him.

Nevertheless, a gold collar was certainly of more use to an almshouse than around the neck of some Grand Master of the Order, of this Keterlyn had no doubt.

26

The Dominican Monastery
19 May, Mid-Morning

THE BELL OF ST CATHERINE'S CHURCH was tolling in a cold and hollow tone in memory of the Prior when Melchior reached the monastery. Today was once again a day of mourning there, yet one more painful and sorrowful than the day before. The Prior's death meant change and also meant that a detailed explanation of the event would have to be dispatched to the Master of the Dominican Order. Those brothers schooled in medicine had stood discussing the causes of poor Eckell's death while his lifeless body was washed, stitched into a linen sack and taken to the chapel, where mass was to be held for the salvation of his soul. Hinricus told Melchior that the brothers had reached the conclusion that death descended upon the Prior either through spoiled food, old age or a poison that Eckell had inhaled or swallowed in a food or drink. Tallinn's Dominicans would, however, continue to consider what to write to their chapter, Hinricus added. Melchior nodded and returned the Prior's amulet to the brother.

'So this contained poison?' Hinricus asked, taking it into his hands with great caution.

'Oh, there undoubtedly *was* poison inside,' Melchior replied somewhat pointedly, although the young monk did not appear to pick up on his tone. 'I wanted to ask how many of the brothers knew about it.'

'None,' Hinricus replied determinedly. 'I spoke to the brothers this morning. No one had seen it. We are protected from the plague by the head of St Rochus – as Prior Eckell often reminded us – and by living pure and careful lives. I do not know if he had ever spoken to anyone else about it.'

'The head of St Rochus …' the Apothecary echoed. He recalled the shrivelled head in the reliquary that he had glimpsed for a fleeting moment. The power of the saints may well be mighty, but the Prior had also secretly put his trust in something else. Not that he could have been blamed for that, Melchior reasoned. 'No doubt the relic is of help, no doubt at all,' he continued. 'I also understand why the Prior never mentioned his amulet, as he didn't want to undermine the brothers' belief in the relic's miraculous powers. He had witnessed a great deal of plague during his lifetime, and he feared it. Maybe he was right about the arsenic; maybe it does indeed offer protection. Alas, it brought death to the Prior instead …'

Before the monk had a chance to say anything, Melchior asked whether any blood had been spotted around the monastery on the day of Wunbaldus's death.

'No, Melchior, I can say in absolute truth that no blood was found anywhere,' the monk replied. 'Not in the passageway, or in the church, or anywhere else at all. But come, see for yourself. No one has yet cleaned his chamber.'

Hinricus signalled for the Apothecary to follow him. The pair made their way once more towards Wunbaldus's chamber, proceeding along the passageway and across the garden. Hinricus asked several brothers along the way whether they had noticed blood anywhere, but each shook his head and looked surprised at the question.

The building work had not halted despite the Prior's death – men were still hauling shale and limestone towards the southern passageway and carpenters constructing scaffolding. Hinricus explained to Melchior that the monks were outgrowing the monastery and that the church was too small, so it was being enlarged as much as could be while staying within the bounds of the cloister. Alas, if anything in this world is declining in value, then it is human life.

'Very true,' Melchior sighed.

'We cannot currently provide room for as many brothers in the monastery as we need to, so many of us are required to hold down several positions. I was the *cellarius* as well as the chamberlain – and sometimes even the sacristan, because Brother Humbertus, who should do that job, is too old and frail,' explained Hinricus. The Dominican Brother's tall and gangly figure seemed to have become even more stooped. The dark rings around his eyes betrayed the fact that he had not slept much the previous night.

'So the monastery has been even more welcoming to those such as Wunbaldus to whom God has given the skills to excel in a number of different roles?' the Apothecary asked.

'We hoped to balance out the debts that we accumulated in constructing the new passageway through selling Wunbaldus's beer. That is true. Alas, the world is temporal, and the monastery is set within that temporal world. We have to find ways to support ourselves no matter how much we would like simply to preach. I would be much happier passing my days in the scriptorium or giving sermons to the country folk outside the town walls, yet I am obliged to spend most of my time accounting and paying money to master masons.'

'Of course. And, according to what my dear wife has told me, and as I glean from your accent, you are of Estonian descent?'

Hinricus nodded. He opened the door to Wunbaldus's chamber, and the two men stepped into the room where the Lay Brother's tools lay on the table just as they had before. Something here still felt wrong. Hinricus gestured to a chair then sat down himself. He swayed a little. He told Melchior that he was born in Harju, the fourth son of a vassal of Estonian blood. His heart drew him towards preaching and bringing the Word of God to the countryside, because that is what he had been taught to do.

'Harju farmers may trade well with the Order and with Tallinn,' he said, 'but they understand nothing of the Word of the Lord, and the vassals give them far too many rights. I want to preach, but my duties keep me within the monastery walls. I digress, however. You did not come here to speak of this, Melchior.'

Melchior shook his head. He had not asked to be led to Wunbaldus's chamber, but he understood that Hinricus brought him here as it was the only place in the monastery where they could talk in private.

'I am interested in Wunbaldus,' Melchior began. 'I want to know why he killed Clingenstain, who he was, where he came from and when.'

'Of course,' Hinricus replied. 'So I thought. Likely you will want to see our register. I will go to the scriptorium to fetch it.'

Left alone in Wunbaldus's chamber, Melchior looked around the dim room and noticed small puddles of water caught in depressions in the stone floor. Wunbaldus had been washed in this room, but Melchior remembered clearly that only his tunic had been bloody. He spotted something white beneath the rough-hewn table, and when he leaned down for a closer look he discovered it was a box containing the chess pieces the Prior and Wunbaldus had played with. He thought for a moment and then opened the box, carefully selected some pieces and set them on the board in the same arrangement as he had back at the pharmacy when Freisinger had so generously shared his knowledge of the game. Melchior then sat waiting for Hinricus, who appeared after a short time, holding a record book bound in leather and sealed with iron rings under his arm.

'You really should have asked the Prior about Wunbaldus,' he said after taking a seat. 'Prior Eckell was the one who accepted him into the monastery and was his overseer in every matter.' The monk's gaze fell upon the chessboard, but he showed no surprise.

'I just ... out of interest ...' Melchior coughed in an off-hand manner. 'I found these under the table. I imagine a lot of chess is played in the monastery.'

'There certainly is,' Hinricus nodded, 'although I have heard that not all brothers in our Dominican Order approve of the game. Prior Eckell and Wunbaldus played often, though.'

'And yourself?'

'I don't play. Wunbaldus always defeated the Prior. For as long as I can remember they had always played chess, and Wunbaldus always won. As far as I am aware the Prior was always white and could thus make the first move to give him a better chance, but he still lost. The Prior also played by himself sometimes, although he was probably not really playing but just moving the pieces around the board.'

Melchior did everything he could not to betray any reaction to this, tensing his hands into fists under the table while nodding casually.

'As if they were meant to represent living people?' he asked. 'They say that the game of chess can be a reflection of life.'

'Indeed they do. The Prior loved to meditate behind the chessboard when faced with a difficult situation. He would, of course, search for instruction from the Scriptures and holy books, but once in a while he would arrange pieces on the board as if looking for guidance on how to act. But the Prior and Wunbaldus ... I think they had probably known one another somewhere before, although

I don't know where. I remember once overhearing a conversation they were having.' Hinricus spoke in a tired voice. An incident had taken place in the garden. A hinder of salt had apparently tipped over from some height, and Wunbaldus managed to push the Prior out of the way before it landed on top of him. The Prior had thanked the Lay Brother and said he had once again saved the life of a Dominican, that it was the fourth occasion. The Prior mentioned some three brothers – three Dominican brothers – who would have been martyred were it not for Wunbaldus. However, the pair had then noticed the *cellarius,* and Hinricus never heard them speak of it again.

'Indeed,' Melchior mumbled. 'The Prior said something to me about the lives of three holy men having been saved when we were here viewing Wunbaldus's body. I did not understand exactly what he meant. Did Wunbaldus ever mention anything?'

Hinricus smiled slightly apologetically. 'Melchior, we Dominicans have not come into the monastery to speak to one another about our lives nor to preach to one other. We have come to declare the Word of the Lord but not amongst ourselves. Our way of living is quiet. Concerning Wunbaldus, well, it is true that – and I know because I do our accounts – our income has risen since he came. Whether trading herring, selling beer or purchasing grain from the countryside, our monastery has never before had such a successful merchant as Brother Wunbaldus.'

Hinricus opened the large register and leafed through the pages.

'Does that also hold records of where Wunbaldus came from?'

'No … actually it doesn't,' Hinricus murmured, narrowing his eyes and looking more closely at the text. 'It simply says "earlier amongst the brothers in Oxford, England". I was just a novice when he arrived, but I do remember that Wunbaldus got along pretty well with Prior Eckell from the start. The Prior even recorded the reception of Wunbaldus as a lay brother here with his own hand and … something has been scratched out.'

Melchior likewise looked closer. He saw that two words before Wunbaldus's name had been crossed out. '"Receive to our monastery without a trial period Brother —" Hm. Then there are two strike marks and only then comes his name. Did Prior Eckell make this entry?'

'He and none other.'

'Very interesting,' Melchior spoke slowly. 'As if he had not been sure of the brother's name, yet they had met one another before?'

Hinricus shrugged.

'And the Prior was Wunbaldus's overseer?' Melchior persisted.

'Yes. I should probably mention also that no other brother or lay brother was ever so close to the Prior. He even gave Wunbaldus this separate room here where he could work and sleep without interruption. But, as I said, Brother Wunbaldus was of great benefit to our monastery.'

'There is no mention here of how many monasteries he had lived in before.'

'On rare occasions he did allude to monastery life elsewhere, although not in any detail. The other monks and I were under the impression that he had served elsewhere as a lay brother with the Dominicans before coming here. As I now read in this book, that time was in England. However, Prior Eckell alone might have been the only man who knew where he was born and in which other monasteries he had lived. Brother Wunbaldus knew the Scriptures and canon law better than any of our other lay brothers, and perhaps even better than our sacristan.'

'And – or so I understand – he was familiar with medicinal practices, too?'

'He knew them better than our infirmarer, yes indeed.'

They both fell silent, as if the conversation had reached a point where neither wished to put their thoughts into words, and they would have been happier if the topic could just be passed over.

Melchior broke the silence. 'Yet, in spite of all this, the man steps out one day, chops the heads off two people, goes to confess at the Church of the Holy Ghost and then drinks down a cup of poison.'

'Stranger things have happened below the heavens,' Hinricus whispered and closed his eyes for a fleeting moment.

'Has a Dominican brother ever taken confession at the Church of the Holy Ghost before?'

'If any has then we would not know because of the secrecy of the confessional. Although, yes, it is an odd thing to have done.'

'I only knew Wunbaldus in passing, but you lived with him,' Melchior spoke carefully.

'He was a man who wore a lay brother's habit. Not all of us are capable of leaving the secular world once within the monastery walls. However, it always seemed to me that, while some of our brothers have simply ended up amongst the Dominicans, Wunbaldus was here because he *had* to be. He probably felt God's calling more strongly than many. And as regards the killings – if he actually did perform those acts – then once again it would have been because he believed he had to do so.'

'Isn't that what all murderers believe?' Melchior asked sombrely.

'I cannot say for certain; I do not know how the murderer's mind works. However, Wunbaldus was a man with a strong will. He always finished something that he believed was just and necessary. As I said, not all of us are capable of leaving the secular world behind. No matter how strenuously we might strive to do so we may still be accompanied by hatred, jealousy, greed and hubris. Some sin or anger from our old life may remain within each of us, something that a person does not quite wish to alleviate through the Word of the Lord. Dominicans are not required to lock themselves away behind monastery walls. The mundane world should recede, but we still engage with it daily.'

Hinricus's voice had grown louder as he spoke, and he now leaned forward with a flash of passion in his tired eyes. Melchior could not tell at first whether this was meant to be a speech in defence of Wunbaldus or whether he was expressing his own thoughts, his own doubts. Hinricus suddenly fell silent and sat staring directly at Melchior, surprised, as if he could hardly believe he had said so much in one go.

Melchior had grasped some kind of subtext in the monk's discourse that he had perhaps not dared to say more plainly.

'Are you saying that Wunbaldus might have experienced something here in Tallinn, something that drove him to kill? That it might not necessarily be anything to do with his past?'

'Perhaps that is what I indeed thought,' Hinricus replied. 'We Dominicans do not shut ourselves in behind the monastery walls. We go out amongst the people. We preach. We see people's toils and their pain … and cruelty and injustice.'

'Some kind of horrible injustice that had to be put to right … You mean something of that nature could have led Wunbaldus into temptation despite having been such a resolved and determined man?'

'Yet we *do not know* that,' Hinricus exclaimed. 'He found it hard to lose his temper, and if you are wondering whether a woman could have led him into temptation, then no, I would doubt that. Wunbaldus was in the monastery because he *wanted* to be here. He was convinced that this place was the right one for him. Not all brothers – and I speak not only of lay brothers – are as unwavering as he was.'

'But you all spend a great deal of time outside the monastery – and people also change over time, Brother Hinricus.'

'No, not him, not Wunbaldus,' Hinricus remained firm. 'He may have transformed several times over the course of his life, but his final change was the decision to enter the monastery.'

'That is an interesting point,' Melchior remarked, 'and I believe that you are correct. Yet now, Hinricus, may I ask in greater detail how the monastery gates are secured and opened? I know the gate is not locked during the day.'

'It isn't.'

'Anyone may enter and exit without the doorkeeper having to remember a person's face?'

'Johannes, our old doorkeeper, probably doesn't even remember his own name. If you want to know whether Wunbaldus could possibly have slipped out from his chamber to kill Gallenreutter, then yes, and we asked Johannes about it. He just crossed himself and chanted, "Lord have mercy", over and over. In short, Melchior, the Swedish king's entire army could have marched in and out of our gates without him noticing.'

'And everyone knows this?' Melchior continued.

'Yes, as one can imagine, this is hardly a secret. He locked the gates at about the usual time, just as he always does following the evening service and after all the townspeople have left and the monks begin to retire for the night. It was an absolutely ordinary evening in our monastery, Melchior.'

'An ordinary evening,' Melchior pronounced slowly. 'Nothing at all unusual took place? Nothing out of the ordinary with the lay brothers' white habits? None was unaccounted for and no unexplained blood spots on any?'

Hinricus raised his head as if he just heard something surprising. 'Habits? You mean the lay brothers' white tunics? Yes, now you mention it, we couldn't find one of Wunbaldus's tunics this morning. Every lay brother has two so he always has a clean one, and for his burial we had to find … that is, once we've reached a decision on how and where to bury him or what to do with his body …' Hinricus broke off, and Melchior nodded.

'I understand,' he spoke quickly.

'Yes,' Hinricus continued, 'we wanted to dress him in a clean tunic, but it was nowhere to be found. Why do you ask? Or do you know where it is?'

Melchior closed his eyes for a moment to conceal the triumph that would have showed in them. When he reopened them he had regained his composure, and only the corners of his lips quivered slightly as if he were smothering a contented chuckle.

'Where it is?' he echoed. 'I believe that it is not very far from here.' The Apothecary then rose to his feet. 'I thank you from the bottom of my heart, Brother Hinricus, in both my name and that of the Town Council. I believe that you have helped me take a small step closer towards unravelling this entire mystery.'

27

Near Seppade Gate
19 May, Around Noon

MASTER GOLDSMITH CASENDORPE heard news of the miracle at the Church of the Holy Ghost as he was walking near Seppade Gate with his daughter Hedwig. He stopped short and asked the journeyman at the mint, who was announcing the news, just what golden collar he was talking about.

'I know nothing more. All I heard is that a golden collar has appeared in the donations box of the almshouse at the Church of the Holy Ghost. As if St Victor himself had walked past and just dropped it in. The Master Goldsmith should go to the church to see for himself,' the journeyman responded and hurried off.

'I only know of one golden collar that it could be, one that I made with my own hands, and Wunbaldus was said to have pilfered that. So, what golden collar?' Casendorpe roared.

Casendorpe had left his journeymen in charge of the workshop to take a turn or two around the town with his daughter to show everyone that nothing was wrong with Hedwig, that she was a beautiful and desirable young girl – and if anyone dared to suggest that she had been dumped by a Blackhead then that was a shameless lie, and the slanderer should have their tongue ripped out. And at that very moment the Casendorpes ran into Clawes Freisinger.

The Blackhead, who was sporting a new feathered cap, had just come through the gate – no doubt from somewhere behind St Barbara's Chapel or a tavern on Tõnismägi that he often frequented. Upon seeing them Freisinger stopped dead and bowed politely to Casendorpe and to Hedwig, who turned away from him.

'Aha, Sire Blackhead,' the Goldsmith snapped, 'are you busy scouring the town for a new bride?'

'No, Master Casendorpe,' Freisinger replied civilly. 'I have just been to St Barbara's Chapel. As we did not have a chance to speak yesterday following that terrible incident, I am asking you now to accept my apologies.'

'Apologies,' Casendorpe barked.

'Indeed,' Freisinger returned. His voice was steady and clear, but his eyes were sad. He discreetly pointed towards a street that ran in the direction of Karja Gate, past the poorer houses that lined the city wall and which had many yards that were safe from the eyes of passers-by. 'I implore you, Master Casendorpe, please be so kind as to give me a minute of your time.'

A few minutes later, standing between the town wall and a copse of lindens, Freisinger bowed deeply again towards Hedwig and said, 'Please accept my apologies and with them my affirmation that I truly have no plans to marry any time soon. May lightning strike me if I lie and I were to search for a bride in Tallinn or somewhere else. I would never want to force anyone into marriage, but nor can I force myself when I feel I am not yet ready to be a good husband – especially to such a beautiful young woman as you, Hedwig.'

Hedwig sobbed, and Casendorpe said angrily, 'Better that you cease tormenting the girl.'

'I genuinely regard Maiden Hedwig to be the most virtuous and lovely young woman within the town of Tallinn, and I would be the happiest man in the world were I able to offer her my hand

and my heart. But I cannot, in all conscience, coax her into a marriage in which she would be unhappy,' Freisinger replied. His eyes now begged for understanding and forgiveness just as intensely as they had begged for Hedwig's gentle touch just a few days earlier.

The girl could no longer hold back the full flood of her tears, but to cover this she shouted, 'Don't even dare to think that I could have ever been happy as your wife. If I agreed to marry you then it was only out of duty to my father and to my family.'

Freisinger nodded, crestfallen, and addressed the Goldsmith. 'Think back to your youth, Sire Goldsmith. Did you not feel doubt gnawing at your heart when you stepped up to the altar? Did you not ask yourself whether love – as sweet and beautiful as it may seem – requires more for growing into a blissful marriage than you could offer at that moment? Did you not say to yourself, "Yes, I do indeed love this girl, but am I able to be a good husband to her, the kind that she truly deserves?" I asked myself exactly that, and I replied, after looking deep into my heart, "Not yet." I am not yet worthy of your daughter Hedwig, who is too virtuous in her youth, in her gentleness and innocence, to be a companion to a man such as myself.'

'In other words,' Casendorpe spat angrily, 'you do not wish to give up the life and freedoms of a Blackhead, which many a pastor would call –'

'In other words, I wish to remain true to myself, to my friends and to the young maiden, whom I truly love. I am honest enough not to want to make her – or her family – unhappy. I wanted to tell you all this yesterday evening, to thank you, after what had happened, for still accepting the invitation to the Brotherhood of Blackheads and for honouring us with your presence. I would have said every word of this yesterday had Prior Eckell's horrific death not taken place.'

Hedwig truly could not hold back her tears any longer. She clung to her father's sleeve and cried, 'If you have the heart to admit that you love me, then where is this show of honesty towards yourself if you wish to marry someone else?'

'I assure you again that nothing would make me happier than to find the courage within myself, right here and right now, to fall down on one knee before you and offer you my hand and my heart,' Freisinger said softly. 'I genuinely ask your forgiveness, Hedwig. I do not know any young woman in all of Livonia worthier than you, and I appeal to all the saints that they guide you to a suitor who is worthy of you.'

'I ... I, on the other hand, would rather become the wife of some journeyman tanner before I would ever become yours.'

'Whatever makes you happy, dear maiden,' Freisinger said despairingly.

'Don't talk rubbish, girl,' Casendorpe reprimanded. 'In any case, it is time for us to leave. I had not planned on wasting my time with you, Freisinger.'

'I, on the other hand, am very glad that we met,' said the Blackhead, 'for my soul aches, and I ask forgiveness for everything that I might have allowed to transpire in my carelessness. Farewell, Maiden Hedwig. I beg you to find room for me in your prayers, just as I shall for you, now and for ever.'

They went their separate ways. On reaching Kuninga Street Casendorpe encountered a Court servant who had had been looking for him. The servant brought a message from Magistrate Dorn. The Magistrate had requested that a number of esteemed citizens of Tallinn come to his official chambers that evening, men who were able to provide testimony regarding the dreadful murders and who had been authorized by the Tallinn Council to decide whether the town's obligation to deliver the murderer to Toompea's authority had been fulfilled. As such, Sire Dorn had the honour of requesting Sire Casendorpe, as the Alderman of St Canute's Guild, be amongst these men.

Casendorpe said that he would certainly attend. A very odd request, indeed, he thought. He believed, however, that the invitation came from Melchior rather than the Magistrate.

28

Mertin Tweffell's House, Rataskaevu Street
19 May, Afternoon

GREAT GUILD ALDERMAN MERTIN TWEFFELL was secure in the knowledge that he could regard himself as one of the wealthiest men in Tallinn. Whether or not this wealth – or rather the donations to churches and the masses paid for with it – had been enough would become clear when he departed this world in the not-too-distant future. There was no doubt in his mind that this would be soon. He felt his vitality gradually leaving his body, his organs falling one after another like soldiers on a battlefield, his soul preparing to depart its aged vessel. He reassured himself that he was an honest Christian, although he was perfectly well aware that he had seen faith just as another trade deal, as a contract. It was only in recent months that he had begun to doubt whether or not his own end of this bargain had been met as diligently as it should have been. He realized that had he attended church more regularly, given larger donations, paid closer attention to sermons, searched for signs that everything was still right with his contract and that the goods would be delivered, that he would enter Heaven. When he spoke with clergymen about this matter they talked of the dangers that lie in wait for all men at the point of death. They told Tweffell that he should not be too proud or arrogant, that he must be humble and patient, that he must hope. Impatience is a temptation, and it is Satan's trick for leading a man off the righteous path of death.

Tweffell had not been satisfied with their words. He was really interested solely in conducting his worldly affairs in peace and knowing that he no longer need worry about Heaven, that his provisions had been noted and the contract fulfilled by all parties. Mertin Tweffell still had a few matters to set right in the world, and this entitlement – to recognize good and evil and to act accordingly – had been given, he was absolutely convinced, to man by God along with a sense of reason.

A court servant had come calling around noon and informed him of the Magistrate's desire that the merchant appear at his official chambers before evening. Tweffell considered briefly whether or not to go to speak of this with the Town Council; however, he decided there was little point in doing so. He had nothing to fear from the Council – the members of the Council were almost all also members of the Great Guild, and he would have received word if his neighbour Melchior had figured something out, something important.

Mertin Tweffell sat in the rear chamber of his house, and, although the weather was clement, he had ordered Ludke to heat up his foot warmer. His old body required extra heat – and he always came up with his best ideas when in a warmer place. The merchant ordered Ludke to bring him a bottle of spiced wine along with a holy book about the life of a saint. He then also requested a sermon inscribed upon a scroll, which he had purchased from St Nicholas's Church and which had been blessed. And, finally, Ludke was to bring him a crucifix.

When he noticed the shocked expression on the boy's face Tweffell added with a chuckle, 'Don't imagine for a second that I'm about to drop dead, you dog. These are meant for you.'

Tweffell then commanded Ludke to tell him where the other members of the household were at that moment. Mistress Gerdrud was in the kitchen preparing supper, the old maid was doing the laundry in the courtyard and Kilian, when last heard of, had been hanging about in a garden near Karja Gate strumming his lute.

'Ah, so,' Tweffell said, drumming his fingers on the tabletop, 'very good. Now, Ludke, tell me. Do you know what it means to swear in the names of all the saints?'

'It is very sacred and important, and one must not swear to a lie or else the saints will punish you,' the boy responded quickly. If Ludke was uneasy he managed to hide the emotion behind his expressionless face. He did not fool Tweffell with this act, of course, otherwise the old man would never have employed the boy as his servant. A sharp intelligence was hidden behind the boy's dim-witted, rough appearance. Curses, the mutt even played chess better than Tweffell.

'Now, tell me whether you understand what it means to lie to your master,' Tweffell continued.

Ludke cast his eyes to the side and recited, 'It is a much worse thing than swearing to a lie in the names of all the saints. It is the worst thing that a servant can do because it will be the last lie of his life.'

'Precisely so. Now, place one hand on this holy book and the other on the crucifix and lean closer to me.'

Ludke did as he was commanded, but as he bent his face to within reach of Tweffell's hands the old man suddenly grabbed the boy by his jaw with his long, stiff fingers, squeezing so hard that his fingernails broke through Ludke's skin and a sharp pain shot through the boy's body.

'Listen to me now,' hissed the old man. 'I want to impart a few words of wisdom because, Lord knows, I believe you need to hear them. Listen carefully now. I am already an old man and am not long for this world. So that things that I have regarded as fair might remain so after my death I have set you a number of tasks that I believe you have fulfilled to the letter. However, if I ever find out that you have lied to me, Ludke, then you will be driven out of Tallinn and forbidden ever to step foot within its walls again – ever. You will continue to live, yet it will be the life of a blind, dumb cripple who must beg, rolling in the mud outside the taverns, for alms with the single remaining hand that he has left. So … You already know this, of course. But now, slave, you will swear to me in the names of all the saints, and your own salvation as well, that everything you told me about Toompea was the truth and nothing but the truth, otherwise you will find yourself a blind and crippled mute, Ludke.'

He released the boy's face from his grip and took a sip of wine. Ludke appeared to consider for a moment how best to hold both the holy book and the crucifix, then placed the book on the table, set his right hand on top and extended his left hand in which he held the crucifix.

'I swear in the names of all the saints,' he said, even, despite the gravity of the situation, managing somehow to maintain an air of dissociation, 'that it was all the truth and nothing but the truth, and not one single word was false. Everything that I told you I witnessed with my own eyes.'

Tweffell stared at Ludke, burrowed into the boy's eyes with his owl's gaze and concluded that it probably had to be the truth. He had witnessed much duplicity and falsehood during his years as a merchant.

'So the whole thing was true, that you remained on Toompea to keep an eye on Kilian after I left?'

'The Almighty's truth.' The boy nodded.

'And you saw him singing and drinking with the Order attendants?'

'With my own eyes.'

'And you saw that …'

'I saw that he was left there alone, and he slipped into the house where that knight was staying and came out again very soon after, went back to the churchyard and carried on singing to the attendants.'

'And afterwards?'

'Afterwards I followed carefully so no one saw me when he started walking down to the town, and I saw with my own eyes that he came to the side of the well here near our house and hid something behind a loose stone at its base. And he believed that no one saw him.'

'And *after* that?' Tweffell demanded.

'After that I did everything precisely as I was commanded – and Master himself knows that this command was fulfilled.'

'Yes, *that* I certainly know now,' Tweffell said. 'That we may know for a fact because matters are indeed as they stand and justice has been done. However …'

He lapsed into thought as Ludke remained standing before him with one hand on the book and the other holding the crucifix. Tweffell meditated deeply, his brow furrowed. Kilian had some of the blood of his lineage, and that was important. Kilian was family, and family mattered just as much as guild. Kilian was of his own blood, which must inherit that to which it is entitled. Yet Kilian had fallen into temptation. He was sick, and this sickness was dangerous to the blood; it could bring everything down some day. Tweffell must speak to him – the boy was still young, he could change. However … Seemingly someone else knows.

Tweffell did not believe in miracles – even if he did, then not in the kind that take place during the final months of his life and right underneath his front window and definitely not those that, in truth, were almost certainly performed by mere mortals.

Someone else knows, he thought, and he was suddenly afraid. All the plans that Mertin Tweffell had carefully laid for this world following his death could be ruined. What else might this unknown person know? Did he know the whole truth?

29

The Tallinn Magistrate's Official Chambers Alongside Town Hall Square
19 May, Evening

IT HAD NOT BEEN difficult for Melchior to convince the Magistrate that things in the town had been carried out in this manner before and that Lübeck law also stipulated, for bigger cases, that counsel may be held with the town's esteemed citizens before the councilmen convene to hold a trial and make their ruling. The Town Magistrate was, in fact, permitted to hold a trial wherever he chose, so long as he carried his livery collar and his sword, and the investigation had not yet reached a point at which someone could be charged with a crime or the councilmen were in a position to demand that the accused be put to the test by torture or ordeal.

'Therefore,' Melchior continued, addressing Dorn, 'it would be beneficial if we call together – in the old Saxon tradition – all those who might know something about the case. It is a complicated matter and at the same time all very simple, and the advice of those wiser than I is needed here on how to act in the town's best interests. The presence of one councilman and the Council Secretary is required because whatever is said with a councilman listening bears greater weight – and if a councilman and magistrate have both witnessed something then their combined word counts the most of all according to Lübeck law.'

'And what should Councilman and Magistrate witness?' Dorn enquired.

'They should witness how the truth rises and falsehood dissipates. *No one has actually lied at all* in this case, if you look at things from a certain perspective – at least neither to the Magistrate nor to me – with the exception of one man, but we can count him out of this whole affair anyway.'

Dorn stared, puzzled, at Melchior for quite some time, then finally said, 'In the names of all the saints, you are hatching something clever here. I agree. There have been too many deaths, and there is no clear end in sight. Why did Wunbaldus need to dispatch that mason, and why did the Prior believe someone had poisoned him?'

'I believe I know why,' Melchior replied, 'but my knowledge falls short on proof. If I go before a Council Court trial and bear witness with what I have now then I would be laughed out of the hall.' He sunk into his thoughts for a moment, but then, as if an unexpected idea had just occurred to him, he added excitedly, 'You know, it is as if we are part of a game of chess. The enemy believes he is carefully protected and that nothing can threaten him, but we must lure him into a trap using our cunning, even if we have to sacrifice a few pieces in doing so. Then we must make an unexpected attack so that his king will find itself in checkmate.'

'I didn't know you played chess,' Dorn remarked with surprise.

'I am learning now,' Melchior replied cheerfully. 'Chess provided me with the key to this case – or, rather, the way that Sire Freisinger explained the game to me did.'

'I don't really enjoy it,' Dorn grumbled. 'Give me a set of dice, and I will play, but chess, no. Every piece moves differently, and it's just one big mess. But wait …' He grabbed Melchior's arm and eyed him seriously.

'You said "enemy". Do we still have an enemy?'

'Yes, and a very dangerous one,' Melchior affirmed. 'He has played very cleverly, so cleverly that we have not even realized which opponent we are playing against. But if you can picture the right faces on the chess pieces then it will all become clear. By the way, did I mention that we need the Commander to attend?'

'The Commander? So this will be some sort of joint consultation between the town and the Order?'

'The Commander must be present, no question, as must Hinricus to represent the monks. Oh, and quite a number of other people who are not exactly town citizens but without whom we cannot make this work.'

Melchior reeled off the names, and court servants hunted these individuals down during the course of the afternoon. So, as the soft May evening fell, a crowd gathered at the west end of Town Hall Square near the Magistrate's official chambers, including every man who had witnessed the Prior's death during the last *Smeckeldach* at the Brotherhood of Blackheads as well as Great Guild Alderman Mertin Tweffell's servant Ludke, the almsman Rinus Götzer, two canons of Toompea, the Vicar of St Nicholas's Church, a mason from St Olaf's Guild, three court servants, the Council Secretary and, last but not least, Councilman Detleff Bockhorst.

Dorn's chambers were located in a spacious rear room on the ground floor of a two-storey house. Long benches ringed the walls of the room, and a speakers' podium painted with the town's crest was set in the middle of the room. Seats for the guests of honour – on this evening the Councilman and the Commander – were placed either side of the Magistrate. Magistrate Dorn usually conducted trials here when the crimes were of lesser importance and it was unnecessary to convene the Council.

Several of the men whispered amongst themselves, asking what sort of odd consultation was to be held when there was no one to try because the murderer was already dead and no one else had been accused of his poisoning. The assembled men cast furtive glances towards both the Magistrate and the Councilman – while Dorn did his best to give the impression that he knew precisely what was going on.

After words of greeting had been offered to the Commander on behalf of the town and Councilman Bockhorst had declared loudly that the deliberations might begin Dorn stood up and declared, albeit ramblingly, 'Yes, so it is, exactly, that if we wish to reach any conclusions in this case at Council Court trial, in truth and spirit and according to Lübeck law – and may God help us in this quest – then the Town Council found that I, as Magistrate, will, here today, discuss, in the company of esteemed sires and the honourable Commander – as these deaths concern the town, the Dominicans *and* the Order – so that in truth and spirit we might indeed discover just who we will take before any such court and so harm may not befall the merchants, or the Blackheads, or the Dominicans by way of those matters of which none of them are guilty ...'

The Magistrate ran out of steam and began to leaf through a fat book of town laws in order to conceal that fact. Melchior looked around the room at those assembled. About twenty men were in the room together with the Council Secretary, the court servants and two Toompea sires. Each displayed an expression of moderate deference and seemed anxious and ready to assist – as was indeed proper under the circumstances – and the man whom Melchior believed to be the killer was no exception. That man's countenance was pure and clear, somewhat humble and untroubled. He believed he had nothing to fear.

When Dorn had finished the Commander spoke, announcing that the Order expected the town to hand over the murderer. 'And if he is deceased, just as we all know that he is, then you may as well hand over his corpse.'

'Undoubtedly, undoubtedly,' the Magistrate affirmed. 'He who is guilty is the man whose corpse we will pass over to the Order. The esteemed Commander is correct, and this is the perfect point at which to begin our council. So, what shall we do with Lay Brother Wunbaldus's body, and should the Council Court recognize him as the murderer?'

'*Naturally* the court should do this, because we all are aware that he killed Clingenstain and that master mason and … himself, to top it all off,' the Commander bellowed, and the Toompea canons nodded self-importantly.

'Let it now be said', Dorn continued, 'that Tallinn Apothecary Melchior Wakenstede, who for the past few days has temporarily served as submagistrate by approval of the honourable councilmen, wishes, in the name of truth and justice, to say a few words about matters that have become apparent to him. He will do this now.'

Melchior rose and slowly walked towards the podium. He felt curious eyes upon him and prayed to himself that St Nicholas give him courage, vigour and luck. A muttering swept through the gathered men, and Sire Tweffell sputtered somewhat crossly.

Melchior cleared his throat and spoke. 'Esteemed Commander, canons of Toompea, honourable Magistrate, good citizens. We believe that the Dominican Lay Brother Wunbaldus killed Clingenstain, a Knight of the Teutonic Order, and Master Mason Gallenreutter. However, do we know *why* he did so? Do we wish for the high lords of the Order to know the full truth, or is the town satisfied with allowing the Order simply to hang Wunbaldus's body and the facts concerning why and how to remain unknown?'

The Commander waved his hand dismissively and bellowed, 'In the name of the Almighty, Melchior, if you know something then tell us.'

Councilman Bockhorst added, 'In the name of the Council Court and by authority of the Council, if our town apothecary Melchior Wakenstede – whom you all know – wishes to swear to the court in the names of all the saints that he knows the answers to these questions then we request that he speak.'

'I will speak,' Melchior replied. 'But first I will ask how many murders have occurred, how many suicides and how many accidents. Do we have two murders, one suicide and one unfortunate death or … or do we have four murders?'

The sounds of surprise filled the room, and Pastor Rode jumped to his feet, waving his hands and exclaiming, 'Melchior, heavenly grace. That scoundrel, that lay brother admitted to everything.'

'Oh yes, that confession at the Church of the Holy Ghost. I will get to that very soon,' Melchior replied and waited for the Councilman to quieten the men. 'Yet if we are to begin from the very beginning, just as St Augustine recommends, let us start by discussing the events step by step. Four days ago someone killed the Commander of the Teutonic Order of Gotland on Toompea. He was travelling to Marienburg and spent some time as a guest in the Tallinn Commander's castle. It is safe to assume that this murderer must have been a strong and vigorous man, a daring man, a warrior, and who had a rage and a hatred for Clingenstain simmering inside and who had undoubtedly encountered the Knight before. This man must have known Toompea well, and his appearance there did not arouse suspicion. He must have had time to find out where Clingenstain was lodging and the route the Knight took there from the castle. He must have had time to steal a sword from the castle smithy. We also know, through the esteemed Commander's statements, that this man could not have been anyone from Toompea. Therefore, this man stalked Clingenstain near his lodgings then boldly entered the house and chopped off his head.'

Melchior fell silent for a moment and almost enjoyed the rapt attention of his audience. Then he continued, 'Just as I have, you will all have heard any number of rumours about the murder. Some said that he was chopped into pieces, that his arms and legs were ripped from their sockets and what have you. Although the Commander forbade anyone from gossiping about how the murderer had desecrated Clingenstain's corpse, one or two facts nevertheless emerged. No doubt someone let something slip, a servant passed word on to an attendant, the attendant to a baker's journeyman and so forth. But not one of the early rumours *said that the Knight's head had been driven on to a hook*. The honourable Commander himself only mentioned this at the Blackheads' beer-tasting, and it spread throughout the entire town afterwards, and with extraordinary speed, given that the Commander referenced it not to the entire company but during the course of a conversation and then only in passing.'

'Curses, did I really do that?' the Commander asked, looking a little sheepish.

'I believe that quite a few men overheard it,' Melchior replied. 'However, there is one fact that *not one rumour mentioned* – and about which the Commander ordered everyone privy to hold their tongues, but which, despite this, an Order attendant gossiped to the Magistrate – and this was the fact that the killer had stuffed a coin into Clingenstain's mouth …'

Someone shouted unintelligibly, and then a deathly quiet gripped the room.

'I see from your faces that this comes as a surprise and only a few people were aware of it. This coin was an old Gotland ørtug, one that rarely circulates in Tallinn today, and this is a very important detail –'

'Hold on now, Melchior,' the Commander cut in. 'It is not impossible that I might have said something about his head being driven on to a stake when beer clouded my brain, but what are you suggesting when you say that word of this spread with extraordinary speed?'

'That someone spread it on purpose,' Melchior replied, 'although I will come to that later. Let us now return to Clingenstain's murder. We know that the killer escaped and managed to slip through the gate between Toompea and the town at just the right moment before the town watchmen came to lock it for the night. The killer threw aside the sword that he had stolen from Toompea *after* he passed through the gate. Why did he do that? Why did he carry the sword with him at all? I believe because if he had been discovered then he would have defended himself with the weapon, which means that he was prepared to fight to his very last breath, that he was a warrior. And why did he throw the sword aside? Evidently because *he no longer needed it.* So if he had planned to go on to kill Master Mason Gallenreutter of Westphalia then he could have used the sword to do away with him as well, but he didn't.'

The Commander raised his hand, and Melchior fell silent. Spanheim looked around at the men gathered then stood up and spoke. 'Yes, that is unquestionably all truth, and we don't doubt it, and we all know that Wunbaldus was the murderer. But why did Wunbaldus kill him then, eh?'

After waiting for the Commander to take his seat, Master Goldsmith Casendorpe spoke up. 'And what happened to the gold collar I sold to Clingenstain? That is, aside from the fact that it now rests at the almshouse of the Church of the Holy Ghost.'

'And which ended up there in a miraculous way after Wunbaldus's death,' remarked Sire Tweffell.

'I've never seen a miracle with my own eyes,' the Commander huffed. 'And that collar ... to hell with that collar; I wouldn't ask for its return from the church in the Order's name. Yet how a *dead* thief carried the collar to the Church of the Holy Ghost, that certainly does interest me.'

'In that case, the only solution – if we do not believe in miracles – is that someone stole the collar and donated it to the Church of the Holy Ghost and in the belief that this way he perhaps might not also be charged with theft at an ordeal,' Melchior replied.

'You say that this *someone* was not Wunbaldus?' the Commander questioned.

'Theft is a transgression. However, the thief has already repented his sin and taken the collar to the almshouse. Since this man could not have been Wunbaldus it must have been someone else.'

'Enough of that collar,' Spanheim barked. 'I want to know why, if it wasn't over the collar, Wunbaldus killed Clingenstain.'

'Greed. It was greed, he said, that drove him to commit criminal acts,' Pastor Rode spoke heatedly.

'Greed?' Melchior echoed thoughtfully. 'How could it have been greed, when the murderer took with one hand and gave with the other? By this I mean stuffing the Gotland coin into Clingenstain's mouth. And, first and foremost, why did the murderer perform this ritual? *Id est*, why did he kill Clingenstain at all? We now reach the confession at the Church of the Holy Ghost. Sire Rode, you say that the Dominican Lay Brother Wunbaldus came to take confession from you. An unheard-of event – a Dominican taking confession at the church. If the man was in a state of mental distress, having just killed and wishing to take his own life, then perhaps he didn't have the courage to approach his own brothers, who would, no doubt, have begged him not to commit suicide.'

Pastor Rode stood up, his face red and his hands trembling lightly. 'I say it was so, as the Lord's is my witness,' he insisted.

'Sire Rode, you said that you recognized this man as the Lay Brother Wunbaldus?' Melchior enquired sharply.

'It was Wunbaldus, yes. It was him.'

'Did he tell you his name?'

Rode seemed unnerved. 'No,' he muttered. 'No, of course not, but I recognized him.'

'So he did not state his name. Did you see his face, perhaps?'

'No, he was wearing a hood. I did not see his face. However –'

'So if you *had* been able to see his face, would you have recognized him then?' Melchior pressed on.

'What are you asking?' Rode said in an agitated voice. 'I don't understand. I tell you, Wunbaldus came to the Church of the Holy Ghost to take confession. I recognized him.'

Melchior was quiet for a moment as he waited for Rode to settle down. He then said, 'Sire Rode, I was at the monastery when you appeared having heard the news that Wunbaldus was dead. You entered the chamber, saw Wunbaldus's body and then you asked, "Is this Wunbaldus? Is he dead?" The Magistrate and I replied that it was he and that he was indeed dead. And then you looked at his face and said, "*He* is Wunbaldus?" Sire Rode, you took a very close look at Wunbaldus's corpse, you saw his face, and you were still unsure whether or not it was him because you did not know him by sight.'

At first no one in the room with the exception of Magistrate Dorn seemed to grasp the significance of this assertion.

'Yes, Sire Rode,' Dorn then said slowly as he recalled the moment in the monastery and nodded, 'you didn't know Wunbaldus by sight, and that means you didn't know for sure whether it was he who came to confession.'

'I knew him … that is, he collected alms and …' Rode mumbled, taken aback.

'But you didn't recognize his face,' Melchior asserted. 'Even during the beer-tasting Wunbaldus remained in the shadows by the wall, and you sat with your back to him. I ask you, Sire Rode, upon what, in truth, do you base your claim to us that the Dominican Lay Brother Wunbaldus took confession at your church?'

'It couldn't have been anyone else.'

'How did you recognize him?'

'Lord have mercy,' Rode exclaimed, 'how many hunchbacked lay brothers do the Dominicans have?'

'Precisely,' Melchior cried triumphantly. 'You recognized a hump; you recognized the white habit of a Dominican lay brother and possibly his height. Nevertheless, you did not see his *face*. Did you *know* what his voice was like?'

Rode looked around the room, confused and appealing for support. The men, however, stared back at him, and there seemed to be no help coming to him from any direction.

'No, no, I did not know his voice,' Rode said in defeat. 'I have not heard him speak, or if I have … The man at confession spoke in a very deep voice and rasping tone, as if he had a sore throat …'

'Aha,' Melchior shouted. 'He spoke in a rasping tone, perhaps as if he were disguising his voice. But why would he have needed to do that if you were not familiar with his voice? And when I spoke to Wunbaldus the previous day there had been nothing wrong with his voice. Prior Eckell was with him the very same day and saw that he was healthy, something Sire Freisinger mentioned, too. So why disguise his voice? The only answer can be that you *would* have been able to recognize the voice because it was someone you *do* know.'

Councilman Bockhorst raised his hand for quiet. 'This is an unexpected development for the Council. What are you suggesting?'

'I simply want to point out that we have no clear evidence that that man was, in fact, the Lay Brother Wunbaldus,' Melchior replied.

Anyone can pretend to have a hump on his back and steal a lay brother's white tunic and scapular. A tunic has disappeared from the monastery, which Brother Hinricus can confirm.'

'In that case,' Dorn spoke up, 'we do not then know who killed Clingenstain. Is that what you are saying?'

A mischievous grin flashed across Melchior's face. 'I didn't say that. I know who killed Clingenstain. There's only one person it could have been.'

'You believe that it was the man who pretended to be Wunbaldus?' Casendorpe called out.

'No, I didn't say that either,' Melchior replied confidently.

The Councilman looked bemused as he listened to the circling conversation.

Melchior continued, 'Sires, I ask, how could it be that Wunbaldus, whose white habit was bloodied, did not leave a single drop of blood on the confession bench? Sire Rode, will you confirm that fact?'

Rode, who looked dizzy, now nodded keenly. 'That is true. The man's white habit did not look bloody, and although the light was dim, still ... And there was no blood on the confession bench. There were no bloodstains there.'

'I can corroborate this. I visited the confessional the next morning to investigate, and there was no blood. How is it possible that a man who claimed to have just killed and beheaded a master mason does not leave behind a single drop of blood when his tunic is absolutely soaked in it later?'

Silence governed the room for a few moments before Kilian spoke cautiously, 'It is possible only in the event that the man did not kill that master mason after all. That he had lied.'

'True, that is possible,' Melchior agreed. 'However, he was truly dead, was he not? Consequently, it is also possible that the confessor either witnessed the murder and lied or that he killed Gallenreutter later, *after* he had taken confession.'

Shouts of astonishment filled the room once more, but the Commander's infuriated voice could be heard above the rest. 'Your story makes no sense at all. Why should someone confess to an act that he did not commit? And, everything else aside, I want to know who killed Clingenstain. That builder's murder has nothing to do with the matter in hand. Was it Wunbaldus, or was it not?'

Melchior bowed to the Commander. 'Once again, what apt words from the mouth of the esteemed Commander. And so, who killed Commander of the Teutonic Order of Gotland Henning von Clingenstain? Who was it that chopped off his head and stuffed a coin in his mouth – a worn Gotland ørtug? I couldn't get that old coin out of my mind. Why did the murderer feel he had to do this? Desecration of the body, abasement ... Revenge possibly? This type of cruel execution does suggest it was a revenge attack. Yet, again, why the coin? The ørtug is rare in Tallinn; it is not often that merchants come upon it. But I will remind you that on that very day Clingenstain had purchased a gold collar from the workshop of Master Goldsmith Casendorpe.'

'Melchior, I fail to understand. What was it about that coin that you couldn't get out of your mind?' snapped the Commander. 'No doubt it was Clingenstain's own. He *had* recently arrived from Gotland after all ...' But after saying this the Commander bit his lip and fell silent.

'I see that you now also remember,' Melchior said, and nodded. 'Precisely. The fact is that Clingenstain had given all his money to Casendorpe. If anyone in Tallinn had any ørtugs in his possession that evening it was Master Casendorpe. You will confirm this, Master Goldsmith, will you not?'

The Goldsmith had leaped to his feet, his face ashen, and searched for words to express his rage.

'Listen, you … you dastardly apothecary and mixer of poisons,' Casendorpe finally roared. 'Do you wish to claim that I, that *I*, the Goldsmith of the town of Tallinn and Alderman of St Canute's Guild, that *I* killed that knight over some measly thirty marks? You despicable liar and –'

Dorn was forced to interfere once again and shout that Melchior certainly had not accused the Goldsmith. He appealed to Casendorpe in the name of the Council Court to behave in a dignified manner.

'I only requested your confirmation of the fact,' Melchior replied, but a dark shadow flitted across his face as he eyed Casendorpe. 'You told me that you and Clingenstain had agreed a fee of sixty marks for the collar, but the Knight haggled down the price. He emptied his chest right down to the very last coin, and it had held those ørtugs worth ten Riga marks apiece. Is that correct?'

'Reply, Sire Casendorpe,' the Councilman said threateningly. 'No one has accused you of anything.'

Casendorpe inhaled deeply, shot an angry glance towards Melchior and then nodded. 'Yes,' he said, 'so it was. He had not a single penny left and sent his servant to the ship, and he brought back those old ørtugs mixed in with the other coins. When I weighed them I had close on thirty marks' worth, which was a ridiculously low price for that collar.'

'So, Clingenstain had the ørtugs with him on Toompea,' continued Melchior. 'He also emptied his coffers entirely to pay Master Casendorpe. When I heard this the identity of Clingenstain's murderer only became clearer in my mind.'

'Tell us, Melchior,' Spanheim demanded. 'What was wrong with those coins then?'

'Naturally, I considered who had visited Toompea that day and who might have had a reason to hate the Knight. And, naturally, I also considered that it might have been the Master Goldsmith, from whom the Order had extorted that collar at half its price that very same day. And, naturally, I also considered Master Merchant Tweffell, who has for some time held a grudge against Clingenstain regarding a ship –'

'Melchior, the whole town knows that Clingenstain of Gotland robbed me,' Mertin Tweffell remarked.

'Master Merchant, that was not exactly what happened,' Spanheim said.

'Robbed, I say.' Tweffell sharpened his tone. 'That was *exactly* what happened, and everyone in Tallinn knows that Clingenstain stole my ship and its cargo for himself to cover some personal debts. And I have also made it known in every corner of this town that I did not wish for the Knight's death, as the Grand Master of the Order would not then be able to demand that Clingenstain issue me any goods in recompense. Nevertheless, he truly deserved such a death. I have nothing to fear – I am an old man, and every townsman knows perfectly well that I am unable to hold a sword in my grasp and that I am too feeble to get the better of a man in his prime, even if he were as full of drink as Clingenstain was that night.'

'Oh no, I would never have believed that you yourself could have got the better of Clingenstain,' Melchior replied. 'However, Master Tweffell, you *do* have a loyal and devoted attendant who is unequalled in strength. You have Ludke, who disappeared from town shortly after your visit to Toompea and who was not seen any more that day. Ludke claims he went to fetch leeches, which may well be true. Just as true as the fact that Ludke served in the Council's armed forces and is highly skilled in weaponry. I do not know a more loyal servant in Tallinn, one who undertakes all of his master's commands, either verbal or those that his master has not actually spoken out loud. Ludke is a seasoned warrior – and he had no reason to love Clingenstain.'

Tweffell stared at Melchior for a moment, frozen, then scoffed at him. 'Pah! I fail to understand what you are getting at here, Melchior. I did send Ludke to bring back leeches and to call in a debt. You may go to the village yourself if you want confirmation of this – if there is still anyone there in good enough health to speak to you, heh-heh-heh. Ludke is a strong-armed boy, and when he realizes that someone doesn't want to repay a debt to his master, then ...' Tweffell fell silent, as if appalled by his own words.

'Precisely so, Sire Tweffell, precisely so,' Melchior spoke. 'Ludke is capable of holding a sword, and Ludke does not tolerate those who have wronged his master. Ludke was also in your company on Toompea.'

'Hold on now, Melchior. You aren't really saying that ...'

'I speak to explain my train of thought. But I always came back to the gold collar and the coin. Could stealing the collar have been the reason for the murder? Possibly, although one does not have to chop off someone's head and stuff a coin into his mouth, as if in compensation, to do that. But then I remembered something that the esteemed Commander Spanheim said.'

'Me? What did I say?' the Commander demanded curiously.

'When the Magistrate and I visited the castle the honourable Commander informed us who else had been on Toompea the previous day. He also recalled Brother Wunbaldus, who just as usual – I repeat, *just as usual* – made his rounds on Toompea with the alms basket and had come into contact with Clingenstain.'

'So he had,' the Commander grunted.

'Brother Wunbaldus had collected alms on Toompea,' Melchior continued, 'and, according to Master Casendorpe, we know that

Clingenstain only had ten marks in ørtugs in his chest at the time he paid for the collar. How else could this rare old coin have ended up on Toompea in the first place if not from Clingenstain's own coffers?' Melchior's voice had now risen to a fevered pitch. 'Only Brother Wunbaldus could definitely have possessed an old Gotland ørtug. *And this had been given to him by Clingenstain himself.* Is it not reasonable to believe that stuffing the coin into the mouth of Clingenstain's decapitated head was like throwing it back at its benefactor out of contempt and hatred and old enmity? Who regularly spent time on Toompea? Who knew all its hidden court-yards and shadowy corners? Whose presence on Toompea did not raise anyone's curiosity? Wunbaldus was as regular a figure on Toompea as any Knight of the Order. He would not have been noticed at all.'

Councilman Bockhorst now piped up again to ask, shaking his head, 'Melchior, you said just a moment ago that Wunbaldus was not the man who admitted to the murder at confession, so how now again …?'

'I didn't say that the *confessor* might have lied,' Melchior spoke on with passion. 'No, he told the truth about Clingenstain's murder. What do we actually know about Wunbaldus? Who was he? When I discussed this with Brother Hinricus he admitted that no one else in the monastery knew anything about him other than Prior Eckell — only the man who had received him as a lay brother and served as his overseer. No one knew where he had been born or in what other monasteries he had previously spent time, with the exception of Oxford in England. However, he was a strong man and had arrived at the monastery about five years ago. Prior Eckell had known him already, though. But from where? Where might they have met? Who was Brother Wunbaldus really, aside from the fact that he was a master of seven arts?'

No one had an answer to that, but then the former captain Rinus Götzer stood up and dared to open his mouth before the high lords without having asked permission.

'A master of seven arts?' he asked, and all turned towards the almsman.

'That he was. Sires, Prior Eckell had previously been at the Dominican Monastery in Visby, at the time that the Victual Brothers governed the island of Gotland. Eckell was there when the Teutonic Order ruthlessly expelled the Brothers and massacred them on the island's shores. And so I began to ask myself – just who was Wunbaldus? Is it possible that …' He shook his head, and then gestured towards Götzer. 'But, Skipper Götzer, maybe you can tell us what you know about Magister Wigbold?'

Magister Wigbold. Gasps could be heard across the room. Everyone knew the name, and invoking it was as if someone had invoked Lucifer himself.

'Oh, no one knows much about him, no one knows much at all,' the old captain spoke gruffly. 'He was said to be the wiliest and cleverest of the Victual Brothers' chiefs, just like an old fox, he was, and no one knew what he looked like – he didn't show his face to strangers – and if anyone *did* see it, well, they didn't last long. And he could avoid every trap –'

'But his head was chopped off near Hamburg, wasn't it?' Freisinger called out.

Götzer continued his tale, awkwardly at first because he was not used to speaking in front of people of such high status, but, as he spoke, he became increasingly confident as he gained courage. There are those who believe that he wasn't beheaded at all, since four separate men claimed to have been Magister Wigbold – all of whom laughed before their executions. Others believe Wigbold escaped, because he was so clever. He was evil to boot, although it was known that he would listen to pleas for clemency and persuade others to spare the lives of prisoners. The Victual Brother called Magister Wigbold was wiser than all the rest and was known as the Master of Seven Arts. All the most notable and cunning acts of piracy were said to have been planned by him. They also say that he had once lived as a monk at an English monastery and university, which was where he had acquired those arts. Others again say that he would knock some sense into the other pirates from time to time but that at other times he could be like Satan himself and would brandish his sword with such fury that heads would fly when he fell into a fit of rage.

When the old man fell quiet and wiped a tear from the corner of his eye, Melchior spoke again. 'Wunbaldus arrived at Tallinn's monastery five years ago, three years after Wigbold's reported beheading. Brother Hinricus once heard Prior Eckell saying that on one occasion Wunbaldus had saved the lives of three Dominican Brothers from the pirates. Wigbold had lived at a monastery in England; Wunbaldus had been a brother in Oxford. Eckell and Wunbaldus had met before. Prior Eckell treated Wunbaldus with special attention, as if he were his own son. Yes, I believe that the man whom we all knew as the Lay Brother Wunbaldus was actually none other than the Victual Brother, Magister Wigbold.'

30

*The Tallinn Magistrate's Official
Chambers Alongside Town Hall Square*
19 May, Evening

M ELCHIOR'S WORDS had the effect of a cannonball crashing into the Magistrate's chambers, as every man in the room suddenly jumped to his feet, shaking his fist and shouting. It was unheard of. It was absolutely impossible that the town of Tallinn might have provided refuge to such a man, that the Dominicans might have taken this manifestation of Satan into their fold. Councilman Bockhorst, himself just as stunned as the others, waved his arms and cried for all to remain quiet, but the Commander's voice overpowered the Councilman's own as he roared, 'That murderer. That scoundrel. How could the monastery have allowed him to live amongst them?'

Brother Hinricus responded, shouting back at the Commander with passion, 'The monastery is a sanctuary. The monastery offers asylum to all sinners who request it. But I swear to you, not one of us had ever heard that Wunbaldus might have been a Victual Brother.'

When the Councilman and the Magistrate, who were equally shocked by Melchior's revelation, finally managed to restore order, Melchior was again given the podium.

'When I viewed Wunbaldus's corpse,' he said, 'and the Magistrate is my witness here, we saw that Wunbaldus had evidently been a warrior. His body was covered in scars. He must have fought in numerous battles, and the last and most painful wound was inflicted by an executioner's axe. This blow should have sliced his head clean from his neck, and only the Lord God knows how he managed to escape that fate. In any case, an axe blow was what turned him into a hunchback. It had been a miraculous escape, and I believe that a man rescued from death in such a way must thank the Almighty and start considering his life, must start to wonder whether avoiding death this way might have been a heavenly sign. Wigbold, or Wunbaldus, had earlier been a Dominican and lived in a monastery. Prior Eckell said Wunbaldus came to the monastery to repent his sins, and I believe that this is true.'

'Repent his sins, ha!' the Commander spat. 'A maggot. A murderer.'

'Murderers can also repent,' Melchior countered. 'Wigbold searched for a sanctuary after his incredible escape. This man, the smartest of the Victual Brothers who on more than one occasion talked sense into his comrades, this man searched for sanctuary. I believe that Wigbold saved the lives of three Dominicans from the Victual Brothers' fury on the island of Gotland, and that this was the reason why he — as a fugitive and a penitent — appeared before Prior Eckell five years ago and the Prior granted him sanctuary in the monastery. Yes, I believe that Wigbold repented.'

'Melchior, are you certain of this?' asked the Councilman. 'It would be a dreadful shame upon the town if we had granted refuge in our own monastery to a murderer and a thief wanted throughout the Hanseatic League.'

'Granting sanctuary does not shame a town,' Hinricus retorted. 'The monastery provides sanctuary on the basis of divine justice. A monastery does not judge, nor does it cut off heads.'

'That monastery is in the town of Tallinn,' Tweffell berated. And if other Hanseatic towns find out that a murderer who was hunted by all was in hiding here in Tallinn, then ...'

'If Wunbaldus *was* indeed Wigbold,' Hinricus remarked.

'All signs point to it,' Melchior said, 'as does the brand that we found at the base of his skull. There was a mark burned into his flesh, two letters that looked to be an E and a K.'

'That's true,' the Magistrate confirmed. 'He had been branded like a criminal.'

'Although those letters were actually not E and K, but rather B and K. A scar cut through the B so that it looked like an E. B and K –'

Rinus Götzer's hoarse shout cut off Melchior's words. *Bunte Kuh*, the *Brindled Cow*. That was the name of Simon von Utrecht's ship.'

'You are correct.' Melchior nodded.

'When Victual Brothers were caught it was customary to brand them with the initials of the warship that captured them,' Götzer explained spiritedly, 'and whichever had the most prisoners with their ship's branding received a bounty per head.'

'And the mark of Simon von Utrecht's ship was branded on to the back of Wunbaldus's neck,' Melchior spoke slowly. 'He had been a prisoner on the *Bunte Kuh*. Magister Wigbold, the Master of Seven Arts, who had pirated ships on the Baltic Sea for ten years and always evaded every trap, had even escaped from Simon von Utrecht's ship and the axe of the executioner on the island of Grasbrook, this most clever and cunning of all Victual Brothers met his end in the town of Tallinn.'

'What were those seven arts?' Freisinger demanded. 'You don't mean the seven free arts taught in a monastery?'

'I do not believe', Melchior responded, 'that Wigbold was titled the Master of Seven Arts through becoming skilled at those seven free arts, which are ... Brother Hinricus, what are they exactly?'

'Rhetoric, Latin grammar, dialect, music, astronomy, arithmetic and geometry,' replied the monk. 'However, I can assure you that Brother Wunbaldus was not skilled at music or at dialect.'

'He was skilled in seven other arts, however,' continued Melchior, 'and every one of us should be quite familiar with the most important of these – Wunbaldus was a fantastic brewer, having studied the art in England. He was also trained as a goldsmith, because upkeep of the reliquaries was under his care at the monastery. He was familiar with justice and canon law, which altogether makes three arts. He had great knowledge of the Scriptures, as Brother Hinricus will tell you. That is four. Wunbaldus was known in the monastery to be an accomplished healer who knew how to prepare salves and medicines. He was well versed in medicine.'

'You have now listed five. Yet what were the sixth and the seventh?' asked the Councilman.

'The sixth was chess. As some of you know, Wunbaldus played chess at a level of mastery. Chess was also what helped provide me with a clue to how the first crime was committed. Perhaps Sire Freisinger recalls the match that was in play on my board when he dropped into the pharmacy?'

Freisinger rose in surprise. 'Yes, I do. It was a strange state of play on the board – but, in the name of God, how could that have given you a clue?'

'Chess is sometimes called a mirror of life. Each piece holds a particular significance, and we know that the Prior and Wunbaldus played regularly. The chess-pieces can be arranged in a way that resembles some kind of life situation. When the Magistrate and I visited the monastery, Wunbaldus – or should we call him Wigbold? – appeared to be involved in an unfinished game with the Prior. I later recreated the positions on a board, and Sire Freisinger happened to see it. He said that –'

'I said that such a situation rarely unfolds in a game,' Freisinger interrupted. 'But I fail to grasp how chess could tell you anything about the killing.'

'It did so because it was not a half-finished match but, in fact, Prior Eckell was communicating with Wunbaldus through the chess pieces. The Prior had a heavy load bearing down upon his soul, and he arranged the pieces on the board in the way he viewed the situation in earthly life. He depicted Clingenstain's killing and his own dilemma. Prior Eckell envisioned himself as the white king, Clingenstain was a white knight and two white rooks signified the monastery as a sheltering house of the Lord. Do you remember, Sire Freisinger?'

'Yes, I remember,' Freisinger murmured in astonishment. 'Although I did not read the arrangement that way at all.'

'Nevertheless, Clingenstain's killing was laid out pictorially. The black pawn would take the white knight on the next move, meaning Clingenstain would be killed. Eckell is threatened with his downfall after a couple more moves because the white queen would not come to his aid in time, the queen being the Virgin Mary or heavenly grace. The only escape route for Eckell's soul would have been to bring the two rooks into play meaning he would shield himself behind the monastery walls and do nothing, yet, in doing so, abandoning his queen, that is betraying his belief. Eckell, playing with white, was losing the game. This position on the board depicted Eckell's thoughts. If the pawn were to kill Clingenstain then Eckell would be deprived of the Lord's sacred grace; he would have to betray all that he held true and conceal himself within the monastery. If he did not do this – if he wished to preserve his queen – then he himself would have to fall, to admit his defeat. Sires, this arrangement showed that white could only be victorious if the black pawn were to abandon his plans to take the white knight. If, however,

Clingenstain were killed then Eckell would have to surrender in order to save his own soul.'

'That is mad talk, Melchior,' the Magistrate remarked.

'Oh no, not in the least,' Freisinger exclaimed excitedly. 'Yes, now I understand. Of course, that was precisely it. Yet that would mean Prior Eckell knew ...'

'*Of course* he knew,' Melchior said gravely. 'He was conveying an allegory to Wunbaldus using the chess pieces when we entered the room. Apparently, he had difficulty voicing his thoughts aloud and conversed with Wigbold through his sixth art.'

'Sixth? But what was his seventh?' Dorn asked.

'His seventh? But surely we know this last one best of all?' Melchior said. 'Is it not the very reason that we are gathered here now? Which art must the Magister have possessed most excellently if not the *art of killing*? This might have been a joke for the Victual Brothers, yet it was the sad fate for hundreds of unfortunate souls along the shores of the Baltic Sea. Yes, Wunbaldus was without question the man who killed Clingenstain – he and none other. He had indeed come to Tallinn to escape and to repent his sins, to thank God for his incredible escape, but, alas, once a killer always a killer ... Clingenstain had killed dozens of Wigbold's friends and brothers, had skinned and burned them alive, had chopped off their heads and driven them on to stakes on town walls. He did this when the Order's forces conquered Gotland and drove the Victual Brothers from its shores. And now, suddenly, nearly ten years later, Wigbold had the chance to get his revenge. The Butcher of Gotland was right before his eyes and completely drunk. And the last straw for Wigbold? The Gotland coin Clingenstain gave him. So, he stuffed it back into the mouth of his mortal enemy. Wigbold knew Toompea intimately. He held back for several days, waiting for the right moment, and this occurred when Jochen, Clingenstain's servant, was away and the man himself was too drunk to stand and incapable of fighting back.

The Councilman nodded, finally, as if he now saw the light. This certainly meant nothing good for the town, but the monastery was none the less a sanctuary, and, what's more, that dreadful man was now dead.

Spanheim also appeared to be content with this. He sat nodding at length then proclaimed, 'In that case, if it is also the ruling of the Council Court, then I demand that the corpse of that Wigbold be handed over to the Order. Yes, just so. And may the Council Court itself reach a verdict on the details of why that Wigbold, or Wunbaldus, killed Gallenreutter …'

'Oh, but he didn't,' Melchior said quietly. 'No, *that* wasn't Wunbaldus.'

The room exploded, and Melchior had to wait for the noise to die down a little before speaking again.

'So now you all know who killed Commander Henning von Clingenstain and why. That story is over. Now, however, I must tell a completely different tale. I began to think that perhaps Wunbaldus was Clingenstain's murderer after learning that it was the Knight himself who had donated the ørtug to the monk. Later, after Gallenreutter's body was found, I just couldn't understand why a Tallinn artig had been crammed into *his* mouth. If it was Wunbaldus, then why? There was no rational explanation. Wunbaldus – Wigbold – had no reason to exact revenge on Gallenreutter. And then there was the fact that the Master Mason had been stabbed to death with a dagger and only *then* beheaded. Once I was convinced that Wunbaldus was actually Wigbold – and the brand was final confirmation of this – then the situation became even more confusing. Wigbold killed to avenge his brothers and the loss of Gotland. Did Gallenreutter know something and threaten to unmask him, as Sire Dorn reckoned? After all, what

Gallenreutter said at the Brotherhood of Blackheads could only have been a challenge to the murderer. Yet why should the man then confess and drink poison? I want to remind you of Sire Rode's words when Prior Eckell freed him from his duty to maintain the secrecy of the confessional. Sire Rode, would you be so kind as to list again the sins that the man confessed?'

'He said that greed drove him to commit criminal acts and that he had killed two people. He said he had chopped off their heads. He said that one had been a Knight of the Teutonic Order and the other a master mason …'

'Two people,' Melchior exclaimed. '*Two* people. Only two. Once I knew for sure that Wunbaldus was Wigbold I knew that the confessor could not have been Wigbold, because that man has killed not two but twenty or maybe two hundred …'

'But who … who was he then?' Rode asked very softly.

'Who? The man who killed Master Mason Gallenreutter; the man who killed the monk he believed to be Wunbaldus; the man who killed Prior Eckell. Four murders have been committed over these last few days, and only one of them was carried out by Wunbaldus. The man who killed the other three sits here amongst us.'

'Melchior, are you going to accuse someone?' demanded the bewildered Magistrate.

'Yes,' Melchior replied, 'but not yet. First, I will remind you of how Prior Eckell freed Pastor Rode from keeping the secrecy of the confessional. Eckell felt very ill, and he knew that he was not long for this world. During the last few moments of his life he freed Pastor Rode from his obligation of secrecy, something that requires the approval of clergymen of high authority and is extremely rare. Nevertheless, he did so.'

'Yes, he did so, and he did so because a man who takes his own life also loses his rights to the holy sacraments,' said Rode.

Melchior shook his head. 'Oh no, that wasn't the reason. He did it because he knew that the man who took confession could not have been Wunbaldus. He did so because he knew that it was a false confession. Someone pretended to be Wunbaldus, so it wasn't a true confession but rather a step in the murderer's cunning plan. This was very astute of the Prior, because the murderer made the mistake of only admitting to only two murders. *He did not know Wunbaldus's true identity.* Prior Eckell, on the other hand, knew exactly who Wunbaldus really was, but he also knew that Wunbaldus would never have confessed to killing Clingenstain, much less at the Church of the Holy Ghost. Also he would never believe that Wunbaldus would take his own life. Yes, Prior Eckell had worked it all out and as he took his final breath he saw … Well, I will address this shortly, but now I want to turn to why someone should have impersonated Wunbaldus, and there can only be one answer. So that Wunbaldus would then be blamed for the murder of Master Mason Gallenreutter. Someone wanted him out of the way, and chance or fate had given him the opportunity to shift the blame on to Wunbaldus. He would dispatch Gallenreutter in the same manner as the Toompea Murderer had killed Clingenstain, and when Clingenstain's killer was apprehended then all would believe he had two men's lives on his soul. Wunbaldus himself was the only obstacle, as he would very likely have worked out who was responsible for the second murder, so he also had to go. Even if the monk lacked any firm evidence, the murderer could not allow any suspicion to fall on him. Sooner or later someone would have worked it out. And so, who killed Gallenreutter, the man building a chapel for St Olaf's Church? Why did he have to die? Was it some mortal enemy, someone he'd argued with, someone of whom he was jealous? All these are possible, but whoever it was must have known that Wunbaldus was Clingenstain's killer — and not only that but *how* the Knight was killed. My suspicions fell on one individual, although I couldn't work out a motive.'

'Who? Who do you accuse?' Freisinger pressed.

'Yes, tell us, Melchior. Who?' croaked Casendorpe.

'Please, I ask for quiet,' said Bockhorst. 'In the name of the Council, Melchior, do tell us who this man is.'

'Someone who knew how Clingenstain died ... but how could he have known that Wunbaldus was the murderer? The solution is very simple. The Dominicans' church is currently being reconstructed, and every sound from the northern nave can be heard clearly in the dormitory and in Wunbaldus's chamber. Is that not correct, Brother Hinricus?' So pointed was Melchior's tone that everyone turned to stare at Hinricus, who had been sitting quietly. The young monk was taken aback. He raised his head, his hands pressed together in his lap in prayer and shock in his eyes.

'What? Yes, I do believe it is. Yes, it certainly is. The north side of the old church has been knocked down, and only the eastern wall of the new passageway has been built thus far, so everything from the northern nave of the church sounds clearly into the lay brothers' dormitory. There aren't any walls separating the two. But I don't understand. How is this significant?'

'Because if everything from the church's northern nave and the Blackheads' side altar is clearly audible in the dormitory then sounds can pass just as easily in the opposite direction. In other words, there is one place in the church where everything that goes on in the lay brothers' dormitory can be heard.'

'That seems right,' Hinricus said, his voice wavering. 'Yet I still fail to understand, in what way –'

'Nor did I at first,' Melchior spoke sharply, eying Hinricus intently. 'But Gallenreutter's murderer had to find out about Wunbaldus *somehow*, and he could have overheard Eckell and Wunbaldus, perhaps as they played chess. This explains some of Eckell's statements and his behaviour – it also explains why he was killed.'

Hinricus wiped the sweat from his forehead and said, 'Now that you mention it, then yes … I must agree … Prior Eckell was rather odd and melancholy during those final days … as if he suspected someone and … But still, Melchior, how? Gallenreutter … no, I don't understand.'

'You see, all of the murders were tied to the monastery. The murderer had to have been connected to the monastery; he had to know that Eckell carried arsenic around his neck; he had to have heard Wunbaldus speak to Eckell about his own act of murder; he had to steal the Lay Brother's white tunic. He had to have been in Wunbaldus's chamber that evening and drunk a tankard of beer with him, a tankard into which he slipped the fatal arsenic.'

'You mean that all this took place in front of us and that we didn't notice a thing?' Hinricus questioned with fear in his voice.

'Someone must have had the opportunity of stealing the arsenic from Prior Eckell's amulet and replacing it with flour,' Melchior continued, his gaze still locked on Hinricus. 'Magistrate Dorn already knows that on the evening Prior Eckell died his amulet contained flour and not arsenic. The murderer swapped the arsenic for flour so the Prior didn't become suspicious. And, by the way, you might recall that Master Tweffell's horse died that same day.'

'What? Ah, my horse, yes. Dropped dead as if hexed. A strapping, strong animal it was, too. How is that relevant?' Tweffell asked.

'Because your horse was probably the murderer's first victim. All the symptoms of its death point to arsenic poisoning. The murderer knew where the Prior put the amulet when he removed it to say mass. He needed to be sure that it really was arsenic and to check that its poisonous effect hadn't worn off with time, so tried it out on

Tweffell's horse because, they say, a compacted ball of arsenic the size of a pea will kill a horse or a man. Isn't that so, Kilian?'

'Yes, at least that's what they say in Italy. Arsenic has been known there since Roman times,' Kilian replied cautiously.

'Who is the man?' Tweffell thundered. 'Give him up, and Ludke will make mincemeat of him. But before that, he will pay me compensation for that dray.'

'So we know that the man took Eckell's arsenic, administered it to Wunbaldus in a tankard of beer, stole the Lay Brother's habit and took confession at the Church of the Holy Ghost *before* killing Gallenreutter, so that he would not get covered in blood, and later poisoned the Prior. But before revealing his identity I want to explain the puzzle of the poisonings and the secrets of arsenic. It is very important that we understand this correctly – and I have to believe that when an evil and malicious man came amongst us then St Cosmas hovered above the town and also sent an apothecary with a great knowledge of poisons.'

Magistrate Dorn remarked upon this that the Council Court would certainly appreciate it if St Cosmas's envoy were to explain the mystery of poisonous flour.

'Prior Eckell wore arsenic around his neck for many years and gradually inhaled its vapours,' Melchior continued. 'This in itself is not immediately deadly, but signs of arsenic poisoning do develop over a long period of time – the victim's hair begins to fall out, white lines appear on his fingernails, his thoughts become somewhat addled and his joints ache constantly. We all witnessed Prior Eckell experiencing these symptoms. Now, while inhaling these vapours may ultimately result in arsenic poisoning and kill the victim, the death would be long and tortuous. But the Prior died suddenly, and he himself was convinced that he had been poisoned. A light scent of garlic wafted from his mouth, which is also a sign of arsenic poisoning … not long-term poisoning, however, but rather the ingestion of a single fatal dose. The rapid onset of pain that causes a man's organs to convulse with uncontrollable vomiting, this is all indicative of arsenic but, once again, not of long-term poisoning. So, what should an apothecary then conclude? The Prior had inhaled arsenic for several years, *and* he had consumed arsenic through food or drink. Yet, as we already know, this did not happen that evening at the Brotherhood of Blackheads because arsenic was not present in our food or drink and neither was it in Prior Eckell's, because Sire Freisinger ate and drank from the Prior's dishes and – as we can see – he is alive to this very day.'

'By the Lord's grace,' Freisinger murmured.

'And we praise Him for this as well,' Melchior concurred. 'But how did the Prior die? Arsenic? Yes, certainly. But his food and drink were not poisoned, and if he had swallowed arsenic earlier – in the monastery, let us say – then he would have died sooner because arsenic works fast. I was troubled by this for a time and could not make up my mind whether or not the Prior had, in fact, been poisoned. But the answer is simple. I found it in Magister de Ardoyn's book, and it explains everything. The murderer did poison the Prior while he was still at the monastery. Each separate strand of this case leads us back to the Dominicans.'

'Melchior – sacred heavens and the Virgin Mary – what are you saying?' Hinricus pleaded.

'What am I saying? I am saying that the arsenic did not work as quickly as it should have because the Prior's body had built up a resistance to the poison as he had already been exposed to it for a number of years. Our murderer knew how much a deadly dose should be and administered it, expecting the Prior to die much quicker. Eckell was old and sick, and his death would have been believed to have been through natural causes. The killer certainly did not want the Prior to die at the Brotherhood of Blackheads, where he himself was also present. But the Prior held out for longer than expected.'

'And this man was someone from the monastery?' the Councilman demanded.

'I asked myself whether it could be someone who had been present at all of these events, always in the background and hatching his dreadful plan. I want to ask whether it is possible that *you*, Hinricus, are this man. The man who accompanied the Prior to Toompea, one so unnoticed there that no one paid you any heed.'

Everyone in the room jumped to his feet, but Melchior's words had been so unexpected that no one was yet capable of saying anything. Hinricus stared back at Melchior, ashen-faced, and then collapsed to his knees.

'Could it have been you who heard the conversation between the Prior and Wigbold sounding in the church when the latter admitted to killing Clingenstain?' Melchior demanded, enraged. 'Could it have been you who knew about Prior Eckell's arsenic? Could it have been you who stole that arsenic and poisoned Wigbold? I want to ask whether it was you who was so enraged that the Prior had received that murdering pirate into the monastery – an insult to St Catherine – that you condemned them both to death for this? You were the last person at Eckell's side during the final moments of his life. You supported him, and could it have been you who forced the final dose of deadly arsenic into his mouth when you saw that the amount given to him at the monastery had had no effect? Could it have been you who disguised yourself as Wunbaldus and then – since all at the monastery would have seen through your masquerade – took confession at the Church of the Holy Ghost in order to transfer the blame for Gallenreutter's death on to another?'

'Gallenreutter?' Dorn exclaimed. 'But why would this feckless monk want to kill him?'

'The question lies rather in how he would have known to put a coin into the man's mouth,' Melchior replied.

A terrified Hinricus kneeled on the cold floor, praying. Dorn was reaching for the handle of his sword in order to command the court servants to take the monk prisoner.

'Sire Freisinger,' Melchior spoke abruptly, and the Blackhead turned a surprised gaze towards him, 'Sire Freisinger, you were the only person in the town besides the Magistrate and I who knew about the coin that had been forced into Clingenstain's mouth. That Order attendant let this fact slip carelessly and against the Commander's orders when speaking to the Magistrate, and *he* mentioned this at my pharmacy, which is where you heard it. You visit the monastery frequently. Tell us, is it possible that you spoke of this to Brother Hinricus?'

'Heavenly grace, oh merciful Lord,' Hinricus whimpered, his face shrouded beneath his cowl. He rocked back and forth on the floor in fevered prayer. The Magistrate approached him, his hand on his sword.

'St Catherine,' Freisinger stammered in alarm, 'did I truly say that?'

'That is what I am asking.'

'I do remember now, that, yes, the Magistrate spoke of this, although it had slipped from my mind, but …' Freisinger stood perplexed, racking his brains. A look of astonishment then flashed across his face. It seemed he now remembered something. 'Of course,' he cried out. 'Yes, now I remember. Yes, I mentioned this to Hinricus in the monastery garden when we were counting the money. Yes, I acknowledge this, in the names of all the saints.'

'That is a lie,' Hinricus shouted in distress. 'That man is swearing to a lie. He never said anything of the sort to me.'

Melchior now spoke rapidly. 'At the time Dorn spoke of the

coin in the pharmacy he did not yet know that it had been an old Gotland ørtug, so Freisinger could not have known that either. The murderer therefore placed any old coin into Gallenreutter's mouth, unaware that it should carry a special significance. And this is what gave him away. This is what confirmed to me that Gallenreutter's killer was another man.'

'It was not me,' Hinricus cried. 'I am innocent. I've never killed anyone. It was someone else.'

'It was the man Prior Eckell accused in his final minute. While he was no longer able to speak, he pointed this man out to us. When he felt the sudden onset of pain, then he understood; he understood everything that had taken place, and he knew the identity of his killer. Sires, the Prior himself pointed this man out to us.'

'Who did he point to?' Dorn bellowed. He gestured towards Hinricus. 'Was it this man here?'

'Melchior, do not put the Council's patience to the test,' Bockhorst said sternly. 'Do you or do you not accuse the Dominican *cellarius* Hinricus of these dreadful acts?'

'The esteemed Prior died right in front of us, and if he had pointed to someone then we would have seen it,' Rode spoke.

Melchior waved his hand and raised his voice, 'I still pose the question. Who needed Master Gallenreutter dead? Who wanted to kill the man building a chapel alongside St Olaf's Church? We should all know this because there is only one person it can be. Each and every act in connection with these murders has taken place right in front of us. I ask you now to name the master who built St Olaf's Church two hundred years ago. What was the name of the man who raised a steeple so high that it could be seen many miles out to sea? What was this man's name?'

A sudden silence filled the room. The men looked at one another in surprise, and Tweffell tapped a finger on his chest.

'Why don't you ask the Council Secretary to look this up in the ledger or ask the Pastor of St Olaf's or something? Of what relevance is this now, Melchior?' Bockhorst asked.

'I would like everyone to recall the first evening of the beer-tasting festival at the Brotherhood of Blackheads. It is possible that not everyone was listening, but Master Gallenreutter recited a song that, as Kilian aptly remarked, was more of a riddle. It was a strange song, and no one knew it – not even Kilian, who knows hundreds of songs. Gallenreutter spoke to us about church construction and how one must dig up the site of the old place of worship before the building can start. And then the Master Mason came to his song. I was already certain at the time that it was not mere chance, that it was not simply to warm his tongue during the course of conversation, but rather that Gallenreutter skilfully worked his speech so he could present his song.'

Melchior took a sheet of paper from his pocket and spread it out on the podium. He read aloud:

'Come, for daybreak is nigh and light gleams from the east
oh, my friend, our seven brothers await thee at the crossroads
nonpareil the Lord's temple, to which they'll show ye the way
radial compass and trowels, they hold
aid them to drink the light that glimmers at the grave
their oaths as ancient as Solomon's wisdom
unto the seven masters, their shields extended
solemn Death drapes in his cloak he who is afore all
Favete linguis et memento mori
relic calls afar for its blood
elegiac yesterday is closer to Christ's blood which floweth down
    the walls.

'And now,' he continued, 'here are four more lines that I found in Gallenreutter's pocket after he was murdered. He inscribed these on paper. The first letters had been obscured by blood, but it isn't difficult to work out what they should be. So this song – and it is one and the same – continues as follows:

'illumined angels will bring our town a protector, higher than us all
sadistic death will dance a jig around their names
in eternal secrecy be affirmed the first's oath of flesh
numen lumen, of the holy flesh, seven will have part.'

The Apothecary was met with blank stares, and even Hinricus had risen to his feet.

'I recall the song,' said Casendorpe. 'Probably everyone does – Gallenreutter even said that it probably originated in Tallinn and was composed by the first guild ever to be founded here.'

'And which guild was that?' Melchior asked. 'Sire Freisinger will assert that it was the Blackheads – although nobody really took any notice of them until Sire Freisinger arrived a few years back, so if the Blackheads were indeed here in the early days of the town then it was probably just a group of old fogeys whom no one remembers. Freisinger was not familiar with the song either.'

'Melchior, you have completely lost me now,' Freisinger said. 'The Blackheads are not mentioned at all in that muddled verse. What are you on about?'

'It is true, they aren't,' Melchior replied. 'But what is it about then? I'll tell you. It is not a song but, rather, an oath and a riddle. Let us solve it. It mentions seven brothers who show the way to the Lord's temple, that is, a church. It is clear that it also speaks of master builders, apparently church builders, who are not ordinary masons. Further on, one can deduce that the master builders have secret oaths that date from the time of Solomon's – and they say Solomon's temple was the progenitor of all modern churches. I believe these lines also mean that church builders have been organized into a single guild that has guarded their secrets since the time of Solomon. *Solemn Death drapes in his cloak he who is afore all.* Who is before all? Who does Death drape in his cloak? We should understand from this that he who is afore all is dead. *Favete linguis et memento mori? Favete linguis* means to hold one's tongue and *memento mori* to remember your mortality. Thus we are instructed to keep quiet about he who is dead but also to remember him. The next line – *relic calls afar for its blood* – we know that Gallenreutter found a box containing bones while digging beneath the old church, so might this be that very same relic? And its own blood that calls afar … if a person's remains call for his own blood then could this verse be talking about lineage? A descendant perhaps? *Elegiac yesterday is closer to Christ's blood, which floweth down the walls.* I believe this means that because Christ lived a long time ago the ancient secrets of the masons originated much nearer to Our Lord's time than ours.'

'Hold on now, Melchior,' Bockhorst said. 'I don't understand why this old riddle is of any relevance to us here.'

'I promise that all will become clear post haste. Let us recall those final four lines that I found in Gallenreutter's pocket:

'illumined angels will bring our town a protector, higher than us all
sadistic death will dance a jig around their names
in eternal secrecy be affirmed the first's oath of flesh
numen lumen, of the holy flesh, seven will have part.

'What is the protector of our town, higher than us all? What shows our position from far out at sea and guides ships into our harbour, keeps the merchants in business and from the pinnacle of which our enemies' forces are also visible from a long way off?'

'Holy Christ,' Dorn murmured, 'you are speaking of St Olaf's Church.'

'Gallenreutter knew that the excavated coffin held the remains of a man, and he must have found this riddle within the box as well. And *he* understood; *he* understood everything. *Sadistic death will dance a jig around their names.* This sounds like a threat or a warning. Death will dance around the names of those who built St Olaf's. The last lines leave no doubt. Who was the first? Why the first? What does this mean? Remember, *solemn Death drapes in his cloak he who is afore all.* Who is before all? And who built St Olaf's Church?'

'Isn't there some old legend that goes something like that?' Tweffell asked. 'I remember something of the sort. My aged head certainly fails to keep hold of most things, but I do recall that people would speak of a master who died during the building of the church.'

'Every legend holds a kernel of truth,' Melchior affirmed. 'An old folk tale tells of a foreigner who arrived promising to build a church, but no one was allowed to know his name. He supposedly also said that if his name were to be found out then Tallinn will never become a large, famed and wealthy town as the townspeople wished but instead a time of unrest, fires, plagues and misfortunes would follow and strife and misfortune would befall the town and the church that he built would not stand for long.'

'I have also heard something similar, although surely it's just some old legend,' Freisinger said, 'just that and nothing more.'

'Are you absolutely sure of that, Sire Blackhead?' Melchior asked. And do you know how the story continues? They say the townspeople did find out the name of the church builder – Olaf – and when this name was shouted by a crowd of townsmen then Satan himself was said to have pulled Olaf down by his legs from the top of the steeple, and the man fell to his death. The master's journeymen were then said to have buried his remains in a place that no one saw and subsequently disappeared.'

'So the story probably goes,' Freisinger replied, shrugging. 'Still, I do not see any –'

Melchior interrupted him, speaking with a passion, 'This may be a legend, and many elements of it will have certainly been imagined, but when we put it side by side with Gallenreutter's riddle and the lines of verse found in his pocket, then … then they add up to a whole in some places. No one really knows who built St Olaf's because the master's name was to remain a secret for all eternity. The man's name definitely could not have been Olaf, because Olaf was king of the Norwegians and the saint after whom the church was named, as a great number of Norwegian and Danish traders passed through this town at that time. Yet the church builder met his death, and no one knows where his remains were buried. Legend brings us a tiny grain of truth, and that truth has to remain a secret. But what do the last lines of the verse tell us? Do they not tell us that this builder had to die in order that the church remain standing and that the masters each received a part of his body, as in holy communion, and that they confirmed this with ritual so that his name would remain an eternal secret?'

'You mean that the master was *eaten?*' Casendorpe cried.

'I mean that Master Mason Caspar Gallenreutter from the town of Warendorf in Westphalia became aware of the name, and so he had to die. Gallenreutter had a vague idea who he was looking for once he found the name out, someone in Tallinn who guards the old secrets of the town. He made some careful enquiries because it looks like he had decided that he wanted payment in exchange for keeping quiet about this secret. And the transaction was made right before our very eyes. Remember, at the beer-tasting festival?'

'I remember,' Kilian exclaimed suddenly. 'I remember the conversation, Sire Melchior. Could you show me the riddle on those pieces of paper? It's as if something tickled my ear ... I am not entirely certain, though.'

'But, Melchior, Hinricus was silent the entire time at the Blackheads.' Dorn spoke gruffly.

'The man Prior Eckell pointed out to us was not Hinricus,' Melchior declared. 'It was not Hinricus who made a trade with Gallenreutter. Think, who was it was that seized upon the verse when Gallenreutter recited it? Who bartered with him right there in the Blackheads' guildhall? Magistrate Dorn, I am now ready to make my accusation. Sires, find favour with the Lord. I stand here according to the provisions of Lübeck law, and I ask that the Magistrate's sword be unsheathed for the first time.'

These were words of Lübeck law, words spoken in the presence of a councilman and the Magistrate, which signified that someone demanded justice and was to accuse another. Dorn unsheathed his sword, the court servants stepped behind him and he sheathed it again. A deadly silence filled the room.

'Sires,' Melchior repeated, 'find favour with the Lord. I request that the Magistrate's sword be unsheathed a second time.'

Dorn raised his sword. 'Here will I hold trial in the name of the Grand Master of the Order, the Town Council, justice and the accuser,' he proclaimed. 'I forbid the violation of order a first and second time. I demand that no one leave this place and that the accuser's speech not be interrupted.' He slid his sword back into its sheath.

'Sires,' Melchior said once again, 'I request under Lübeck law that the Magistrate's sword be unsheathed a third time.'

Dorn raised his gleaming sword for a third time. 'Town citizen Melchior Wakenstede has demanded that the Magistrate's sword be unsheathed on the basis of Lübeck law. Allow him to speak, and may no one interrupt him under threat of a fine.'

'I remind you of Sire Freisinger's words during a conversation at the Brotherhood of Blackheads. "Tallinn is a prosperous town, and a peril such as a shortage of coins has never nipped at the Brotherhood of Blackheads' heels. We Blackheads have always had quite sufficient funds for maintaining our dignity and significance, as ours is the oldest guild in Tallinn." He then went on to say that the Blackheads helped dedicate this town's holy sanctuaries to the Lord Christ and that "when death dances around the town it is the Blackheads who are the first to reach for their arms". Those were his exact words, "when death dances around the town". This was a signal to Gallenreutter, who now knew he had found a buyer. He asked whether the Blackheads are then so warlike that they reach for their arms immediately. Freisinger responded that more is accomplished with good counsel and a barrel of silver Riga marks than with a halberd. Yes, this was a trade that took place right before our very eyes. Gallenreutter got a response to his question because someone acknowledged that he knew the ancient secret of St Olaf's Church. Someone recognized the words of the old verse. In the name of Lübeck law, it was you, Sire Blackhead, Clawes Freisinger, who killed the former Victual Brother Wunbaldus, Master Mason Caspar Gallenreutter of Westphalia and the Dominican Prior Balthazar Eckell. And under Lübeck law you must now be held accountable for your acts before the Town Council.'

Magistrate Dorn stepped towards Freisinger with his glinting sword raised, followed by the court servants.

'What do you have to say in response to the accusation?' he asked.

'Is this is some kind of a joke?' Freisinger asked in an icy tone. He stood proudly with a defiant sneer on his face and his arms crossed.

'This *apothecary* cannot truly swear by the names of all the saints that this is really the absolute truth,' he added.

'Oh, but it is the truth, and by the names of all the saints I accuse you, Sire Clawes Freisinger, of these murders. And, in my mind, I had accused you of killing Gallenreutter from the very moment that I found the Tallinn artig in his mouth, because you, Sire Freisinger, were the only person in the town other than the Commander, Magistrate Dorn and me who knew that a coin had been placed in Clingenstain's mouth and that his head had been driven on to a stake. Yet you did not know what kind of coin it had been. And you swore to a lie when you claimed to have spoken of this to Hinricus. You spoke of it to no one – Brother Hinricus had nothing to do with these killings. And it was you, Freisinger, who asked about a bounty immediately, as if you knew the identity of Clingenstain's killer. You *knew* that it was Wunbaldus because you had been near the Blackheads' altar in the Dominican Monastery the previous evening when you overheard Brother Wunbaldus confessing his crime to the Prior.'

'Yes, I was there – yes, I was – but I didn't hear a thing,' Freisinger snapped.

'You must certainly did – at least enough to know that Wunbaldus had killed the Knight. But you didn't approach the Council with this knowledge because you were waiting for a bounty to be offered. Then, however, during *Smeckeldach* you heard what Gallenreutter had dug up from under St Olaf's, and a man within you awoke – the man you were when you arrived here, the man you were sent here to be: a murderer. What I heard was you two making a trade. Gallenreutter reckoned that one of the guests at the Brotherhood of Blackheads, one of the guilds' aldermen, might be the man he was looking for. He made a false claim that Tallinn was a poor town where hardly anyone would want to pay him to keep quiet. And it was you,

Freisinger, who said in reply that Tallinn – and the Blackheads – had an abundance of wealth. You threatened Gallenreutter, saying the Blackheads would reach for their weapons – sadly he took no notice. With this statement you told Gallenreutter that *you* were the very man for whom he was searching and that you had enough money to pay for his silence. And the deal was done. A barrel of Riga silver, and Gallenreutter would remain silent. Oh yes, yes, he fell silent all right, although he did so for all eternity because you could not allow the fact that he had read the verse and would now know the master mason's name. The Blackheads have always been secretive, and not much is known of your own past. You Blackheads came to this town at some time yet have always kept to yourselves. I must now believe that some ancient pact ties you to brotherhoods of church builders, whose symbol is a trowel and a compass and which are similarly organized into their own brotherhoods, veiled in mystery, that are scattered throughout German towns. This pact requires you to keep watch to ensure the name of the builder of St Olaf's Church remains a secret. So Gallenreutter had to die. First, however, was Wigbold, whom you knew as Wunbaldus. You were a daily guest at the monastery, Freisinger, because the Blackheads' altar is there. No one paid the least attention to you when you called on Wunbaldus and doubtless set a fantastic brew before him for the tasting, having slipped the arsenic stolen from Eckell into the beer. It was for this reason that you tested the arsenic on that unfortunate horse. The arsenic *was* deadly. Eckell spoke often of his fear of plague and at some point had told you what was in his amulet. When Wunbaldus was dead you stole a Dominican habit. You dressed in his clothes and rushed off to take confession because the secrecy of the confessional is not sacred for a man who commits suicide, and so all would soon find out that Wunbaldus killed both the Knight of the Order and the Master Mason. Then Gallenreutter's time was up. You had stolen an axe from the workshop at St Nicholas's earlier and hidden it not far from the meeting place. Before you used the axe, however, you killed Gallenreutter with a dagger. St Nicholas's churchyard is well hidden from prying eyes – an appropriate place for two conspirators to meet, and Gallenreutter would not have suspected any foul play. You had by this time made sure word had spread throughout the town about the Knight's head being staked to the wall. What next? Only Eckell remained. You were both at the monastery the next day, and you dissolved arsenic into his food or drink while you were there. Why? Because Eckell would have found out the truth sooner or later. You knew that he and Wunbaldus were friends and Eckell would not believe the story about the Lay Brother's confession. You poisoned him in the hope that he would perish immediately at the monastery and that no one would have the slightest suspicion of poisoning because the Prior was known to be old and sick. Yet you were unaware that the Prior's body was already accustomed to the arsenic after having inhaled the poison for many years. He did die, but he died less quickly than you would have wished. He died, but he still managed to tell us who his murderer was before his final breath. "You poisoned." Those were his last words.'

Freisinger listened to Melchior contemptuously and shook his head. Only Dorn noticed that a cold sweat had broken out on his forehead and that his cheek twitched slightly.

'What a load of mindless nonsense,' he snorted. 'The Apothecary is always going on about poison. He swore by the names of all the saints, and so now I, too, swear by the same oath that it is untrue. Yes, take me before a Council trial and allow them to judge according to Lübeck law whether an apothecary's yarn trumps an honest merchant's account when he swears by the names of all the saints.'

'Do not insult the saints or swear to a lie in their name,' Melchior shouted, livid. 'You certainly swore to a lie earlier when you vowed to Master Casendorpe's daughter that you would take her as your wife. You came to this town as a bachelor and thus became an alderman of the Brotherhood of Blackheads, just as your pact with the church builders apparently prescribed. And you were supposed to remain a bachelor. However, you fell in love with Hedwig, and the secret of St Olaf's Church seemed to be buried for all eternity, so you began to forget the true reason for your presence here. You wanted to marry Hedwig and become a citizen of Tallinn, and you would happily have given up your association with the Blackheads. No doubt someone new would have been sent, and you would have been freed from your obligation, but Gallenreutter's discovery struck like a bolt of lightening from clear sky. One day you had vowed to wed Hedwig, and the next you told her that you were now not ready for marriage and did not want to make her unhappy. You thrust away the love of a young woman – for whose hand half the young goldsmiths in the Hanseatic towns would have run their legs to the bone – because you were already bound by a blood oath. Gallenreutter, Wunbaldus and Eckell had to die, and you would remain the Sire Blackhead and guardian of the secret of St Olaf's.'

'That is only your claim? Your fairy-tales and contrived fantasies?' Freisinger retorted. 'Yes, let Lübeck law weigh up this apothecary's tale. No one can be accused of murder because of legends and because he did not marry a girl. The Blackheads number many in Tallinn and in other towns as well. They will rise in my defence, because the claims of one apothecary –'

'It is not only the claim of one apothecary,' Melchior said, cutting off Freisinger's words, 'because we all witnessed Prior Eckell's last testimony. He knew the identity of his killer just as we all do now. Why did you do it? Maybe because it was so simple. To mix odourless, tasteless arsenic into his drink – it was so simple. You were already used to killing. A murderer is like a weed in a garden. He will sprout time and time again because he believes he has the right to do so, that he *must* do so. Let us revisit the Prior's last moments. He was no longer able to speak, but he was still capable of commanding his body. He ripped the treacherous amulet from around his neck and cast it towards us; he showed us where the poison came from. He accused someone, he pointed towards someone – towards whom exactly? He demonstrated it to us. He managed to pull the Commander's black scapular down on to his head – black head. He told us it was a Blackhead and accused him. "You poisoned."'

'That is absurd,' Freisinger shouted. 'Absurd. A mad old monk's convulsions before death – ha! Black head … This apothecary is out of his mind.'

'What was absurd was your foolish attempt to make us believe that no poison had been in Eckell's food and drink,' Melchior continued. 'It was childish and idiotic, because no person in their right mind would dare taste food consumed by a man who had just died of poisoning. You wished to demonstrate to us the Blackheads' integrity and innocence, but you merely demonstrated your own foolishness. You showed us that you knew Eckell's drink had not been poisoned, and you knew this because you had administered poison to him several hours earlier.'

Freisinger's words became lodged in his throat. He continued to stand defiantly but was unable to reply when faced with Melchior's confidence. Every man in the room stared at him blankly, except Dorn and the Councilman, who exchanged a glance. Dorn did not know what to do now. Should a Council trial be convened immediately? He did not notice Melchior wink at Kilian – as if giving him a signal or looking for assistance – and the boy, who up until that time had been poring over Melchior's sheets of paper, waved his arm.

'Wait just a moment, wait now,' Kilian appealed and continued speaking without waiting for Dorn's permission. 'I wish to say that this riddle, this song written here … something had already tickled my ear before, although you wouldn't notice it before *reading* these lines … That is, I know who is he, who is *afore all*. It's written here that *solemn Death drapes in his cloak he who is afore all*, and then later that *in eternal secrecy be affirmed the first's oath of flesh*. He who is afore all is before these *lines*, these *lines of text*. If you read down the first letters of the sentences one by one from top to bottom, then … then a person's name lies here.'

'The name of the builder of St Olaf's Church, yes,' Melchior confirmed. 'Who died and whose bones were buried beneath St Olaf's.'

'And the name is, well, that is … it is incomplete.' Kilian continued heatedly.

'Because we do not have the last three lines of the song, although those are unimportant.'

'But one can nevertheless still read here …' Kilian exclaimed. 'That the name is C-O-N-R –'

Kilian had barely managed to pronounce the letters, when he was interrupted by a ghastly roar erupting from Freisinger's throat. He had pulled a dagger from his breast pocket at lightning speed and was rushing towards Kilian.

'Silence, you idiot minstrel,' Freisinger howled. 'That name is a secret if you want the church to endure. Shut your mouth.'

Dorn was none the less defter than the younger Blackhead. He leaped in front of Freisinger, barging him with his shoulder and knocking the dagger from his hand as the two court servants seized Freisinger from behind.

The merchant thrashed in their grip, struggling to break free, and screamed in rage, 'You fools, you don't understand what you are doing. It is forbidden to say that name. It must remain secret or your church will fall into ruin, your town will fall into ruin …'

Dorn pressed the tip of his sword against Freisinger's breast and demanded, 'Stand still. Do you now admit it? Do you admit your guilt? Do you admit to killing Wunbaldus, Gallenreutter and the Prior? Do you admit it, or shall Kilian read the name aloud? Kilian, read.'

Kilian had no time to do so. Freisinger's voice burst with loathing and rage.

'I admit, yes, I admit it. Yes, I killed them. Order that minstrel to stay silent.'

'To the prison cell. Take him to the prison cell,' Dorn commanded. 'In the name of the Grand Master of the Order, the town and Lübeck law, take him to the prison cell.'

31

St Michael's Convent, the Brewery Tavern
22 May, Afternoon

EVERY NOW AND AGAIN Melchior really enjoyed spending time here at the St Michael's Convent brewery – which nestled right up against the wall between the Nunnadetagune and Gut Dack towers – where the nuns sold beer to the townsfolk. It was a quiet part of town, and a somewhat higher class of customer – journey-man artisans, vassal servants, town watchmen and members of the monastery – drank here compared with those who went outside the town walls. The holy sisters' beer had a pleasant, bitter taste, and Melchior was especially partial to one of the brews that the nuns flavoured with mint. On this tranquil afternoon the Apothecary sat with Kilian and Brother Hinricus, who had finally managed to slip away from the monastery. The last few days had been quite difficult for the *cellarius*, as he had been tasked with a great deal of written correspondence, organizing a funeral service and the reorganization of monastery affairs. Sub-prior Gerbhardus was an old man, and so the younger brothers were required to take on the running of the monastery, while he spent his days praying in the chapel. Melchior was glad that he had been able to get out of the pharmacy for a spell, because word had spread throughout the town that it was he who had assisted the Council in capturing the murderer, and so a steady

352

stream of townspeople had been stopping by his pharmacy demanding news – and, of course, to buy his goods. Melchior's business was booming, but it was tiring. Still, he was certainly now a step closer towards his dream of a house on Town Hall Square.

At the moment, however, Melchior, Hinricus and Kilian took swigs of beer and discussed the incredible events that had occurred over the last few days in Tallinn. The Commander, the Dominicans and the Town Council had held a fierce debate over what to do with the body of Wunbaldus, or Wigbold, so that relations between the town, the monks and the Teutonic Order should not be too disrupted. In the end Wunbaldus's body was handed over to the Order – it was hanged at the gallows then dumped in the mud at Tõnismäe. His body was then disposed of as the Dominican Lay Brother Wunbaldus, because neither the Commander nor the town – not to mention the monks – wanted it known that he was once a Victual Brother thought to have died years before. There was no hard proof to support that theory anyway; Wigbold's name was not mentioned in any monastery document. The town of Tallinn did not want the reputation of having provided sanctuary to a thief notorious across the Baltic Sea. The Council simply announced to the townspeople that Wunbaldus and Clingenstain had an argument, and the monk beheaded him in a fit of rage and later breathed his last during a harsh bout of penitence at the monastery. The Toompea Murderer was dead, the Order had received the killer's body from the town, and it was executed in an appropriate manner. And may that dreadful story be forgotten henceforth.

What Hinricus now told Melchior, however, was that the man had been confirmed as having been the infamous Wigbold. Old Gerbhardus had known. That old man – Eckell's peer – had also been at the monastery in Visby and remembered Wigbold well. Hinricus saw tears amongst the wrinkles below Gerbhardus's eyes when the

Order attendants arrived at the monastery to drag Wunbaldus's body up to Toompea. The old man admitted to Hinricus in private that the prayers he had said for Wigbold had not helped – once a murderer, always a murderer.

'He escaped the executioner's axe, but Satan had marked the murderer's soul,' the old man whispered. 'St Catherine sees that he repented his sins. He saved three Dominicans from the fury of his own brothers, yet he was not forgiven for those other souls whose bodies rest at the bottom of the sea. His greatest sin was that he called himself a friend to the Lord.'

'Wigbold survived one death and will live through another,' Melchior said to Hinricus. 'I wouldn't be surprised if some will see him as a kind of hero one day, although he will for ever remain a mystery. But, Hinricus, tell me, have you forgiven me for my ignoble scheming?'

'I wasn't angry with you,' Hinricus replied with a smile. 'Of course, it all happened so fast that I was truly unable to believe that you were really accusing me of the killings. I have always believed that you are a sensible man and that such madness could have come upon you … However, when Freisinger lied in the names of all the saints then I understood immediately that it must have been a trap. Why else would he have had to tell such a dreadful untruth?'

'I had to be certain,' Melchior replied, 'certain that if he were given the chance to shift the blame on to someone else that he would do it. The man thinks very quickly, but this time he thought too quickly. I had to be absolutely confident that he was lying because otherwise I would not have dared to approach the Council with my accusations. Your surprise also had to be genuine for him to take the bait. After his lie I knew I was right, and then everything fell into place.'

Kilian sipped his beer and cast a few glances towards the window, through which his young friend Birgitta could be seen cutting grass in the nunnery garden. The boy held his lute in his lap, knowing that sooner or later someone would request that he play and that quite a few nuns would stop to listen until propriety got the better of them and they returned to their holy duties.

'And about that golden chain,' Hinricus continued, 'well, I have come to understand that no miracle took place in the town of Tallinn.'

Kilian shook his head sadly. 'It seems not,' he said. 'Sire Melchior was right once again. That flaw has hounded me since my childhood; in fact, it was the reason I was forced to leave Milan. That time it was over a silver brooch that belonged to a nobleman's daughter. The moment I saw it I just had to have it … I really couldn't help myself. I wanted it so much. The urge to steal is as strong within me as my desire to sing, but I genuinely repent it and have vowed one day to go on a pilgrimage.'

'Singing might make you famous,' Melchior said. 'It might not make you wealthy, but people will love you. If, on the other hand, you steal a golden collar belonging to a Knight of the Teutonic Order then you will have your hand chopped off.'

'The urge overpowers me in an instant,' Kilian moaned. 'It compels me and burns within my soul. When I steal it's like I'm watching myself from a few paces away, as if it's not really me at all.'

'You must battle your inner self,' Melchior advised. Something sombre and painful flashed in his eyes for a brief instant. 'If you stole something from behind Sire Tweffell's back then you will be cast out of the house and Ludke would beat you to within an inch of your life. He has been ordered to keep his eye on you – but you've probably already worked that out.'

Kilian eyed Melchior for a moment in amazement but then nodded and asserted, 'No, I would never steal anything from Uncle Mertin's house. It is my home, and I do not need to steal from my home. I came to understand that long ago. What *I fail* to understand, however, is how you knew that I took the collar.'

'Stole,' Melchior corrected.

'Well, yes, stole. I know that you found it and took it to the Church of the Holy Ghost, but still … how?'

'One must believe in miracles, too, Kilian – in miracles, too,' Melchior replied. 'As St Augustine once said, if a miracle does not match what we know from nature then we know too little about nature. If you do not believe in miracles then you do not believe the biographies of the saints and what they teach us, yet we all need the saints. As for the collar, I will say this. I know how much you like to sit on the well wall, and as I looked out of my window over those days I noticed that you were picking at that loose stone in the wall when you thought no one was looking. And once I realized it was you who had stolen the collar then I began to consider that you would hardly dare to hide it in Sire Tweffell's house because Ludke keeps you under surveillance. So I decided to take a look at the well.'

'But, all the same, how did you know? That collar was like a curse. When I heard that the Knight had been killed, then … then I became afraid. I wanted to throw it down the well, but I couldn't bring myself to do it.'

'I don't know whether I could have either. Gold has an incredible capacity to weigh on a man's soul. But how did I know? Quite simply, I noticed that you have a lust for stealing pretty things – you even stole a spoon from my pharmacy. (It is made of silver, by the way, and I would like it back.) You were on Toompea that day and had seen the collar. You wanted an attestation from Clingenstain.

You saw him go into his residence, and I thought about what might have happened were you to follow him, thinking perhaps to ask humbly once more for the attestation, because you do possess courage and perseverance. Clingenstain had left the collar behind and gone to confession. The collar might have been there somewhere and – just as it was with the spoon – you would have been unable to resist the compulsion, have stuck the collar into your breast pocket and run off. What betrayed you, however, was your lie that the Knight was wearing the collar around his neck when you saw him later. And actually, Kilian, you were also given away by the song that you sang to those young town maidens as well.'

'Song? Which song?' Kilian asked in astonishment.

'That song of nothing at all. You said that you thought it up on the spot, but actually you had sung the same song the previous day on Toompea. This meant that you were lying, albeit not very well. Minstrels should be better liars if they want to make it in life ...'

'I am not a minstrel,' Kilian retorted, 'I am a Meistersinger – well, I'm still a journeyman – but either way, I'm not a minstrel.'

'Fine, then, Meistersinger. Anyway, after I realized that you had stolen the collar then it was clear that the Knight had not been murdered for that, so what could I to do then? I could not tell the Order that it was you who had stolen the collar because Spanheim would have believed you to be the murderer as well. I had to find the right murderer and help you get rid of the collar in some way. The Church of the Holy Ghost almshouse seemed to be the most proper place for it. The Order will not demand its return from the poor.'

Hinricus chuckled lightly, turned his head so that the spring sunshine splashed over it and squinted. 'So you agreed ahead of the meeting that Kilian would act as if he were about to read out the name of the builder of St Olaf's, yes?' he asked after a pause.

'True, I admit that it was one more small trick I employed to force Freisinger into telling the truth. If he protected that name so dearly then he was forbidden to let it be heard in public.'

Melchior removed the piece of paper on which he had written the song of the ancient church builders from his breast pocket. He unrolled it and traced his finger along the lines of text.

'But you knew the name anyway, didn't you?' Hinricus continued.

'Yes, I saw it. *He who is afore all*. And we can work the name out from there. As far as we can surmise, it is a distant forefather of the former Alderman of the Blackheads. *Relic calls afar for its blood*. The Blackheads sent him here to guard the secret of his own name. Those men so full of secrecy, the ancient church builders with the wisdom of Solomon, a trowel and compass ... I find it difficult to believe the things that people are prepared to kill for ... the world is so full of mysteries. Perhaps it might have been better if I'd never become aware of the name.'

'They had their ritual,' Hinricus said, 'gruesome as it was, although this is not the first time I have heard of such things. Some say that the word "guild" itself relates to an old Saxon tradition in which a clan ate a sacrificial victim together. They also say, of course, that many strange practices and arcane secrets were brought back from the Holy Land.'

'I have made a sacred vow to myself never to tell a soul the name of the man who built St Olaf's Church,' Kilian said seriously. 'Do you think it's true that the town will be plagued by troubles and ruin if anyone ever finds out?'

'Who knows?' Melchior returned pensively. 'Our town is not defended by sturdy walls, Lübeck law and the Teutonic Order alone. A town must possess an idea, which all of its citizens have to understand. At church, when we pray to the saints and the Almighty for our town's fortune, whether this is enough ... Who knows, Kilian?

A town will not endure if its churches fall into ruin. But what is it that gives a town the strength and the will to last for centuries, longer even? Perhaps *that* is Solomon's wisdom, because Jerusalem is the city of paradise on earth, and maybe the crusaders brought back some knowledge from the Holy Land that really can help a town's churches to survive. I do not know, and neither does Freisinger. He believes. He believes that the Blackheads' secret must remain a secret, that no one may know the name of the Master of St Olaf's, and he killed only so that St Olaf's and the town might endure. He could have taken the Maiden Hedwig as his wife and joined the Great Guild, but no, he had to remain a Blackhead and stand guard over their ancient mysteries.'

'Did he say anything?' Kilian asked. 'Freisinger, I mean, when you went to visit him at Bremen Tower. And before he ...' A frown spread across the boy's face. 'Before, well ... he left for good or whatever became of him.'

'That's right,' Hinricus said softly and leaned towards the Apothecary. 'Melchior, you promised to speak of your conversation with Freisinger. Did he repent?'

Melchior motioned for new beers to be brought to the table. He would pay their tab today.

'Yes, I spoke to him. I questioned him. He had already been tortured,' Melchior said after their tankards were refilled.

The previous day Melchior had requested permission from the Council to be allowed to visit Freisinger in the Bremen Prison Tower, a new structure behind the Dominican Monastery that had been completed just a few years ago. The Council kept all of the town's worst criminals there, and that is where Freisinger had been taken after being led through the town in chains. Freisinger was not a Tallinn townsman. He was not a citizen; he was a foreigner. The townspeople knew that it was he who had poisoned their beloved prior and killed a church builder, and the man was not worthy of better treatment or a more comfortable cell. No, he was taken to the Bremen Tower while the people of Tallinn screamed at him, spat at him, glowered at him and cursed him. The formerly proud and popular Blackhead, to whom in the past only shouts of praise were exclaimed at war games and tournaments and whose valour was appreciated by all, had now been trampled into the dust, was now a hated enemy.

It was impossible for a prisoner to escape from Bremen Tower without help. The gaol was located just below the tower's upper defensive level. One entered the prison along a stairway winding up from the tower's southern edge and then through an entryway and past two doors made of oak timbers that were fixed to the wall with iron hasps and bars and which, in turn, were secured by a heavy padlock. The tower had two storeys, and one could pass between the two floors only through a hatchway in the floor. Freisinger was held in the lower cell, which had no windows. The only daylight filtered into the space through the hatch in the ceiling. Melchior had squatted down at the edge of the hatch to speak to Freisinger. He had been tortured on the rack, and one of his arms hung at an unnatural angle by his side.

'Yes,' Melchior repeated. 'I spoke to him. I asked him about the Brotherhood of Blackheads, about their history and their secrets. I asked about the three lines of text, about which we know nothing.'

'And? What did he say?' Hinricus and Kilian asked in unison.

'He said – and I will attempt to repeat this as accurately as I can – that he does not bear any hatred towards me. "If you have taken any sort of apothecary's oath, then you will understand the oath that I have taken as well. From the moment my forefathers seized the cross and marched to the Holy Land, ever since that time the oath has been taken, and it must not be broken if Christians want their churches and their towns to survive and flourish." He went on to say that there are many of them and that the Blackheads are only one of numerous guilds that guard and maintain secrets that go back as far as the time of Solomon. He told me he had taken a vow to come to Tallinn to watch over these ancient secrets and that "that idiotic, greedy mason brought misfortune down upon himself". Gallenreutter had wanted money in return for his silence. He had chanced to overhear that there were men who keep guard to ensure that the names of the ancient church builders remain secret. There must be one such church in every Christian town, the very oldest church sanctified by the proper rite, because the town could not keep going otherwise.'

'So he did not repent?' Hinricus asked.

'He felt no shame at all over Gallenreutter's death. I asked him why he killed Prior Eckell, a man whom he was supposed to respect and honour. He replied that the Prior had figured out that Wunbaldus was not responsible for his own death or that of the Gallenreutter and that he had once accidentally mentioned to Freisinger what was in his amulet. Freisinger said he did this with a heavy heart, adding that the Prior was so old and sick that he would have died quite soon anyway.'

Hinricus took his head between his hands and sighed deeply.

'A murderer always finds justification,' Melchior said gently. 'He makes himself believe that it had to be done, that it was the only course of action.'

'But did he already know? Was he certain that ...' Kilian began but trailed off.

'He said he was sure that he would not be hanged on Town Hall Square nor at Võllamägi. The Blackheads are too old and powerful a brotherhood for such a thing to occur. There are many of them and they have untold numbers of friends – so Freisinger said, although

I did not at that stage understand quite what those words meant. He said, "They may torture me with pliers, but they will not take me to the killing platform. Go, Melchior, and know that I do not bear any hatred against you. Yet keep in mind that you must be careful, you and that minstrel. Cast from your memory the name that you deciphered. My words carry not the greatest weight in our brother-hood, but I shall make an appeal for both your lives.'"

'And you believe this?' Kilian pressed. And should I really be afraid as well? After all, I *do* know the name.'

Melchior shook his head. 'We have nothing to fear in Tallinn. That I promise you.'

'Regardless,' Kilian continued, 'I will be as silent as the grave. I wish no harm to befall our town.'

'"Our town", you say?' Hinricus asked.

'Yes. Tallinn is my town now as well. If I should ever leave here then my heart will for ever weep.'

'Yes, I believe you will never leave here again,' Melchior said, grinning slyly. 'Sire Tweffell has already taken care of that.'

'How so? I don't understand.'

'Sire Tweffell has no heirs, and he is too perceptive not to notice for whom your heart beats and for whom Gerdrud's beats in return. And his meanness would not allow him to let his assets leave his bloodline. Keep in mind, Kilian, that Ludke guards your every step and maybe mine as well. At some time, possibly quite soon, you must choose whether you will become a Meistersinger or a merchant. Tallinn could use both. No matter what Solomon's wisdom might be, I know with certainty that no town can last for long if it is populated by too few masters of song and too few merchants – despite the fact that a merchant must sell his soul in the pursuit of profit.'

Kilian blushed but exclaimed stubbornly, 'Then I wish to remain a Meistersinger.'

'And may all the saints bless you in this quest,' Melchior replied. 'A town that does not have enough Meistersingers is a dead town. Yet a town will also wither away without merchants.'

Hinricus reasoned that this was doubtless the case, although every town also needed monasteries and churches, otherwise it would have no soul. 'The more merchants, the more monasteries, so perhaps merchants do not truly have to sell their souls. We certainly pray for them and remind them to care for their eternal salvation.'

'But Freisinger, did he say nothing more?' Kilian asked again. 'Nothing about those three missing lines?'

'Nothing much,' Melchior replied. 'I asked where the testament that Gallenreutter dug up had disappeared to, but he said I did not need to know about that. It was as if he wanted to warn me off and reassert that he did not hate me. I did not fully understand what he was talking about. I heard the news in the morning, just as you did, and that news will surely echo long here in Tallinn ...'

That morning Magistrate Dorn had gone with the tower guard to ask Freisinger who he wanted to represent him at his trial, but all they found was an empty cell. Yes, there are certainly many Blackheads, and they do have a lot of friends – possibly even on the Town Council, possibly on Toompea, possibly somewhere far away and high above.

'Freisinger is already far from here. He was right, Tallinn's Town Council will not hang him because the Blackheads have many powerful friends,' Melchior spoke firmly.

The town had been shaken by Freisinger's mysterious escape, but a town quickly forgets, as everybody has their own work to do and lives to be getting on with. The other Blackheads swore they knew nothing of their Alderman's escape, and no doubt they told the truth. The Brotherhood of Blackheads denounced Freisinger and his secrets. The jolly Blackheads would remain in Tallinn; they knew nothing of ancient rituals and church-builders' oaths; they would continue to trade and arrange their jousting tournaments. They – the new Blackheads – already existed in Tallinn, and perhaps they *had* to be a part of the town as everyone had already become accustomed to them. Freisinger had been like a malicious abscess that was now cut free from the body. His trial had not been held, and not one entry including his name would remain in the Council records. The town would endure; the churches and monasteries would endure.

Hinricus rose and took his leave. Through the window it was apparent that Katrine and Birgitta had entered the convent court-yard and were calling for Kilian. It seems it is time for us all to leave, Melchior resolved, but before he did he threw that scrap of paper – dug up from a grave and on which was written the song of the old Blackheads – into the holy sisters' tavern fireplace. He stood before the hearth and watched the flames greedily seize upon the paper, turning it grey and razor thin before it broke into thousands of fragments of ash transformed into a trail of smoke winding up into the chimney.

Melchior stood and gazed at the flames that sent the secret of the builder of St Olaf's Church high up into the sky.

Twenty-four years later, grey-haired and a widower, Melchior stood on Pikk Street and recalled those flames as fires raged through the town. Terrified townspeople ran around in front of him as the steeple of St Olaf's Church – soaring almost as high as the heavens – crack-led and shot fierce flames up towards the clouds.

AVAILABLE AND COMING SOON
FROM PUSHKIN VERTIGO

Jonathan Ames

You Were Never Really Here
A Man Named Doll
The Wheel of Doll

Simone Campos

Nothing Can Hurt You Now

Zijin Chen

Bad Kids

Maxine Mei-Fung Chung

The Eighth Girl

Candas Jane Dorsey

The Adventures of Isabel
What's the Matter with Mary Jane?

Margot Douaihy

Scorched Grace

Joey Hartstone

The Local

Seraina Kobler

Deep Dark Blue

Elizabeth Little

Pretty as a Picture

Jack Lutz

London in Black

Steven Maxwell

All Was Lost

Callum McSorley

Squeaky Clean

Louise Mey

The Second Woman

John Kåre Raake

The Ice

RV Raman

A Will to Kill
Grave Intentions
Praying Mantis

Paula Rodríguez

Urgent Matters

Nilanjana Roy

Black River

John Vercher

Three-Fifths
After the Lights Go Out

Emma Viskic

Resurrection Bay
And Fire Came Down
Darkness for Light
Those Who Perish

Yulia Yakovleva

Punishment of a Hunter
Death of the Red Rider